The Judgement Book

Simon Hall

Published by Accent Press Ltd – 2009

ISBN 9781906373733

Printed in the UK by CPI Bookmarque, Croydon, CR0 4TD

Cover design by The Design House

Acknowledgements

My detective friends, for their endless patience, guidance, and not being too phased by my weird imagination, also my medical advisers for stretching their Hippocratic oaths to help with my murderous plots. The librarians and literary festival organisers who do so much for writers and books lovers, often with little recognition, and Jess and all my friends for keeping me writing and reassuring me that turning 40 hasn't been quite such a rocky voyage as I feared. Finally, and perhaps most importantly, my readers – getting published was a big surprise, people actually reading the books was a shock, and the fact that most seem to enjoy them was stunning. Thank you!

SH, Exeter, Summer 2009

For Niamh

Prologue

THE JUDGEMENT BOOK SLIPPED from its secret place and sighed open on the old wooden table. It had been almost two weeks since it was last freed and it felt starved and greedy, as if it again longed to gorge itself on depravity. It would soon have its fill of rich deceit.

The pages turned and the list of the condemned passed, their names spelt out in capitals on the top of each sheet. Below was lovingly written the text of their cheating, corruption, envy and hate, a vibrant spectrum of destructive human failings. Today, it was a familiar diet, but no less delicious for that. Today, sex would fill its hungry pages.

Lust, sex, lies and hypocrisy.

He would become the star of the great show that was about to begin. The first truly famous name to feed the Judgement Book, the one for whom it had waited so patiently. And how he had blessed it. He'd been a wonderfully despicable man. The neat newspaper cuttings of some of his speeches and pronouncements littered the table, a pile of shouting banner headlines and tight black print.

"FREEDMAN FIGHTS BACK FOR THE FAMILY!"

It was a speech to the Traditionalist Party's Women's Guild, a table-thumper the reporter called it. He'd attacked the ever-slackening morals of modern society and promised a return to old-fashioned family values when the party was back in government. The audience had devoured it. A standing ovation, cheers of delight. The interviews with some of the women called for immediate promotion. The reporter concluded that such an elevation would not take long. Will Freedman was a new political star, rising fast.

The Judgement Book would see to that.

The calm hands shuffled the cuttings, straightened and stacked them tidily in the corner of the battered old table. The glossy colour picture of Will and Yvonne Freedman had worked its way to the top. It was fate's confirmation of the righteousness of what was about to unfold, the justice that could finally be delivered.

The couple's fourteen-year-old daughter Alex stood between them. All three were smiling at the camera. It was a feature from a magazine, a double-page spread, fawning and sickening.

"The Perfect Political Family."

He dominated the picture with his height and the jutting, angular jaw of leadership. His eyes brooded, seemed to draw in the camera's lens. She was the classical antidote to his masculinity; blonde, petite, holding his hand dutifully, looking up to his mastery. Alex stood between them with the slight awkwardness of a teenager, the strength of her father's features seeding an etched beauty in her face.

The perfect family indeed. The Judgement Book knew better. It understood the reality, and would soon reveal it to the world.

It was time for the truth to be written.

Will Freedman is an adulterer, a frequenter of prostitutes, a liar and a hypocrite.

In March he attended a three-day mini-summit on economics in Blackpool. It was organised and funded by the Traditionalist party. There, he spent a night in a hotel with a high-class call girl. He paid the woman five hundred pounds in cash for the privilege of two hours of her services. She was a young woman, probably no more than nineteen or twenty years of age. It's hardly necessary to point out this is only a handful of years older than Mr Freedman's daughter, but I do so anyway, just to be sure the implication is not missed.

The prostitute uses her youth to aid her profession by specialising in dressing and acting as a schoolgirl. It is, in the economic terms of the summit, her unique selling point.

Will Freedman believed he had safely hidden his indiscretion by meeting the girl at a hotel, which was not the one he was staying in. He wore a false pair of glasses and a hat when checking in to further limit the small chance anyone might recognise him. It was not the kind of hotel where great attention is paid to the guests, so he calculated the chances of getting away with his deception were good.

She arrived in a long, beige raincoat, her school uniform concealed underneath. He paid for the room in advance, in cash, to ensure no trail was left. His excitement when she knocked on the door he described as 'volcanic'. He later referred to the two hours he spent with the girl as being among the best in his life, the fulfilment of a long-cherished fantasy.

As an aside here, I note that when interviewed by the media, Will Freedman would say the best times of his life were his wedding, the birth of his daughter, and his election as an MP – a rather different response.

He had sex with the woman twice, and wished he was a younger man so he might have been able to manage more. He would have preferred not to use a condom, but did so to reduce the risk of contracting infection. The woman carried a cane in her bag, which he used to spank her. She described that as an optional extra. It was one he found irresistible. It cost him another fifty pounds, but he said it was very well worth it. They had sex on the bed of the hotel room and in the bathroom.

Will Freedman said he knew he should not have done this, with Yvonne and Alex at home and his career to consider. But he'd seen the woman's services advertised on the internet when he was doing some "research" on his laptop computer in his room. He'd had a few drinks, and couldn't resist the lure of the fantasy. He also said that he may do it again, if the chance arose. It would be one of the perks of having to travel for his job. The experience didn't leave him feeling guilty he said, but newly alive.

Will Freedman is an adulterer, a frequenter of prostitutes, a liar and a hypocrite.

The pen rested and the emotionless eyes stared at the words, unblinking, until they lost their focus, shifted and slid across the page. Just forms and patterns but with such momentous power. The force of truth.

A rare commodity in this rank society.

The Book was so disarmingly mundane, just an ordinary pocket diary, bound in cheap black leather, but with a world of sin festering inside, the neat words carefully inscribed on the rows of faint blue lines. A calm finger rested on the coolness of the cover. It felt wonderful.

It was a work of art. And it would soon be appreciated.

By millions.

Will Freedman MP was not alone in occupying the Judgement Book. By no means. He was accompanied by many others of his kind. The Book was swollen with their lies and longing to disgorge their secrets.

And it would. Soon now, so very soon.

Freedman had the honour of being the first chosen. As he would discover tomorrow. The grand game was about to begin.

But first, it was time for the joke, to leave them all in no doubt about what was to come. Public humiliation, ridicule and scandal. For the pompous, they were the most telling of lessons and they would be ruthlessly applied. The little Book would fill hours of television and radio time, acres of newspapers and magazines, thousands of internet pages and would infuse the huddles of people in each gossip corner of every office and street and bar across the country.

The note was written, the typeset letters stuck firmly in place on the sheet of paper. The wiring was convincingly untidy, the tangle of red, blue and green spilling from the top of the rucksack, and the battery was bulky and heavy.

The bomb was ready.

Thursday mornings were one of his favourites. The week was more than half done, the working mountain scaled, now it was the descent towards the brief release of the weekend. No more murders, rapes and robberies for a couple of merciful days.

He'd been sitting in his office, sipping at a coffee and

working through a surveillance report on a gang of suspected people traffickers when the call came in. He was the most senior officer in the station. He had to react, and fast, and he had.

'Police! Clear the area! Now! I said now!!'

Some faces stretched with awakening alarm, others crinkled with amusement as he ran towards them, shouting and waving his arms. They thought he was mad. That was the trouble with CID. The lack of a uniform meant a loss of the instant authority of the shiny buttons of a beat cop.

Detective Chief Inspector Adam Breen reached into the pocket of his suit jacket, found his warrant card and held it high. 'Now!' he bawled. 'Clear the area! There's a bomb!'

At last they were shifting, some walking fast, some stumbling into lumbering, unfamiliar runs. There were a couple of shouts of alarm, the lightning forks of panic spreading quickly in the crowd. The dense pack of people oozing through the shopping centre was dissolving. The reflected sun blazed from the shining steel of the Sundial sculpture in the growing gaps of the fast-thinning crowd. Other cops converged from different directions, arms waving, all moving the milling shoppers away from the danger.

Not bad, thought Adam, as he caught his breath. He'd run from Charles Cross Police Station, just outside the shopping district, shouting gasped instructions to the handful of officers they could quickly muster. Only nine minutes ago the warning was phoned through and the shopping centre was almost cleared. They'd been ready for anything like this since the London suicide bombings of 2005. Every police force was.

The navy's Bomb Squad was already here, a couple of men standing outside their grey armoured jeep, pulling on heavily padded flak jackets and helmets with dense black visors. Another pair held up binoculars, trained them on the Sundial.

A few hundred yards up each of the four spurs of the High Street crowds of onlookers were being held back by blue-and-white police tape and uniformed officers. Some of the crowd were holding out mobile phones, videoing the scene.

A rucksack leant on the top of the four concrete steps that

led up to the Sundial. A tangle of wiring spilled from it. The bag bulged, looked heavy, menacing. Adam wondered if he should have the crowd moved further back. There was plate glass in the shop fronts, heavy and reinforced, the splinters lethal if propelled by the force of an explosion, thousands of flying daggers.

He grabbed the radio, gave the order. Along the spurs of the streets officers started herding the pack of people. Adam wasn't surprised to see many complain and resist. A bomb threat was an irresistible spectacle, well worth the risk of your life. Or it might have been the stories of the tens of thousands of pounds the media offered to people with pictures of the moments after the London bombings.

Sometimes dealing with human nature could be such a delight.

The two Bomb Squad men in their heavy khaki coveralls began a slow walk towards the Sundial, a surreal sight in the familiarity of the lines of shops, bright special offers shining from each window. One stopped, put a pair of binoculars to his mask, leaned over to the other man. They held a brief conversation, then moved on, faster now.

A crowd of pigeons fluttered out of their way. The men walked straight up the steps, leaned over and delved into the rucksack. Adam resisted the urge to turn away, step back, curl up, hide his face, ready himself for the shattering attack of the blast.

One of the men rummaged in the bag, fished out a piece of paper, stared at it, then took off his helmet. The other sat down on the top step, also removed his helmet and leaned back, looking at the clear blue sky. He lit a cigarette, blew smoke into the air. Adam hesitated, hissed under his breath, then walked carefully over, but found himself stopping thirty yards away. He shouted an introduction.

'I'm the officer in charge. Is it safe?'

The balding man with an old-fashioned handlebar moustache shook his head.

'It was never a danger. Come have a look, you don't need to worry.'

Adam paused, then walked on, climbed the steps to the sundial. The man held out the piece of paper.

'A pretty crude hoax,' he said, sounding disappointed. 'Easy enough to do. Pad out the rucksack with paper and rags, stick a heavy battery and a few bits of wire in the top and it's enough to make sure we have to turn out and treat it as the real thing. We'll be off now. Over to you to try to work out who did it.'

Adam looked down at the paper. It was full of individual letters cut from different newspapers, a jumble of fonts of headlines.

"The REAL ExplosiONs Start soON. The JUDGEment BOOK is Opening."

Chapter One

'KEEP BIDDING,' DAN GROVES hissed forcefully to the man in the ill-fitting black jacket by his side.

'For my best camera's sake, we're up to twenty grand,' he moaned back, shifting uncomfortably from foot to foot. 'I can't afford to get lumbered with that kind of bill. I'll be bankrupted. I've only got a few quid in the bank.'

'Keep going,' whispered Dan again, checking quickly around him.

There were a couple of hundred people packed into the room and it was getting hot, a hovering fug of sticky atmosphere feeding the anticipation in the crowd. He'd stationed them in the dimly lit corner farthest from the auctioneer and was trying to look as if he wasn't with the man next to him. He couldn't risk being recognised as the source of the bids.

'You'll be OK,' whispered Dan, trying to sound reassuring. 'Just keep going until I say stop.'

The auctioneer looked over expectantly, and Dirty El raised a reluctant hand.

'Twenty-two thousand pounds. Thank you, sir.'

Dan tried to glance nonchalantly at the other side of the room. He screwed up his eyes to peer through the throng of people jammed in under the low ceiling. He couldn't see the auctioneer's assistant making a bid. Dan felt his body tense.

He had got it right, hadn't he? If not, he and El had some explaining to do. They'd be twenty-two thousand pounds worse off, a sum Dan couldn't imagine raising. He had only a few hundred in savings. They'd probably be under police investigation too. It was effectively fraud, what they were doing. Forcing someone to part with a very large sum of money, albeit for a good cause.

Dan checked his memory of earlier in the day. Half the newsroom's staff were away on a teambuilding course. He prided himself on avoiding such worthy initiatives, always said he was quite content working in a team consisting of himself.

stiletto heel into the long-suffering carpet.

'You didn't get very far with that interview, did you?' she snapped. 'It didn't exactly illuminate the issue.'

'I thought I exposed him as not being able to answer the questions.'

'I thought you had a row.'

That night, at home, lying on his great blue sofa, his faithful Alsatian Rutherford at his feet, when he'd finally calmed down, Dan had to admit Lizzie had a point. If you stripped away the irritant of the perfectly manicured jabbing fingernail and idiosyncrasy of the stabbing high heels, she usually did. It might have been entertaining television, but it was hardly informative, and that was supposed to be the point of his job.

Dan prided himself on lovingly nurturing grudges and he'd never forgotten that interview with Parkinson. So, it was revenge day.

'Twenty-three thousand pounds on the telephone bid,' the auctioneer called triumphantly. He looked over at El. 'Any advance, sir?'

Gasps rose from the crowd. A host of expectant eyes turned back to them. El cut a comical figure. To accompany the black suit jacket which Dan had leant him, he wore his own tatty jeans and black shades. The idea was to make El look like an eccentric millionaire, but Dan wasn't sure the photographer came close to carrying it off. He looked more like an out-of-work undertaker.

Dan had planned to pull out at about twenty thousand pounds, just to be safe, but the memory of the broadcast spurred him on. 'Keep going,' he hissed from the edge of his mouth.

'Hell,' moaned El, lifting an unsteady hand again.

'Twenty-four thousand. Thank you, sir,' called the auctioneer. 'Do I have an advance on that? It's all for charity remember.'

Dan stared over at the auctioneer's assistant, standing still, phone clamped to his ear, willing him to raise his hand. Everyone was staring at the man. It was getting hotter.

'Hell,' moaned El again. He was sweating hard. 'What have you got me into? I'm going to be bankrupt. I'll have to flog a kidney.'

'Any advance on twenty-four thousand pounds?' called the auctioneer again. 'No? Are we all done then? Going once – going twice.'

Dan felt a spreading sweat. What if he'd misheard? Or Parkinson could have called back later to lower his bid.

'Last call for the Bass,' yelled the auctioneer. 'Any advance on twenty-four thousand pounds?'

'Hell,' moaned El, his chubby face quivering. 'We're screwed. I'll have to sell a lung too. And maybe a slice of me heart, if I can find it.'

The auctioneer's assistant raised a hand. Dan felt his legs buckle with wonderful relief.

'Twenty-five thousand on the telephone bid!' called the auctioneer. 'Any advance on that?'

'No bloody way,' grumbled El under his breath, shaking his head so vigorously that there was no chance whatsoever of any misunderstanding.

'Agreed,' whispered Dan. 'Let's get out of here. We've done our bit and raised an extra fifteen grand for charity. And we've screwed Parkinson. Mission accomplished. Come on. I really need a beer.'

Suicide was the only way out. There was no other choice.

It was such a shame. It had been a productive day. What a sad way to end it.

He'd finally secured the funding for the new kids' playgroup, after a marathon wrangle with the city council. And they'd even agreed to new swings and more street lighting for one of the parks. He'd left the office as one of the researchers was typing up a press release, proclaiming yet another triumph for his constituents.

"Freedman wins through for the children!"

It was a good headline. But he couldn't help wondering how tomorrow's release announcing his death would run.

All day long he'd debated whether there was any possible escape. By the afternoon he'd just allowed himself to begin to hope the blackmailer didn't really mean it, that it was all a game, to teach him a lesson. Now that his invisible tormenter had made his point, Will Freedman would live a better life and his sordid secret would be buried and forgotten, an unspoken agreement reached.

Then came the story on the local radio. The evacuation of Plymouth city centre. A bomb hoax. The suspicion that it was the work of someone who was seriously unbalanced, a note found inside the rucksack, some bizarre threat about a Judgement Book opening.

That was the moment he understood his life had only hours left to run.

The goodbye note was written, neatly folded, and placed in the bedroom under the bottle of Yvonne's favourite perfume. His will was checked and up to date. His family would be fine without him, perhaps even better off.

He tried not to think about that.

The bottle of whisky stood beside the hot bath. He caught a hint of its sweet, heady fragrance in the swirling steam rising from the gushing water. The smell brought so many memories of the life he was leaving, of university balls, party conferences, family holidays. The white capsules of the painkillers formed a pretty pyramid next to the sink, the syringe of insulin beside them.

Slip into the foamy water. Swill down the tablets, then sip away at the whisky. Be careful not to make yourself sick by overdoing it. When the warm waves of drowsiness come lapping, don't fight. Just relax, inject the insulin, and let it take you, to the release of a better place.

And that will be that.

He turned off the taps and reached for the tablets. He'd given up hating the person who was blackmailing him. In a strange way, he had to admit it. They were right. The only person to hate was himself. He stared at the spider plant in the corner of the bathroom. He'd always disliked it, but Yvonne had bought it at one of their trips to the local church fete and had insisted they kept it.

It was all part of the image. Now to be splintered, smashed and shattered.

Well, at least he wouldn't witness it.

He saw no reason to spare himself any punishment. The memory of the schoolgirl prostitute would be the last to linger in his dying mind.

Nineteen, she was. It was so exciting at the time, so shameful now. Just five years older than Alex. He knew what the papers would make of that. He recalled the details of the uniform the girl had worn. A tight grey blazer, navy skirt, grey knee-length socks.

He heard himself whimper.

Will Freedman felt the tears gathering in the corners of his eyes. The loneliness was making him tremble. He hoped his family would forgive him, his party would try to understand and the obituary writers would find something kind to say. But he could see the headlines, as if written in the steam on the bathroom window.

SCHOOLGIRL SEX SCANDAL MP
IN BLACKMAIL SUICIDE

He lowered himself into the bath and closed his eyes. It was a little too hot, but that hardly mattered now.

He eased back into the welcoming water and wondered whether his fellows in the Judgement Book would come to the same end. He'd never believed in an afterlife, despite all those hypocritical mornings in church, but if it existed he imagined them all meeting up, an exclusive little club. He wondered who they could be and what they had done. They were faceless in his mind, surrounded only by the writhing serpents of their sins.

Will Freedman MP wished them luck as he lay back and counted away the last seconds of what had been such a promising life.

They walked to the Heather Park Tavern, five minutes down the road from the Auction House. Seagulls wheeled in the calm of the spring evening air, calling gleefully to each other, delighting in the freedom of their flight. Dan bought them a couple of pints of ale, a dark and foreboding brew. It was stronger than he'd usually go for, but after the stress of the auction he thought they needed it.

sounding harassed. 'In fact, it's going to be huge. This is a quick tip-off to let you know, and because I get this feeling I'll need your help – again. The media's going to be all over it.'

'Go on,' said Dan, fumbling for a pen and piece of paper.

'This didn't come from me.'

'As ever and always.'

'Will Freedman, high-flying local MP.'

'Uh huh,' mumbled Dan, balancing the phone under his chin while he tried to write. He motioned to El to finish his pint. The photographer nodded and drained the glass.

'He's dead. Topped himself at his home.'

'Suicide you say? That's a decent story, but it's not huge. It happens.'

There was a pause. The mobile line hummed.

'Yeah, but not when his death appears to be connected to a bizarre bomb hoax. And not when he seems to have been driven to it by a blackmailer who knows some dynamite sex scandal about him. And not when he leaves a note saying he pities the other prominent people whose sordid secrets are about to be revealed, courtesy of something called the Judgement Book.'

Another pause, then Adam said huffily, 'Now, does that sound like a story to you?'

Dan was already out of his seat and heading for the door.

Chapter Two

THEY RAN OUT OF the pub and tried to hail a black cab. Two drove by, despite their frantic waving. One driver even gave them a cheery smile as he passed.

'Bloody Plymouth cabbies,' grunted Dan. 'They don't want to know unless you're young, female and cute.'

The evening was still, the fading light mixing with the orange of the streetlamps. Dan spotted another taxi rumbling up the road. They had to move fast. If a big story was breaking, getting there as soon as possible was vital. Some creativity was required.

'Come here El,' he said, stepping out into the middle of the road. The photographer remained determinedly on the pavement. 'Big money for good piccies,' Dan cooed, rubbing his fingers together, and El reluctantly joined him. The cab slowed.

''Ere, what the hell you doing?!' shouted the driver, waving a fist from the window. Then his tone changed, surprise replacing the anger. ''Ere! Aren't you that bloke off the TV?'

For once, Dan thought the dreaded words could just work for him. Usually followed by a jabbing finger and, "What you should be reporting on," or "What you don't understand is," this time being recognised might be useful. They clambered in to the back of the cab.

'Yeah, I'm the man on the telly and we've got a story breaking,' said Dan. 'Quick as you like please.'

The man whistled. 'Cool. I've always wanted to do something like this. Wait until I tell the Mrs! Hold tight.'

The taxi's wheels squealed in protest as the driver forced it into a spinning U-turn. Dan and El instinctively grabbed the door handles to steady themselves. Dan started going through his Scramble plan. He called Nigel to get him to Freedman's house, then the newsroom. There was a satisfactory panic at the end of the line. The outside broadcast truck would be despatched. They wanted a live report for the 10.25 bulletin.

The cab's engine gunned as it headed through the city centre, past the bombed-out Charles Church, lonely memorial to the Blitz of Plymouth, up to the University, all glass and concrete towers, and on to El's flat on North Hill.

The taxi pulled up on the double yellow lines and the photographer jumped out, jogged up the path and waddled back less than a minute later, panting heavily, camera slung around his neck. He cradled it lovingly as he climbed back into the cab. Despite the warmth of the evening, El wore his familiar battered body warmer, its pockets filled with flash bulbs, lens cloths, light meters and spare batteries. The paparazzo was ready for action.

Dan checked his ever-unreliable second-hand Rolex. Almost nine o'clock it said, so probably about ten past. Only an hour and a quarter until the late news. They'd have to move quickly.

El handed Dan the jacket he'd borrowed for the auction. 'Here mate, think you'll need this.'

Dan took it and checked the inside pocket. The black tie he kept for sudden VIP death stories was safely there. Good. He found a few scraps of paper in his jeans pocket. Enough for some hasty notes. He had all he needed.

Blackmail, sex, a fake bomb and the suicide of a well-known MP. It sounded like the sort of story journalists dreamt of. He looked at El. The photographer's face was soft with the whimsical contentment that said he sensed a scandal erupting, and the scent of big money to be made.

The cab sped through a turning traffic light, screeched around a corner. The flats and terraces of the city centre faded, replaced instead by semi-detached houses. All were in the impeccable decorative order so beloved of estate agents, all with two or more cars in the drive, and all with neatly trimmed lawns, both front and back, naturally. They'd reached Hartley, probably the most upmarket area of Plymouth, although many locals joke that might be a contradiction in terms.

The taxi growled to a stop in Hawthorn Lane and Dan hopped out, El managing more of an untidy clamber. Elegance had always eluded him. Within seconds of their arrival, curtains began twitching.

It was that kind of an area.

'Thanks, mate,' said Dan, giving the driver a ten pound note. 'Keep the change, but do me a receipt would you?'

'Done,' said the man, grinning and exposing a couple of gold front teeth. He handed Dan a piece of paper. 'Me mobile number's on there. Call me if you need anything and I'll drop what I'm doing and come. I've always wanted to get into TV. The birds love it.'

Dan couldn't disagree. He knew he was a reasonable-looking man, had his own teeth, most of his allocation of hair still hanging on, albeit forlornly, was neither fat nor thin; in short, very average. But many of his romantic entwinements had been kindled by women recognising him from the television. They seemed to assume it guaranteed a level of quality that he usually failed to come close to living up to.

And now those days were gone, Dan reminded himself. He was in a serious and contented relationship, about to buy a house with Claire. It was the first time he would live with a woman and attempt that intimidating and long-avoided phenomenon only ever whispered by men – and even then looking over their shoulders, as if in fear of the fabled bogey man – the thing known as "commitment".

Dan expected to feel a nudge of nostalgia for his carefree bachelor days, just a hint of regret, but was pleased to find none came. It must be right, this new way.

He hoped.

He and El walked quickly over to the house. A couple of uniformed cops stood outside on sentry duty. There was a line of cars and a white van on the road outside, Greater Wessex Police CID and scientific support staff standard issue, but there were no other journalists or photographers.

'Great!' hollered El, stroking the long lens of his camera lovingly. 'We're first on the scene and not another snapper in sight. I can whazz the pics off to all the nationals and clean up.' He mimicked the sound of an old-fashioned cash register. 'Kerching!'

The photographer's face warmed into a sleazy grin and he launched into one of his bizarre limericks.

'There once was a dead MP,
Who made poor El happy,
He was mired in scandal,
Which lit up El's candle,
As he did his snap snappy!'

El raised his camera and began clicking off a series of pictures of the house. Staccato white flashes lit the darkening night.

Freedman's home was a politician's choice. Pleasant and respectable, but not ostentatious, just right to fit in with his people. Semi-detached, circa 1930. Whitewashed stone, new slate roof, probably four bedrooms, safe and enclosed garden at the back for the kids. Couple of lemon trees and a patch of grass in the front garden, bird table with a half-full wire mesh feeder hanging down. It said family and contentment.

Dan had never interviewed Freedman, but remembered he talked a good game of compassionate politics, not letting yourself get too far removed from your constituents. Living here he could claim to be one of them, even if his life was nothing like the nine-to-five office grind of most of theirs.

A diesel engine rumbled and groaned. A large white van with Wessex Tonight painted on the side bumped up the pavement, slewing heavily from side to side. A thickly bearded face poked out from the driver's window. 'Loud' Jim Stone, the outside broadcast engineer had arrived.

'Bloody late for a call out,' he grumbled accusingly. 'I was getting ready to go to bed. Even had me pyjamas on.'

The hairy head disappeared back into the cab. The truck jumped into reverse, lurched backwards and snapped a sapling. The two policemen watching from the drive exchanged glances and shook their heads. Dan smiled his best placating look at them and shrugged. He fumbled his mobile from his pocket and called Adam.

'Not a good time,' the detective replied, emphasising the first word.

'Sorry, I know you're busy, but …'

'And I know you've got a bulletin in an hour,' Adam cut in. 'Working with you has ingrained them in my thoughts. I'll give you a call in a while with some info. Don't worry, I can guarantee you it'll be in time and interesting.'

Another car pulled up fast, a green estate. Nigel jumped out, ran around to the back and grabbed his camera and tripod from the boot. Dan noticed he was wearing slippers, but managed not to comment.

'Evening,' said Dan. 'Welcome to the latest episode in our frantic "run around like trained hamsters to get a story on air" show. That's Freedman's house, and the only pictures we've got so far. So I'll have as much of it as you can shoot to start us off please. Lots of the cops guarding the place too.'

The two officers straightened their tunics and caps and stood up straight at the sight of the TV camera. It had that magical effect, could create a parallel world of polite, smart and efficient illusion in the ambit of the lens.

Nigel set up the tripod, checked the camera's focus and exposure. 'OK,' he said, his eye fixed to the viewfinder. Dan noticed he already felt more relaxed having his friend here. A few years older than him, Nigel and he had been through countless stories together, many difficult and emotional, but had always managed to produce some decent television. Nigel had also appointed himself father-figure to his errant reporter, and his wise counsel was often invaluable.

Dan stood behind him, watching Nigel's back as a good TV reporter should. The cameraman was oblivious to much of the world when looking down the lens. Now it was time for some research. Dan called the newsroom library for a quick biography of Freedman. It'd be useful for background and context and they could also use an archive story to show pictures of the man.

Forty-four years old, Dan scribbled on the back of a flier for a nightclub. Began in politics as a "special adviser", or spin doctor, at the age of 25. Elected Traditionalist Party MP for Plymouth Tamar in the General Election of 1997. Good majority too, almost eight thousand votes. Only the second mixed-race MP the party had. Well regarded by his constituents, several items about him campaigning hard on local issues, winning the refurbishment of a local junior school, the building of a new swimming pool, and traffic calming for one street that suffered from being a rat run.

One sad story dominated his past. Just over ten years ago, Yvonne had become pregnant and given birth to a boy. He was named Andrew James, after Freedman's father who had died the previous year. There was a series of articles in the local press about the couple's delight at having a son.

In a magazine interview, Freedman joked, 'I'm delighted because now it evens the family up, and I'll have an ally in the house to make sure I get to watch the football on TV.' Yvonne had playfully retorted, 'Don't bet on it!'

The next story, covered in all the papers, was the news the baby had died. Dan could sense the shock. There was no interview with the Freedmans, just some quotes from friends talking about the couple wanting private time to come to terms with their loss, and being 'devastated'. It was the standard word produced at a time of any personal disaster, the nearest most could come to expressing their despair, but this time Dan found himself nodding. He could hardly imagine the pain. A new life so quickly ended.

He'd never wanted children, in truth had never even thought about it, but now realised he'd begun wondering if perhaps, just maybe, one day he and Claire might … He stopped the run of thought. First, find a house and see how living together goes. That was a step quite sufficient for now.

A gap of several months and then another story, about Will Freedman becoming patron of a charity dedicated to research into the causes of cot death. And now many more reports about him repeatedly raising the issue in parliament and tireless fundraising for the cause. The most prominent was a cycle ride from Land's End to John O'Groats. It was a familiar enough tale, barely newsworthy any more, but Freedman had found a new angle to make sure he attracted plenty of interest. He'd done the whole trip on a Penny Farthing.

There was one quirky item, from a couple of the national papers. Freedman had become chairman of the All Party Commons' Gardening Group. Apparently he loved to relax with a bit of pottering amongst the greenery. Dan wondered whether it helped keep his mind from the death of his son.

The librarian read excerpts from more profiles and stories. Freedman certainly received a healthy press. He was regarded as a rising star of the Traditionalist Party. Speciality economics, which he'd read at university in Southampton, part of the Traditionalists' Treasury team. Tipped to join the Shadow Cabinet by the next election. Strong on family values, a recurring theme in his speeches.

"The family is all, the foundation and heartbeat of our society. Anyone who betrays it, betrays us all", was a quote that resonated. Dan juggled the phone under his chin and added it to the end of his list.

He thanked the librarian and hung up. The flier was almost full, a good measure he had enough background material. It certainly helped to explain why Freedman might be pushed to suicide if he was caught with his trousers down. It would destroy his reputation and career in an instant.

Adam stood in the bathroom of the Freedman family home and forced himself to study the corpse.

The man's eyes were mercifully closed and he looked oddly at ease. A half empty whisky bottle lay on its side on the floor, spreading a sticky, amber puddle across the stripped wooden floorboards. There was still condensation on the bathroom window.

'Dead,' said Silifant, the police doctor. He sniffed hard, stood up slowly from the body and pulled unattractively at a tuft of silvery hair protruding from his left ear.

'Very dead in fact,' he added. 'This was no cry for attention. He saved up a lovely cocktail of all sorts of pills. They would probably have done the trick on their own. Combine them with the insulin and whisky and it's a quick goodnight. One of the more efficient suicides I've seen. Nine out of ten for lethal effect, I'd say.'

Adam rolled his eyes. He'd never come to terms with Silifant's way of dealing with death. 'Still marking corpses for efficiency of dispatch then, doctor?' he asked tetchily.

It was a familiar argument, and Silifant produced his

standard reply. 'It lessens the tedium of being a mere worker on the factory line of mortality.'

'What's a ten then?' asked Adam. 'Spontaneous human combustion?'

The doctor edged out of the room, holding his back. 'Something like that. But this was a good effort. Not as dramatic as plunging off a building or throwing yourself in front of a train, but just as effective and certainly less messy. Nine out of ten for him. Goodnight.'

Silifant stepped carefully down the stairs, one hand still on his back. He'd injured himself playing golf. That in itself was something of a mystery. It wasn't the easiest game in which to maim yourself, hardly replete with physical risk. He was one of those men whom it was impossible to accurately age, but was probably somewhere between 50 and 65. Adam tried, but usually failed, not to hope the figure was closer to the retirement age. Silifant had become the local police doctor by simple virtue of the fact that no one else appeared to want the job.

Adam thought he heard a faint sobbing from below. Mrs Freedman and their daughter Alex, being comforted by a police Family Liaison Officer. The usual pathetic attempts to soften the shattering shock. An endless supply of cups of tea, a uniformed stranger's arm around the shoulder. They did their best, but it never worked. What could?

Detective Sergeant Claire Reynolds stood in the doorway behind him, her hands intertwined over her stomach. 'Who found the body?' asked Adam, still staring at the frozen form.

'Mrs Freedman, sir. She came upstairs to find her husband like this.'

'Any possible doubt about it being a suicide?'

'Not that I can see, sir. The house was locked up, very secure and there's no sign whatsoever of a break in. I've called out Scenes of Crime to check the place to be certain, but I don't think there's any doubt. And there's a note too.'

Adam sighed, nodded, picked at a stray fibre which had the temerity to have attached itself to his suit. 'So, what does the note say?'

'I haven't touched it, sir. It was left in the Freedman's bedroom. Mrs Freedman read it, then threw it down on the bed. I thought I'd wait for you to have a look. What I told you on the phone about blackmail and that Judgement Book thing came from Mrs Freedman.'

Adam pursed his lips, then said, 'Let's see for ourselves then. It's time to delve into the despair of a dead man's soul.'

Chapter Three

THE FREEDMANS' BEDROOM WAS unremarkable, the sort you'd find in a million family homes. A couple of built-in wardrobes, a dresser and a chest of drawers. A double-glazed window looked out over the back garden. Adam pushed open a curtain. A spill of light from the windows downstairs revealed it was immaculately kept, bordered with neat earth beds.

The walls of the room were painted cream. Two sets of pine bedside cabinets, a digital radio and alarm clock on one. His side, Adam thought. It was usually the man who had the gadget. The clock's glowing red numerals said 9.46.

He picked up the note, holding it carefully by its top corners so Claire could read it too. The handwriting looked shaky, but was painstakingly legible, as if produced by a child trying to impress a teacher.

> *Dear Yvonne and Alex,*
> *Please forgive me. I've been the most stupid and selfish of men. I hate to have to tell you this, but I'd rather you heard it from me than the newspapers. I know that's where it will end up. I'm so sorry.*
> *In a moment of weakness, on a conference, I spent a night with a young prostitute. I don't expect you to understand and I don't try to excuse my behaviour, but I'd had a few drinks and couldn't stop myself. I can still hardly believe I did it. I've never ceased hating myself for it. But even worse, somehow, someone got to know about it. I've been blackmailed. The blackmailer didn't ask for money, but seemed to want to humiliate me. In an odd way that was worse than some outrageous financial demand. The power he had over me was a torture. He set out very clearly in a letter what I had done and said that if I wanted to save myself, I had to solve a riddle. It was as though he was enjoying toying with me, watching me suffer. I*

can't describe to you the depths of the pit of despair I've known in the last few days.

Forgive me if I've been behaving strangely, but recently I've been doing little except trying to solve the riddle. I'm afraid I have failed and the time limit the blackmailer set is up. I have no doubt he is about to expose me, so this is the way out I've chosen. I could see no other. At least this way the screams of scandal will be brief. The press will not have the fun of chasing me down the street every time I venture out and the blackmailer will be denied the enjoyment of seeing the pictures. Most importantly, you two will be spared it.

Again, I ask for your forgiveness. I couldn't bring myself to tell you what I had done and what I've been going through in person. Despite all this, please never doubt that I love you both very much and wish I could have been a better man for you. Please try to find it in your hearts to forgive me.

My love always,

Will

PS. I know the police will have to become involved. To them I say this: Please do everything possible to catch this person. He has taunted me with the knowledge of my own stupidity and weakness, and used his power over me in a sick and ruthless way. He has also told me that four other well-known people have behaved in similar immoral, criminal or corrupt ways, and that they too will suffer the attentions of what the blackmailer calls the "Judgement Book". Please try to help these people, find this Book, and destroy it.

Adam laid the note gently back down on the double bed. He breathed out heavily. Claire said nothing. From downstairs, there was another muffled sob. Adam pointed to a couple of streaks on the paper, icicles of ink where the writing had smudged and blurred.

'Tear marks,' said Claire quietly.

Adam nodded slowly. 'He was crying as he wrote. And he was a decent man, you know. He did a lot for this city. He helped us stop plans for a hostel for sex offenders being set up in a street not far from my house. And he championed a police sports project which turned a load of kids away from crime when the council didn't want to know. He'll be missed.'

The detective's voice hardened. 'Get the search teams in. Get them going over the house. Begin in whatever room he used as a study. Get the Square Eyes technical boys in too. They can start on his computer to see if he's been using it to try to solve this riddle. We've got to find the note this blackmailer sent him.'

He hesitated, ran a hand over the dark stubble on his cheeks. 'I'm going to talk to Mrs Freedman.'

Yvonne Freedman was sitting in the living room in the corner of a beige sofa, her legs scrunched up tight to her body, her arms wrapped around them. Her eyes were narrow slits, edged red and angry. Alex sat in a matching chair, staring at her mother. She wasn't crying, and there was no sign she had been.

Yvonne was a little younger than her husband, around 40 or so. She had chin length, ruffled blonde hair and was probably beautiful, but it was impossible to tell through the fog of her misery. Her face was swollen and sallow. She hadn't changed from the white dressing gown she was wearing when she found her husband's body.

Alex had inherited her father's dark looks. Her eyes were brown and her complexion smooth and Mediterranean, the kind that makes other women stare in jealousy. A spray of auburn hair tumbled over her shoulders. She looked a little overweight Adam thought, but that could just be teenage changes. She wore blue jeans and a red-and-white striped rugby shirt. A square silver stud shone in the side of her nose.

WPC Helen Masters, the Family Liaison Officer, pulled a high-backed wooden dining chair from under a table and Adam sat down. It was unforgiving and uncomfortable, the sort you might offer to a guest who you hoped wouldn't stay too long. He shifted in the seat, took a few seconds to phrase his questions as gently as he could.

'Mrs Freedman, I'm sorry to have to talk to you now,' Adam began. 'I know how much you're suffering.' Her mouth started to open, and he continued quickly, didn't want to get into a discussion about her husband's suicide note. 'I just need to ask a couple of questions.'

Yvonne nodded, a barely perceptible shift of her head.

'Did you have any inkling at all that anything was wrong with your husband? Did he raise anything you thought unusual? Do anything strange?'

A pause, no reply but a slight shake of the head.

Adam thought his way through the note. 'Was he spending a large amount of time working?'

Yvonne's tired eyes closed, but she managed a tiny nod.

Adam waited for her to look back at him, then said softly, 'Was there anything unusual about that? More time than normal?'

'He was always working.'

The harshness of the voice was a shock. It came from Alex.

'That was what he did,' she went on, spelling out each word. 'He worked. That was all he did.'

On the sofa, Yvonne Freedman bowed her head and began crying, soft flutters of breath, then shaking sobs. Alex glared at her and snorted unpleasantly.

WPC Masters sat down beside Yvonne, reached for her hand, held it gently, whispered some soothing noises. The momentum of the new widow's misery was growing. She was struggling to breathe through her tears.

Adam studied her, folded his arms. He knew they would learn nothing more from Yvonne Freedman tonight. 'I'll leave you now,' he said quietly, getting up from his chair. Like most men, despite years of experience, he'd never grown competent at handling a woman's crying. Besides, tears were an unassailable defence against questioning.

He softened his voice, but laced it with a warning. 'I will

need to speak to you again though, and soon. Probably tomorrow morning. For now, just one more thing.'

Adam paused, turned to Alex. Given what they knew about Freedman's liaison with a teenage prostitute, testing the relationship between father and daughter was important.

He said as gently as he could, 'I know he was your dad, but were you particularly close?'

Yvonne Freedman looked up, her mouth falling open, but all that emerged was a whimper. WPC Masters placed a tentative hand on her shoulder. Alex opened her arms theatrically and shook her head. 'Close?' she asked contemptuously. 'How close can you get to someone you never see?'

Adam didn't answer, took a couple of steps towards the door. Almost as an afterthought he added, 'Where did your dad do his work? Did he have a study?'

'Out there,' Alex said sullenly, pointing to the hallway. 'By the kitchen.'

'Thanks,' replied Adam. 'You should both try to get some sleep. A police doctor will help you if you need a sleeping tablet.'

He held her look. Alex shrugged and mumbled something under her breath.

'I'm sorry?' asked Adam, taking a step towards her.

'I said arsehole,' she spat, her dark eyes suddenly wide. 'He was an arsehole. My father. An absolute arsehole. OK?'

10.20. They were on air in five minutes. Dan had to get ready for the bulletin, even if he had nothing to say. Deadlines don't negotiate.

Adam would call, he knew it. But the detective was leaving it damned late.

Dan squeezed the moulded plastic tube into his left ear, tucked into the back of his shirt the cable that connected it to the radio receiver on his belt. The link crackled, then buzzed.

'Testing the line to Dan at the outside broadcast,' came the harassed voice of the director. 'This is Emma in the Wessex Tonight broadcast gallery in Plymouth. Oh, for God's sake, where are you OB?!'

Dan gave a thumbs-up to the camera. 'Hearing you loud and clear,' he said, taking the microphone Nigel was proffering.

There was a groan of relief. 'About time! You're top of the bulletin and we're on air in just under five minutes. Standby. The next time we talk to you it'll be for real.'

Dan felt the adrenaline run, tingling his body and quickening his breath. Live broadcasting, always the most exhilarating part of his job, but by far the most dangerous too. Get it right, and you were admired and respected as cool, composed and authoritative, the man who brought the big news to the hundreds of thousands watching and waiting, hanging on your words of wisdom. But get it wrong, and it was a very public humiliation.

He wondered what the hell he was going to say. All he knew was the thinnest of information from that rushed conversation with Adam. Freedman was dead, suicide, linked to some sex scandal and blackmail. He had no details and no confirmation. What if there'd been a misunderstanding?

It happened. The fire of breaking news could shoot off a thousand sparks of misinformation.

You learn that fast as a hack. First reports were often garbled. In the early minutes of a story, often the only certainty was uncertainty.

What if Freedman was watching and walked out of the house, very much alive, to demand to know what on earth Dan was talking about?

He didn't like the thought of the consequences. Zero credibility and a laughing stock would be the best possible outcome. Unemployment was more likely. Lizzie wasn't a forgiving editor, far from it. He glared at his mobile, but it remained obstinately silent.

'Shift to your left a little Dan please,' called Nigel, from behind the camera. 'There's a tree branching out the top of your head at the moment.' Dan took a step to his side. 'That's better,' said Nigel. 'Got the house nicely behind you if you want to refer to it.'

So, what to say? He'd have to couch his words, pad it out and fill as best he could. He could definitely say the police had been called to Freedman's home earlier that evening. And that detectives were inside at this moment, beginning an investigation into … what?

That was the key question. Whether he could he go further and talk about death, suicide and blackmail. It was the juicy part of the story, what made it so very newsworthy, but the biggest risk.

Nigel flicked on the small but powerful light on top of the camera. Dan blinked a couple of times to allow his eyes to adjust. Three minutes until he was on air. He took a deep breath to calm himself and closed his eyes to focus.

His mobile rang.

Dan jumped, grabbed at his trouser pocket and dropped the phone. Swearing, he scrabbled on the ground, trying to find it in the black and white lines of the shadows.

'Will you stop clowning,' came Emma's piqued voice in his ear. 'We're on air in two minutes. Stand still, man.'

Dan found the phone and answered it. His hands were sweaty and shaking. Adam.

'Wow, am I glad to hear from you. We're on air in minutes. Some ultra-quick questions. Is Freedman dead?'

'Yes.'

'You sure?'

'Very.'

'Suicide?'

'Yes.'

'Where?'

'Bath.'

'Left a note?'

'Yes.'

'Can I say anything about blackmail without harming your investigation?'

A pause on the line.

'Dan, one minute to on air,' yelped Emma. 'Drop that bloody phone and look at the camera.'

'You can say the police are investigating whether Freedman was being blackmailed,' replied Adam calmly. 'Nothing about the sex bit though. I want to keep that quiet for now.'

'OK. Got to go, will call you later.'

'Thirty seconds!' came the director's voice again. 'Drop that phone Dan!'

Dan turned his mobile off and threw it to Nigel. Experience took over. He felt suddenly calm, his mind clear.

Remember the golden rule of broadcasting. If in doubt, just KISS. Keep it short and simple.

'We begin tonight with some breaking news,' came Craig, the presenter's voice in his ear. 'We're getting reports of the death of a prominent local MP in strange circumstances. Our Crime Correspondent Dan Groves joins us from the Plymouth home of Will Freedman. Dan, what more can you tell us?'

'Craig, extraordinary developments here tonight,' said Dan, putting on his most sombre tone. 'A senior police source tells me Mr Freedman has been found dead in his bath and that he committed suicide. A note has been recovered and detectives have begun an investigation. One of the most important elements of that inquiry is to discover whether Mr Freedman was being blackmailed. Now, this news will cause great shock. As you'll appreciate, Will Freedman is a very well known local MP. He's highly regarded in his Plymouth Tamar constituency, a prominent campaigner for traditional family values and is also reckoned to be one of the rising stars of the Traditionalist Party.'

Craig thanked him and they were on to the next story, something about passenger numbers at Exeter airport. Dan hardly heard it. He popped out his earpiece and breathed deeply.

If only the viewers knew. So often the control of the calm and authoritative on-air persona was a tissue-thin layer of bluff.

A police van pulled up by the house. Nigel spun the camera and started filming. A dozen men and women, all dressed in black, hopped down from the back and marched up to the front door. The police officers on guard opened it and they filed in. Dan noted only two wiped their boots on the mat.

'Who's that?' hissed Nigel from behind the camera.

'TAG. Tactical Aid Group. They do all the searches. They must be here to take the house apart.'

Dan picked up his mobile and called Adam.

'I know you're busy,' he said, 'but I just wanted to say thanks for the tip-off and for getting me that info for the bulletin. We got it on – just.'

'No worries. I've been waiting for your call. Now I've got something to ask you.'

'Really?' said Dan, surprised. 'What?'

'This is going to be all over the press and some inside track on how to handle it wouldn't go amiss. Plus the blackmailer's apparently been talking about some Judgement Book of people's secrets, and he seems to have set a code which we're going to have to try to break. You cracked those others we came up against. Do you fancy pitching in with us again? It'd be the same deal as before. You only get to broadcast what I say, but you'll have some exclusive angles on the case in return for your help.'

Dan felt a familiar, stirring excitement. A big case and the inside story – he could hardly ask for more. He'd finally managed to admit to himself how much he loved detective work, perhaps even more than being a reporter. It had changed his life, coming at a time when he'd been a journalist for almost fifteen years and was starting to grow stale, to wonder about doing something new.

Was it really only three years ago he was moved from Environment and given the Crime Correspondent job? And to think, at the time he hated the idea, felt lonely and vulnerable in the new post. Now though, he couldn't get enough of it. It was how he'd met Claire too, and finally just about tamed the debilitating swamp of the depression that had stalked him throughout his life.

'I think we'd be delighted to help you Adam,' Dan replied, trying to keep the excitement from his voice.

'Good. Because we need to get this blackmailer. Freedman was a good man. Whatever he might have done, he didn't deserve to die like this. Come down to Charles Cross for the morning briefing tomorrow. By then I should have a good idea what the blackmailer wants, what's in the so called Judgment

Book, and what this code is.'

Dan grinned, couldn't help himself. He was already looking forward to tomorrow immensely.

Chapter Four

DAN WOKE EARLY, STIRRED by the aura of spring sunlight stretching across his bedroom. He yawned, and was surprised to find himself feeling relaxed and content. He knew he'd been dreaming of Claire, but he couldn't remember the details of the elusive, sleeping images. They flitted on the edge of his memory like smiling ghosts.

He'd have to call her later. They hadn't had a chance to speak yesterday and they'd planned a day out tomorrow. Saturday, his favourite day of the week. A whole day off and the chance to eat and drink well and have a lie-in on Sunday. The weather forecast was benign too. Perhaps they'd go for a walk on the coast.

He swung himself out of bed, leaned down and stroked Rutherford's head. The Alsatian sat up and stretched his mouth into a jaw-cracking yawn. Dan chuckled.

'Classy, my faithful friend,' he said. 'Fancy a run?' Rutherford's tail thumped on the carpet at the sacred word.

They walked over to Hartley park. It was early, just before seven and there was no one else around, so Dan let Rutherford off his lead. The dog sprinted across the jewelled, dewy grass, skidded to a halt, then careered back. Dan steeled himself and broke into a jog.

'Twenty laps of the park hound,' he called to Rutherford, whose head was buried in a thicket of bushes.

It was a beautiful morning, a Devon speciality. There was still an edge of the night's chill in the air, but the ascending sun was fast chasing it away. Hartley Park was one of Plymouth's highest points, rich with fine views on a clear morning.

Dan grimaced as a stick jabbed him in the back of his legs. He stopped jogging and wrestled Rutherford for it. The dog locked his jaws, insurmountable determination in his unblinking eyes.

'I'll never understand why you bring me a stick, then don't want to let go of it, stupid,' Dan told the growling dog. 'But

I've got a trick for this, haven't I?'

He let go of the branch, picked up another from the hedge and held it up like a great prize. Rutherford immediately let go of the stick he was holding and jumped for the new one. Dan threw it, the dog sprinted after it, and Dan picked up the original.

'And I'll never understand how you don't get wise to that con either,' he called.

A gang of starlings squabbled in the trees as he jogged, jostling amongst the brave new buds. The park felt awash with springtime. On the steep slope covering the underground reservoir a pair of magpies hopped and chattered. It was a morning made for contentment.

There was just the one trial to endure, and he had a strategy ready. Dan took Rutherford back to the flat, showered, and put on a clean shirt and his best jacket. His tyrannical editor could require serious manipulating and he had to get it right. He didn't want to risk her turning down Adam's offer to join the blackmail inquiry.

Dan walked into the newsroom just after half past eight. Lizzie was already there, and wearing low heels today, only a couple of inches. A good sign. He ticked off a line on his mental checklist. Only the bravest or most foolhardy approached Lizzie when she wore her favourite four-inch daggers. They were harbingers of peril.

Next, some flattery to oil the approach. 'Morning. I have to say, you're looking good today. Is that a new hair-do?'

A momentary suspicion he thought, but she seemed pleased, tossed her dark bob. 'No, I've just styled it. That's all.'

Dan had learnt early in life that asking a woman if she'd had her hair done was a strategy which couldn't lose. If she had, she was flattered. Ditto if she hadn't. The real risk was saying nothing.

Next on the list, some self-promotion. 'Good story that last night, I thought,' he said, trying not to sound sly.

She nodded. 'It was acceptable.'

'Obviously as I was out covering it – out late that is – and in my own time, of course – I didn't get to see the opposition's bulletin. Did they have the story?'

'No.'

'So it was our exclusive.'

'Yep.'

'On a huge story.'

'Yep.'

'Could be an award-winner, that one.'

'Yep.'

An eyebrow arched. Another good sign. He was making headway, albeit slowly. As with so many of Dan's conversations with his editor, it felt like being on board an ice-breaker, the ship trying to make its way through the Arctic Ocean in the middle of a frozen winter.

They held a look. Lizzie narrowed her eyes and raised a finger from the desk. Long experience had taught Dan that she found unqualified praise impossible. He sensed one of her familiar "Not rest on our laurels" speeches coming, the kind which she used every time Wessex Tonight scored a success. Complacency was never an option with Lizzie.

Dan took a gamble, got his spin in first. 'Well, I don't want to rest on my laurels, naturally. It's too big a story.'

She nodded again and Dan sensed the final target on his range was within sight.

'It's so good for the ratings,' he added. 'I bet people are turning to us in their thousands for the latest on what's going on with Freedman and this blackmail plot.'

Lizzie nodded dreamily. The ratings were her church. Every morning she'd sit in her office for half an hour, scouring scores of statistics from last night's programme for clues as to the viewers' current likes and dislikes.

'Well, that's why I've lined us up a follow-up story for today,' Dan continued. 'And I reckon we've got a great chance for some more corking exclusives.'

He outlined Adam's offer of joining the inquiry, then quietened, waited for the reaction. A perfectly manicured fingernail tapped on the desk.

'What are you up to?' she asked eventually.

'Nothing.' Dan tried for a hurt expression, but he'd never

got the hang of them. 'I'm just trying to do my best for you and the programme – as always.'

She laced her look with acid suspicion, as only Lizzie could.

'Done,' she said finally. 'But on one condition. I want wall-to-wall coverage. You got that? Wall-to-wall, then floor-to-floor, then back to wall-to-wall again. Oh, and ceiling-to-ceiling too. I want the lot, I want it first and I want it exclusive to us. And I don't want you disappearing into the investigation like you have before. You're a hack, remember, not a detective. This is a fantastic story and the viewers will be hooked.' She stood up and wagged the fingernail at him. 'You got that?'

'Yes boss,' Dan replied meekly.

He'd have been disappointed with anything less.

Dan walked into the Major Incident Room, or MIR, just before nine o'clock. Heads turned with the curiosity of a bunch of detectives and he looked away to hide a smile. He'd laid two bets with himself as he drove down to Charles Cross Police Station. That Adam would be wearing his best suit in expectation of a television interview, and that the detective's beloved green boards would have been retrieved from storage.

Dan sometimes wondered if the world of the media and television had beguiled his friend as much as he himself had fallen for the realm of the detective.

Adam stood at the front of the room, dressed in an immaculate navy suit, white shirt and blue-and-white diagonally striped tie. Always a handsome man, with his dark and rugged looks, today he could have passed as prepared for a modelling shoot. Four green felt boards stood on their chipped wooden legs beside him.

It was one of the first things Adam had said to Dan when they'd met, and even now he could remember it, almost word for word. He'd been nervous, new to the Crime Correspondent job, an eager amateur, and Adam had taken it upon himself to impart some wisdom.

The detective had straightened his tie, that odd quirk of his when he felt life was running his way, and launched into his little speech, the justification for the anachronism of his boards.

'Computers are vital in modern policing, don't get me wrong. But sometimes, to crack a case, you have to see the web of links between people set out in front of you. Too many detectives mistake computers for brains. Crimes are committed by humans, not machines, and only people can solve them. Computers are tools to help, but they can't see the invisible threads that connect people and events, which in one lightning strike of realisation give you the key to the crime.'

It had become a familiar oration.

The room was filled with about thirty people, mostly detectives in well-worn suits, but there was also a sprinkling of uniformed officers at the front. A rumble of expectant conversation resonated. It felt like a tribal gathering, the excitement of the meet before the hunt.

Dan weaved his way to his customary position at the back of the room and propped himself up against the window ledge. No matter how many times he was invited to join an inquiry, he'd never got over the feeling of being an interloper. He was always more comfortable secreting himself at the back, knew many around him felt he had no place here. A couple of detectives nodded a half hearted greeting, others whispered hostility or shook their heads contemptuously. Most just seemed to regard him as a curiosity.

Claire stood at the front, to Adam's side. She was wearing her standard black trouser-suit, looked professional, authoritative, and simply beautiful. They exchanged a brief glance. They'd agreed to be discreet about their relationship when working, even though everyone else knew. You couldn't keep a secret from detectives.

'OK, everyone, let's make a start,' Adam said, and the room quietened. 'This is going to be quick, as we have to get out there and get the inquiry running. We need some momentum to carry us to our killer. And that's what we're looking for. We're hunting a killer – not perhaps with a knife or a gun like we're used to, but a killer nonetheless. Someone who drives people to their death.'

He paused, looked around the room, eye contact for every officer. It was Adam's way at the start of a case, to energise his team with a vision, make them feel they had a righteous mission to pursue. The nods and mutters of agreement indicated the words had done their work.

Adam pointed to a photo stuck to the centre of the middle board. 'Will Freedman, MP. Killed himself yesterday at his home. Two key points to start with.'

Another pause, letting the words settle. 'First, his family,' Adam went on, pointing to two more pictures next to Freedman's. 'Wife Yvonne and daughter Alex. They were downstairs when he killed himself. Was he getting at them in some way? Why choose the house, when it could have been a cliff, or railway line? He could have spared them that distress, couldn't he? Or was it just that he wanted to be in his own home when he died?'

A few of the younger detectives took notes. Most just listened. The room was silent, rapt.

'I had a chance to speak briefly with Yvonne and Alex last night,' Adam continued. 'They were upset, of course. But with Alex, it was more than that. She was scathing about her Dad. So what's that about then? Is it just the shock and upset of her father's death? Or something more sinister?'

No one spoke. Outside, a plane droned by. Adam watched it thoughtfully for a few seconds, then continued.

'Right then, let's start thinking. I want ideas how we find our killer. First, let's have a look at the letter the blackmailer sent Freedman. The TAG teams found it a couple of hours ago. It was well hidden, stuck between some constituency research papers inside a folder in his study.'

Claire passed around a sheaf of papers. Dan took one of the last copies and began reading. He knew from the hisses of breath from the detectives around him that what he was about to see was shocking.

Dear Mr Freedman,
You are a despicable man. Like many of your kind,
you pretend to be one thing in public, when the
private reality is very different.
You are an adulterer, a frequenter of prostitutes, a

liar and a hypocrite. All that, despite your fine talk of family values. You are utterly odious.

I know what happened in Blackpool. A nineteen-year-old prostitute, dressed as a schoolgirl. How will you explain that to your fourteen-year-old daughter? Let alone your loving and devoted wife?

It was a nice trick, using a different – and sleazy – hotel to the one you were staying in to meet her. Paying for the room in cash was a wise precaution. The false glasses and the hat were pretty touches too. But still I know what you did.

I'm surprised you only managed to have sex with her twice. That's not exactly great value for money – as I believe you Traditionalists espouse – when you've paid five hundred pounds for her services, is it? Particularly not given how excited you were. The fulfilment of a long-cherished fantasy, wasn't that how you thought of sex with a schoolgirl?

I can't bring myself to pass any comment on the extra fifty pounds you paid to spank her.

So, Mr Freedman, we have established you are a thoroughly despicable man. The question is, what do I intend to do about it?

You'll be expecting me to ask for cash. Wrong, totally wrong. I don't want your filthy money. My only interest is in exposing you. You and your rotten kind.

Will it be any comfort to know you are not alone, Mr Freedman? Your sordid secrets fill my beautiful Judgement Book. But there are others there too. Others of your kind. You are the first, but you will not be the last. I've chosen four others to share your fate. Is that any comfort?

You don't deserve this, but I will give you one chance to save yourself. The following riddle, if solved, will give you a word. It's a classic game. If you can break it, use that word to begin your speech to the Plymouth Traditionalist Association on Thursday night. If I do not hear it, news of your little indiscretion will be

spread far and wide.
61, 43, 21, 51
For your information, and for the police who will no
doubt eventually come to see this note, I add this. The
solution to the riddle, and those which I will set for
the other four chose ones, will take you to the hiding
place of the Judgement Book.
Good luck.

Dan breathed out heavily and looked up from the photocopied sheet. Some of the detectives were still reading, others staring sightlessly ahead, lost in their thoughts. A series of gasps and low whistles punctuated the silence of the room. It took something extraordinary to surprise such experienced officers, but Dan could tell from their reactions they'd never seen anything like this before.

Adam waited until everyone had finished reading, then asked, 'So, what do we make of that?'

'A bloody nutter,' growled one uniformed officer at the front.

'Perhaps,' replied Adam, slowly. 'Or someone coldly sane and with a grand purpose – in their eyes at least. You all remember that hoax bomb in Plymouth? That contained a note which talked about a Judgement Book opening. We dismissed it as a crank at the time. But now we have to ask ourselves – was that a warning of what was to come?'

Another silence. Most of the crowd in the MIR kept glancing down at the blackmail note. Next to Dan one woman whispered what they all seemed to be thinking. 'What the hell are we up against here?'

A middle-aged detective in a crumpled suit spoke. 'It's that stuff about the schoolgirl that's worrying, isn't it, sir? If Freedman liked them that age, what could have been going on with his daughter?'

There were a couple of groans from around the room. 'My thoughts exactly, Jack,' replied Adam. 'An unpleasant possibility, but something we have to look at. It's a sensitive one. You and Claire can handle it.'

The man nodded, as did Claire. Dan noticed she was rubbing her hand over her stomach. He wondered if she was feeling ill. She looked a little pale. He reminded himself to call her as soon as he could.

'Come on then, team, what else?' Adam demanded. 'Where else do we go?'

'What about the riddle, sir?' asked a young detective at the side of the room.

'What indeed?' replied Adam. 'Well, as it's such a high profile case, we've got codebreaking experts coming in courtesy of the National Crime Faculty. We can let them work on the riddle. Us mere mortals will stick to the mundane old detective work.'

Dan stared at the pictures of the Freedmans on the felt boards. He knew he wouldn't be leaving the codes alone. He'd always found puzzles enticing, and was bloody-minded enough not to give up until he knew the solution. He studied the numbers on the photocopied sheet.

61, 43, 21, 51

He wondered how they could form a word. His first instinct was that they looked like coordinates, but to where? And why so many number ones? Dan tried to let the numbers swirl in his mind, to see if they'd form any patterns, but Adam's voice drew him back to the MIR.

'So where else do we go then, team? Come on, let's start making some progress. The media are all over us, not to mention our beloved High Honchos at headquarters. And it looks like the blackmailer has other victims in mind. We've got to stop him. So, what about how he knows all this? Could he have been there at the hotel, when Freedman was with this prostitute?'

There were some murmurs of no. 'I agree,' said Adam. 'How could he? He'd have to have been in the actual room. And kinky though he might have been, Freedman wouldn't have been up for giving a show. So, could he have bugged the room?'

'Or she, sir,' said Claire quietly.

Adam nodded. 'Quite right. Our blackmailer could be a man

or a woman. So, come on then team. How does our person get their information?'

Dan started to speak, but stopped himself. He was an observer here, however much he might like to think of himself as an amateur detective. But Adam had spotted the movement and turned, head tilted expectantly. Dan felt his face reddening.

'Yes?' Adam prompted. 'Come on, if you've got an idea, share it with us. You're amongst friends.'

A lick of laughter rolled around the room. Everyone was staring at Dan. There was no way out.

'It sounds like a conversation to me,' he made himself say, trying to keep his voice calm and level.

'Explain,' replied Adam.

Dan looked down at his photocopied sheet, gave himself time to think.

'Well …' he began, and, annoyed to hear his voice croak, swallowed hard. 'It sounds like the details are taken from something Freedman himself said. It's all from his perspective, isn't it? How could some observer know it was his fantasy, to have sex with a schoolgirl? And everything about the disguise, the cost of the room and the extra fifty quid for the spanking? It sounds like a level of detail and insight that could only come from the man himself.'

'So what are you saying?' asked Adam. 'That he told someone about it? Wrote it down somewhere?'

The room was still oppressively silent. Dan avoided eye contact with anyone but Adam.

'Not wrote it down,' he said finally. 'That'd be too risky. I'd guess he told someone about it. And that's how the blackmailer got to know.'

Adam nodded thoughtfully. 'But it's a very detailed account, isn't it? That's what makes it so convincing. And we have to assume the blackmailer got it right, otherwise why would Freedman kill himself? It doesn't sound like a rumour, something someone heard second or third hand.'

Now it was Dan's turn to nod. Suddenly he was more relaxed. It felt like just the two of them talking, as they had so many times before, friends discussing a case in a quiet corner of a pub.

'Yes,' Dan said. 'It sounds like the blackmailer heard it all from Freedman himself. But who would he tell about something like that?'

'Who do we tell our innermost secrets to?' asked Adam. 'Our family usually, but clearly not here. So let's see if Freedman had any close friends he might have confided to. Boasted to, even.'

'And there's another possibility, isn't there?' mused Dan. 'Is Freedman religious?'

'Why?'

'What if he's confessed what he did to a priest? What if that's how the blackmailer got all this?'

'Good thought,' said Adam. 'And let's take it one step further. Who else do people speak to in professional confidence? What if Freedman had a counsellor? Might he have talked to them? What about a lawyer? Or a doctor? Maybe he was worried about catching something from the prostitute and had to go to his doctor and explain. Let's get working on anyone Freedman could have told about his fatal indiscretion.'

Some of the detectives, mainly the younger, more keen ones, took more notes, others just nodded.

'Right,' Adam said, with a tone in his voice that said it was time for the discussion to end, 'there's just one more thing for now then. Our little game. What do we call our blackmailer?'

In his experience of major investigations, Dan had quickly learnt it was a tradition to give the criminal they were hunting a nickname, and often an unpleasant one.

'How about Blackie, as it's a blackmailer?' an older man at the back said, and laughter rolled around the room.

'Not in these days of painful political correctness,' Adam replied. 'No matter how harmless the idea it could be misinterpreted, and I don't need some daft row with the PC brigade. Come on, give me something else.'

There was a silence, filled with thinking, then Claire said, 'Worm.'

'Worm?'

'Yes. We don't know if we're hunting a man or woman, and

worms are hermaphrodites. Plus – well, Worm seems to sum up the kind of person our blackmailer is.'

Adam nodded. 'Worm it is.'

The door swung open and rattled against the wall. A uniformed sergeant bumbled in. He was chubby and red-faced.

'Sorry to interrupt you, Mr Breen,' the man said, with a hint of a Welsh accent.

'Yes, Taff?' replied Adam. The police had never been renowned as the most imaginative organisation, particularly with their nicknames.

'Something you should know about, sir. Two of the bobbies on patrol have just reported something bizarre. They've arrested a bill-poster. He was sticking up a board near the city centre, one of those huge ones out in the middle of the Marsh Mills roundabout.'

The sergeant looked around at the expectant faces. 'Go on,' replied Adam.

'This billboard, sir. It only had writing on, not like those fancy posters with pictures that you see, just these great big letters. But it was what it said that made me think, sir, given what happened yesterday ...'

'Just tell us, man,' snapped Adam, losing patience.

'Yes, sir. Sorry, sir. It said –'

The sergeant squinted at his note book. Everyone was watching him intently. Dan was tempted to ask the assembled to hold a quick vote on whether Taff's nickname should henceforth be changed to procrastinator.

Adam folded his arms, glared. A perfectly polished black brogue tapped irascibly on the floor.

The sergeant looked up and finally the elusive information came. And, remarkably, it was worth waiting for.

'I've got it now, sir. Here it is. It said – "Vote Will Freedman MP, Prostitute Party."'

Chapter Five

ADAM RAN DOWN THE police station stairs, Dan following. Their clattering footsteps echoed from the cold concrete and chased them along the flights. A series of uniformed officers and traffic wardens stood back to let them through. The MIR was on the fourth floor, but Adam wasn't at all breathless.

'Come on,' he called over his shoulder. 'I've had the world's press on the phone to the station this morning wanting interviews. You can tell me what you reckon's best to do while we go see this poster. I think we just found out how our Worm planned to expose Freedman.'

Adam jogged over to a battered blue Vauxhall Cavalier and climbed in. The car smelt strongly of stale cigarettes. The detective pushed a series of buttons until one rolled down a window. He breathed in the clean air, gunned the engine and accelerated out of the police station.

'What are you going to do with the poster?' Dan asked, as they followed Exeter Street eastwards, out to the edge of the city. He fumbled to clip the seat belt around him. Adam's driving wasn't reassuring.

'Look at it, get it photographed, then taken down and bagged up for forensics to check.'

Perfect, thought Dan, but didn't say so. Not yet. He was thinking his way through the scoop he wanted, and how to sell it to Adam.

Yet again he was serving two masters. He needed to bank some credit with Lizzie, appease her with a sacrificial story to be sure of securing time to work on the case. Over the past few years he'd had to learn to become adept at balancing the two interconnected worlds, hack and amateur detective, keeping both Lizzie and Adam happy. It could usually be done, but sometimes required near-shameful cunning and the kind of deviousness which would make Machiavelli rise from the ground and applaud enthusiastically.

The car's clock said it was coming up for half past ten. The timings might just work out.

'And what about the media?' Dan asked, holding on to the door strap to fight the force of Adam's cornering. A couple of horns blared from the blurs of the cars they passed.

'Haven't thought about that yet. Got more important things to worry about.'

They turned onto the embankment, the sun laying a carpet of diamonds on the wandering River Plym. The green slopes and spreading trees of the parkland around Saltram Country house rose from the opposite bank. It should have been one of the city's most beautiful areas, in many places it would have boasted a promenade, cafés, shops and bars. Not in Plymouth, city of missed opportunities. Here there was a railway line and dual carriageway.

A couple of canoeists paddled hard through the smooth waters, leaving waves of glitter in their wake. An occasional fisherman sat hunched over his rod. Dan suspected they were more enjoying the day than in serious pursuit of an elusive fish. The effort of catching and landing one of the unfortunate creatures might only spoil the mood.

Adam accelerated around a milk lorry and the car bounced on the bumps in the uneven road. Dan's stomach lurched with it. They'd be at the Marsh Mills roundabout in a couple of minutes. Time to make the move.

'I've got a suggestion about the media,' Dan said, trying to make his voice sound nonchalant.

'What?'

'A press conference. That way you'll sort them all out at once. Give them half an hour of your time and they'll go away with a story and leave you alone for a while.'

'Not a bad idea. But I've got lots on with the investigation and can't really spare the time.'

'It'll be worthwhile,' Dan quickly interrupted. 'We can make the media work for us. I reckon if I come up with what you should say, we can hit big articles in all the papers, national and local, and get it on all the TV and radio news too.'

'How would that help?'

'We could work in a way to try to get anyone who knows

50

Freedman to come forward. Particularly the people we discussed at the briefing. Lawyers, priests, that sort of thing. And any of his mates. It could be a useful shortcut to finding them. It might even raise something at the Blackpool end.'

They were approaching the roundabout. Adam slowed the car and changed down a gear. The engine growled in protest.

'Mmm,' he said thoughtfully. 'Sounds good. What would I have to say to make sure all the media ran it?'

'Don't worry, I'll sort that bit out. I've got a few ideas.'

Dan ignored the warning voice in his mind that told him he was yet again crossing the line. From impartial hack to … freelance detective and media adviser. It went against all the journalistic principles of impartiality and neutrality. He could see Lizzie berating him, a sharpened fingernail wagging.

The thought succeeded only in making him smile.

A couple of police cars had pulled up on the side of the road ahead. The traffic slowed as other motorists gawped and pointed. For some people, this was high excitement. Only last week Dan had realised the numbing mundanity of many lives when he'd sat in the Old Bank pub on Mutley Plain, waiting for El, and overheard three women animatedly advocating the merits of various deodorants. The discussion had lasted almost half an hour.

Adam indicated and tucked in behind the police cars.

'And what's the price?' he asked, reaching for the car door.

'I don't know what you mean,' Dan replied lamely.

'Just get on with it please, time's against us. Remember how well I now know you.'

Dan tried to keep a straight face. 'Fair cop. OK, let me get Nigel here to film the billboard before you take it down. It'll be a scoop for me. That's the trade off for the advice on how to handle the media.'

Adam didn't reply, so Dan continued his salesman's patter, 'Then I'll work up a way of getting the story everywhere. It'll really give the investigation some momentum.'

They got out of the car, walked over to the roundabout. Dan pointedly took out his mobile, caught Adam's eye, waited. The detective frowned, but managed a slight nod.

'It'd better be a bloody good splash of a story,' he muttered.

'It will be.'

Dan had no idea yet how he'd make it happen, but he could worry about that later. Sometimes it was better to win one battle at a time.

Claire sat down on the same dining chair Adam had the night before and felt no more welcome. Detective Constable Jack Roffey stood beside her, notebook in hand. Yvonne Freedman and Alex sat side by side on the sofa. Both had their hands folded in their laps, just like they were preparing to face a firing squad.

'I'm sorry to bother you again, but I know you'll appreciate we have to ask certain questions,' Claire began. They both nodded, but didn't speak. 'It's important I get a full picture of Mr Freedman's movements and behaviour in recent days.'

They nodded again in unison, the movement dislodging a tear from Mrs Freedman's eye. She was wearing a black skirt and jacket, patent black shoes and a white blouse. Alex wore jeans and a T-shirt. She had to split the two of them up, Claire thought, couldn't ask the important questions with Mum here.

She tried to put on a sympathetic smile and began. 'Was there anything at all you found unusual in Mr Freedman's behaviour in recent days?'

Yvonne shook her head again, another tear rolling down her cheek, chasing the first towards her chin. Alex managed a low 'No.'

'Was he spending a lot of time away? Working?'

Alex jumped up from the sofa. 'Jesus, I told you that last night. He was always bloody working. That was all he did.'

She stalked out of the living room, slamming the door behind her. An expensive looking blue vase rattled on the mantelpiece. Jack made to follow, but Claire held out an arm to stop him. Her limited experience of teenagers suggested being followed was exactly what was wanted, and all that was required to justify another outburst against adult persecution. Let her calm a while.

'Mrs Freedman?' Claire asked. 'Was there anything unusual

about your husband lately?'

'No,' said the woman softly, dabbing at her face with a handkerchief. 'It was a complete shock. Everything was normal. Our lives were all normal until …'

Her voice tailed off, but her mouth remained half open, glossed lips quivering. Claire sensed she wanted to say something else.

'Go on,' she prompted gently.

'Until he started with all the party thing – the politics.'

Her cheeks coloured, the anger starting to show through the pain, the words coming more easily now. 'Climbing the greasy bloody pole! He got caught up in it. That was when we lost him. When all these toadies told him how talented he was – how far he could go. When he started to think he could be prime-bloody-minister! We stopped being his family … started just becoming the decorations a bloody MP needs to help in his career!'

Claire hid her surprise, raised a calming hand, but the tirade hadn't finished. Nowhere close. Yvonne Freedman's face creased with lines of misery and anger.

'Do you know what happens to wives and daughters of so-called special men? We're not people in our own right any more. I stopped being Yvonne and started being "Will Freedman's Wife". And Alex – well, it was the same for her. "That MP's daughter" they called her. How do you think that feels? So what are we now he's gone, eh? And left us with the legacy of shagging some teenage – bloody – tart!'

Yvonne buried her head in her hands and began to sob. Claire nodded to Jack to sit with her and walked out into the hallway. From upstairs roared a thumping beat and howling electric guitar. She climbed the stairs and knocked on the vibrating door. There was no answer.

She pushed at the door and it swung open. A pointedly unmade bed, the duvet in a pile, posters of tanned, muscled young men grinning down from the walls. She must be getting old, Claire thought, they looked adolescent. The music was overwhelming, an instant headache. But then, every generation thought that of the anthems of the new young. Her parents had said the same to her. Claire reached across to the stereo and turned it off.

'Alex?' she said. 'Alex?'

She opened the wardrobe door, then knelt down and checked under the bed. A few old board games, balls of fluff and dust, but no Alex. Claire walked over to the window. It was open, and the garden shed was just below. An easy jump. She leaned out. No sign of Alex. 'Shit,' she said to herself.

Claire sat down on the bed, suddenly felt tired, longed to lie back and close her eyes. No chance. No time. They had to find Alex. But first, she allowed herself the luxury of a few precious recuperative seconds.

Claire rubbed her eyes and caught a sight of herself in the wardrobe mirror. It might have been the angle, or the light, but she was convinced she was growing fatter.

She was going to have to tell Dan soon.

It was one of the busiest press conferences Dan had seen. The room was packed with journalists, cameramen and photographers. Dirty El stood at the front, grinning happily. Dan noticed he'd bought himself a new pair of jeans, the fashionably grimy and battered look. He'd never fancied a pair himself, didn't see the point of something new that was produced to look so worn. It was hardly value for money. They'd be falling to pieces in weeks. He prided himself on resisting the more absurd dictates of fashion.

A friend once remarked that Dan Groves had found a style he liked in the mid 1980s, and had stuck with it ever since. He'd been about to remonstrate when the fire of his argument was dowsed by the realisation that the claim was entirely and annoyingly true.

'Beers on me next time we go out,' El gushed, stroking the long lens of his camera, then added, 'Like my new jeans? All courtesy of our dead MP.' He did a little twirl, ran his hands unappealingly down his ample backside and launched into one of his impromptu and forever dreadful rhymes.

'The MP may be totally dead,
But he's feathering Dirty El's bed,

He snapped up his shots,
Gave the tabloids the hots,
And lifted his bank balance way out of the red.'

For once, Dan struggled for words. He thought it was one of the worst he'd heard, and that was against some very strong competition. El didn't seem to notice, still less care.

'Your tip-off meant I was the first one with pics of Freedman's house and the cops on the scene,' the photographer continued gleefully. 'I hoovered up the cash. Sold the snaps to everyone. Even better, all the papers want a follow-up too. They love their dirt. Especially when it's an MP who's been caught with his pants down. Naughty naughty!'

Adam walked in at exactly midday. Dan had never known his friend be late, another of his quirks. He sat down to a blaze of photographers' flashes and blinked hard. A cluster of microphones rose threateningly on the desk in front of him, all propped up on a strip of white plastic bearing Adam's name and the Greater Wessex Police crest.

Dan had sat himself at the back of the room, Nigel alongside, bowed over his camera. He and Adam always tried to make sure it wasn't obvious how well they knew each other. It could raise awkward questions from the other journalists. And it was particularly important today, given how they'd agreed to stage-manage the press conference to make it their own little drama.

Adam straightened his already perfect tie and welcomed the gathering. 'Ladies and Gentlemen, thanks for coming here. We are investigating a highly distressing case and we need your help in finding the person responsible.'

Dan checked his notes. Adam was sticking exactly to the script he'd written a few minutes earlier.

'Will Freedman was a popular and talented Member of Parliament for the Tamar constituency of Plymouth. Yesterday evening, he was found dead at his house. We can now confirm he committed suicide.'

Adam looked around the room. All the journalists were taking notes, the cameramen intent on their shots.

'Mr Freedman left a note, which said he was the victim of

blackmail over an issue in his private life. I believe it was the actions of this blackmailer that led Mr Freedman to kill himself. I have two things to say about that. The first is that a man has been pushed to his death over an indiscretion. Whatever anyone may think about that, it is a personal matter, and to use it against him is both illegal and immoral. In fact, I go further. We have all done things we are ashamed of. I say the actions of this blackmailer are disgusting and reprehensible and have no place in a modern and caring society.'

Adam paused to check the room again, let the drama build. The reporters were all still scribbling, lapping it up, just as Dan knew they would. Strong quotes, he'd said, give them spice. Don't do the police's usual leaden, "I was proceeding along the road in a northerly direction when I came upon the aforementioned felon," canteen-talk-type cliché. Make it direct and gripping, and Adam was delivering it beautifully. Many times Dan had wondered if his friend was a frustrated actor.

There was just the sole issue they'd argued over. But that wasn't surprising. It was the same one which bothered so many in British society. Fascinated with it they may be, but that could never be mentioned, let alone admitted. The subject was usually unspoken, but if it really had to be brought up – only if there truly was no choice, naturally – it was done so with taut faces and stilted words.

Just three letters, but so dominant, driver of so much in life. And unfailing in always attracting interest.

Sex.

Give the hacks sex, Dan had advised. Sex makes stories and sells papers. But Adam was wary. He didn't want to get the police involved in a sex scandal. Dan again checked his notes outlining Adam's little speech. As with everything, there was a way around the problem.

And here it came.

'The second thing I have to say is this,' Adam continued. 'A person who can blackmail someone so coldly, and with such evident enjoyment, is extremely dangerous. We need to catch them and as quickly as possible. I would appeal for anyone who Mr Freedman may have spoken to about what was happening to him, or who knew him well and can give us an insight into his life, to contact us. Your information could be vital.'

Adam stood up and there was the burst of questions from the journalists that Dan had expected. The detective ignored them and shuffled the papers on the desk, played for a little time. Dan waited for a moment to let the reporters' flurry die down.

Journalists began reaching for their phones, keen to file their copy. In the era of 24-hour news being first with the story was all. Dan knew it was a good tale, but not quite good enough to guarantee a nationwide splash. Not yet – but it would be in a moment.

He readied himself for his part in the drama.

Adam turned towards the door. Now, it had to be now. The room was still noisy with reporters, photographers and cameramen talking to each other. But it had to be now and loud too.

Dan swallowed hard, then shouted, 'What about the prostitute?'

The room was suddenly silent, the hubbub instantly halted. Everyone turned. Adam stared too.

'What about the prostitute?' Dan repeated, more quietly now. 'Come on, that's what my sources say. That the blackmailer knew Freedman had sex with a prostitute. Are you deliberately keeping important information from us?'

Adam held his stare. Dan felt his heart pounding. All the other reporters stayed silent, were watching the exchange. But they were getting their notebooks ready again, pens poised above paper, faces watchful and waiting.

They sensed the story.

'Certain details of the investigation are being kept back so as not to hamper it,' said Adam quietly, his face impassive. 'And certain areas I did not want to go into out of respect for the late Mr Freedman. But as you ask the question so directly, I will give you a direct and honest answer. Yes, it is alleged that Mr Freedman had sex with a prostitute, and that was the reason he was being blackmailed.'

That, thought Dan as he drove quickly back to the studios, was

57

one of his masters sated. But despite being a senior detective, hardened by the horrors he'd seen and investigated and driven by his compassion for victims and commitment to justice, Adam was nonetheless often the easier of the two.

Lizzie, though, was the definition of never satisfied. Dan often thought of her as like a nest of baby birds, no matter how many juicy morsels he brought she always wanted more and wouldn't hesitate to produce a cacophony to demonstrate it. He once dreamt of finding an exclusive on a cure for cancer, complete with interviews with the scientists responsible and people whose lives would be saved, only to have her wanting an extra interview with some undertakers to emphasise the downside of the discovery.

Dan found his expectations were not disappointed.

'What the bloody hell were you doing?' Lizzie yelped as he jogged back into the newsroom. He glanced at the radio-controlled clock. Half past twelve. Just an hour to edit the story for the lunchtime news. He had the structure and script for the report in mind, but didn't have time to hang about.

She stood up from her desk, looked taller than earlier. The other hacks pretended to be engrossed in their work, but Dan knew they were watching. Lizzie bawling out an errant reporter was a favourite spectator sport. He'd enjoyed it often enough himself. It was most entertaining, given the one proviso – that you weren't the hapless victim. Today though, he seemed to have a target painted on his chest, and she was taking careful aim.

'Don't know what you mean,' Dan replied, edging towards the edit suites. He could defuse her anger by revealing his scoop, but didn't have the time. He wondered if it was more the case that he didn't have the inclination. The best tactics might be to let her work herself up, then produce his surprise. The result could be wonderfully deflating.

A sharpened fingernail began jabbing at the air, those thin lips working themselves into a blur. 'I mean telling the cops to call a press conference. And then revealing the prostitute angle! The story's running everywhere. Every hack in the bloody country has got it.'

A stiletto ground into the carpet to complement the fingernail. She'd changed from the lower heels of earlier to four-inch stilettos, gleaming black and sharp as an icicle. Lizzie kept at least half a dozen pairs of shoes in her office and had been known to change them several times a day according to the oscillations of her mood.

'I let you go help them to help us,' Lizzie raged on. 'Instead you end up blowing our exclusive!'

He edged further towards the door. 'Would I do something as stupid as that?'

She didn't answer, just summoned up a laser stare which suggested that was exactly what she thought. Dan raised his hands calmingly. 'Look, I'd better get on with this edit. There was no way the rest of the media wouldn't get on to the story. It's just too big. The cops had no choice but to call a press conference.'

Her lips tightened and Dan could sense the explosion coming. He continued quickly before the detonation. 'But I can guarantee you I've worked it so I've got you an exclusive angle, which every other hack will be cursing themselves they missed. And even better, they've got no chance of getting it now either.'

The stiletto stopped grinding the carpet.

'Go do your edit then,' she said menacingly, sitting back down. 'I'll suspend judgement, for now. But it had better be good.'

It was, Dan thought, as Jenny edited the last shot of the lunchtime report. Even if he did say so himself, it was damn good. He wondered whether to give the Royal Television Society Awards Panel a call, to make sure they didn't miss it. Perhaps it would be best to log their number in his phone. It felt like that kind of a case, filled with the promise of more extraordinary developments to come.

The report followed the classical formula for telling a TV story. Start with your best pictures, then move on to your strongest interview. Hook the viewers from the first seconds.

It opened with the striking shot of the billboard, screaming letters, red on white. It effectively told the story on its own.

VOTE WILL FREEDMAN MP, PROSTITUTE PARTY

Dan added a few lines of commentary about how Wessex Tonight could reveal this was the way the blackmailer planned to expose Will Freedman, and the reason why, the MP's liaison with the prostitute. Then it was a clip of Adam at the press conference, talking about how disgusting the crime was.

'That's amazingly human for a cop,' Jenny said as she edited the extract into the report. 'It's the first time I've ever heard one say anything so powerful and sensible.'

Sitting behind her at the computer, still working on his script, Dan favoured himself with a wink.

After that came a few pictures from last night of the Freedman house and the police activity with Dan recapping on how the MP was found dead. Then another clip of Adam, about the blackmailer being dangerous and the urgent need to catch them.

Dan walked back into the newsroom at 1.25 and made a show of sitting next to Lizzie to watch the bulletin on one of the bank of monitors on the wall. She didn't speak, just stared at the screens.

The titles played, the story was introduced, ran and ended. There was no reaction from his editor.

Dan sensed a challenge, so he didn't comment but kept his face set and watched the rest of the bulletin. Calls for more help for alcoholics in Cornwall, a big water-main burst in north Devon, Exeter City Council increasing efforts to recycle more domestic waste and the inevitable "And finally", an appeal to help hungry hedgehogs awakening from hibernation.

'Right, here's the plan for tonight,' Lizzie said, when the bulletin was over. 'I'll have more of the same from you. I was thinking of sending the outside broadcast truck for you to do a live update from Freedman's house, or the cop shop. But I've got an obituary on him being put together and a live from Westminster about the reaction there, so I won't need it.'

Dan pointedly folded his arms and adopted an expectant expression. Not a word of thanks, he noted. Certainly not an apology for her outburst of only an hour ago. But that wasn't Lizzie. The sorry word wasn't in her vocabulary. The best you could hope for was a disguised apology, sometimes so well hidden it was nigh on impossible to discern. A miniscule needle in a mountainous haystack.

But Dan sensed it coming, and kept quiet. Smugly quiet, he suspected.

'You worked late last night,' she said. 'You can go home when you're done.'

And now, Dan told himself, comes the caveat. It was ever thus. As reaction follows action, and night day, so any ground given must instantly be retaken, or, at the very worst, marked for unfailing attention later.

'But – but! – I want you on call at the weekend. I want you ready for anything. I want you out there at the slightest hint of a development. And I want it on air as soon as it happens. This story's got real legs. It's not just a runner, it's a sprinter. If anything comes up, I want you straight on it.'

'Lovely, thanks,' said Dan, trying to sound enthusiastic.

He slowly got up from his chair, gave her plenty of time. He wasn't finished, wanted to force just the slightest hint of recognition, make a nudge of headway in one of his seemingly eternal battles with his editor.

Dan fumbled for his satchel, picked it up and they stared at each other. He tried to keep a straight face.

'Oh, and not a bad report either,' Lizzie added finally and painfully begrudgingly.

Dan took that atom of victory as his leave to depart.

Chapter Six

A TRAFFIC JAM WOUND up the hill from the Charles Cross roundabout. Dan joined the back, wondering on a whim whether one day, if he continued working so closely with the police, he might be entitled to a flashing blue light that could help him cut through such irritants. It was only four o'clock, but the weekend exodus from the city had begun.

No such luck for him, despite Lizzie's promise of allowing him home. He had more work to do. Adam wanted another chat about the case and how it was playing in the media and naturally no, it couldn't wait. Around Dan, the faces in the windscreens wore a mix of resignation and frustration at the hold up, and relief that the long-awaited Friday afternoon had finally arrived.

Dan stared at the ruined Charles Church as he queued to get through the roundabout. The traffic was moving in random staggering steps, like a drunkard's uncertain progress home. The sun was still strong in the sky and all the cars' windows were down, a line of elbows leaning out. He'd lived in Plymouth for ten years now, but still found it hard to believe that, despite the nationwide abundance of evidence of their insensitivity, the faceless planners could ever have thought the fitting way to treat such a powerful and dignified memorial as the church was to encircle it with a roundabout.

Dandelions spotted the thin lake of grass around the ruin with their vivid yellow heads. A bare-chested man worked at cutting back some of the waxy ivy weeping from the empty stone arches of the windows. The church was blind, the rainbow eyes of its stained-glass windows lost to the screaming shrapnel of the Blitz. Almost 70 years ago it was now, the monument standing as a reminder of Europe's descent into barbaric darkness, and the terrible price paid in the struggle to stay in the light.

Dan realised he'd driven around the church so many times, but never got out of his car to walk through the ruins. He must, he told himself. He owed it to the past and the bygone people who had suffered for his present. Maybe he would explore it with Claire when they were next in town. It would be an experience the better for sharing.

Dan reminded himself to call Claire later and was pleased at the thrill the thought brought. He was looking forward to their walk tomorrow. Him, Claire and Rutherford, atop a windy cliff, gazing down on an azure sea, with an old inn, dinner, and a few pints of ale to follow. A perfect Saturday.

Adam stood waiting in the MIR, staring out of the windows, arms folded and apparently drifting in thought. A couple of uniformed officers worked away at computers, but otherwise the room was deserted. Dan noticed several new pieces of paper had been stuck onto the felt boards.

The detective sensed his look. 'Some progress,' he said. 'I'll tell you about it in a minute. Don't get comfortable,' he added, as Dan went to sit down. 'I thought we'd go out for a beer and have a chat. I've had enough of this place. Worked all right, didn't it?'

'Our little scene in the press conference?'

'I thought so,' said Adam.

'Me too.' Dan nodded. 'I couldn't see any other way to make sure the prostitute angle was confirmed unless it was by you. The way we played it saves you the hassle of being accused of sullying a man's reputation and getting drawn into a political row about sleaze. But it still ensures the story's splashed everywhere.'

'Spot on and just what we need,' replied Adam. 'It's been all over the national radio and TV, and the internet news sites too. I'm told all the papers are running it tomorrow. You're a cunning one, aren't you? Maybe you should have been a crook.'

Or a detective, Dan thought to himself wryly.

They walked into the city centre, towards the waterfront and Barbican. It was one of the few areas of Plymouth that hadn't been levelled in the war and still boasted the white buildings and dark wooden beams of the Tudors. The jam at the roundabout had eased and the traffic flowed smoothly out of the city.

'We've all got them, you know,' Adam mused.

'What?' Dan asked, a little thrown by the pronouncement.

'Guilty secrets. Everyone has. I certainly have – look at the ways I've connived with you on some investigations.'

'You're talking about Freedman, and why he killed himself?'

'Yep. One moment of weakness. Giving in to himself. It gets found out and that's it, life over.'

'We're hardly talking the same degrees though, are we? We've always bent the rules for the right reasons. Catching criminals.'

'But what we've done has been illegal. And it's certainly been an abuse of our positions. For both of us it's hardly the way we're supposed to work.'

'What we've done has been harmless though, surely. In fact, more than that – it's for the greater good.'

'As no doubt Freedman thought what he was doing was harmless. No one suffered, no one had to know. All I'm saying is that we all have secrets. I think that's what rankles with me about this case. Freedman was a good man, he made one slip, and that was it. If there was any comeback, it should have been between him and his wife, and no one else. Not some threat to make it a national scandal.'

They stopped at the bank by the post office for Dan to get some money from a cashpoint. The detective took off his jacket and even loosened his tie. The phenomenon was almost worth a news story. The wonders of the magic of the weekend.

'Where do you fancy for a drink?' Adam asked. 'I'm not fussed about sitting outside. I don't want anyone overhearing us.'

Dan thought for a moment, then said, 'What about the Ginger Judge? It's about the best Plymouth's got and excellent if you want to be discreet. It's where the lawyers go to talk about cases over lunch. You can see them all glancing over their shoulders before they speak. It's like animal behaviour, better than going to the zoo.'

They walked on, past the 1970s court complex, a squat, two-floor block of concrete and glass. Adam stopped to admonish a couple of young lads on skateboards who were trying to use the side of the building as a ramp. He waved his warrant card before they had a chance to loose off any abuse and they slouched away. An old man shook the detective's hand, congratulated him, saying too few people intervened these days. It had become a walk-on-by society. Dan nodded his agreement.

'Nice place,' said Adam, as they pushed open the Ginger Judge's door. There was a scattering of people at the tables, mostly men. Dan noticed nearly all wore the pinstripe suit and striped shirt of the lawyer's uniform. Some even boasted red braces too. It was the classical case of the professional bubble; what was accepted within a career was comical to the rest of the world.

Dan picked a table in the corner farthest from the door, got the drinks, a couple of pints of guest ale from a brewery on the Isles of Scilly. He'd first met the beer when he was in the Scillies doing a story about the islands' vulnerability to climate change and rising sea levels. When he was unwillingly moved from Environment Correspondent to Crime he used to feel a powerful tug of nostalgia at thoughts of his previous professional life. No longer.

The lurid underworld of lawlessness had him hooked.

He had his new existence to thank for meeting Claire too. The memory of his early clumsy, stumbling chat-up lines made him wince. How life can change in one brief moment. Environment to crime, one job where he was getting stale to another where every day held a surprise, and, that great wonder he thought would never come, finally perhaps even finding a partner.

Dan often tried to stop himself thinking it, scarcely dared to hope, as if it might frighten away the elusive prospect of happiness. He could have thanked that prostitute he paid for an interview, a transgression which gave Lizzie the excuse she was looking for to switch his job.

From the ridiculous can indeed grow the sublime.

'Very good,' said Adam, sipping at his drink. 'And a fine place. Do you come here often?'

Dan grinned. Hadn't he used that one with Claire?

'Cheers. Good line. Better than some of mine, anyway,' he said. 'Yes, I do come in fairly often. I like it because the tables aren't all crammed together, the way they do in places more interested in making money than looking after customers.'

A middle-aged couple walked in. She headed for the bar and he the toilets. Unusual role reversal, Dan mused. He noticed the place had had a make over since he'd last been in. The stripped wooden floor shone from a polish and a couple of large pine-rimmed mirrors had been added to the walls. The big glass windows were cleaner too. A blackboard hung behind the bar with "Today's Specials" written floridly at the top in chalk. There was a tempting looking list of dishes. Fried local shark, rib eye steak, Caesar salad, vegetarian lasagne. Dan felt his stomach rumble.

'So what's this progress you mentioned then?' he asked Adam.

'Not a great deal, really. We've interviewed that bill poster guy, but didn't get anything from him.'

'Nothing at all?'

'No. The chap's not too bright. The posters get delivered to his house, along with instructions about where to put them up and he does it. The Freedman one came with a letter on headed paper, saying put it up at Marsh Mills. He chucked the letter away in some bin in the shopping centre he says, and the search teams can't find it. They get emptied too often. So no go there.'

'What about the poster itself?'

'Made by a company in Bristol, big group. They got a call asking them to design a poster like the one you saw. The caller said they needed discretion as it was a trial for a political party, and they wanted to keep the idea secret. The company's quite used to things like that, apparently. So they got paid in cash, designed the thing and some despatch rider came to pick it up. Again, that's standard. We've had no luck finding the rider. It was probably someone picking up a few quid on the quiet. So no go there either.'

Dan sipped at his beer. 'It's one hell of a way of exposing someone though, isn't it? The Worm would have known the moment the poster went up that thousands of people would see it. The media would start asking questions, the police would investigate, and that'd be it. Secret blown.'

'Yep,' replied Adam. 'It's certainly creative criminality. It tells us we're dealing with someone clever and ruthless, who's planned this well. He had that poster made, so when Freedman didn't solve the riddle he could expose him straight away. Merciless. But in a way Freedman cheated him by killing himself first.'

Dan sat back on his chair and breathed out heavily. 'Not much of a victory for Freedman I'd say. What about his agenda then?'

'Meaning?'

'Well, this is no ordinary blackmailer, is it? The only ones I've ever heard of want money. Not ours. For him, it's something else. Publicity. Some cause. Something more important to him than money.'

Adam nodded. 'Yes, and that's reflected in the note, isn't it? It goes on about your filthy and rotten kind. So what does the Worm mean by that? Politicians? Men? Successful people? Powerful people?'

'I guess we'll find out, won't we? When the next blackmail note arrives with the next unsuspecting victim.'

Adam loosened his tie further, then took it off and hung it on the back of his chair. 'And another thing. Why the riddle? Why torment the victim further by setting a riddle he can't solve?'

'It's a power thing, isn't it? Increasing the Worm's power over him, and probably the police too.'

A gush of laughter erupted from a table in the far corner. As if on cue, the three lawyers sitting there all looked over their shoulders. A waitress walked out from the kitchens and propped open the front door. It was getting hot in the bar. Dan tried, but mostly failed to blame it on the sunshine. In a place so popular with the legal profession, there was bound to be an excess of hot air.

Adam rubbed a hand over the stubble on his cheek. It never took long to accumulate. Like many dark-haired men, a clean-shaven look would always be a distant dream.

'What do you make of the Worm saying that if we solve the riddles, we find the Judgement Book and save the victims?'

Dan shrugged. 'Maybe exactly what it says. That we could save them if we break the codes. But would you trust the word of a blackmailer?'

'Not a chance.'

'Me neither. But we've got to have a go at Freedman's riddle, haven't we? Because it's part of the investigation, and it might lead us somewhere.'

'And not just that one riddle, either,' said Adam. 'According to the blackmailer's note, we've got four more victims to come. So, four more little puzzles.'

Dan took the photocopy of the blackmail note from his pocket.

'Careful with that,' said Adam quickly, looking around. 'I want the riddle stuff and the threat to the other victims kept quiet. It'll cause panic if it gets out.'

'OK,' said Dan. 'Understood. But I've been thinking about it.' He pointed to the numbers.

61, 43, 21, 51

'I have to say I haven't got much of a clue.' Dan looked up at Adam. 'I thought maybe coordinates, but that's just guessing. Any ideas?'

'Not a sniff.' Adam sounded exasperated. 'I hate riddles. Those other ones we've had to tackle nearly drove me mad. I'm a detective, not a puzzle freak.'

'Fair enough. But I take it you don't mind if I keep working on it?'

'Go ahead. You've got that kind of weird brain which enjoys these things. You're welcome to it.'

Dan thought he'd take that as half a compliment. It was better than none. He finished the remains of his beer and swirled the glass. 'Another drink?'

Adam stood up. 'No, I'd better be getting back. There's lots to do. I shouldn't really have come out. I just needed to get away from the office for a while. It gets on top of you.'

'Sure,' said Dan. 'No worries, I could do with getting home. Your round next time then? Speaking of which …'

They were interrupted by a shout from the corner of the bar. 'Dan! You're not going after just the one? That's not like you!'

A woman bustled over to them. Medium build, but carrying it elegantly, spiky dark hair with blonde highlights, perhaps forty years old or a little more. She smiled, but in the weary way of the professional host.

'Hello, Sarah,' said Dan, kissing the proffered cheek. 'Let me introduce my friend Adam. Or to be more exact, Chief Inspector Adam. He's a detective, so none of your usual naughtiness please.'

They shook hands. 'How are you doing now, Sarah?' Dan asked. 'Getting back on your feet OK?'

'Yes, fine now thanks, Dan. Life's much more sorted. I know where I'm going again and I'm happy. Well, content anyway.'

'That's good to hear.' Dan noticed Adam edging towards the exit. 'Sorry I can't stop for a chat, but I've got to get back to work. Big story on.'

'No problem, Dan.' She escorted them towards the door. 'Come in again soon. And drink more next time. It's my livelihood! Good to meet you, Adam.'

Adam slipped his jacket on as they walked back towards Charles Cross. A gathering mob of clouds had surrounded the sun and a cool breeze stirred and ruffled the oddments of litter in the gutter. It was the time of year when the fickle weather was one thing or the other, hot or cold, no ideal in between.

'How do you know her?' asked Adam. He was walking fast and Dan struggled to keep up. He could see the detective's mind was back in the depths of the case.

'She's been working there about six months. She's the bar manager. Before that, she had her own place, but the business went bust. She told me all this when I was in there one night having a beer. She seemed very bitter and keen to pour it out. Or maybe it's just that people seem to like to talk to me.'

They reached Charles Cross. Adam took the grey concrete steps two at a time.

'I'm not going to come in,' said Dan. 'I want to get back and take Rutherford for some exercise. I've been neglecting him with all that's been going on this week.'

'No worries,' called Adam, disappearing through the swing door. 'I'll call you if anything happens over the weekend.'

Dan drove home, gave Rutherford a brush as an apology for not spending much time with him, then took the dog for a run. When he got home, he showered and rang Claire's mobile. Her answerphone clicked in. Nothing unusual, she often wouldn't pick up a call when working on a case. He left a message.

He found a pizza in the bottom of the freezer, tried not to look at its best-before date, sliced some greening ham to go on top and ate it in front of the TV. The pizza tasted of nothing, but at least it was food. His report took the top slot on Wessex Tonight, followed by Freedman's obituary and the live political reaction to his death that Lizzie had arranged.

It was detailed and comprehensive coverage and an impressive show. They had their disagreements, but in truth Lizzie was an excellent editor. He wondered what she thought of him. She never said, but he thought he understood, or hoped so anyway. She always wanted him on the most important stories. That was about the highest compliment she could pay.

What would life be like, living with Claire he wondered? No more frozen pizza, he hoped. Would she finally get him organised enough to eat some fresh food? And how would Rutherford cope with the move? Not to mention having another master? What about packing up the flat? He was hopeless at such chores. And what about renting or selling it?

He'd have to find an agent to help, and notify the council and the bank and all the others about his change of address too. But no matter what problems he thought up, he knew how much he was looking forward to them moving in together.

'Times are changing, old fellow,' he told Rutherford, stroking the dog's head. 'And do you know what? I'm enjoying it.'

Claire called just after eight. It was a brief chat, she was still working on the blackmailer inquiry. They had a missing girl to deal with too, but she didn't go into details and Dan didn't ask, despite the sharp bite from his journalist's instinct. They'd agreed early in their relationship that she wouldn't talk too much about her job so as not to compromise her. In return, Dan had promised Claire that he wouldn't talk about her with Adam. And then Dan had agreed with Adam that he wouldn't talk about him with Claire. It was a complex set of arrangements, probably a unique relationship triangle, but it seemed to work.

It was busy, Claire said, but she'd agreed to work on Sunday so they could have Saturday together as they'd planned. Would it be better to forget the weekend and let her get on with the case, Dan asked? He would understand. It happened. No, she said, she very much wanted to see him. Needed to see him, in fact. There was lots they had to talk about.

He thought he sensed something behind the words, a need to free an invisible tension, and a tingling of concern began to awaken. But as the evening slipped by and he sipped at another can of beer and half-watched an old war film on the television, Dan came to believe it was only his imagination.

If there was a problem, something bothering her, Claire would have said. She was fine. He was fine. All was well.

Or so he hoped.

Chapter Seven

A FLAWLESS SHEET OF silver sea encircled them. Dan had never liked heights, and tried not to look down. He stared determinedly at a passing tanker, so small in the distance. Around them screaming gulls circled and wheeled, delighting in the freedom of the air. A mischievous wind pulled playfully at their clothes, flapping them back and forth. Between its buffeting blows they could hear the rhythmic wash of waves on the rocks below.

A tang of salt from the swirling spray dampened their faces with its sticky, dancing mist. Even Rutherford was stilled by the moment. He stared at the view, his face turned instinctively into the wind, his sleek fur smoothed by its caress.

St Agnes Head was stunning, even on an overcast day like this. Dan reached out an arm and pulled Claire closer. She half turned, and smiled. He tried to avoid driving at the weekend. He always felt he spent more than enough time in the car for work. But the panorama made the hour and a quarter journey from Plymouth to the north Cornwall coast worthwhile. They'd set out early and the traffic was light.

It was more than the view. There was a "feeling" about this place, as the great legends told. No wonder it gave rise to so many tales of magic. He sneaked a glance at Claire. She had her eyes closed and was breathing deeply.

'That way Wales,' said Dan, pointing north. 'That way America,' he added, turning his finger to the west. He waited a moment for her to look, then pointed back to the car. 'And that way the pub!'

She dug him gently in the ribs. 'In a while. Let's enjoy a bit more of the walk and a chat first.'

He found himself surprisingly content to agree. 'Fine by me. It's magnificent here. I can feel it massaging away the tensions of the week.'

They turned from the headland and followed the coastal path along the cliffs. It was well-worn, in places more patches of dry and cracked earth than thriving grass. Further inland were the stone ruins of old mine workings, grey tumbledown towers of engine houses rising from the yellow gorse and grey and brown brambles.

'There was a big mining industry here once,' Dan said. 'The tunnels used to go right out for miles, under the sea even. Dangerous business, but lucrative at the time.'

'What were they mining?'

'All sorts of stuff. Copper, tin, arsenic.' Dan hoped he'd remembered right. It was a long time since he'd covered a story on Cornwall's mining heritage.

Rutherford found a stick and scampered circles around them to show off the prize. Dan wondered where he managed to conjure it from. There wasn't a tree for miles. He tried to wrestle it from the dog, then gave up, found a tiny twig, picked that up and Rutherford dropped his and jumped for it. Dan bent down and picked up the stick.

'Stupid dog,' chuckled Claire. 'He never learns, does he? Why is someone else's stick always better?'

'It's the canine equivalent of the grass always being greener.'

He threw the stick towards the mine workings and Rutherford sprinted after it. The dog vanished into the gorse. All they could see was a dismembered head floating about the bushes, appearing and disappearing as he hunted for the prize. His mouth hung open in what Dan always thought of as his smiling face.

'Don't be too hard on him,' said Dan. 'It won't be long before you'll have to take him out too. If we're sharing the bills, cooking and chores, we're sharing the dog-walking duties. I'm not the only one who's going to be embarrassed by my stupid friend.'

'I'm looking forward to it.'

'So am I.'

They stopped for a quick cuddle. To an observer it could be a sickly sight, a couple entranced and entwined. But when you were a part of it, you didn't notice and didn't care. It was one of the joys of the hypocrisy of love. Rutherford bounded up and nosed his way between them. He'd lost the stick. Claire stroked his back and Dan patted his head.

'He doesn't like missing out on anything,' Dan explained. 'I think he's looking forward to us all being together too. I broke the news to him last night. I was a little worried what his reaction might be. For as long as he's been around, it's been just him and me, you see. I thought he might be jealous. But he was delighted.'

'Idiot,' said Claire. 'But cute idiot.'

She yawned, stretched out her arms. 'You OK?' Dan asked.

'Just a little tired from last night. I was up late.'

'The missing girl?'

'Yep.'

'I know I shouldn't ask, but …'

Claire sighed. 'The perils of going out with a hack. Promise not for use in stories?' Dan agreed and she told him about Alex Freedman's disappearance.

'We found her though,' Claire added. 'At a friend's house. Upset, but fine. I took her home – after I'd had a little chat.'

'About her dad's fondness for younger women?'

'Yep.'

Dan steeled himself to ask. Despite years of being a journalist, raising some of the toughest of questions, there were still areas where it felt uncomfortable to tread.

'And?'

'No hint of anything like that. I didn't ask the question directly, but she knew where I was coming from. She said he wasn't a great dad, that he wasn't around enough, but he'd never ever … well, you know.'

Claire raised a hand to her mouth and stifled a laugh. 'What?' Dan asked.

'What Alex said. I don't think I'll ever forget it.'

'Which was?'

'She said her dad was "an arsehole", but he wasn't "that big an arsehole".'

Dan smiled too, couldn't help it. 'Kids, eh?'

Claire looked at him, paused, said softly, 'Yeah.' Another hesitation, then, 'Kids.'

She seemed to want to add something, but instead pushed a stray lock of windblown hair back behind an ear, looked at Dan expectantly. He nodded.

'I know exactly what you're thinking. You reckon her anger towards her dad was just the usual teenage rebellion thing?'

She studied him, and he couldn't read her expression. Finally, she said, 'Yes, I do, thankfully.'

'And Mrs Freedman?'

'Well, she said Will was a good man who worked hard and meant well, and all that kind of platitudes stuff, but ...'

'But?'

'It didn't even rise to the heights of being damned with faint praise. I could feel the anger. It's fast taken over from the grief. That he could do that to her, and to Alex, seeing that prostitute and then leave them both alone in that way – leaving them to find his body ...'

Claire stopped abruptly, shook her head as if to clear it. 'Look, can we talk about something else? I'd really like to leave work behind for a bit.'

They walked on in silence. Sometimes no words were required. The cliffs, the sky, the sea were all. Dan glanced over his shoulder to where they'd parked the car.

With a lover's forbearance, Claire said, 'Just a few more minutes. Then we can go and get you a beer. I'm really enjoying being out here.'

'I must keep reminding myself I'm going out with a detective,' mused Dan. 'There's no point trying to get away with anything. What am I going to do when it comes to buying your Christmas presents? And what if I ever have to arrange a surprise for you?'

She pushed his shoulder playfully. 'Like any good police officer, I know when to turn a blind eye. Don't let any of that stop you spoiling me. If you do, then you'll really be in trouble.'

Claire pointed to a path that wound inland towards an old engine house. 'Can we go and sit there for a while? I'd like a few minutes just relaxing and looking at the view before we head back. It's so wonderfully calming.'

Dan nodded his agreement. The brief moments of their weekend escapes were the perfect antidote to their working days. No savagery, crime, grimness and cruelty, just the pure and clean countryside. It was the ideal remedy for the human world.

The track was thinner than the coastal path and bounded by gorse bushes. One pricked Dan's calf. 'Ow,' he yelped, petulantly kicking out at it.

'That really showed it,' said Claire. 'It won't forget that lesson in a hurry.'

'It made me feel better,' was the best retort Dan could manage. His leg throbbed, but he scarcely noticed. It wasn't that kind of a day.

They reached a pyramid of fallen blocks, the ground around them shorn of overgrowth. Claire turned and scanned the surroundings. They could still see the band of blue-grey sea and the rugged line of cliff top. 'Here,' she said. 'This is perfect.'

Dan laid his coat on the ground. They sat down, leant back against a stone and cuddled together. Rutherford sniffed his way around the pile of blocks, then trotted back and lay down beside them, his head resting between his paws.

'Happy family,' said Dan contentedly.

Claire rubbed her stomach. 'You feeling OK?' he asked. 'I noticed you were holding your tum yesterday. You're not feeling ill, are you?'

She held his look. 'No,' she said gently. 'No, I'm absolutely fine. Full of life.' She nodded hard, added, 'Blooming in fact.'

'That's good.'

They sat and admired the view. Claire looked about to say something else when a growing noise interrupted her. A yellow helicopter thudded its way through the air, following the coast from west to east. Rutherford stood to watch it fly slowly past, his head tilted to one side.

'Rescue chopper,' said Dan. 'I wonder what that's about. Maybe a fishing boat in trouble, or a holidaymaker fallen down the cliff.'

'Mmm,' replied Claire, cuddling into him.

'What was this you said you wanted to talk about then?' Dan

asked. 'House things, I guess? I've had a quick look at some of the finance and mortgage deals going at the moment, but I was going to tell you about that later. It doesn't feel right now, all that mundane money stuff in the midst of this beauty.'

Claire cuddled closer and nuzzled his neck. She whispered something he couldn't catch.

'Pardon? I didn't get that.'

She sat back and looked at him, but didn't speak. Her expression was impenetrable, a mix of drifting mind, happiness and fear of reality.

'Claire?' he said, unnerved. 'Are you OK? Claire?'

She flinched. 'Fine, yes. Sorry, I was miles away.'

'Where? What? Are you OK?'

'Yes, fine. I'm fine. You won't believe what I was thinking.'

'What? Go on, try me. What?'

Claire hesitated, rubbed her stomach again. Finally she said, 'I was thinking about whether we might get an Aga. I've always wanted one.'

Dan breathed out with relief. 'Is that all? Well, I don't know about it in our first house. It depends how big it is and what we can afford. But one day, certainly, yes. I'd love one too. They make great toast.'

She smiled at him, but mistily. 'Yep. Great toast. What more could we ask for?'

He was about to reply when a thundering barrage of noise assailed them. The helicopter had risen from below the cliff like a great yellow bird of prey. It hovered just a couple of hundred yards away. The side door was open and a figure leaned out. He seemed to be looking at the edge of the cliff. Even from where they sat they could feel the rushing downdraft of the helicopter's rotors. It poured out, beating and bowing the grass and gorse around them.

They stood and Claire pointed along the coastal path. A line of yellow-jacketed figures was striding fast towards the helicopter. There were a couple of uniformed police officers at the back.

'What's going on?' she shouted.

'No idea, but they're spoiling the peace and quiet. Shall we go and have a look?'

Dan put Rutherford on his lead and they walked towards the group. They'd gathered on the cliff top where the helicopter had hovered. It had flown west, following the line of the coast.

'What's happening?' Dan asked one of the police officers.

'Suspected suicide, sir,' the constable replied in a Cornish burr. 'Nothing to worry about. It's common along here. It's a pretty spot to jump to your death.'

Dan reached for Claire's hand and turned to walk away. It felt ghoulish to stay. He'd had enough of death for one week. The weekend was supposed to be a respite. But she stopped him and said, 'Hang on a minute. A suspected suicide? Given what happened on Thursday with Freedman I'd better check that's all it is.'

She reached into her pocket for her purse and showed the policeman her warrant card. He couldn't hide his surprise.

'Not really one for CID, ma'am,' he said, straightening his cap. 'It's just a suicide. Sad, but it happens a lot around here.'

'I'd like to check anyway,' she replied. 'What happened?'

'We had a call from a woman saying there was someone standing on the edge of the cliff, with arms outstretched, who pitched forwards and fell. We turned out in case the jumper was lying badly hurt at the bottom of the cliff, but there's no sign. The helicopter hasn't found a body, but that's not unusual. The tides and currents around here are ferocious. We only find the remains of about half the suicides.'

On the cliff behind the policeman the rest of the group had clustered together and were examining an object. Claire strode over. One was holding a small plastic lunch box.

'What's that?' she said sharply. 'Where did you find it?'

'Just on the cliff, love,' the man replied, looking up at her. 'It was weighted down with a big stone. There's a bit of paper in it. I reckon it's the guy's suicide note.'

'Drop it,' said Claire in a commanding voice. 'Put it down on the grass and don't touch it again. Any of you.'

'Who the hell are you...?' he began, but Claire cut him off.

'CID. Just do it.'

The man hesitated, looked as if he was contemplating

challenging her, but did as he was told. Claire walked forward, squatted down and stared into the box. Dan did the same. The plastic was opaque, but clear enough to make out some of the note inside.

The piece of paper was folded in half. There were lines of scrawled handwriting, but the words "Judgement Book" were clearly visible.

Chapter Eight

TWO SHOCKS AWAITED THEM when they got back to Charles Cross.

Adam, Dan and Claire watched as a forensics officer carefully opened the lunch box and used tweezers to extract the note. The man slipped the piece of paper into a clear plastic evidence bag, sealed it, and handed it to Adam. They jogged up the stairs to the MIR and he held it out so they could all see it. The message was brief, just a few lines, and took them only seconds to read.

Adam laid the bag down on a table and swore loudly, then again, a stream of snarling profanities such as Dan had never heard him use before. The detective walked over to the window and stared out at the ruined church. Claire just stood, shaking her head in disbelief. She had turned pale.

The second victim of the Judgement Book, the person who'd committed suicide by jumping from the cliffs of a Cornish beauty spot was one of their own, and it was a woman. Inspector Linda Cott.

'I knew her,' groaned Claire. 'She was a great woman, talented, principled, thoughtful, kind, dedicated to the job. Everything you could ask for. She believed in policing. She always said the local police officer should be a part of the community, just like the priest or doctor. We used to talk about how difficult it could still be, as a woman in the force. She even talked me round once when I was thinking of quitting.'

Dan was surprised, had never heard Claire mention it before. 'Really?'

'Oh yes. She told me not to quit because the police needed women like me and that we really made a difference. She said she'd prove it and took me for a walk in the city. We popped into a couple of shops and pubs run by women. They were all really pleased to see her. They went on about what a difference it made to have a women's perspective in policing. The men loved her too. She could mix it with anyone, from a tramp to a government minister. A real people's police officer. I even saw a scarf I liked in one of the shops we went in, and she said she'd turn a blind eye if I wanted to buy it. It's still one of my favourites.'

Adam nodded, picked up the plastic bag, held it out in front of him and stared at the note again. 'She was a fine singer too, did you know that? She used to front a folk band. They were well known locally, always in demand for gigs. In fact, she was quite a character all round. She came in to Tom's school once to talk to the children. All the kids were shepherded into the hall, thinking they'd got to listen to this boring talk, and she stood up at the front and said, "It's a lovely day, why don't we go outside and have a kick-about instead?"'

He smiled at the memory. 'This poor young beat cop she'd brought along had to go in goal, and she played football with the kids. And all she said at the end was, "Remember, the police are your friends." They still talk about it at the school. It was one of the best lessons they've ever had.'

The room went quiet. Then Adam spoke again, his voice harder now. 'She was a top cop, tipped to go on to a very senior rank. What the hell can the Worm have had that stopped her from reporting it to us, and made her kill herself?'

He banged his fist on the table, making a line of computers shudder.

'She's about the least likely blackmail victim I can imagine. Shit! What was her personal life like, Claire?'

'I'm not sure, sir. I know she didn't have a partner. But I didn't get the feeling she was unhappy. She always said she'd find one when the time was right. We used to talk about how difficult it was to meet a decent bloke, the hours we have to work. And if you do, they tend to run a mile when they find out you're a cop.'

Dan sat down on the window ledge and kept quiet. He fiddled with some change in his pocket and stared at a pigeon which was preening itself on the flagpole outside. Again, he felt an intruder here, like a child listening to an intimate conversation between adults.

'Well, we're going to have to go through her background,'

said Adam. 'And that's never a pleasant task, especially with a colleague. We'd better call the search teams in. They'll have to take her house apart. Don't worry about the weekend overtime. I'll sort that with the High Honchos. They won't complain. We're effectively hunting a cop killer now.'

Claire picked up her mobile, walked to the corner of the MIR and started making calls.

'At least Linda's given us one thing,' Adam growled to Dan. 'She solved the riddle the bastard Worm set her. But it didn't save her, did it?' The detective's neck had turned puce, a vein throbbing angrily. 'Come and have another look at the note. Tell me what you think. We've got to get this guy.'

Dan eased himself down from the window ledge, walked over to Adam and looked at the plastic evidence bag. He traced the words with a finger as he read.

> *I'm sorry it has to end this way, but I don't see any other choice. Given what I've done, there is no way I could ever continue as a police officer. I have only myself to blame for falling into the Judgement Book. I'm sorry, so very sorry. My job is my life, and without it I have no life.*
> *For those officers who investigate my death, I have solved the blackmailer's riddle. The answer is ORIGINAL. I hope this helps you to prevent any more deaths.*
> *Linda Cott*

Dan read through the note once more. The handwriting was a little scrawled, but still perfectly legible. It looked like someone who was under pressure, but was trained or used to coping. It was similar to his own style when writing a script against a looming deadline.

He imagined where the note had been written. In a car, parked by the cliffs, in the last few moments of Linda's life, or at home, in her kitchen with a cup of tea, preparing for that final act, the fatal decision made.

'What do I think?' Dan said slowly. 'Well, like you, I can

only wonder what the blackmailer must have had. It would have to be dynamite, something like the magnitude of Freedman's sex scandal. But why, if she solved the riddle, didn't she use it to save herself?'

'Maybe she did,' said Adam. 'Maybe the Worm just laughed at her and said I'm going to expose you anyway. Maybe she simply didn't trust him and didn't bother trying.'

Dan thought for a moment, tapped a finger on the edge of the desk, then said, 'Anyway, how was she supposed to show she'd cracked the riddle? We're only going to know that by finding the Worm's letter, aren't we? So far, we're working on half the story, just having her suicide note.'

'Yep,' replied Adam. 'Come on then, let's get down to her house and find the other half.'

He looked over to Claire. She was still on the phone, but gave him a thumbs-up.

'The search teams will be assembling within an hour, I'd say,' Adam continued. 'All our detectives will be here soon too, weekend or not. I won't be able to keep them away and I won't try. A dead colleague is the best motivator you can get.'

Claire insisted on driving. Dan knew she often liked to make a point of taking control, although he couldn't help but wonder if this was something to do with Linda's death. They stopped on the way to her house to buy some newspapers. Adam hopped out of the car.

'Won't be a mo,' he said. 'I want to see the Freedman coverage.' His face and neck were still flushed, his tie hanging well down from his collar.

Dan waited for the detective to disappear into the shop. 'You OK?' he asked Claire, leaning forward to whisper into her ear and rub a hand over her shoulder.

'Yeah, just shaken. It always gets to you, something like this, no matter how tough you think you are.'

She reached back from the driver's seat and squeezed his knee.

'There'll be no chance today, but maybe we can have dinner tomorrow night?' Claire went on. 'My place? I'd like to cook.

Maybe we can have a chance to talk about some of the stuff we didn't manage earlier?'

'Agas and toast you mean? Sure, I'd like that. It'd be a great way to round off the weekend.'

Adam opened the car door. He was carrying a pile of newspapers. Will Freedman's face stared out from all the front pages. The story dominated the headlines.

"MP'S SEX, LIES AND SUICIDE"

"PROZZIE MP TOPS HIMSELF"

Adam leafed through the papers. Tabloid or broadsheet, the story was the same.

"MP IN SEX BLACKMAIL SUICIDE"

"MYSTERY OF SEX BLACKMAIL SUICIDE MP"

"TRAGEDY OF SEX SUICIDE MP"

'I wonder if all these stories made Linda's mind up,' Adam said quietly. 'It would have been her in the headlines next.'

Linda Cott lived in a small, terraced house in a quiet cul de sac off Mutley Plain, less than a mile from Charles Cross. It was an oddly mixed area, lines of Victorian terraces, many converted into flats and bed-sits for students, but also plenty of middle-class families, although the numbers were dwindling in the face of the students' relentless invasion. The tensions between the two lifestyles formed a staple story for the local media.

Linda's front garden was paved, apart from the edges where a few well-tended rosebushes reached out from the flowerbeds. Their buds were starting to blossom. The house was whitewashed, with pale blue windowsills and looked neat and well cared for. A Neighbourhood Watch sticker was slightly askew in the double-glazed glass of the front door. A police locksmith fumbled with the mechanism for a couple of minutes and it opened.

Adam stepped inside, onto a 'Home Sweet Home' mat. He wiped his feet respectfully and Dan and Claire did the same. The hallway was carpeted in beige, as was the living room. A white-tiled kitchen at the back looked out onto a small garden. The lawn was evenly trimmed, coloured sprays of wakening flowers lined the wooden fences.

Upstairs, there were two bedrooms, both with double beds. The bathroom was also white and stark. A yellow rubber duck sat on the edge of the bath, the first hint Dan had seen of any real spark of character. No one spoke. There was no discussion of what they were seeing, no banter, no attempt to lighten the mood. They found no sign of any blackmail note or frantic attempts to solve a riddle.

They walked slowly back downstairs. Adam sat heavily on the white sofa in the living room. There was a long silence, then he said, 'Depressing, isn't it? You feel like you're trespassing through the layers of someone's life. And you're doing it because there is no life any more.'

Dan looked around. There was a print of Dartmoor's Hay Tor on the wall above the television. A group of people stood triumphantly atop the great granite rock, arms raised to the camera. Walking had been one of Linda's hobbies. The lack of family photos was unusual, but Adam had said that both her parents were dead and she had no siblings.

'The search teams are here, sir,' said Claire, walking over to the window. Dan felt a sudden urge to hug her, to protect her from the savagery of the world. She was holding her stomach again. He hoped she wasn't ill, ignoring it for the sake of the investigation.

A police van had drawn up outside and the TAG team piled untidily out. A couple of neighbours watched from the safety of their gates.

Dan couldn't stop his mind from slipping back to earlier. A moment's fatal resolution, a woman plummeting from the dizzying cliffs, a body shattered by the shocking impact with the unforgiving rocks. A gentle tide slipping in to claim the final physical memory of another broken hope, and a desperately lonely end to a once promising life.

He shuddered and sat down next to Adam, watched as the search teams began their work.

'Nothing, sir,' said the black-clad TAG sergeant. 'Not only not a sausage, but not even a chipolata.'

'Are you sure?' asked Adam.

The question made the man grimace. He took off his cap and scratched at his balding head. When he spoke, he sounded hurt.

'Quite sure, sir. We've tried all the hiding places there are. There's no computer, no reference books, none of Linda's personal papers and definitely no blackmail note. All we found was one drawer with bills, TV licence, passport, driving licence and that kind of thing. Nothing else at all.'

Adam looked at him, then turned and stared at Linda's house. Twilight was gathering and windows shone in the neighbouring homes. An occasional curtain twitched, but the interest in the show was waning. The weekly treats of take-aways and Saturday night TV took easy priority over cops going about another depressing investigation.

The evening was mild and still. The faint blare of an advert drifted from an open window. A ginger cat made a more obvious show of its curiosity, watching intently from a wall, its striped tail swinging.

'OK, Sergeant, stand down your team,' said Adam finally. 'You've done everything you could. Thanks for trying.'

'No problem,' said the man, saluting. 'Linda was a great boss. She once covered for me when my son was beaten up at school so I could go and be with him. A top officer. We all want to nail this bastard blackmailer. Go get him, sir.'

Adam nodded, but didn't reply. He turned and stared again at the house. The police van's diesel engine growled and spluttered into life and it grumbled up the road. The bite of diesel fumes lingered in the air.

'Sir?' tried Claire tentatively. 'Sir?'

'Sorry,' said Adam. 'I was thinking. I don't understand.' He addressed the empty house. 'Why give us the answer to the riddle, but nothing to show us how you got it, Linda? And what have you done with the blackmail note? You knew it would be vital for us. What was in it that was too horrible for you to let anyone else see?'

Dan leaned back on the bonnet of the CID car and arched his aching back. The twin assaults of tiredness and hunger had ambushed him. It was coming up to half past eight. They'd set out for Cornwall at eight this morning and he hadn't eaten since. A couple of breakfast slices of toast and a yoghurt was all he'd had all day. The excitement had kept the hunger caged, but now he needed to eat.

Adam was still staring at the house, his hands in his pockets. The ginger cat hopped down from the wall and swaggered up the road. Claire bent down to stroke it, but the cat slipped past her outstretched hand. Inside her bag, her mobile rang out a muffled tone. She stood up and answered it. Adam didn't move.

'Sir,' she said, when she'd finished the call. Then more insistently, 'Sir?'

'Sorry, Claire, yes?'

'It's the labs. They've got some news about St Agnes head.'

Adam turned to them. 'Come on then,' he said wearily. 'We're getting nowhere here. I reckon Linda sanitised the place before she ... well, you know. It's a silent house. It's not telling us anything. Let's get back to Charles Cross.'

Arthur Lamont, the technician, was waiting for them in the labs in the basement of the station. He had reached 65 and been forced to retire despite his protests, but still worked part-time and loved being called out in emergencies. He often covered weekends to give the other forensics officers some time off.

'Hello, Mr Breen. Good to see you again.' They shook hands. 'And the lovely Claire too.' He pecked her on the cheek. 'And this is the man on the telly.'

Dan tried to hide his irritation at the detested words. 'Dan Groves,' he said, keeping his voice level and holding out his hand. 'Pleased to meet you.'

The technician straightened his battered white coat and led them to a bench top. A line of test tubes stood in a rack, clear liquids inside them. Some sheets of paper were scattered around the bench. Arthur shuffled through them.

'It's so good to be back, Mr Breen,' he prattled. 'I've tidied the place up and sorted out some of the sloppy paperwork of the younger technicians. The labs need experience, you see, and they just haven't got it ...'

'Arthur,' interrupted Adam, his voice a warning.

'Almost there, Mr Breen. Almost there. I just still can't

believe they made me retire. A travesty it was. An absolute scandal. You can't replace experience, you know. And I work just as hard as …'

'Arthur!' Adam snapped.

The technician sniffed hard, produced a handkerchief and blew his noise. Adam took a step backwards.

'Sorry about that,' Arthur wheezed. 'It's unhealthy, being forced to retire. Not good for a man.' He caught Adam's look. 'Yes, now, the Scenes of Crime boys found some blood at St Agnes Head, Mr Breen. It was on a rock just below where Linda was seen jumping. They reckon she probably hit her head as she fell. We've tested it against some hairs I took from her desk upstairs. It's bad news I'm afraid.'

Arthur looked at them expectantly. No one spoke. 'It's a match,' he went on gravely. 'The jumper was definitely Linda.' He raised a hand to his chest and placed it over his heart. 'May she rest in peace.'

Arthur closed his eyes and there was an odd silence. Dan wasn't sure whether it was a poignant or comical moment.

'OK,' said Adam heavily. 'Let's keep going. Claire said you had some other things for us.'

The technician fumbled for another piece of paper. He held it up and peered at it. 'Sorry, the old eyesight's not what it was.'

'That's OK, Arthur, just take your time,' said Adam in a strained voice.

Arthur traced his finger down the paper. 'Here it is. Her car. We found it in a car park half a mile along the cliffs. The boys in the workshop took it apart, Mr Breen. They knew you were looking for something as small as a piece of paper. But I'm afraid they didn't find a single thing.'

Adam breathed out hard. His shoulders sagged. Arthur looked crestfallen, as though he was personally responsible for the failure. Adam thanked the man, they left the lab and walked slowly back up the stairs.

The police station was quiet, the classic calm before the weekly storm. Soon the night shift would clock on, resigned and ready for the wrestling matches with belligerent drunks that might have been the job description for a Saturday night beat in any English city.

Their footfall echoed around the stairwell. To Dan, it sounded heavy and disheartened.

'I'm tired out,' came Adam's voice over his shoulder. 'And I'm starving. I need to think, but I'm too tired and hungry. Is there anywhere close we can get a bite to eat?'

'It's well past nine,' Dan replied. 'Most decent places will have stopped serving by now. We could get a kebab or a burger.'

Claire quietly groaned. His eating habits had always caused friction.

'I need something better than that,' said Adam, stopping on the stairs. 'Burgers aren't thinking food. How about that Ginger Judge place?'

'Stops serving at nine, I think,' replied Dan. 'But I could give Sarah a call to see if she'd mind keeping the kitchen open a little later for us.'

'Go for it. Pull the TV fame card. Yesterday she was all over you. She looked like she couldn't wait to have you back in there.'

Beside him, Dan heard Claire catch her breath. Thanks Adam, he thought.

'Roll up, roll up, hurry on in,' said Sarah in a mock showman's voice. She'd been standing at the door waiting. 'I promised the chef he'd only have to be here another half hour. He's a young lad, and it's Saturday night. I've saved your table.'

They sat down gratefully. 'It's all on,' Sarah said, handing them each a menu. 'And the specials are still on too. If you wouldn't mind being quick, that'd help.'

'Mixed grill please,' said Adam instantly, leaning back on his chair.

'Lasagne for me please,' added Claire. 'With salad, not chips.'

Dan stood up and checked the Specials board. There were only three dishes left, some salad concoction which he hardly registered, chicken in black bean sauce and fresh local ham.

'Don't think me unadventurous,' he said. 'But I really fancy the ham. Is it good?'

Sarah folded her arms and gave him a look. 'It's all good, Dan. The ham has been newly hacked, and off a local pig too if you're interested. With the egg and chips I take it?' Dan nodded eagerly. 'You all looked tired,' said Sarah. 'Busy day?'

No one needed to answer. 'OK then, let's see if we can nourish a bit of life back into you. I'll get your food sorted and as it's you I'll even bring your drinks over. Beer again for you boys?'

'Yes please,' chorused Dan and Adam.

'Let me guess. A glass of wine for the lady?'

'Sorry,' said Dan. 'You haven't been introduced. Sarah, this is Claire. Or Detective Sergeant Claire.'

'Pleased to meet you,' said Claire, a little frostily. 'White wine would be lovely. Just a small glass though please.'

Adam took a deep draw on his pint and rolled his neck. Dan sipped at his beer and looked around. All the tables were taken and there was a line of people standing at the bar. The room bubbled with conversation and laughter. It wasn't quite the Saturday night he had had in mind, but it felt better now he had a drink and dinner was on the way.

Adam excused himself and went outside to call home. He hated people talking on their mobiles in pubs and restaurants. It was one of his little themes, how etiquette hadn't yet evolved in line with new technology. He'd once had an argument with a businessman making a call in a bar, asked him to keep his voice down.

'It's not against the law,' the man had countered. 'No,' said Adam. 'But I bet if I send our accountants round to your office, and our vehicle examiners to your car park, they'll soon find something that is.' The businessman had quickly cut the call.

Adam walked up and down as he spoke and Dan could see from his gesturing that he was firmly on the defensive. Annie was a patient woman, quite used to losing her husband for days when a big case came up, but she wasn't shy in pointing out how little he could be at home. Her lodger, she'd joked, on one occasion Dan had been invited round for dinner. Adam hadn't laughed.

Annie's most potent weapon was mentioning how Tom, Adam's teenage son, missed him.

The detective walked back in, looking sheepish, and Dan could see it had been strategically deployed.

The detective took another long drink of his beer. 'So, where are we then in the hunt for the Worm?'

'Not very far, sir,' replied Claire. 'We've got two victims, now both dead, and the prospect of three more still to come.'

'Right,' interjected Adam. 'And one of our corpses is a fellow cop. I don't want any more deaths and I want this person caught. We've got an idea about how the Worm works and some vague thoughts about what kind of a person he is, but that's it. What we don't have yet are suspects. So – where do we find them?'

There was a pause, then Claire spoke. 'We're looking for someone who'd know intimate details about people. What Dan said about the contents of the letter to Freedman sounding like a conversation chimed with me. The idea about priests and lawyers and doctors sounded like a good one.'

'Agreed,' replied Adam. 'So that's where we go next. We've started work on who Freedman used as a lawyer, or whether the family had a priest or a counsellor. Now let's do the same for Linda and see if we come up with any matches. Anyone who might know both their secrets. Any other thoughts?'

Dan sipped hard at his beer. It didn't bring any inspiration. Unusual that. He must be tired.

'Not really,' he said. 'The media coverage might bring people forward with information. If we need more, we can release the details of Linda's death.'

'Not yet with that,' said Adam. 'We've got enough on at the moment. I don't need another session with the press. First let's just do some quiet work on the case in the boring old traditional way.'

'OK,' agreed Dan, not even bothering to acknowledge the nudge of his conscience that said he was a journalist and Linda's death was a great story. 'I'd like to have another look at the first code too. It might help now we know the answer to the second one.'

The numbers returned to his mind. 61, 43, 21, 51.

Dan imagined them spun around, turned them back to front, tried to see a hidden meaning, but nothing came to his lethargic brain. The ones, he was sure the number ones were important. Otherwise, why so many?

Adam was speaking and he focused back on the detective's weary face. 'Fine. It's worth a try. When we go back to Charles Cross we'll have a chat with our codebreakers to see what they've come up with.'

Dan stood and headed to the gents. 'Excuse me. Back in a minute.'

Sarah intercepted him as he returned to the table. 'Are you working on this blackmail case?' she asked, pointing to the rack of newspapers by the bar. They were full of Freedman's face. 'It sounds awful.'

'It is,' replied Dan. 'Really nasty. Excuse me if I can't talk about it. It's quite a sensitive one.'

She gave him that tired smile. 'I understand.'

'Thanks for squeezing us in and keeping the chef on though. It's really kind of you and much appreciated.'

'It's no trouble at all. I like to keep my customers happy. They've always looked after me, unlike others I could mention. The government for example, with their endless taxes and regulations.'

Dan sensed Sarah wanted to talk again, and wondered how to escape without being rude. There was a dam of resentment and anger she needed to release. But all he wanted was some food and drink.

He saw Claire watching. She wasn't usually the jealous kind, but she had been a little odd lately. He wondered what was bothering her. It couldn't be second thoughts about living together, surely?

Dan blinked hard and pushed the thought away. He couldn't face it. He knew exactly what effect it would have on him if it all went wrong with Claire. The swamp of his depression would return, and with all the putrid fury it had fermented in its banishment.

A buzzer sounded. 'That's your meals,' said Sarah. 'I'll get them.' Dan tried not to look relieved. 'We can talk some more next time you're in. It's about time you did a story on how tough it is for the little person, with the government and everyone else on their case.'

Dan walked back to the table, reflecting that when so many people said talk to, what they actually meant was talk at. He'd known plenty who mistook a monologue for a conversation. He often thought that was one of the foundations for his success as a journalist. Interested or not, he could listen.

The food tasted fantastic and they tore into it. Even Claire, usually a gentle diner, ate quickly. Dan squeezed her knee under the table and she looked up from her plate and smiled. All was well.

Adam was wiping up the remnants of his tomatoes with a piece of bread when his mobile rang. He answered it, listened for a few seconds, then spoke.

'We'll be right there.'

He put the phone back into his jacket pocket. Dan and Claire looked on expectantly.

'The codebreakers,' Adam said, swallowing the last of the bread. 'They've cracked Freedman's riddle. Let's go.'

Chapter Nine

THEY MARCHED BACK TO Charles Cross, fighting the ballast of the dinners they'd only just finished. The city was rowdy with weekend revellers and they picked their way through the current of excitement as it flowed around them.

A party of policewomen in unfeasibly short skirts waved blow up truncheons at the passing traffic, attracting a cacophony of wolf whistles. Dan felt Claire's eyes on him and made a point of not admiring the parade.

Adam got a cheer and round of applause from a group of young lads for wearing a suit, but he ignored it. Dan wondered if he'd even noticed. He was walking mechanically, his eyes unfocused with his thoughts. If they now had two of the five parts of the code, it could be an important breakthrough. They might even have enough information to find the Judgement Book.

He found himself wondering what it looked like and what secrets it held. So far they only knew about one, Freedman's. What was Linda Cott's? Her house had offered no hints, deliberately so he suspected. If she wouldn't leave them the Worm's note, she'd make certain there were no clues in her home as to what it was she'd done.

Just how many people were in this Judgement Book? Dan's imagination threaded together a picture of a leather-bound, A4-sized address book. There was an index at the side with each letter of the alphabet. He saw himself open it at G. There was his own entry, lines and lines of neat black handwriting.

There was plenty of material to fill the page, and that in the last few days alone. Pushing a businessman to spend thousands of pounds on a painting because of some inside information Dan had overheard. Conniving with Adam to force the blackmailer case into the headlines. Lots more too, if he went back over the history of the cases he had worked on. Not exactly major crimes, but enough to destroy his career.

Adam could be in the Book too, the innocent lines of tidy

writing describing the rape of his sister, Sarah, and how it had driven him to become a detective. A kind of legitimate vigilantism he called it. Some of the things he'd done to catch criminals were well short of being lawful and scrupulous. If they became known, his future as a police officer would be in doubt, to say the least.

The Book struck at an innate fear. Just as Adam had said, everyone had their guilty secrets. Dan vaguely recalled an experiment he'd once read about. A hundred men received anonymous phone calls, the unknown voice saying simply, "All is discovered. Flee! Flee!" Around 80 per cent had shown signs of preparing to run.

Cabs filled the roads, their amber taxi lamps speeding like rushing fireflies. Music pumped from a couple of pubs, mixed with shouts and laughter. The weather had remained kind, a duvet of low cloud keeping the city warm. The men who passed wore their best peacock shirts, the women tight dresses and cropped tops. Their newly bared flesh shone in the orange glow of the sodium streetlights.

Dan glanced at Claire, walking beside him. She was beautiful, her dark hair bobbing with the rhythm of her stride. She didn't return the look, but winked at him from the corner of her eye. Dan couldn't suppress a smile. She was a detective all right, and a good one. He couldn't even sneak an admiring look without her spotting it.

Adam jogged up the steps into the police station and disappeared through the automatic doors. Dan exchanged looks with Claire and they hurried after him. They were both out of breath and glowing with sweat.

Michael Hunter and Eleanor Yabsley were sitting at a table in the MIR. She wore another of her flowing floral skirts, stretching yellow tulips curving up from the floor to her hips. Her lined face was as kindly as Dan recalled from when they'd met in the Evil Valley case. She was in her mid to late 50s, silvered hair, but with a soft and fine look and strikingly brown eyes. She floated up from the table and shook hands with them, her skirt slowly straightening itself in lapping waves. Michael hopped from the edge of the desk and did the same.

Dan still couldn't help being surprised by how young he was. Not yet thirty, and already on the books of the National Crime Faculty as an expert codebreaker. He wore his uniform of white trainers, black jeans and a black T-shirt with AC/DC printed on the front. A Celtic tattoo snaked around his bicep, an intertwined grey-green band. His spiked hair looked a different shade of black from last year, a hint of purple tinting its peaks. He smiled continually, with a hint of nerves.

The pair always worked together. Dan knew the detectives thought of them as a classic mother and son relationship, but never said so. She, with her more advanced years and academic background, still an emeritus professor of mathematics, he with his extraordinary puzzle-solving talent, knowledge of computers and modern life. Their skills complemented each other perfectly.

'Well, Eleanor,' said Adam when the introductions were over. 'What have you got for us?'

'Michael found it,' she said, smiling gently. 'Although he cheated a little.'

The codebreaker coloured under their looks. 'I did not cheat. I just enlisted some help. Using the best tools available is not cheating.' He patted the keyboard of the laptop computer in front of him, as if it were an old dog who had been his companion for long years.

'Enlighten us then, Michael,' said Adam, rather impatiently.

The young man took the hint. 'It was a fairly straightforward puzzle. Once you saw the key to it, that is.'

'Which is?' asked Adam.

'It's in the Worm's letter.' Michael pointed to a section he'd highlighted on his copy. The words were, "It's a classic game."

He looked at them and smiled knowingly. The blank stares he got in return prompted him to continue.

'I missed it to start with,' he said. 'I tried to make it too complex. I was busy looking for acrostics, or anagrams or algorithms. It was much simpler than that. "It's a classic game," gives you the key. I thought initially those words referred to the blackmailer playing with their victim. That is a classic game, after all. But in fact that's the way into the puzzle.'

Adam folded his arms. 'Explain please,' he said sharply.

'OK. Look at the numbers.'

61, 43, 21, 51

'And?' said Adam, heavily.

'There are a lot of ones. So I started to think about what classic games used numbers and contained plenty of ones.' He looked at Dan, Claire, Adam in turn, clearly finding it difficult to believe they hadn't got it. 'Any thoughts?'

'Battleships?' asked Adam with a heavy slice of sarcasm.

'No.'

'I thought something to do with grid references,' said Dan.

'Nope,' replied Michael. Dan noticed himself starting to feel annoyed too.

'Scrabble,' said Claire.

Michael looked at her and smiled, sounding relieved. 'Correct. Scrabble.'

Adam frowned hard. 'I'm sorry. You're trying to tell us this blackmailer has set us a code in scrabble?'

'That's exactly what he's done. It all adds up.'

The detective couldn't keep the disbelief from his voice. 'Sounds daft to me, but if you say so. OK then how do you read it?'

Michael picked up a pen. 'In Scrabble, each letter has a score. The most common, like "a" and "e" only score one. The rarest, like "z" score 10. There are only a couple of letters that score 10. But there are quite a few which score one. So, to differentiate them, perhaps you'd label the first letter that scores one – a – as 11. The second – e – would be 21. The sixth to score one is "o". So under this system, "o" would be coded as 61.

They stared at what Michael had written.

'61,' said Dan finally. 'The first number in the sequence of the code.'

'Yes,' said Michael.

'Spare us the rest of the lecture, please,' grunted Adam, tetchily. 'What's the answer?'

'61 is o, 43 is p, 21 is e and 51 is n.'

'Open,' said Claire. 'The answer to the riddle is "open."'

'Yes,' replied Michael, sitting back down on the edge of the desk.

There was a silence. 'So,' said Adam slowly. 'We've got open and original. What does that mean? Open original? Original open? What does that mean? It doesn't tell us anything. Not a bloody thing.'

No one replied. Adam stalked over to the window and stared out at the city. It was still alive with darting cabs and staggering revellers. Chinks and blocks of colour glowed from the shop windows. White floodlights illuminated Charles Church. The stark wash of cold white light made the ruin seem more hollow and lonely.

'Not a bloody thing,' said Adam again, slapping his palm on the window ledge in time with each word. 'And here was I hoping for a breakthrough.'

Adam sent them home for the night. They had a short discussion about the code and what the answers they had could mean, but no one had any realistic ideas. Dan noticed they were becoming irritated with each other. It was getting on for midnight, and he could feel the weight of tiredness numbing his mind and body.

'There's nothing much else we can do tonight,' Adam said. 'We'll need to start talking to Linda's friends and going through all her personal stuff. We'll have to put together a statement for the press as well. But the best thing we can do for now is get some rest. The first two blackmails have been close together. I don't think we'll have long to wait until the next one.'

In the car park, Dan and Claire had a quick chat. They slipped into a narrow gap between two police vans and she reached out to him for a cuddle.

'I don't want to sleep alone tonight,' she said, her head pressed against his shoulder. 'Not after what happened today with Linda. I know it's late, but I wouldn't mind sitting for an hour before we go to bed and having a chat, just to clear my mind.'

'Sure. I'd like that that. Your place or mine?'

'I'd prefer mine. I have to get some things ready for the

morning.'

'OK. I'll have to go home first, see to Rutherford and get myself some clothes for the morning too. I'll be at your place in half an hour.'

Rutherford was asleep when he got back to the flat. The dog looked dazed and his fur was sticking up on the side where he'd been lying. He managed a half-hearted bark.

'Sorry to neglect you after our day out was cut short earlier, old friend,' said Dan, cuddling him. 'And I've got to go out again. Claire needs me tonight. I know you'll understand. I'll make it up to you next weekend, I promise. We'll go for a good long walk on Dartmoor.'

Dan found some clean trousers and a shirt while Rutherford was in the garden. He sat on his bed to get some socks and pants out of a drawer, and felt a longing to lie back and close his eyes. They ached with tiredness. He forced himself to get up and splash some cold water on his face.

He drove back into the city and let himself into Claire's flat. It was just after one o'clock. She was asleep on the sofa in the lounge, a blanket over her legs, her hands folded across her stomach. Her breathing was almost imperceptible, just butterflies of whispered air.

Dan quietly slipped into the bathroom and washed, then came back to check on her. Claire was still asleep. He put a hand on her shoulder and rocked her gently. Her eyes fluttered open and she looked at him, recognition gathering in her waking mind.

She smiled. 'Sorry. I must have fallen asleep. I was so tired.'

He helped her up and said, 'Come on then, proper sleep time for you. I've set the alarm for just before eight.' They got into bed and she lay back on the pillow.

'Guess you don't need that chat to clear your mind then,' Dan said, cuddling in to her and stroking the hair behind her ears. 'Was it anything specific you wanted to talk about, or just more Agas and toast?'

'Something like that,' she replied. 'It can wait until tomorrow.'

Chapter Ten

DAN WAS LOST IN the warm haze of a pleasant dream when he was yanked cruelly back into reality by the phone.

'Hello?' he managed, sleepy and startled.

'It's Adam. Get in here, quick as you can. And Claire as well. We've got the next note. Another cop's the victim. Another bloody cop! But this time, I think we may have a break – a picture of the Worm. The media are all over us again too. We need to work out a strategy.'

The phone went dead. Beside him, Claire stirred and turned on to her side. Dan blinked at her alarm clock. Its red digits said half past six. He'd been asleep for only five hours and felt as though he hadn't rested. The fleeting release wasn't enough for rejuvenation. His legs ached in protest as he stretched them.

A fringe of early sunlight framed the curtains. Outside, he could hear the triumphant cries of a gang of seagulls, squealing in delight at the dawn and its rich feast of discarded take-away food from the night before. The sanctity of Sunday mornings was nothing to them. That was the trouble with Claire's flat. It was much closer to the sea than his, and meant sleeping in was impossible. Not that that was even an option this morning.

Dan reached out and gently shook Claire's shoulder. She mumbled something. He shook her again, a little harder this time. She turned and opened her eyes.

'Work?' she asked.

'Yep.'

'Yours or mine?'

'Both.'

As so often, their two worlds were interconnected. Where the police were called, there were usually journalists following. Dan often thought of the similarities between their professions as the reason for his success as a detective. At a basic level, the arts were the same. Ask the right questions, read the reactions, spot the lies and evasions and pick your way to the hidden truth.

In the shower, he thought about Adam's call. Another police

victim. No wonder the detective sounded angry. The case must be starting to feel personal. How did an attack on another cop fit in with Linda and Freedman? Two police officers and an MP. Where was the pattern?

He borrowed a squirt of Claire's special and expensive conditioning shampoo. He must remember to leave some of his own here, to keep the blue sentinel toothbrush company. He kept forgetting shampoo every time he brought an overnight bag. But at least he felt as though he was waking up.

As he dressed, he wondered what Adam really thought about him and Claire being a couple. They'd agreed not to talk about it, but he couldn't help but ask himself the question.

Adam was protective of his officers and well aware of Dan's disastrous history with women. They'd talked about it often enough, particularly in those long-gone days when Adam was estranged from Annie. All that was resolved now, happily. Dan found himself hoping he'd one day be as content as Adam. But his friend must be worried about what could happen between him and Claire. Dan knew Adam was fond of Claire, thought of her as a perceptive and diligent detective with a promising future.

From the bathroom, he heard the buzz of Claire's electric toothbrush. He smiled. He even found the way she cleaned her teeth cute. He must be enamoured.

Well, he didn't have to worry about what Adam thought or what would become of his relationship with Claire. They were getting on great and would soon be moving in together. Dan felt his mood warm and his tiredness lift. Life was good, and he shouldn't lose sight of that. If you went looking for problems and concerns, you could always find them. Better to live for now and appreciate what you had.

He walked into the kitchen to make them some toast. They'd need the energy. Another busy day was in prospect. Dan moved some of Claire's discarded leftovers from the work surface. He'd half-heard her get up in the night, vaguely remembered she said something about needing a snack.

A chocolate wrapper, the remains of a banana, some oat flakes, raspberry jam, natural yoghurt and the crust from a piece of white toast. He shook his head. What a bizarre combination for a midnight feast. No wonder she had a bad stomach.

Adam was waiting for them in the MIR. His face was drawn and he looked tired and pale. He'd shaved badly, with patches of bristles still shading his cheeks, and his tie hung a couple of inches down his neck. He didn't say anything, but handed them each a photocopied sheet. They sat in silence and read the blackmailer's note.

Dear Superintendent Osmond,
You are a despicable man. Like many of your kind, you pretend to be one thing in public when the private reality is very different.
"You are a liar, a hypocrite, and you are corrupt. You boast of being an upholder of the law whereas in fact you have broken it and used your position to cover up that fact. You are utterly odious.
I know what happened on your little celebration in December. It was a lovely night out, wasn't it? You and your wife, toasting the birth of your first grandchild and the impending arrival of Christmas. A beautiful evening, and just cause to celebrate. So you chose one of Plymouth's finer restaurants. Who would begrudge you that?
Except you went a little too far, didn't you, Superintendent? You love that Jaguar car of yours, don't you? And you live out in the country. You could have easily booked a cab. A man in your position could afford it without any trouble. But you chose not to. You decided to drive in, and you got a little carried away.
You assured that poor wife of yours, Janey, that you would only have a glass or two of wine. But you couldn't stop at a glass. You had to have a bottle. And then another. You could always get a taxi home, you said.
But then comes the end of the night. Getting a cab is

a hassle, isn't it? And you don't want to leave your lovely car in the middle of Plymouth. It could get vandalised, stolen even. Who'll know if you drive home?

But it wasn't your lucky night, was it Superintendent? Some of these traffic police are smart. A patrol spotted you. You were driving just a little too carefully. You made the officer suspicious. And so he pulled you over.

You get out of the car, and suddenly our traffic policeman has a problem. You're one of his superior officers. He doesn't need to make you do a breath test, does he? He can smell the drink. He knows.

You see the confusion in his eyes, Superintendent, and you suggest a way out of this tricky little problem. Perhaps he could forget all about the last few minutes and go about his business, while you drive very carefully home. And when he applies for that sergeant's position which is coming up, well, you can't promise, of course, but you can make sure his application is viewed most favourably.

And there's one postscript to this tale of woe, Superintendent. What's this I find in my research on your illustrious career? That for the past six years, you have been in charge of Greater Wessex Police's Christmas campaign against drinking and driving. And here you are, quoted.

'Drink driving is a scourge. Anyone who takes to the wheel after drinking deserves society's strongest condemnation. It's akin to taking a loaded gun out and not caring who might get hit by the bullets. It kills. It wrecks innocent lives. We must stamp it out and we will stamp it out.'

What fine words! But, I suppose you forgot to mention that drink driving is fine if you're a high-ranking police officer who fancies a few and can't be bothered to get a taxi home. An understandable omission. It would spoil the quote rather, wouldn't it?

So Superintendent, we have established you are a thoroughly despicable man. The question is, what do I intend to do about it?

You'll be expecting me to ask for cash. Wrong, totally wrong. I don't want your filthy money. My only interest is in exposing you. You and your rotten kind.

You'll know by now that you are not alone. You could hardly have missed your detectives running around so amusingly in their pursuit of me. Your sordid secrets fill my beautiful Judgement Book. But there are others there too. You are the third, but you will not be the last. I've chosen two more to share your fate. Is that any comfort to you?

You do not deserve this, but I will give you one chance. I confess I am enjoying my game. I give you one hope to save yourself. The following riddle, if solved, will give you a word. If you can solve it, place a personal advert in the Western Daily News' Births, Marriages and Deaths section, starting with the word that forms the solution, and going on to use your surname.

So then, your riddle. As a clue, I give you this advice. It might help you to think back to last Sunday to solve it. Now tel me the answer to this.

1112, 7257, 1173, 22584

For your information, and for your detectives, I re-emphasise this. The solution to the riddle, combined with those to the other four, will take you to the hiding place of the Judgement Book.

Good luck.

The three of them finished the note at the same time. They looked up, all quietened by what they'd read. The flagpole outside the window rattled.

Claire drew in a hiss of breath. 'Osmond, eh?'

Adam said knowingly, 'You've had dealings with him?'

'Only a few, sir, ages ago. From when I was in uniform.'

'And?'

'Well, I …'

'Come on Claire. You're amongst friends. If it's any help, I can't stand the man, and it's a common feeling around here.'

She nodded. 'He was the one who came closest to making me quit. When I was a probationer. He bawled me out because I filled in a fixed penalty notice wrongly. It had me in fits of tears. Some druggie had been shoplifting. I gave him a ticket, just like we were supposed to. But the shop complained that was too lenient and demanded to see the paperwork. The manager wanted to take the case to court, but I'd put the street name on the form in the wrong box and it meant he couldn't.'

Dan whistled through his teeth. 'He bawled you out for that? It's a tiny mistake. Easy to make.'

'Maybe, but it doesn't feel like it when you're just starting off in your career. It was the first time I really met Linda. I was sitting in the canteen, trying not to cry, and she came and chatted to me. She talked me out of quitting. She even went to see the shop manager to smooth it all over.'

Adam nodded. 'Osmond's not exactly known for his touchy, feely style. He's an ex-army officer and still thinks he's in the forces. I've had a few run-ins with him myself. He thinks every problem's solved by shouting at it. He's a walking anachronism.'

'So,' said Dan. 'You think the drink driving allegation in the note's true?'

Adam didn't reply, just gave him a look.

'Bloody hell,' said Dan, who couldn't think of a more eloquent contribution.

'Quite,' replied Adam, his voice quiet and strained. 'My already impressive list of problems just grew longer. Now I've got a very serious allegation against a senior and belligerent officer to mix in with my already tortuous blackmail case. Osmond doesn't know yet. He's on his way in. I'm going to talk to him, then he'll be suspended pending an investigation.'

'How come he doesn't know about the note yet?' asked Dan.

'The letter was put through the post box here at the police station at about five o'clock this morning. On it was written "To Supt. Leon Osmond. Enclosed, the latest chapter of the

Judgement Book." They called me when the duty sergeant found it.'

Claire raised an eyebrow, then said, 'And what about this picture of the Worm?'

'As you know, the front office here isn't manned throughout the night,' replied Adam. 'But there is CCTV on the entrance. I think we've got an image of our blackmailer delivering the letter.'

'Breakthrough?' Dan asked.

'I'd like to hope so, but ...'

'But?'

'Let's wait and see. The Worm's smart. I can't imagine him smiling up at the camera in a nice pose for us.'

The detective wiped his shining forehead with a sleeve. 'Just to add to my burden, the media have twigged the link between Linda's suicide and Freedman's and are baying for interviews. You'll have to work out a way of dealing with them. I'll do another press conference, but that's it. The High Honchos have been on my back twice this morning, demanding results. I can't afford to lose more time. And I've now got to confront Osmond, and that won't be pretty.'

Dan was about to reply when Claire suddenly retched, threw her hands to her mouth and ran out of the MIR. He stared in disbelief, then jogged after her, down the stone stairs to the toilets. From inside he could hear more retching.

'Claire? Claire!' he called. There was no reply. He stared at the thick wooden door and wondered what to do. He hardly wanted to walk into the women's toilets at a police station. He pushed the door ajar and called her name again.

The retching subsided. 'I'm OK,' she shouted from inside. 'Just feeling a bit under the weather. I'll be with you in a minute.'

Dan walked slowly back up the stairs. The two flights felt a long way. The tiredness was back with him.

'She's OK, just feeling a bit queasy,' he said, in reply to Adam's quizzical look. 'She ate some odd food last night. Chocolate, bananas, toast, weird stuff like that. I expect it's just caught up on her. She says she'll be back up in a minute.'

Adam blinked a couple of times and stared at him. 'OK,' said the detective eventually, and in a strange tone. 'But if she's feeling odd, make sure you look after her. And I mean look after her well.'

There was a silence, before Adam continued, 'Right, time to confront dear Superintendent Osmond.'

He stretched his arms, took a long breath, pursed his lips and walked slowly out of the MIR.

Chapter Eleven

ADAM SAT ALONE IN his office, door closed, fingers on his temples thinking. He was going through his plan, testing it, checking it.

He had an idea, but it was risky.

The criminal psychologist's report lay on his desk. Doctor "Sledgehammer" Stephens was so named within Greater Wessex Police because he suffered an antipathy to subtlety and an irresistible desire to make sure his views were conveyed with painful clarity. His thoughts on the blackmailer were couched in none of the usual caveats and equivocations so beloved of his profession.

"I consider blackmailer HIGHLY DANGEROUS", Stephens had written. "Clearly very DRIVEN in his actions. Obvious PSYCHOPATHIC TENDENCIES – that is a person who has no empathy or sympathy for others."

'Yes, I know what psychopathic means,' muttered Adam.

"Burning sense of GRIEVANCE and INJUSTICE. This person has a SELF IMPOSED MISSION which he is utterly dedicated to carrying out. He WILL NOT STOP until caught."

Not for the first time, Adam reflected that Stephens had managed to tell him little, if anything, that he didn't already know or suspect. He flicked tetchily at the report, pushed it into a filing tray.

The phone rang. The desk sergeant, as instructed, telling him Osmond had pulled in to the car park. Adam got up from his chair and jogged down the stairs. He needed to have the initiative. It was going to be a bitter confrontation, quite probably simply a shouting match. He had to see the Superintendent's reaction to his revelation before the man had a chance to gather his thoughts, refuse to answer and walk out.

Osmond could easily hide in taking legal advice about the drink drive and corruption allegations. They were perfect barriers to questioning, allowing him weeks to consult, gather his thoughts, prepare his defence. But there were three blackmail notes now, and two dead victims. The threat of another two victims to come. The inquiry was too urgent. It couldn't afford to stall.

It was too much to expect Osmond to confess. But all they had to be sure of was that there was truth in the claims against him. And fast.

Adam reached the bottom of the staircase and headed for the back of the station. It was quiet, Sunday morning, skeleton staff. The night shift had gone home to recover after the familiar hours of arresting drunks. Charles Cross always seemed hollow on a Sunday. It was the only day of the week there weren't shouted conversations echoing around the corridors and the continual pounding of heavy police feet on its long-suffering staircase. The sounds were the station's heartbeat and it felt lifeless without them.

Adam forced his mind back to Osmond. He had to concentrate. The word that came to mind was ambush.

He was setting a trap.

The superintendent was hauling his bulk out of his car, locking it. He was even checking to make sure the central locking had engaged, rubbing a smear off the side mirror and checking his reflection.

Adam waited.

Now Osmond was almost at the door. He walked with a slight hobble, a legacy of his military service, or so he liked to say, but in fact the product of falling off a ladder when doing some DIY. He fumbled in his jacket pocket for his security pass and the clumsy grappling exposed the bulging roll of his stomach. He wore a crumpled old single-breasted navy suit, his usual.

'Superintendent,' Adam said, as brightly as he could. 'Thank you for coming in. I very much need your help.'

'What the hell is this about, Breen?' the man grunted. 'It's Sunday. It's supposed to be my day off.'

'I'm sorry, you were the only person I could think of who could help me.'

Osmond made to walk along the corridor towards his office, but Adam stopped him.

'Would you mind coming to my office please? I've got something there I need you to look at. It is urgent.'

Osmond huffed, but followed Adam's guiding arm and started up the stairs. He was embarrassingly overweight for a police officer and was panting within a few steps. OK, it didn't matter so much when your patrol was only ever a desk, but it couldn't be good for the public to see such a fat cop.

The superintendent's face was embroidered with a tiny network of broken veins, the faint trickles of blues and reds that marked many of the old school of senior officers. Slaves to the ritual opening of a special drawer in the inner sanctum and the chink of a whisky decanter. There were less of his kind now, but some still inhabited forgotten corners of remote police stations, unmoved by change, waiting only for retirement.

His dark hair was greasy and thin and his ears oversized, as if they'd been designed to match the figure he had grown into. He was about fifty, but looked older.

'Please do sit down,' said Adam pleasantly, offering Osmond one of the padded visitors' chairs. The superintendent lowered himself heavily onto it.

'What's all this about then, Breen?' he huffed again. 'Whatever it is, can we get it over with? I've got lots of other things I'd rather be doing.'

Adam opened a drawer and took out a photocopy of the blackmailer's note.

'This arrived here this morning,' he said calmly, passing it over. 'It was addressed to you.'

Osmond took the piece of paper and began to read. Adam watched him intently. The man's eyes worked their way down the page. If what he was reading was true, he was good, very good. No real reaction so far. He thought he saw a twitch of Osmond's cheek and a blink, but that was it.

The room was still. The clock on the wall ticked loud.

Osmond was halfway though the note.

Still nothing definite. Nothing to give him away.

Not yet.

Adam shifted in his chair, tried to do it silently. He didn't take his eyes from Osmond's face. The man was still reading, almost finished now, continued to show no reaction. There was nothing to indicate that what the blackmailer had written was true.

'Pathetic,' grunted Osmond, dropping the piece of paper onto Adam's desk.

He flicked at it dismissively, then switched his look to Adam. 'You called me in here because of that? The pathetic ravings of someone I've banged up, no doubt. Some small-time criminal with a grudge.'

Adam held the man's stare. There was still nothing to suggest he was even worried, let alone guilty. But he was an experienced cop. He knew how to handle pressure. He could be bluffing.

Adam steadied himself, then said, 'You'll appreciate this note forms part of an inquiry into a very serious crime, one which we believe has led to two people taking their own lives. So, it's my duty to ask you if there is any truth in the allegations.'

Osmond struggled up from his seat. 'How dare you!' he roared, and his voice was surprisingly loud.

'This is contemptible. I am your superior officer, Breen. I was policing this city when you were pissing your nappy! I am going home.' A pause, then more sinisterly, 'When I return to work, I will decide whether to lodge a formal complaint against you.'

Adam stood to face Osmond. 'So you deny the allegations completely?'

The Superintendent turned for the door. 'I have no intention of lowering myself to even reply,' he hissed. He was sweating, his face furrowed and red.

Adam studied him, thinking fast. That anger sounded genuine. Osmond could be totally innocent.

But ... he didn't deny it. Just blustered.

'Superintendent,' Adam heard himself say. Osmond stopped, half in, half out of the doorway. 'What?' he grunted. 'You want to apologise? Not a bad idea, Breen. It might just help your cause if you did.'

Adam stared at him. There was the slight hint of a tic under

Osmond's eye.

'Superintendent,' Adam repeated, his voice soft. Osmond took a step towards him. 'One final thing.'

'What?'

Adam held his look. Neither man spoke.

The pit was yawning. It was only a question of luring the victim towards it.

But what a risk.

Finally Adam spoke. 'Leon.'

'What? How dare you, Breen! I'm Superintendent ...'

'Leon, please. I've always looked up to you.'

The flattery quietened him. Osmond was listening now, suspicious but intrigued, despite himself.

Vanity, such an irresistible lure.

'Superintendent, you've been a cop here for years, and the things you've done for this city ...'

'Just get on with it, Breen. If you've got something to say, say it.'

Adam nodded, kept his voice calm. 'Sir, between us and out of respect for you, before you leave I think it's only fair to warn you we have a witness who saw you and your car pulled up by the traffic officer on Exeter Street.'

Osmond glared at him. 'It wasn't Exeter Street ...' he began, then stopped himself.

And now there was a stark tic, jumping and angry under his left eye, hammering away, sending tiny waves through the pasty flesh.

'You bastard,' Osmond hissed, his face flushing fast. He turned, hobbled out of the office and slammed the door.

Dan was surprised to realise it was the first time he'd been alone in the Major Incident Room. He walked along it, past the desks with the blank and silent computers and to Adam's beloved felt boards. The picture of Freedman stared out at him. Dan couldn't stop himself from shuddering. What a way to die. Alone in a bath, your family downstairs, oblivious.

The door crashed open and Adam burst into the room. He looked as though he'd been in a bar room brawl, his eyes wild, hair tussled. Dan didn't say anything, just gave him a questioning look. Adam walked to the boards, pinned up a copy of Osmond's blackmail note and a small photograph of the Superintendent. It had been cut from a newspaper and showed him standing by a police patrol car, holding a breathalyser.

'It's true,' was all he said.

There was a silence. Dan tried to keep his face impassive, but the detective must have noticed the hint of an expression. Or perhaps Adam just knew him too well.

'But!' he added. 'No reporting, no story. Not yet, anyway. We've got too much on with the investigation. That has to be the priority.'

They both gazed at the boards and the photographs staring back at them. Freedman, Linda Cott, now Osmond. Dan saw Adam going through the same thoughts. What linked them? What was the golden thread that connected two police officers and one MP? And when they found the link, who was the blackmailer it would lead them to?

The door opened again, gently this time and Claire slid in. She moved slowly and looked pale. Dan raised his eyebrows and she lifted a calming hand, then lowered it and rubbed her stomach.

Adam watched as she gingerly sat on the edge of a desk. 'Being sick in the morning,' he said, thoughtfully. Claire nodded. 'Something unusual in the stomach area?' he went on. She closed her eyes and nodded again. 'Better see the doctor and talk it over with him. I'm sure Dan will take you. It sounds like it might be something that could last for quite a few months.'

'Of course I will,' Dan replied, indignantly. 'But usually with sickness they just tell you to drink lots of water, eat simple foods and it'll pass. That's what I'd do.'

Adam sighed heavily. 'I'm not sure that'll work here.'

'Well, what do you suggest then?' Dan said. 'I didn't know you'd suddenly become a doctor, as well as a cop.'

If he expected a feisty response, it didn't come. Instead Adam looked pitying.

'You know what I don't understand about you?' the

detective asked. 'It's how you can be so smart in so much of life, but your emotional intelligence barely registers a blip on the meter.'

Dan was about to retaliate, but Claire spoke first. 'I'm OK,' she interrupted forcefully. 'I'll talk to Dan about it later. We've got a Worm to catch first.'

Adam stared at her. 'Fine. I understand. OK then, let's have a brainstorming session. I want to look at exactly what we've got and work out where we're going.'

He pointed to Freedman's handsome face, captured in the studio photograph. 'He's where it started. Linda's the second element.'

Adam moved his hand to the next board and her picture. She was a plain looking woman, almost the definition of nondescript. Mousy coloured hair, shoulder-length with a fringe, thin face, but somehow kind and trustworthy. It was her eyes that won belief, grey-green and clear, but with a nascent web of crows' feet spreading from each corner. She wore no make-up or jewellery in the picture. It looked like a blown-up police photo from her warrant card.

'And Osmond is our third,' Adam continued, pointing to the other board. 'He's not going to say anything more to us. We'll let Professional Standards investigate the allegations against him. We've got the note though, and that's the third piece in our puzzle. So, let's look at what connects Osmond, Linda, and Freedman.'

The detective pulled up his tie, checked his reflection in a window, made certain it was straight. Dan hid a smile, knew there was some good news coming, as sure as if Adam had written it across the boards.

'We already have one lead, and it could be a good one,' he said. 'Late yesterday, the inquiry teams found that Linda and Freedman shared the same priest. So, could this all have come from the confessional? From the priest himself, or someone who overheard what was said? We'll see this Father Maguire when he's finished his service.'

Claire took out her notebook and unfolded her copy of Freedman's blackmail note.

'The letter to Osmond is almost exactly the same format as Freedman's, sir,' she said. 'Word for word, much of it. The Worm's working to a template.'

'And the information in it sounds like it's taken from a conversation again,' added Dan. 'That's still my hunch.'

There was a quick, polite knock and the door opened and Eleanor and Michael walked in. Adam greeted them and they sat down, Michael on the edge of a desk, Eleanor on a chair. Dan made a point of pulling it out for her. He'd had enough of Adam's criticisms of his chivalry.

'So then,' continued Adam. 'First, what do we make of the order of victims? An MP, then two police officers. Anything strike you?'

They looked at each other.

'I couldn't see much in it either,' Adam went on. 'I reckon it's what we originally thought. The victims are connected by being some kind of authority figure. That fits with what the Worm goes on about in the letters. That stuff about exposing you and your rotten kind.'

'There is the publicity angle,' said Dan. 'If the Worm wants to make an impact with their crimes, an MP's a great one to start with. The media love a story about a politician caught with his trousers down. And Freedman's the only one who's actually been exposed so far, isn't he? The billboard was quite some way of doing it. But there's been no similar move against Linda.'

'Perhaps because the Worm knew she was dead, so didn't need to,' said Claire.

'Yep,' agreed Dan. 'And we don't know what's going to happen with Osmond yet, do we? How he might be exposed.'

Adam nodded at them. 'Good thoughts. We're getting an idea how our man works.' He caught Claire's look. 'Or woman,' he added. 'So, what about leads? We've got our priest. But what else? How about the riddles? Eleanor and Michael, that's your department. You've got a new one to solve.'

Adam pointed to the copy of Osmond's blackmail letter and explained how it had arrived. The pair got up from their seats and looked at it. Dan noticed Michael pressed his face almost up to the note, as if he was scrutinising each word individually.

"'So then, your riddle,'" Eleanor read softly. "'As a clue, I give you this advice. It might help you to think back to last Sunday to solve it. Now tel me the answer to this.

"1112, 7257, 1173, 22584.'"

'Any thoughts?' asked Adam eagerly.

'Numbers again,' mused Eleanor, walking dreamily back to her seat, hands on her flowing skirt, the climbing tulips again. It was a clue she'd got up in a hurry this morning thought Dan, the first time he'd seen her wear the same skirt two days running. She and Michael must have received the same early call as he and Claire.

Eleanor settled herself down, crossed a languid leg. 'Numbers ...' Her voice changed, became sharper. 'Yes, I think I might have an idea how this code works. I'm pretty sure in fact. Give me a few hours.'

Adam couldn't hide his surprise. 'Really?'

She smiled kindly. 'I'll need access to a library, but I suspect it's not too tricky, this riddle. Perhaps even deliberately so. The key's in the sentence before the numbers. "Now tel me the answer to this". Misspellings are often a giveaway in codes.'

Adam stared at the note on the felt board. 'You mean the "tel"? Just a mistake, surely?'

'I don't think so. Our blackmailer doesn't strike me as the type who makes mistakes.'

She walked lightly out of the room, her skirt flowing behind her. Michael followed with a nervous grin. He hadn't said a word, just watched and listened like an overly disciplined child, the kind a Victorian parent would have approved of.

'Well, that'd be a turn-up,' said Adam, when the door had closed. 'If we've solved three parts of the five in the riddle, that could be the breakthrough we need.' He suddenly looked less tired. 'So, what else have we got?'

'Did anything come of the dig into Linda's life?' asked Claire.

Adam shook his head. 'No. We went through all her colleagues, but no one was really close to her. We found some friends' numbers at home and on her mobile phone accounts, but apart from the priest they didn't turn up anything. We checked her finances and there was no hint of any problems there either. So what the Worm had over her is still a complete mystery.'

Dan waited, and then said quietly, 'Sex.'

Adam tapped Linda's picture. 'Yep,' he said, ruefully. 'That's about all I can imagine. It's the usual reason. Maybe she was seeing a married man, or something like that. But if so, surely there'd be some hint of it? And would that be bad enough for her to kill herself, and not want the blackmail note to be found? What it said must have been awful, for her to keep it from us.'

'Something kinkier than a married man?' prompted Dan. He tried to ignore Claire's disapproving look.

Adam nodded. 'You mean like male prostitutes? Or fetishes? Something like that? Again it's possible, but we've got no evidence. I think we're better off working on what we do know, not speculating on what we don't.'

Claire stood up and stretched. Dan was relieved to see the colour had returned to her face. She was keeping that protective hand over her stomach, but she looked much better.

She turned to Adam. 'What about forensics, sir?'

'Not much there. We got a few bits of skin off the first note, but they don't match anyone on the DNA database, so we're looking for a new offender. There was one oddity. The labs found faint traces of cooking oil on the note.'

'Cooking oil?' queried Dan.

'Yes, in small traces,' replied Adam. 'It suggests the note was written near a kitchen. But that doesn't help us. All houses have kitchens.'

Claire asked, 'What about Osmond's note?'

'With forensics now.'

There was a soft knock at the door. It sounded hesitant.

'Come in,' called Adam. Arthur's greying head appeared and he ambled in, almost like a penguin. He was carrying a sheet of paper.

'Got that photo for you, Mr Breen,' he said. 'Taken from the CCTV, as you requested. It's the best shot we could get.'

Adam grabbed the sheet and laid it carefully down on a desk. 'It's not great ...' began Arthur, but Adam interrupted. 'OK, Arthur, thanks. We'll take over now.' The technician nodded and slipped back out of the door.

They studied the picture. It was monochrome and grainy, as if sprinkled with salt and snow. A streetlamp threw a flare of white across the top. In the centre, a hunched figure was bent over the doors of the police station. It wore a baggy top with a hood, which was drawn tightly around the face. A baseball cap sat on top of the hood, the peak pulled down low. A scarf covered the mouth up to the nose, and a pair of large, black-lensed sunglasses hid the eyes. The figure looked about five feet seven or eight tall and with an average build, but it was almost impossible to tell through the thick clothing.

'Damn,' Adam moaned. 'I suspected as much. He'd have guessed he'd be caught on CCTV. It's just about useless. You can't make out anything.'

Claire angled the picture towards her. 'I think you're right, sir. I can't even tell if it's a man or woman.'

Dan stood back and heaved himself up on to his customary window ledge. It was always the place he found best to think, perhaps because of the panoramic view across Plymouth.

He looked out at the ruined church below. Its white stone was glowing in the spring sunshine. The traffic encircling it was light, and above the grumble of cars he could hear a symphony of Sunday bells summoning worshippers to churches across the city. For a moment, it was as though the long derelict Charles Church had been resurrected, regained its voice and rejoined their choir.

It was just after ten o'clock. Dan yawned. It felt like he was already at the end of a working day, but there was still so much more left to do. He'd have to file a story, as well as dealing with the demands of the investigation. How were they going to handle all the media, and still leave an exclusive angle for himself, to appease Lizzie? Not to mention finding some way of presenting the report that could help the inquiry.

Life was beginning to feel very crowded.

Dan sensed Adam looking at him. 'You OK?' the detective

asked. 'You look a little out of it.'

'Just thinking.' He paused, rubbed his forehead, then added, 'I've got an idea. What about if we call another press conference? The nationals wouldn't normally carry the same story twice so soon. But if we tell them we're going to reveal a picture of the blackmailer, I think they'd go for it. And you can use it to appeal to anyone who might recognise the person in the picture.'

'Not a bad idea,' mused Adam. 'It would get all the interviews done at one go, and leave me free to carry on with the real work.'

'How do you fancy pushing it a bit further?' asked Dan. 'Trying something unusual.'

Adam straightened up from the CCTV photo. 'Like what?'

'Well, I think you'd agree that so far the Worm's been setting the pace. We've just been left to trail around after him.'

Adam nodded ruefully. 'Can't argue with that.'

'And so far our Worm hasn't made a single mistake that might give us a chance to catch him.'

'Agreed again. But what are you getting at? Come on, time's against us. Get to the point.'

Dan held up his hands. 'Just bear with me, I'm thinking it through as I talk. How do you think the Worm might react if you insult him at the press conference? Give the media such tasty quotes that they'd definitely use them. Maybe we could make our Worm angry and he might do something stupid, perhaps even make a mistake and give us a chance to get him.'

Adam stared at him thoughtfully. 'Done. I like it. It's certainly worth a try. And if it doesn't work, at least it'll be us taking the initiative for once. Good thinking.'

The detective made for the door, but then stopped and turned back.

'What's the price?' he asked. 'What exclusive are you after this time?'

Dan hesitated. 'I'll think of something,' he managed, trying to keep his face set.

He quickly debated whether to mention it now. No, wait a minute. Let's get the press conference arranged first, then talk about it.

He was fairly sure Adam would go for the idea. But Dan was much less certain about Claire, and it was her that he needed for it to work.

Chapter Twelve

IT SHOULD HAVE BEEN an easy Sunday morning drive to the outskirts of the city. It turned into an ordeal which haunted Dan for months.

Their first warning of the crash was an agonised screech and squeal, as if an animal was being tortured. It took a couple of seconds to realise it was a car's brakes locking in their futile effort to prevent the impact. A booming smash and a sickening metallic grinding echoed across the street. Then there was silence, the empty seconds as powerful at the cacophony which preceded them.

A red car had crumpled head on into the thick stone pillars of the library. In the front, through the white web of shattered windscreen, Dan could make out the figure of a person slumped over the wheel. The car was so badly damaged it looked like one of those he'd seen piled high in teetering, wrecked towers at a scrapyard. A snake of smoke rose dark and threatening from underneath. A couple of people had stopped, spellbound in their shock, a young woman with hands at her mouth, a middle-aged man starting to stumble towards the wreckage.

Facing them, half up the pavement was an old blue Ford Escort. Gouged streaks of silver ran along its side, as though the talons of a great beast had swatted it. The car sunk sideways on a flat and shredded front tyre. One headlight had splintered, diamonds of plastic patterning the pavement. A horn blared above the pumping beat of a stereo. The front doors sprung open, two young men jumped out and began running towards the city centre.

'Pull up,' snapped Adam. Claire did, swerving the Vauxhall on to the pavement. 'Claire, you're a first-aider, aren't you?'

'Yep.'

'Go look after the victim. Dan, with me. Let's get the villains.'

Adam sprinted off after the two men, his hard soles clattering on the flagstones. Instinctively, Dan followed. His heart was beating so hard he could hear the blood pumping in his ears. But his mind was clear, sharply aware of his fear. He was a TV reporter, not a cop, however much he liked to dabble. He had never been a brave man, and was acutely aware of it.

The two men turned down a side alley, one half-stumbling and cannoning into a brick wall. They were about fifty yards ahead, ducking and weaving between parked cars. Dan was relieved to see they didn't look tall or muscular.

Adam pushed past two old ladies, shouting an apology over his shoulder. His exaggerated politeness when dealing with the public extended even to the heat of a chase. One woman waved an arm at him. The alley opened into another street. One of the men veered left, the other to the right. Adam didn't hesitate. He ran left.

'With me or take the other guy,' he called. Dan didn't hesitate either. He followed Adam. They were closing, their prey only twenty yards ahead now. The man took a fast glance back, increased his pace, turned sharply down another lane.

They followed, careering around the corner. The joyrider passed a line of green and brown wheelie bins, threw out an arm, pulled a couple down. They thudded into the pavement, one lid falling open, spilling tins and bottles.

Adam wheeled elegantly around the debris. Dan slowed, jumped, made it but caught his knee on the corner of one of the bins. He yelped in pain, stumbled, but managed to right himself.

'You OK?' gasped Adam.

'Yeah … think so.'

In front, the man glanced round again, saw them closing. He sprinted across a road, ignored the blaring horn of a car, ran up the concrete ramp of a multi-storey car park and disappeared into the gloom. They were only a dozen yards behind now.

'Police officer sonny,' Adam shouted breathlessly. 'Stop! Now!'

The joyrider kept going. He looked only eighteen or nineteen and had short dark hair, which shone with gel. Dan surprised himself how well he was keeping up in the chase. Little sleep and feeling so tired only a few minutes ago, now it was as though he could run for miles. Adrenaline was amazing stuff.

A couple of people shouted from their car as they ran past, but Dan couldn't make out the words. The multi-storey was mostly empty, too early yet for the onslaught of the day's shoppers. It smelt of stale piss. He wondered what they must look like, two middle-aged men wearing jackets and ties chasing a young lad.

The man ran through a swing door to the stairs. He slammed it hard behind him, the crash thundering around the hollowness of the car park. Adam barged through. He was just yards behind. 'Stop!' he shouted again. 'Stop, police!'

The figure blurred as it jumped down the stairs, then he was off, running again. He had the advantage of wearing trainers, but Adam wasn't letting up. He jumped too, skidding and stumbling at the bottom as he hit the concrete floor. Dan quick-stepped down the stairs and caught up with Adam. He was panting hard.

'Keep going,' the detective hissed. 'Not him letting get away now.'

They burst through another door, back into the car park. The man was just ahead of them, but he was moving more slowly now. He was fumbling in his jacket.

Adam sensed the danger, slowed too. 'Watch it,' he panted, reached out a warning hand.

The joyrider turned. He was holding a knife. He held it out, pointed it at them. Adam stopped instantly, Dan just behind.

'Drop it, sonny,' growled Adam. 'Don't make it any worse for yourself.'

'Fuck you, copper!' came the panted reply. 'You want me – come get me.'

Dan couldn't take his eyes from the knife. The blade looked about nine inches long, and tapered to a viciously sharp point. It was shining dully in the half-light of the car park. He wondered what it was like to be stabbed or slashed. He imagined a pain like being burned by a scalding iron, not just through his flesh but inside his body, slicing into organs and arteries, and then the darkness of impending death.

'There's two of us,' grunted Adam. 'We're both handy in a

scrap and you're surrounded. Drop the knife and give yourself up.'

Dan just managed to stop himself looking around for the mythical back-up. He tried to control his shaking, pull himself up to his full height and look mean. He forced his gaze from the knife and stared into the man's eyes. They seemed vague and unfocused. Drugs? Shit, he hoped not. If he was high, what was he capable of?

The blade of the knife was wavering slowly up and down. The joyrider's hand was wrapped tightly around it, his knuckles white. There was a blurred ink tattoo across his fingers. It looked like it spelled out "Mum".

Adam edged forwards. 'Put it down now, sonny,' he commanded. 'It's bad enough for you as it is. Keep that knife on me any more and I'll make sure you go down for a long, long time.'

The man stared at him. He was sweating heavily, his white T-shirt streaked with grey stains of dampness. He hadn't shaved and the speckling of dark whiskers made him look desperate. Still he held the knife out in front of him, just a few feet from Adam's face.

'Last chance, sonny,' he said, more calmly now. 'Knife down or very big trouble indeed. Your choice.'

The man looked quickly around. Checking for some way to escape. There was nowhere. They were in the lower floor of the car park. The concrete walls penned him in. The only way out was the stairs, behind them. He was cornered. If he was going to try it, he had to come through them.

'Fuck you!' he screamed, and lunged at Adam. Dan jumped back instinctively, his hands shooting up in front of his chest as if to ward off the blow.

Adam sidestepped the lunge, caught the joyrider's arm in his hands and twisted it hard behind his back. The knife clattered to the floor and lay there, still.

It was one of the most beautiful sights Dan had ever seen.

The man bent double under the pressure of Adam's armlock. He started screaming streams of wild abuse, his free arm flailing helplessly behind him, trying to get a grip on the detective. A foot kicked backwards at Adam's legs, but he dodged it easily.

Adam checked carefully around. Dan wondered what he was going to do. He smiled unpleasantly, then wrenched the man's arm again. A shooting crack echoed from the grey concrete walls of the car park.

'Resisting arrest,' said Adam calmly over the man's agonised screams. 'You saw it. I had no choice but to incapacitate him.'

Never had the interior of a car felt so welcome.

Dan didn't care for driving, associated cars with pollution, pointless macho competitiveness, endless traffic jams and the ugliness of the lines of parked metal boxes blighting every street. But this Sunday morning he was very glad to be in the sanctuary of a car, insulated from the world of joyriders and knives.

'So then, on to Father Maguire,' said Adam easily from the Vauxhall's passenger seat. He looked remarkably relaxed, arm resting on the open window, enjoying the morning breeze. 'We're going to be a little later than planned, but I think he'll understand, given the circumstances.'

Dan eyed his friend, wondered how well he really knew him. The detective had clearly enjoyed the chase, the danger, and the injury he'd inflicted on the joyrider. They hadn't talked about what happened, and Dan sensed it was one of those subjects which would never be mentioned. A classic non-event, it simply didn't happen.

He was a little concerned he wasn't more shocked by what Adam had done. With the adrenaline pumping, facing a man who'd be happy to stab them to escape, the survival instinct had taken over. Even now, feeling calmer, he was mildly surprised, perhaps taken aback, but that was all. Adam had always been passionate about justice. Dan thought he understood that meant the detective wasn't above enforcing a little justice of his own.

They'd marched the man up to Charles Cross and Adam booked him in to custody.

'Reminds me of my old days on the beat,' he said. 'I don't

get to do enough of that kind of thing any more.' The detective smiled as the joyrider directed another tirade of abuse at him. 'Enjoy your time in prison,' he said cheerily. 'Hope the arm doesn't heal too fast.'

The traffic division had taken over the investigation into the crash. Silifant was called to check on their suspect's dislocated shoulder. He gave it eight out of ten for painfulness, prompting Adam to nod in a satisfied manner.

Dan stayed quiet and hoped he'd kept a straight face when Adam explained how the man had resisted their attempts to arrest him. The other lad was still free, but the traffic officers thought they knew who he was and were confident he'd soon be picked up.

Claire had tended to the woman in the smashed car. Ms Joanna Watson had been taken to Plymouth's Tamarside Hospital for a check-up. She was suffering shock, but her injuries were superficial, just a few cuts and bruises. She'd been on her way to church and was upset but remarkably forgiving. Ms Watson even intended to say a prayer for the two joyriders.

'I didn't mean anything sexist or any of that kind of nonsense by leaving you out of the fun of the chase,' Adam told Claire. 'I'd be happy to hunt suspects with you anytime, you know that. It was just that as a first-aider, you were better off with the crash victim. Anyway, we have to be a little careful with you, don't we?'

From the back of the Vauxhall, Dan craned his neck to look at Claire. She seemed fine now she'd got over the sickness of earlier. What was Adam talking about? He was always protective of his staff, but this was getting excessive.

Dan sat back across the rear seats and tried to breathe deeply. His heartbeat had just about returned to normal but his throat still felt dry. He couldn't quieten the memory of that knife pointing at him. Sometimes he forgot he was just a journalist, shadowing a criminal investigation. The confrontation had reminded him he wasn't a police officer and had no desire to be.

Whenever there was conflict overseas, his friends asked if he was going to cover it. The Second Gulf War was the last occasion. They all seemed to think that being a war correspondent was the peak of a journalist's career. He felt a little ashamed explaining that he didn't fancy it at all. For Dan, it was no contest. Sleep in a tent in a desert, baking hot by day, freezing by night, with the ever-present risk of being shot at or bombed. Or live in his beautiful Victorian flat, always cosy and comfortable, sleep in his super-king-size bed, his faithful dog by his side, all in reassuring safety.

Claire drove them to Crownhill, on the northern edge of Plymouth, turned down to the old village of Tamerton Foliot and parked the car outside St Joseph's Church. They walked up crunching gravel to the dark, arched wooden doors. Dan wondered if they should be respectful and knock, but Adam just pushed them open and strolled in. Behind them, a white swirl of cherry blossom followed, ushered in by a playful breeze.

A man stood beside the altar, bent over a rack of fat red candles. Triangular flames flickered from their ranks, silhouetting his cassock. Many of the candles had brief notes underneath. The church was quiet, a couple of worshippers praying in a corner, but otherwise deserted. It was warmed in a spectrum of light, the flooding sunshine tinted by the rich colours of the stained glass windows. Dan noticed himself trying to tread softly. The feeling of reverence was pervasive.

The man stood up to face them. He was short, with silver hair, balding on the top, about fifty years old. He greeted them with a warm smile, revealing a chink of gap between his front teeth. Combined with the chubbiness of his cheeks, it made him resemble a beaver.

Adam went to speak, but the priest put a finger to his lips, pointed to the kneeling couple and led them outside. They shook hands and Adam introduced them.

'I've been thinking about your call,' said Father Maguire. 'You've given me quite a dilemma for a Sunday morning, when I should be thinking about him above.' He raised his eyebrows towards the blue sky. 'I know what you want, of course. And I know you'll appreciate it's something I'll find almost impossible to give. The confessional is sacrosanct. It's a foundation of our beliefs.'

'I understand,' replied Adam. 'But it's my duty to ask you about it anyway. So far, you are the only link between two of the three people who have been the subject of blackmail demands. You're sure you've never met Leon Osmond?'

'Quite sure.'

'OK. Well, as you know, both of the other victims have gone on to kill themselves.'

Father Maguire crossed himself, rather theatrically Dan thought. He felt like the sort of priest a television director would cast for the role. He looked and acted the part.

'Poor Will and Linda,' he intoned. 'Fine people both. May they rest in peace.'

Adam nodded his agreement. 'Let me start by asking you a couple of general questions about them. I hope that won't infringe on the confidences of your parishioners.'

Father Maguire tilted his head to one side, said warily, 'Go on.'

'Was there anything that seemed to be specifically worrying them?'

'Yes.'

'Will Freedman first then. You'll have seen the newspaper reports about the prostitute. Was it along those lines?'

Father Maguire pursed his lips and held a finger to them. He took another glance towards the sky, but gave a slight, sad nod.

Adam nodded too, then asked, 'Anything else?'

'Not that's material to your investigation.'

'Father, with respect, it's better if I'm the judge of that.'

'No!' the priest snapped. 'I'm already fighting my conscience in trying to help you as much as I can. Don't push it, man.'

The lilt of an Irish accent bubbled into Maguire's voice when he was annoyed. His silver eyebrows arched and jumped, as though they were competing with each other to touch his hairline.

Adam stared silently at him. Dan knew the technique. Quiet was unsettling. The detective was inviting him to fill the void, give something away. It was a tactic Dan himself had used many times in interviews. But the little priest was not to be intimidated. He held Adam's gaze and said nothing.

'OK then, Father, how about Linda?' said Adam, finally. 'You're aware she appears to have committed suicide too?'

'Of course.'

'Was there anything she was specifically worried about?'

'Again, I don't think that'd be relevant to your inquiry.'

'Father please,' said Adam. 'This is vital in catching someone who is ruining lives.'

'I know that, Breen,' snapped the priest again. 'That's why I agreed to see you at all. I don't have to tell you anything, as you're very well aware. I'm bending my faith just talking to you. Don't try to break it.'

Adam held up his hands in a calming apology. 'Then let me rephrase the question. Perhaps that would help us both. Did Linda mention anything about blackmail?'

'No.'

'Anything about sex?'

The priest closed his eyes.

'No,' he barked finally.

'Anything about work?'

Father Maguire paused, slowly opened his eyes and raised his face to the heavens.

'God help me,' he whispered. 'And on a Sunday too.' He looked back at them, his eyebrows jumping again. 'Yes,' he snapped. 'She was worried about her job. Now that's it. No more.'

Adam waited, then said, 'Father, we need to know ...'

'No more!' he barked. 'None! Not a word. You got that, Breen?'

Adam nodded. 'All right, Father, thank you. I very much appreciate your help. There's just one final thing I must ask. May I take you into my confidence?'

Maguire nodded wearily. 'If you must. Confidences are part of my job. And they're not always an easy weight to carry, I can tell you.'

Adam managed a weak smile. 'We think the information the blackmailer has may have come as a result of conversations between the victims and other, unknown, people. Is there any way what happens in the confessional here could be overheard?'

'No.'

'You're sure?'

'Yes I'm bloody sure, Breen! No one else comes near when you're in the confessional. We respect it completely. And if your imagination's running away to listening devices and spy stuff like that, you can forget it. We always check the booth before we use it.'

'Last question, Father.' Adam saw the man's look. 'I promise this is the last one.'

'Go on.'

'Where were you at five o'clock this morning?'

'Funnily enough, I was in bed.'

'Can anyone confirm that?'

He gave Adam an exasperated look. 'It's not very likely, is it? I'm a Catholic bloody priest, Breen. We sleep alone remember? And before you think it, I don't even bother the choirboys, unlike some of my colleagues. I imagine you're asking to see if you can take me off your list of suspects?'

'I can't lie to you, Father. Yes, that is why I wanted to know.'

'Well, I was asleep in bed, alone, like a good Catholic boy. I didn't do it, but I'll bear the idea in mind the next time the church needs a new roof. Blackmailing people from what you hear in the confessional isn't a bad thought at all. It beats all these miserable jumble sales and coffee mornings I have to put on a fake smile for.'

Dan studied the ground to hide his amusement. For once, Adam looked lost for words.

'Well, at least that's one suspect,' said Adam as Claire drove them back to Charles Cross.

'You don't really think so, do you, sir?' she asked.

'Not really. Didn't feel right, did it? Couldn't see the motive. Yes, the opportunity might have been there to blackmail Linda and Freedman, but where is it for Osmond? What he said about Linda being worried about her job was interesting though,

130

wasn't it?'

Claire slowed the car for a set of traffic lights. 'Could be just that she was concerned about whatever it was she'd done getting her the sack, or disciplined.'

'Could be,' replied Adam. 'But what if she'd made a mess of some case she was handling and that's what she was being blackmailed for? What if she'd got too involved in something? We'll have to go through all her current and recent work to see if anything comes up.'

An ambulance screamed past them, its siren wailing. The noise made Dan think of the joyrider's knife again, its blade glinting in the half-light of the car park. He could have been in the back of that ambulance, gasping for life, a knife handle protruding from his chest.

Adam turned. 'What was this exclusive you were thinking of for your report tonight then? We'd better get that sorted, if we can.'

'I don't know if now's the right time …' Dan began, but Adam interrupted.

'Get on with it. We haven't got time to fumble around.'

Dan looked at Claire. In his eyes, she even managed to drive elegantly. He must be in deep. He was hoping to have a few private minutes to raise it with her first, but Adam was in no mood for delay.

'What I was thinking – what I had in mind was this …' Dan began, and tailed off again.

'Yes?' prompted Adam. 'Come on. Even you can't have thought of something that bad.'

'Well, everyone will have the story of the blackmail link between Linda and Freedman and the CCTV of the blackmailer from the press conference. But what I wondered was whether, to make my report different and better, and I know this is asking a lot, but …'

'Just get on with it, will you?'

Dan hesitated, then said, 'I'd like to do a tribute to Linda.'

'Fine,' replied Adam. 'Good idea. She deserves it. What's the problem? Why are you making such a fuss? I'm very happy to say a few words about her after the rest of the media have cleared off. That way you get your beloved exclusive.'

'Well, that's the point,' said Dan, uneasily. He shifted in his seat and sneaked another glance at Claire.

'What is?'

'You doing the interview.'

'Why?'

'Well, you'll be doing the news conference attacking the blackmailer, won't you?'

'So?'

'So, it would be good to get someone else to do the tribute.'

'Why?'

'Because TV likes variety, and two different faces on the screen always work better than one. Plus you didn't actually know her very well, did you? I'd like to talk to someone who can give me an anecdote or personal experience of her.' Dan looked at Claire again, waiting for the reaction. 'Like someone she's helped, for instance.'

Adam turned back to the front of the car and drummed a couple of fingers on the dashboard.

'Fair point,' he said. 'But no one really knew her that well.'

'Some knew her better than others though, didn't they?'

'Like who?'

From the driver's seat Dan heard Claire draw in a sharp breath.

'Ah,' said Adam. 'Like Claire?'

'Yes. Like Claire.'

Adam folded his arms, gazed out of the windscreen. Dan noticed they were picking up speed. Claire stared straight ahead, her face set. The car felt as if it had filled with storm clouds.

'I don't have a problem with that,' said Adam at last, placing a heavy emphasis on the "I". 'I suppose you knew her as well as anyone Claire. What do you think about doing an interview?'

There was a pause, then Claire said tersely, 'Can I have a few minutes to think about it please?'

For the first time, Dan truly understood the meaning of the phrase "through gritted teeth". He wondered how much trouble he was going to be in later. He thought he saw a slight smile flicker across Adam's face.

'Fair enough,' said the detective. 'It's bad enough being interviewed by Dan when he's your friend. I wouldn't want to think what it's like when he's your boyfriend.'

Dan shifted again in his seat. It suddenly felt sticky. He didn't know what to say, so he kept quiet, counted the landmarks. They passed the old Crownhill Fort, its great earth ramparts and gun emplacements part of the Victorians' attempts to defend Plymouth from a French attack, then turned south, heading into the city, along the Manadon flyover, for once living up to its name and not choked with traffic. He took a couple of obvious looks at Claire and knew she was aware of him doing so, but she didn't acknowledge him, just kept her eyes set ahead. Dan sighed to himself.

They drove on in silence until the radio crackled with a call for Adam. He picked it up and listened, nodded a couple of times.

'Good,' he said finally. 'We're making progress. We have another suspect. The teams have found a solicitor who worked for both Linda and Osmond. And the press conference has been arranged for an hour's time. All the media are going to be there. So then, what do I say?'

Dan looked up from the notes he'd written earlier. 'It's quite spicy,' he said, tearing off a sheet of paper and handing it forwards. 'See if you think it's too much.'

Adam read through the scrawled words, emitted a few murmurs of approval. 'I like it. It should certainly put some wind up our Worm. I might even add a couple of little jibes of my own. Let's really take the fight to our foe for once. It's about time.'

Chapter Thirteen

DAN SAT AT THE back of the press conference and fretted. He kept picking a snagged nail, smoothing it, then finding another to worry away at. He tried to concentrate, but unpleasant thoughts kept surfacing and nagging. Does she still love me? Or have I blown it? Anyway, what was he doing? Loves me, loves me not – it felt like being twelve years old again.

Claire hadn't said a word to him in the hour they'd been back at Charles Cross. He'd tried to engineer a couple of minutes alone so they could talk, but there was no time. Adam was buzzing with his speech to the press conference. Every new line he thought of he wanted to test on Dan to see how the media would react. Dutifully, but uninterestedly, Dan had offered his view.

The detective had also agonised about his tie, whether it was too bright for a sombre occasion. Dan had to stop himself pointing out that he didn't really care, and eventually agreed. Adam was right, appearances were very important on TV. The sprouting red and green flowers would have to be replaced. Semiotics, the unspoken language of film, dictated that they didn't fit with a story of blackmail and suicide.

A probationer detective was despatched to the city centre and told it was the most important mission he would undertake – not to come back until he'd found a smart, diagonally striped tie, with a mainly navy base colour to match Adam's suit. It must be silk too, of course. Dan, who usually found his friend's vanity and fixation with his wardrobe amusing, couldn't help but feel a growing irritation.

To cheer himself up, he called his downstairs neighbour and was reassured that Rutherford had been fed and was currently running around the garden with a tennis ball clenched between his teeth. Dan smiled. He felt a sudden desire to join his dog. The thrill of chasing the joyriders had long since ebbed and a leaden tiredness was weighing him down again. The memory of the menacing knife was still strong in his mind. The simplicity of being outside, in the spring sunshine, throwing a ball for his stupid dog to sprint after was wonderfully alluring.

But there was no chance of escape. It was going to be a long day and it felt as though everyone wanted a piece of him. There was the press conference to cover, then the interview with Claire, if she decided to do it. A big if, and even then in capitals, italics, and probably underlined too. He'd also have to appease Lizzie, go back to the studios to cut the story, then probably back to Charles Cross to help out with whatever Adam decided they needed to do next. Dan yawned and stretched, tried to force some spirit back into his sullen body.

Eleanor said she hoped she'd be able to reveal the answer to the third part of the riddle later. Dan wanted to be there for that. So far, he hadn't even had a chance to work on it. "Now tel me this" was the key, she'd said. What did it have to do with last Sunday?

He went to get his copy of Osmond's blackmail note from his pocket but stopped himself. He didn't feel up to trying to solve it. His mind was too full of Claire, the press conference, Lizzie, and the story he'd have to write later. That was quite enough.

Beside him, Nigel bent over the camera, checking its focus. The room was full again, snappers, newspaper, radio and TV reporters, many grumbling about being called out on a Sunday. Dirty El was at the front, caressing the long lens of his camera. If Claire was playing it cool, maybe they could go out for a few beers. That would cheer him up. He sometimes thought of El as the court jester in his life. Always up to something comical, but often full of surprising wisdom too.

At exactly two o'clock, the door at the side of the room opened and Adam strode in, wearing his sombre new tie. He sat down at the desk, with the blue and white Greater Wessex Police screens behind him and looked around at the press pack. The rumble of conversation died away.

He apologised for the late notice and for asking the hacks here on a Sunday, then paused, shuffled some papers, and hit them with the story.

'We believe we have a picture of the blackmailer.'

Adam waited again, let the pack react. There were a few gasps, a couple of whistles and several nudged each other. It was pure theatre.

'It's taken from CCTV pictures,' Adam went on. 'For those of you in television, I will be making a copy available. For those of you in print, I have a series of stills taken from the video. I have some more information for you, then I'll take a few questions.'

A uniformed sergeant began walking around the room, handing out CDs and photographs of the CCTV film. Dan noticed El took a handful. He must be looking after several papers and making good money from them. No wonder he wore his trademark sleazy grin.

'We believe the blackmailer has now claimed their second and third victims,' continued Adam, his voice grave. 'I regret to inform you the second was a police officer, one who worked here in Plymouth. Her name was Inspector Linda Cott. Her car was found in a car park on the north Cornwall coast, near St Agnes. We have an eyewitness report of her jumping from the cliff. The identity of the third victim I cannot release to you as inquiries are continuing.'

Adam looked around the room. It was silent, all the journalists scribbling at their notes, the cameramen and photographers intent on their shots. And still the punch line was yet to come.

'I have one further thing to say,' the detective continued. 'This blackmailer is very dangerous. He, or she, is wrecking lives. He needs to be caught before he destroys another. I would appeal for anyone who thinks they might recognise the person in the pictures to get in touch with us and help us put an end to these dreadful crimes.'

The silence returned. Adam caught Dan's look and gave him a slight nod. It was working perfectly. Now he'd take some questions. They'd hoped one of the hacks would ask the right one, but if they didn't Dan was ready, just in case.

There were a couple of questions about Linda and her career. A newspaper reporter wanted a photo of her and Adam promised he would get one. Dan silently chastised himself for not thinking of that. A radio reporter asked about progress in the inquiry, and Adam managed to sound upbeat without giving anything away.

The detective pointedly checked his watch. 'Now, ladies and gentlemen, if that's all?'

'Keep recording,' Dan hissed to Nigel, who had stood up from his camera. 'Go in tighter on him, get us a big close-up. This bit could be good.'

Dan rose from his seat and put up his hand. 'Mr Breen, just one final question, if I may?'

Adam turned to him and nodded. 'Go on.'

Dan waited for the whirr of the camera's motor, zooming in. The closer the shot, the more powerful the image, the tension and passion revealed in each line and motion of the face.

'What do you think of the blackmailer? What do you believe are the reasons for his crimes?'

Adam looked down at his notes, composed himself.

'This is what I think,' he said finally. 'The blackmailer is clearly sick. He might think he has some grand purpose in what he's doing, but he, or she, doesn't. He's just a common criminal. In fact, it's worse than that. At least common criminals have the decency to show themselves. This blackmailer hides behind poisonous little notes. That makes him a coward, a pathetic one who can't make a mark on society in any other manner but to sneak around, looking for ways to have some sordid hold over decent people. As to what drives him to do it, I can only speculate. But I can say this. He or she must be a very lonely, sad and utterly inadequate person.'

When the other hacks had left to file their stories, the door opened again and Claire walked in. She kept her head high and didn't even glance at Dan, but strode over. He looked at her and tried his best smile. It wasn't returned.

His efforts at bringing a thaw felt as effective as holding a lighter to an iceberg.

'I will talk to you about Linda,' Claire said frostily. 'But I want to make it clear I'm doing it for her, not you.'

'Fair enough,' Dan replied, trying to keep his voice level.

Nigel sat Claire down and clipped a tiny personal microphone onto the lapel of her jacket.

'What do you want to ask?' she said.

'I want to know what kind of a woman Linda was, and if you have any special memories of her. It'll give the viewers a sense of her personality. Two sound bites will do me fine.'

'OK.'

'Recording,' said Nigel, from behind the camera.

Dan asked his questions and Claire answered, fluently and easily. She'd been rehearsing it, he thought.

'Linda was a dedicated police officer. She joined the force because she wanted to make a difference to people's lives. She was a great champion of neighbourhood policing and she wanted to make communities safer and happier places. She wanted people to see the police as friends who they could turn to for help. I think the best way to remember her is someone who achieved that. She really made a difference in the communities she served and she'll be sadly missed.'

Dan tried not to smile. Good answer. So she was listening all those times I ranted on about how important it is to make an interview vivid and human, not the usual robotic police spiel about "apprehending the aforementioned suspect to assist us in our inquiries".

He'd never understood why they did it. Officers who were perfectly normal when you chatted to them before the interview suddenly became automatons when the camera was rolling. Not Claire.

He hesitated to think it, but did anyway. It felt good. His Claire.

He hoped so, anyway.

He forced his mind back to the job. 'And how will you personally remember her?'

Claire clasped her fingers together, gathered her thoughts. Beside him, Dan heard the whirr of the camera's motor as Nigel zoomed in the shot.

'Linda was a friend to me in times of need. Even today, it's not always easy being a woman in the police. In the dark moments, she'd sit down with me and let me pour it out. She told me she'd gone through just the same and that I should stick at it. The bad days passed and good ones came to take their place. It's always stuck with me. Bad times go and good times come to replace them. It's what I cling on to now when I'm having a rotten day. She was a great woman. A fine and dedicated police officer and a good friend. I'm proud and privileged to have known her.'

Nigel drove them back to the studios to cut the story. Sitting in the edit suite, Dan had to struggle hard to concentrate. Claire's face on the monitors was a terrible distraction. For the first time in many years he properly understood a universal truth. Why was it that you only really appreciated what you had when you felt threatened with losing it?

Lizzie was having the weekend off, a rare phenomenon, renowned only to be forced upon her by the demands of her family, but that didn't mean he could relax. It was an oft-repeated joke that her ghost patrolled the building. Like many journalists' tales, it was heavily embroidered, but still retained an element of truth. If she wasn't at work, Lizzie always watched every bulletin from home and had a block setting on her TV system to record them in case she happened to be out.

Dan debated how to start the story. It was a fine call. The two broad rules of television reporting collided on this one. It was generally agreed you should begin your report with the best material you had, and that often came down to a powerful personal story or some striking pictures. He had both, Claire's moving comments about Linda and the CCTV of the blackmailer.

Dan went back to basics, something he'd first begun doing as a cub reporter, all those years ago. He jotted down the pros and cons for each on his notebook but still couldn't decide, so he flipped a coin. The CCTV pictures won, so given the luck he'd had lately he went for the human interest.

He began the story with the photo of Linda and explained what had happened to her. They used some pictures of the cliffs where she had jumped, Dan talking about an eyewitness seeing her fall and her car being found close by. Then it was into

Claire's interview. After that came the CCTV, a recap of what had happened to Freedman and Adam talking about what he thought of the blackmailer.

They watched it back. Dan still wasn't sure he'd got the report the right way around for the TV purists, but, whatever, he knew the viewers would find it compelling and that was what counted. Claire's words were powerful and Adam's attack on the blackmailer was captivating. It could well prompt a reaction and give them a chance to catch him. Even better, the story had the exclusive angle that Lizzie so craved.

He could imagine her at home, playing with her kids while watching the bulletin, nodding with the nearest she ever came to contentment. It should keep her off his back for a couple of days longer. The case was fascinating and he didn't want any risk of being taken off it.

The clock on the wall said it was just after four. Dan realised he was hungry. With all that had happened he'd forgotten to eat. Time to get a sandwich. No, even better, how about a burger from one of the take-aways on Mutley Plain? Claire wasn't here to nag at him and he deserved a treat. It could even be a small measure of revenge for the way she was treating him. He managed a weak smile at the thought.

His mobile rang, Adam's name flashing on the display. As Dan answered, he knew his chance of a sly snack had gone.

'What's that?' he said, as the phone buzzed with the detective's excitement. 'Really? Wow! That's two big developments then. OK, I'll be right there.'

Dan grabbed his satchel and jogged down the stairs to the car park.

Chapter Fourteen

A WONDERFUL WASH OF warm relief enveloped Dan as he walked into the MIR. Claire smiled to see him, and it was genuine. His chest lost its tightness and he could breathe again. He smiled back, tried not to make it too pathetically delighted, and felt a sudden ache behind his eyes. Tonight they would cuddle up together at her flat and talk about the new house. If she wanted an Aga, she would get it, no matter what it took. She deserved it.

Adam sat on the edge of a desk, Claire stood next to him. Michael was leaning against the windows at the back of the room, looking down at the passing traffic. He turned and gave Dan his nervous smile. Eleanor stood at the front, by the green boards. She looked like a teacher about to give a lecture, and played the part.

'Settle down please class,' she said with her gentle smile. 'Now, I haven't said that for a few years.'

Dan quickly perched on the edge of a desk next to Adam. He could feel the anticipation in the room. On the table beside Eleanor was a pile of Sunday newspapers.

'This code wasn't too tricky to break,' she said. 'And I'm suspicious that was deliberate. In fact, perhaps there's even a pattern emerging.'

'Like what?' Claire asked.

'That first code, Freedman's, it was a tough one to crack. I wonder if it was designed that way, so he couldn't solve it. The second one, Linda's, was probably easier, as she cracked it. This one wasn't difficult either.'

'And why would the Worm do that?'

'Perhaps because of meaning what they say about giving people a chance to crack the codes and save themselves. So the Worm needed Freedman to fail, to justify exposing him. And with that, came all the publicity to start off the game. For the Worm, it was like the official and spectacular launch, if you like.'

'But the next two codes?'

'Easier because they don't matter so much. The game is underway. You know five notes are coming. You're working against the clock. The media interest is building. The pressure on you is growing.'

Claire smoothed a lock of hair behind her ear. 'Which would answer a question that's been bothering me. Why set the codes at all? So it has to be a taunt. Aimed at us, the police, as a figurehead for the "authorities" the Worm's hitting out at.'

Eleanor smiled again, her face softly lined with a grandmother's wisdom. 'That would be my guess. But I'm straying outside my specialism here. That's a matter for you, and Adam.'

He nodded thoughtfully, looked more relaxed than earlier. His face had lost some of its tautness, but his voice was hoarse and he sounded tired as he said, 'All thoughts welcome. So, come on then, Eleanor, tell us about the code.'

She picked up a couple of the papers. 'It was the misspelling of "tel" that gave it away. I immediately thought our blackmailer wouldn't make a mistake like that. So, look at the sentence.'

Eleanor pointed to it, highlighted in Osmond's note on the board behind her. 'Why would "Now tel me" have special significance on a Sunday?'

The room was quiet as they all stared at the words.

'Newspapers,' said Dan slowly. 'Now means News of the World. Tel means Telegraph. M and E mean Mail and Express.'

'Or Mirror and Express,' said Eleanor. 'But you're right, yes, it did turn out to be the Mail. The words all refer to Sunday newspapers.'

'Clever,' said Dan. 'Simple, but clever.'

'So what about the numbers?' asked Claire. 'What do they mean?'

Eleanor picked up a copy of the News of the World. 'That was what took me a little while. I wasn't quite sure and it needed a bit of experimenting.'

Dan silently cursed himself for being so slow. He should have seen that code, he thought. But then, he had been rather

142

preoccupied with other things. Covering the story, managing the media for Adam and worrying about Claire. He glanced at her, and she winked from the corner of her eye.

The sun shone in his sky. Life was feeling so very much better.

'Take the first number, 1112,' continued Eleanor. 'I think each of the blocks of figures refers to one of the newspapers the blackmailer's given us. So we're looking for four words, one from the News of the World, one from the Telegraph, one from the Mail and one from the Express. The numbers give us the location of the word we want within the paper they refer to.'

'Blimey,' grumbled Adam. 'How?'

Eleanor smiled indulgently, a classic teacher's look for a struggling pupil.

'Take 1112,' she said. 'It means go to the News of the World, page one, column one, line one, word number two.'

She held up the paper to show them and traced her finger along the front page, past the screaming "Three-in-a-Bed Sex Shocker" headline about some snooker player Dan had never heard of.

'Column one, line one, word number two, and you get the word "the"'.

'The?' repeated Adam dubiously.

'Yes,' Eleanor replied. 'Bear with me. That's only the first part of the answer.'

Adam drew in a heavy breath. 'Well, I'm glad we've got you here to solve these things for us. I would never have cracked it. But as time is pressing, rather than taking us through the other words would you mind putting us out of our misery and just telling us the answer?'

Eleanor tutted. 'That goes against my teacher's principles. I should make you work through the other numbers to show me you understand. But as you asked so nicely, when you do all that the code reads, "the answer is memorial"'.

There was a silence. 'Memorial?' said Adam, finally. Dan couldn't tell if his voice was more full of disbelief or scorn, but there was certainly plenty of both.

'Yes,' replied Eleanor calmly. 'Memorial is your answer for

part three of the Worm's riddle.'

Adam stood up from his desk and walked over to the green boards.

'Memorial,' he said again. 'So put that together with the other clues and we've got "Open original memorial", plus two missing words to come.'

He folded his arms and stared at them. "Open original memorial." How the hell does that help us?'

The expression on each face made it clear that was exactly what they were all thinking.

The damage wasn't serious, but it looked impressive. The image on the TV screen steadied and focused on a window, a fist-sized hole in its centre, a radial pattern of jagged cracks spreading from the wound. The camera panned quickly to the next window. It had suffered a similar assault. Shards of glass littered the patio surrounding a couple of half bricks, the missile of choice.

The front of the old Victorian building had been a proud white, but was now daubed with sprays of royal blue paint. The black wooden door had taken a splash of streaks of blue too, but the mainstay of the pot had been reserved for the brass name plaque. The legend "Plymouth Traditionalist Association" was barely discernible through the repeated attacks of the flying paint.

Adam stopped the DVD player. 'Recorded earlier by the bobbies who were called. They found Yvonne Freedman waiting outside to be arrested. She's down in the cells. Let's go have a chat.'

They followed him down the stairs to the basement. Dan was so tired he had to concentrate on each step. He noticed Claire was holding the banister carefully. She must be struggling too, particularly if she wasn't feeling well.

At the thick black metal bars which marked the entrance to the cells complex, Adam paused. 'Claire, will you take the lead on this please? I think she responded better to you the last time we spoke.'

Yvonne Freedman was sitting on the edge of a thin blue

plastic mattress covering a hard, metal shelf which passed for a bed. She looked up expressionless as they walked in. It couldn't have been often the custody suite hosted such an unlikely criminal. She was still dressed smartly in the outfit of widowhood, a white blouse, black jacket, knee-length black skirt, and black shoes.

The cells were cold, but she didn't seem to have noticed. Her expression was vague, as though her focus was inside herself, the world around merely of passing interest.

Dan and Adam stayed standing in the cell doorway, Claire sat beside her, said gently, 'Hello again, Mrs Freedman.'

She didn't reply, just stared straight ahead at the whitewashed brick wall, her hands in her lap.

'How are you feeling?' Claire asked. 'How's Alex?'

Again no reply. 'How are you coping?'

Still no response. Claire and Adam exchanged looks. 'Why did you do it, Yvonne?' Claire persisted. 'Why attack the building? Was it because of Will?'

Now her head slowly turned and she muttered something they couldn't catch.

Adam took a step forwards. 'I'm sorry, Mrs Freedman. I didn't hear that?'

She looked up at him, her eyes widening. For a few seconds there was silence, then the shock of her voice, sharp and strong.

'I said, because they took my husband away! Because they turned him into someone who could only think about their damned party and his bloody self and not his family. Someone who could go off with some teenage tart! And then take the bloody coward's way out. Now charge me. Charge me and I'll go to court and tell the world what these people are like.'

The venomous words echoed from the hard brick walls. From the cell opposite came a couple of drunken cheers and the sound of arrhythmic applause.

Claire reached out an arm, placed it around Yvonne's shoulders. She initially resisted, tried to shrug it off, pull away, then collapsed into Claire's shoulder and began a muffled sobbing.

Adam sighed, folded his arms. 'There won't be any trial,

Mrs Freedman,' he said gently. 'There won't even be any charges. The Traditionalists don't want to take the matter further. You're free to go, but please, no more of this. It doesn't do anyone any good. I'll get someone to drive you home.'

She looked up at him through tear-soaked eyes, swallowed hard and gasped, 'No charges?'

Adam shook his head. 'No.'

Yvonne Freedman struggled to catch her breath and her face darkened into a scowl. 'Then I'll find some other way … some way to tell people what they're really like. I'll get them somehow.'

Dan felt a dense, smothering fatigue overwhelm him when they got back to Claire's flat. He'd been fighting it all day, but now it had grown into an irresistible force. In the half-light of the stairwell, he briefly closed his eyes and the memory of chasing the joyriders and that knife lunging at Adam's chest flashed back into his mind. He shuddered.

He could see Claire was exhausted too. She slung her jacket untidily over the back of a chair, slipped off her shoes and put her feet up on the coffee table. She lay back, rested her head on a cushion and cupped her hands over her stomach. Dan made them both a cup of tea and looked for a take-away menu in the kitchen drawers. Neither of them would be up to cooking tonight. He wondered if he was too tired even to eat.

Her Art Deco mantelpiece clock said it was just past eight. After seeing Yvonne Freedman, they'd spent a couple of hours at Charles Cross working on the parts of the code they'd cracked, but made no progress. Open original memorial – what memorial? Where? And why original? Were there two? Or more? They'd started to get irritable with each other and Adam had sent them home for the night, telling them to get a good sleep so they could start again early tomorrow.

Then, they would talk to Julia Francis, the solicitor who represented Linda and Osmond. Dan had met her before, back when he'd first worked with Adam. She had a ferocious reputation and had already made it clear they shouldn't expect much help. But the detective had insisted on seeing her. Dan got the feeling he was looking forward to another confrontation. He was in a bloody mood.

A mix of harsh streetlight and the gentle glow of the dusk seeped through the windows.

Dan closed the curtains. It felt time to shut out the world.

Claire opened her eyes. 'Don't worry about food for a minute,' she said. 'Come and sit with me.'

Dan did, cuddled into her on the sofa. She wrapped herself around him. Claire looked flushed. She was sweating a little and wiped a frond of hair from her face.

'You OK?' he asked. 'You look hot. Is your stomach bothering you again?'

'Kind of,' she replied, closing her eyes and lying back.

'Shall I give it a rub for you?'

'No, probably not a good idea. It's growing more and more sensitive each day.'

Dan nodded understandingly. 'Sure. I know what it's like when you've got a bad stomach. You don't want anyone near it. It's a horrible feeling. Maybe Adam was right. Perhaps you should see a doctor. It's been going on for a while.'

'I am going to see a doctor. But I thought I'd talk to you first.'

Claire reached up and cuddled into his neck. She said something he couldn't catch.

'Sorry, what was that?'

'Nothing,' she replied. 'It was nothing.'

'Sure?'

'Yes.'

Dan struggled up from the sofa. 'Well, I'd better start seeing about some food before it gets too late to eat. I thought we might get a take-away delivered.' He walked over to the kitchen and opened a couple of cupboards.

'Where do you keep your take-away menus?' he said, over his shoulder. 'I can't find them anywhere.'

There was no reply. He rummaged on, still without success. When he looked back at Claire he stopped, stricken. She was crying, silent tears streaming down her cheeks. Her chest shook and she sobbed gently, the noise rising until she began gasping and coughing.

'Claire, what is it?' He strode back over to her. 'Claire? What's the matter? What is it? Claire!'

Her face was soaked with tears, crumpled in deep, miserable lines. He held her tight, tried to make her talk to him.

'Claire? Claire! What is it? What's the matter? Claire! Is it your stomach hurting you?'

She grabbed some tissues from the coffee table and dabbed at her face, tried to breathe deeply to calm the sobbing.

'Yes,' she managed finally. 'Yes, it is my stomach.' She took both his hands in hers and looked into his eyes. 'It's my stomach. There's something I have to tell you.'

'Shit!' he gasped. 'Oh no – you're not saying …'

'Yes.'

'Oh shit! I can see it now – how did I miss it …'

'Yes.'

'I don't believe it – it can't be …'

She nodded. 'It is. It's true.'

'You're serious – I can't believe it … it can't be … it's …'

Dan hesitated, couldn't find the words. Finally, he spluttered, 'It's … it's cancer, isn't it? You're dying. Please don't tell me you're dying. Please, no, please. It can be cured, can't it? Don't say you're dying.'

She looked at him and seemed to laugh, a breathless, disbelieving noise. He just stared, uncomprehending. Her hands ran over his and gripped them hard.

'No. No, I'm not dying. Quite the opposite. I'm full of life.'

'What?' Dan put his hands on her shoulders. 'What?!' He couldn't hide his bafflement and alarm. 'What? I don't understand. Tell me! Please, tell me!'

She reached out and wrapped her arms around him, held him close. He felt her take a deep breath, then another. She was shaking and her voice trembled.

'Dan, I'm pregnant. Pregnant.'

The words seemed to bounce around his mind, flashing in bright neon pink and green, always elusive, floating just in front of him, lingering for hours before he could finally stretch out to catch them, hold them, examine them and understand what they meant.

Later, in the countless times he thought back on the moment, Dan could only compare it to being hit by an avalanche, a solid wall of sweeping emotion. It rendered him utterly helpless, numbed and paralysed with its power. It was a defining moment in his life. Nothing would ever be the same again.

It was one of those rare seconds when his universe changed for ever. He saw the stars spin around him, and felt the world and all its billions of people stop to stare at him and Claire, cuddled into the corner of a sofa in a small first-floor flat in Plymouth. There was no sound, no motion, nothing, just a second eternally stilled in time.

Later, he also rued how appallingly he handled it.

'Blimey,' was all he managed. 'Blimey,' he gasped. 'Is it mine?'

She stared at him, her mouth opening. He wished more than ever at that moment he could fly and grab the words back from the air, swallow them and erase them from existence.

Claire burst out laughing, her face suddenly shining through the tears. 'Yes, you idiot,' she said kindly. 'Of course it's yours. He's yours, in fact. I think it's a boy.'

'Blimey,' Dan repeated. 'Blimey. I need a drink.' He got up and walked over to the kitchen. He noticed his legs were wobbling and seemed to be only partially under his control. She watched him, shaking her head, but smiling.

'Actually, what I probably mean is I need a cuddle,' he said, walking unsteadily back and taking her into his arms again. 'I mean, you need a cuddle. Or we both do. Yes, that's what I mean.'

'That's better,' she sighed into his neck. Her breath was hot and she was still shaking. 'God I was so nervous about telling you. I've been trying, but you didn't pick up the hints.'

'What hints?'

She sighed. 'Never mind.'

They cuddled, held each other tight. Claire started crying again, the warm tears seeping through the shoulder of Dan's shirt. He wasn't sure how long they stayed meshed together. He seemed to have lost any sense of time. Nothing felt real. It was a waking dream. He tried to force his brain to think about what she'd said, but it was blank.

'Did Adam know?' Dan asked finally, remembering how the detective had questioned his emotional intelligence.

Claire leaned back against the sofa and dabbed at her eyes with another tissue.

'I think so.'

'So I was the only one to miss it.'

'Don't blame yourself. Adam's got experience of having a kid. You haven't. Plus you've been wrapped up in the blackmail case. Don't worry about it. You know now. That's the main thing.'

Dan could feel a familiar burgeoning annoyance with himself.

'It must have been horribly lonely for you, bearing it on your own. I'm so sorry I missed it.'

'No, it's fine. Forget it. You know now. That's all that's important.'

Dan reached out and ran a gentle hand over Claire's stomach. She watched him, then placed her hand over his and held it there.

'How pregnant are you?'

'I don't know. Probably only a few weeks I think, but I'm not sure. I'll have to see a doctor to check.'

They both stared at her stomach.

'I don't know what to say,' managed Dan finally.

'You don't have to say anything,' she replied, stroking his forehead. 'I'm fine and I feel so much better for having told you. Tonight I think we should just try to relax, have something to eat and we can talk about it when it's sunk in.'

'OK,' replied Dan, standing up. 'But you stay there. I'll sort the food out, and …'

'And don't think you have to wrap me up in cotton wool,' she interrupted. 'I don't need molly-coddling. I'm pregnant, not terminally ill.'

She got up and found the take-away menu. It was in a drawer Dan had already checked. They ordered a Chinese. On the phone, Dan managed not to ask whether there were any

150

ingredients or additives which could be harmful to an unborn child. He also stopped himself questioning whether Claire should drink the tiny glass of wine she poured for herself. They sat and watched a film, held hands throughout and didn't talk about it any more that evening.

Dan had expected to suffer a restless night. His mind should be full of the news, buzzing with what it meant and what they should do. But he slept deep and easily and dreamt of playing football in the park with a boisterous eight-year-old with dark hair, an unpredictable temperament, a pronounced and immensely irritating selfish streak and dreadful egotism.

In essence, a boy very much like his father.

Chapter Fifteen

DAN SCARCELY RECOGNISED IT as a Monday morning. He didn't feel the familiar, tedious lethargy of the return to routine after the weekend, the struggle to find time for food shopping, ironing shirts and trousers. None of that mattered. It didn't even register in his mind.

In that moment, in Claire's flat last night, the world had been transformed. It looked the same, but it felt new. He struggled to take his eyes from Claire's stomach. All he could see was her. Everything else was blurred, a meaningless background. She caught his look and gave him a brief, sideways smile.

It was eight o'clock and they stood in the MIR, drinking the pungent canteen tea and discussing the day ahead. Adam wanted to talk about the interview with Julia Francis, but Dan was finding it hard to concentrate on anything except Claire. He longed to reach out and place a protective arm around her wherever she went.

His mind still hadn't come up with any sensible thoughts about what her pregnancy meant and what they would do about it. But that wasn't bothering him. He felt adrift in a gentle tide of easy contentment, a valium dream. The coming day, the interview with the solicitor, even Lizzie's call earlier to demand a follow-up on yesterday's story, none of that mattered. All he could see was Claire and his son growing inside her.

'I don't expect to get much from Francis,' Adam was saying. 'But we've got to try. She's a link between Osmond and Linda, although she says she didn't know Freedman. She'll hide behind client confidentiality, but we'll give it a go.'

A plane droned by in the sky above the city. Dan looked out at the lines of cars, commuters queuing dutifully to get to a place almost all probably didn't want to go. He wondered what percentage of people actually liked their jobs. Not high, probably.

The ruined church stood to welcome them with its loneliness. A couple of crows perched on the edge of the tower, scornfully watching the mundane rituals of the human world. Dan's eyes wandered up to the plane. It was small, just a single propeller engine. A banner trailed behind it. One of those promoting a new bar or car dealership, he suspected. It had become fashionable to advertise by air.

Dan squinted to look at it, then stared. He blinked, looked again.

'Adam,' he said slowly. 'Adam!'

'Yes,' snapped the detective, looking up from a sheaf of papers. 'I'm busy. Is it urgent?'

'I think you should come and look at this.'

'What?'

'It's easier if you just look.'

Adam put the papers down heavily and walked over to the window. Dan pointed to the plane. He said quietly, 'I think we've just found out how the Worm planned to expose Osmond.'

'Bloody hell,' Adam gasped. 'Claire, get on to Plymouth air traffic control and get that plane down. I want to talk to the pilot.'

Claire picked up a phone, still staring at the plane. The banner trailed behind it, shining in the morning sun, bold black letters on shimmering white plastic. Dan could imagine the thousands of eyes looking up at it and wondered what they must be thinking of the message.

SUPERINTENDENT LEON OSMOND DRINK DRIVER

Dan followed Adam into Julia Francis's small, modern office. It was stacked with books, all in orderly rows and piles and smelt of pine air-freshener. A couple of prints hung on the walls, colourful geometric intertwinings of lines of cats, backs arched, tails erect, smiling out into the room. There was also a small photo of a Siamese cat on the solicitor's desk.

It was a familiar theme. Dan could count three cat-obsessed women with whom he'd had brief relationships. All lived alone, apart from their pet, and every single one talked to and treated the lucky feline more like a close relative than an animal. Naturally, the slightest of attempts to expose such ridiculousness – usually in an attempt to win some well-deserved attention for himself – would be greeted with disdain, if not horror.

One particular house had excelled in its felinity. There were pictures of the cat on the mantelpiece, by the side of the bed too, and assorted feline paraphernalia scattered around the house, from cat door-knockers to cat welcome mats, cat corkscrews, cat ornaments, even a cat duvet.

Dan had made a point of ensuring that particular relationship didn't last.

He was about to begin enjoying a familiar superiority complex when that annoying corner of his mind which he presumed housed his conscience whispered a sly suggestion. What about Rutherford? The creature Dan always thought of as his best friend. The only one he could ever really rely on. Who was always loyal. Of whom he had countless photos.

The nag of self-awareness could be so irritating.

Julia Francis stood up from behind her desk to shake their hands. It was one of the most reluctant gestures Dan thought he had ever seen. Her chubby fingers stretched out quickly, made a brief, transient contact, and were immediately withdrawn. He noticed she wore no rings and her fingernails were short and bitten down.

Her desk was clinically tidy, no human disorder to soften its austerity, and her appearance matched it. Dan had first thought of her as like a matron, but without the kindliness, and that image stuck with him.

She wore a plain black suit with an equally plain white blouse, had short blonde hair, greying over her ears, and pale, watery blue eyes which rarely blinked. Her features were sharp and severe, her face prematurely lined. She radiated hostility.

Facing her felt akin to standing in the path of an enemy tank.

Francis opened her attack before even they'd sat down. 'Chief Inspector, is it usual to arrive for an interview in a criminal investigation with a journalist in tow?'

'Dan's been co-opted onto the inquiry,' said Adam levelly. 'It's a case which has attracted great media interest and he's helping me handle it. He understands that all he witnesses is confidential.'

Francis stared at him, said frostily, 'Well, I'm not happy with him being here. And given what I have to say to you in a moment, you may prefer for us to be alone.'

Adam held her look. 'Thank you for your advice. However, how I conduct my investigations is my business. He stays. Now, regarding Linda Cott and Leon Osmond.'

'Very well, Chief Inspector, but don't say I didn't warn you. Not that it matters. As I have said, I won't be able to help you. Discussions with my clients naturally have the protection of law in their confidentiality.'

'Even dead clients?'

'Yes.'

'Even on matters as urgent and important as this investigation?'

'Difficult as you may find it to understand, the law makes no exceptions for your convenience.'

Adam took a deep breath and crossed his legs. 'Let me ask you this then, to see if it doesn't impinge on your duty of confidentiality. Apart from you, who might Superintendent Osmond have spoken to about matters concerning his private life?'

'Mr Osmond has instructed me in the most unambiguous of terms not to answer your questions about him. He believes your methods are unethical, and from what I know of you, I must agree.'

Adam ignored the dangling and tempting bait, tried again.

'Then let me try this,' he said heavily. 'On what matters did you act for Cott and Osmond?'

'That's confidential.'

'Did you have any discussions with them about matters which involved them being blackmailed?'

'Confidential.'

'Did you discuss anything they had done they were worried about, or feared being blackmailed for?'

'Confidential.'

Adam leaned forward and dropped the palm of his hand heavily on the desk.

'I am investigating a very serious crime which we believe has led to the deaths of two people and I have to say I believe you're being deliberately obstructive.'

The attack made all the impact of a water pistol on the tank's armour.

'And yet again in my discussions with you, Chief Inspector, I find you acting like a child. If you can't get your way, you throw a tantrum. Will you ever appreciate that not everyone jumps to your commands? You are not the law, merely its tool. I am not being obstructive, I am being professional.'

Adam cleared his throat noisily. His neck was starting to redden. 'Then let me ask you this. Did you know Will Freedman, or act for him in any way?'

She sat back on her chair. 'On that matter I can help you, Chief Inspector. As it does not in any way impinge on my professionalism or the law, I can tell you I did not act for him. I was of course aware of him as a local MP, but I did not know him.'

Adam nodded. 'Then I think it only fair to warn you that as you are linked to two of the blackmail victims and could have been privy to sensitive information about them, you will be considered a suspect in this investigation.'

The solicitor shook her head slowly. Dan wasn't sure whether the gesture was more contemptuous or pitying.

'That's quite ridiculous, but as you wish, Chief Inspector. I must, however, wonder how your investigation is progressing if you consider me a possible perpetrator of these dreadful offences. I hardly need say I had nothing whatsoever to do with them.'

Dan tried not to enjoy the joust. He kept his face set and wondered what Adam would try next. If he was being an impartial referee, he'd have to say Julia Francis was winning.

The detective stood up. 'Well, thank you for your help, Ms Francis ...' he began, his voice heavy with irony, but she interrupted.

'I did mention there was one thing I had to say to you.'

Adam stopped by the door. 'Do go on,' he said with sarcastic politeness.

Dan thought he saw a hint of pleasure cross the solicitor's stony face.

'My client, Mr Osmond, has asked me to pursue a case against you for entrapment regarding an interview you carried out with him yesterday. The matter has taken on added importance given the defamatory nature of the claim being trailed behind a plane over the city earlier. You will be hearing from us regarding legal proceedings, and if I were you, Chief Inspector, I would be more than a little concerned.'

Adam walked fast and determinedly back to Charles Cross, as if he were trying to burn off his anger. He didn't say anything, seemed lost in his thoughts. Dan kept thinking of Claire and his unborn son. Why was it he imagined the boy as being eight years old? He suspected it was because that was the happiest time of his own childhood. The days of living in a pub and playing football with his dad in the beer garden. The innocent age when the sun always shone.

It was a great life for a kid, growing up in a pub. The regulars would always include him in their rounds. He'd never be short of ginger ale, orange juice or even bitter shandy. They must have been his first tastes of alcohol. Dan sometimes wondered if he could trace his love for beer back to those days.

The coppers of change from the locals' rounds usually made it into his pocket too and had quickly added up to help buy his first bicycle. He'd ridden it round a corner of the pub car park time and again, his face frowning with determination to learn how to balance. It was such an important mission that even the skinned and scarred knees of the inevitable accidents hadn't seemed to matter.

What life could his son expect, with a detective and a journalist as parents? Dan felt the sunshine of his imagination dim. Endless days at a crèche to start with, then babysitters, after-school clubs, relatives and friends to stand in for him and Claire on the inevitable days they worked long and late.

Would he give up some of his career to bring up a child? Would she? He couldn't imagine either of them doing so. The thought seeped its bitterness through his mind.

He tried to push it away. They could talk about all that. They would work something out.

Dan's mobile rang twice on the walk back. The first time it was Lizzie, repeating her demand for a story. She'd heard about the plane and its banner. They had a big pensioners' protest about the ever-rising levels of council tax to keep them occupied for the lunchtime news, but she made it very plain he was expected to provide a report on the blackmail case for Wessex Tonight.

'I want a full splash. I want the works. And I don't want you giving it away to all the other media in some press conference! You got that? I want the inside track on this Osmond. I want people switching to us in their thousands to find out what's happening. I want stories, I want lots of them and I want them good.'

So it had gone on. He didn't bother arguing. With Lizzie in that mood, it was like trying to paddle against a tidal wave. But the barked orders down the phone left Dan feeling irritable.

The next call was from El. He'd seen the plane and its banner and taken a few snaps. But what he desperately needed now was a new photo of Osmond, preferably beside his car to match the story of the drink-driving allegation. Did Dan have any thoughts about how to get one? It could be worth thousands. All the national papers were interested.

Dan felt like snapping at his friend. It seemed that everyone wanted him to sort out their problems. He stopped himself. El was a good mate and they always looked after each other.

He thought about it for a minute, then sensed an idea growing, one which could help them both. It was immoral and probably illegal too, but so what? Osmond was a drink driver, a bully too. He'd need Adam's help, of a kind the detective never should give, but after that interview with the solicitor and Osmond's threat of legal action, he might just get it.

They were almost at Charles Cross. Adam was still striding hard. Dan realised he was out of breath, trying to keep up.

'Just before we go,' he said, 'there's one little thing I'd like to ask.'

Dan explained about El's call and his own need for a story

for tonight's programme. Adam stared at him. Dan couldn't read what the detective was thinking. He sensed it wasn't the time to question or try to persuade, just to keep quiet. They walked on, but slower now.

The ruined church loomed ahead, its tower silhouetted against the brightness of the spring blue sky. The grey sixties block of the police station lurked incongruously behind, like a waiting mugger. A group of people stood around its steps. Adam stopped, squinted, swore under his breath. There were photographers, cameramen, reporters, sipping at take-away coffees, chatting to each other, but watchful too.

'Press pack,' Adam hissed.

'Yes,' Dan replied.

'Waiting for …' He didn't have to finish the sentence.

The two men turned down a side street before the pack could spot them.

'Yep,' said Dan. 'They're all waiting for you. That plane and its less than subtle banner means they want to ask you about Osmond, the investigation, the works.'

Adam swore under his breath. 'I haven't got time for all this. I've got the High Honchos on my back demanding progress, Osmond making a complaint against me, and now the bloody press hunting me too. Have you got any ideas what to do?'

Dan sensed his opportunity. 'You need a diversion. To give them a new quarry to hunt. Someone to distract them.'

'Like who?'

Dan didn't reply, just gave his friend a look. 'Regarding what we were discussing a few minutes ago,' he said eventually.

Adam ran a hand over the stubble on his chin. 'Come over here a minute, there's something I want to show you.' He led Dan around the corner of the street. They crossed the road and stood looking into the window of a camping shop. A range of half-price tents was on offer, all guaranteed waterproof.

He pointed at one. 'I can't under any circumstances tell you where Osmond lives so you can go and stake him out,' he continued. 'It would be entirely unethical. No matter how it might help you get a story and distract the rest of the pack.'

Dan looked at the tents, then back at Adam. Again he felt something else was coming, but didn't know what. He turned back to the shop window and stayed quiet.

Adam indicated a four-man tent and said, 'You and Claire are looking for a place together, aren't you?' he said.

'Yes,' replied Dan, puzzled by the change of subject. 'But I wasn't thinking of a tent ...'

'Found anywhere yet?'

'No, not yet. We haven't really started looking.'

'Well, let me give you a tip. I know some lovely places. Ermington for example. Particularly those big houses up by the church. They're well worth a look. You never know what you might find.'

They decided to go together in Nigel's car to attract less attention. Dan wondered how successful that would be. He was well known from his TV appearances, and El and Nigel both had their conspicuous kit to carry. If they had to start asking around, in a small village they would look exactly what they were.

Predators.

El clambered untidily into the back, carefully cradling the long lens of his camera. He was grinning and mumbling about how much he loved naughty Superintendent Leon Osmond. The muttering became more distinct and another of the photographer's dreadful limericks was launched on to an unsuspecting world.

"A cop who's too fond of his drink,
Can cause a quite terrible stink,
With El on his tail,
Then how can we fail?
To see him immortalised in ink!"

Dan groaned. He had thought he was almost inured to El's awful standards of rhyme, but that had to be one of the worst. Even the diplomatic Nigel looked pained.

En route, Dan put one hand over his ear to dampen El's background burbling and called Claire to check how she was. She was absolutely fine she said, but sounded a little abrupt. He got the message. No matter how pregnant she was, don't fuss. That wasn't going to be easy. It seemed the most natural thing in the world to try to take care of her. The worries about looking after a child were still picking at his mind, but he didn't mention them. Wrong time, wrong place. They could talk about it soon enough.

He found a couple of bits of Nigel's emergency clothing on the back seat and donned a spare baseball cap in an attempt to disguise himself. Combined with his sunglasses, he might just get away with looking less obvious and vulnerable to the dreaded shout, "It's that man on the telly".

It was another fine spring day, the sunshine dappled by a high gauze of tissue cloud. Nigel drove them east, out of Plymouth, along the dual carriageway of the main A38 and then turned south, following the path of the pebble-bed River Erme to Ermington.

Dan unwrapped a sandwich he'd bought from a petrol station and began eating. He heard El whine plaintively in the back, sighed, tore off a piece and handed it to him. It was like being a parent. Well, he'd better get used to it. The photographer munched gratefully. He reminded Dan of Rutherford.

A line of trees bowed over the Erme, as though bending to sample its crystal waters. They were heavy with paper-white blossom, some escaping and dancing in the breeze. Dan wound down the car's window and breathed in the warm air. A sweating thatcher sewed golden straw into a cottage roof while an old lady stood at the bottom of a silver ladder waving a tea cup at him. It was pure Devon.

The famous crooked spire of the church appeared through the trees. Nigel slowed and the car crawled past it, just as so many tourists did. El's head leaned hungrily out of the window, scanning each house for any sign of Leon Osmond or his Jaguar. Dan relaxed. If there was a hint of Osmond anywhere, El would spot it.

They passed a pub and the junior school, a babble of joy and excitement in life with the children running and shouting in the playground. A row of cottages shepherded the narrow road, all perfectly kept and adorned with hanging baskets of bursting colour. Cars manoeuvred carefully to park outside a small line of shops.

Ermington had fought hard to retain the sense of community that so many villages had seen fade over the years. It made such a difference. Too many now had residents, people who passed silently in the street, not neighbours and friends. But not here. It was a living village.

The continued on, through to the outskirts. The houses changed, grew larger, all in their own grounds, detached with drives, some modern, some conversions of farmhouses and barns. Nigel kept driving slowly, their faces sweeping from left to right.

'Bingo!' yelped El suddenly. 'Target in my sights.'

He pointed ahead to a modern, detached and whitewashed house standing at the end of an asphalt drive. Parked by its front doors was a gleaming maroon Jaguar.

'Gotcha,' chattered El happily. 'One half of mission Naughty Drinky Cop accomplished. Now the tricky bit. The man himself.'

They got out of the car and discussed their plan. There were sturdy black iron gates at the end of Osmond's drive, firmly closed, and it was more than a hundred yards to the house. The drive curved away from them in a sweeping arc so a hedge obscured the front door.

'Too far for me to get a decent shot of him,' said Nigel, hands on hips, studying the scene. 'Even if he decided to come out.'

'Me too,' grumbled El. He hopped from foot to foot and stroked the lens of his camera. 'Even with this beautiful all-seeing eye. Got to get closer. Got to lure him out of the house too. That won't be easy. Bet the bugger's gone to ground.'

They both looked at Dan. He rolled his eyes and muttered, 'Down to me then, is it? Thanks, lads.'

He gazed at the house and its surrounds, thought for a moment, then pointed to a shallow ditch that ran alongside the edge of Osmond's land. It was thick with bushes and overgrowth.

'There,' he said. 'That's our way closer. Let's do a recce.'

They waited for a hiatus in the passing cars, then tried to walk nonchalantly along the road until they found a gap in the hedge. It was dense and leafy, but after a while they came upon a break and pushed quickly through into a field full of stubble. They crouched, waited for the challenge, the angry shouts wanting to know what the hell they were doing, but none came. A car passed, then another. They squatted down, waited, then slowly slid back towards the ditch.

It was mostly dry, but Dan did get a couple of shoefuls of cold and stagnant water. They crept along, bent double, Nigel and El carrying their cameras, Dan with the ungainly weight of the tripod. Lively young branches snapped at them as they pushed their way through, landing a couple of whipping blows and the odd thorn tore at their clothes. A blackbird sang out its alarm and fluttered away across the open fields.

Dan paused and looked back over his shoulder. They were all sweating heavily, Nigel panting and El sporting a chain of leaves in his shock of hair. He held up a hand, let them have a moment's breather, moved on.

About twenty yards from the front of the house the ditch widened into a dry hollow. There was a clear view of the door and the car. Perfect. Nigel and El trained their cameras on the house and they waited. It was a quarter past one. Plenty of time for their prey to emerge.

They only needed a few seconds of pictures to get their exclusive. Just enough of Osmond by his car to start Dan's report for tonight. No one else would have that. It would be fresh and entertaining and should suffice to keep Lizzie happy. El could snap all the shots he needed in the time it took the Superintendent to venture out of his door. For whatever reason; to check the weather, stretch his legs, get some air, it didn't matter. All that was important was that he appeared.

Dan had lost count of the number of stake-outs he'd endured. He'd never cared for them. It was always waiting which was the worst. Action he could handle, reacting to a breaking story, busking his way through a live report. But waiting made you feel impotent, knowing you could get a fine scoop or simply nothing, depending on the vagaries of your luck.

Two hours ticked slowly by. Dan leaned back against some grass at the rear of the hollow, Nigel and El bent over their cameras at the front. It was like some military scene, he thought. Not a bad way of earning a living, sitting in the Devon countryside in the sunshine, but he was getting increasingly twitchy about the time.

If he was going to get a story, Osmond would have to come out soon. Wessex Tonight was on air at half past six. Dan reckoned he'd need an hour to edit the report, and they'd take half an hour or so to get back to the studios. So five o'clock was their deadline.

It was getting on for half past three.

'Come on, come on, come on,' El mumbled over and over again, stroking his camera lens for luck. 'If I don't get the snap of him to London soon, it'll be worthless. That's thousands of quid down the drain. Thousands!'

'He's not daft though, is he?' whispered Nigel. 'He'll know the media will be after him for a picture. I reckon he's staying put safely inside.'

They waited on. Another half hour edged by. Dan tried to occupy himself thinking about Claire and his baby boy. What name might they choose? He went through a mental list and found he didn't really like any apart from his own. What would Claire think of Dan junior? He could imagine her face if he even dared raise the question.

El let out a low moan of frustration. Dan checked Nigel's digital watch, cheap, but always accurate. It was getting on for a quarter past four. Time was running out.

A pigeon landed in a tree above them and let loose a dropping. It hit El's foot.

'Blimey,' he groaned, looking up. 'Even the bloody birds are against me. Thousands of quid just slipping away in front of my eyes.' He took a sly look at Dan. 'Any ideas?'

Dan stared over at Osmond's house. He was sure he'd sensed life in there. Perhaps just the twitch of a curtain and the faint sound of hammering. Nigel was right. The Superintendent was safely inside, probably doing some DIY. He'd gone to ground to stop the media getting a fresh picture of him.

'I could just be straightforward and try ringing the bell,' he said. 'You two could get a shot of him when he came to the door.'

'No chance,' replied Nigel. 'He's not stupid. He'd either send his wife or just not answer.'

Dan nodded. It was a vain hope. Osmond had seen enough of journalists in his career to expect such a trick. He had to come up with something better.

He scanned the house and the car shining outside. So, what would tempt Osmond out? Everyone had a weakness. What did he know about the man that he could use?

His thoughts again started to drift to Claire and playing football in the park with his son. Days like this would be perfect for a kick-about. It would be just the way his father had once played with him. Dan wondered how Claire's interview with the pilot of the plane had gone. Were they getting any closer to catching the blackmailer? He blinked the thoughts away and forced himself to concentrate.

He stared at Osmond's Jaguar and an idea started to tug at his mind. The blackmail note said Osmond loved his car. And it certainly looked impeccably cared for, standing here, shining brightly in his drive.

Dan checked Nigel's watch again. Almost half past four. They were nearly out of time. If he was going to do it, it had to be now.

Dan stood up and clambered out of the front of the hollow. Time to move before he changed his mind.

'Cameras at the ready, boys,' he whispered. 'This is our one chance, so let's give it our best.'

Dan crouched low and followed the line of the hedge to the side of the house. Not for the first time he was glad he always bought soft-soled shoes. They were indispensable for a TV reporter, smart enough to be worn on camera, but still practical for running after reluctant interviewees or away from irate victims of their filming.

He felt his heart thumping and had to concentrate to control his breathing. He crept across the drive and knelt down beside the Jaguar. No sound or movement from the house. They hadn't seen him. He waited for a moment to compose himself, then slid around to the back of the car. He took his handkerchief and stuffed it into the exhaust pipe.

Dan looked over to the bushes. He could just make out the shine of the camera lenses protruding through the leaves. The snipers of the media. They were well camouflaged, but Nigel and El were ready. Good. Now it was just down to him. He'd have to move fast.

Dan stood up, rested his backside on the Jaguar's bonnet and bounced it up and down.

The screaming siren of the car's alarm split the air. Dan was instantly away, sprinting, back towards the bushes. He felt his legs ache with the effort. He crashed through the greenery, landed heavily in the ditch and ducked down, caught his breath and turned to look back at the house.

The front door flew open and out strode Osmond. He was wearing a pair of long blue shorts and a white T-shirt with the logo of a local brewery on it.

What a wonderful irony. Dan silently thanked the Gods of News. Truly they had blessed him for his boldness. He couldn't have asked for more.

Osmond glanced suspiciously about, held out a key fob and stopped the siren. He walked over to the car and checked it twice, circling carefully around, running a hand over the bodywork, examining it. He even knelt down to check the underside. Then he opened the car's door and tried the engine. It coughed and turned over, but wouldn't start. He tried again with the same result. The blockage in the exhaust pipe was doing its job perfectly. Their quarry was out in the open, and for more time than they could ever need.

Dan crept carefully along the ditch to Nigel and El. He could have sworn the paparazzo was purring with delight.

'Got enough?' he whispered.

'Yep,' they both replied without taking their eyes off the viewfinders of their cameras.

'Beautiful,' added El. 'Wonderful. Heavenly. I'm in

166

snapper's paradise.' He sounded entranced and broke into another limerick.

'Oh, how Osmond loves that car,
It's taken him so very far,
But when he's fuelled up with drink,
Looking all so fat and pink,
El cashes in and laughs – Ha ha!'

'Shhh,' urged Dan, trying not to chuckle. 'Let's hope he just thinks there's something wrong with the car. I reckon he'll go back into the house in a mo to call a garage. When he does, we're off, OK? And be quiet about it. The last thing I want is for him to spot us.'

'Wait until he sees the news tonight,' whispered Nigel.

The traffic was light on the drive back to the studios and they made it by quarter past five. El waddled off happily to file his pictures, still burbling to himself, and Dan sat in an edit suite with Jenny and put the report together. As he wrote it, he had to stop himself giggling. It was certainly entertaining.

Again he had a dilemma how to begin. The most recent pictures, and the most dramatic were those they'd just shot, of Osmond charging out of his house and checking his car. They also had that added delight of his T-shirt. But the shot that told the story – the golden image – was the one El had taken, the snap of the plane trailing the banner. Then again, stills were never as interesting as moving pictures. Quickly, Dan jotted down the pros and cons, weighed them up.

Ten minutes ticked past. Half past five. An hour to on air. Jenny coughed pointedly.

Dan took the hint. The best of stories, the most stunning of pictures, the finest of elegant scripting meant nothing if the report didn't make the programme. He was thinking too much.

Eventually, he reverted to the basic question – what is news? It came down to the old adage, the difference between the mundane "dog bites man", and the headline-grabbing "man bites dog". The viewers were unlikely to ever before have seen a plane trailing a banner accusing a senior police officer of drink driving. Argument settled.

Over one of El's snapshots of the plane, Dan talked about how the blackmailer had decided to make it very clear who his latest victim was. Then Jenny cut to another photo, this time from a newspaper article in which Osmond was interviewed about his campaign against drink driving. It was pure counterpoint, and made the man look an utter hypocrite.

To follow, they used some pictures of Osmond checking his car, Dan talking about the allegation that he was driving the Jaguar when he was caught. He added the police press office's official statement; that Osmond had been suspended, was under investigation by the Professional Standards department, and that no further comment would be made.

Finally Dan recapped on the case, how Freedman had killed himself, as had Linda. He signed off by saying detectives would like to hear from anyone with information that could help their investigation. Adam had been very keen that should feature. It was a police cliché, said in just about every inquiry, but it did often help bring forward new witnesses.

And so another assassination by television was completed.

Claire was working late on her inquiries into where the plane's banner had come from, so they agreed to spend the night apart. She wasn't getting very far, she said, just about nowhere in fact, but she didn't want to go into details. She sounded busy, tired and irritable. Dan asked if Claire felt they were coming any closer to finding the Worm and received an unattractive snort. He wasn't surprised. He'd reached the same conclusion himself.

Dan ate some beans on toast on the great blue sofa in his flat, Rutherford at his feet, and realised he didn't know how to feel about not being with Claire tonight.

Logically, it made perfect sense. He could do with a good sleep and some quality time with Rutherford. It was never certain when she'd get home when she was working on an investigation. He was sure she wasn't punishing him because of his clumsy reaction to the pregnancy. Claire wasn't like that. She didn't use emotions as a weapon, unlike some women he'd met. Men too, in fairness. They could both probably do with time and space to think. But he still couldn't calm the squealing of the instinct which said he should be there with her.

Dan ironed a couple of shirts and some trousers for the week as he watched Wessex Tonight. His story was second on the programme, after the protesting pensioners. He wondered how shocked Osmond would be, but he couldn't focus his mind on the Superintendent.

When his stomach had successfully digested some of the weight of his tea, Dan took Rutherford for a run around Hartley Park. The dog spun wheels of yelping joy around him as he rummaged in the hallway cupboard for the lead. He bent down to give Rutherford a cuddle. He felt better for spending time with his beloved friend. The guilt always stung when work forced him to neglect his dog for a couple of days.

They jogged slowly around the park. Twilight was creeping in, stretching the shadows of the lime and oak trees that guarded the boundary of the green. It was a wonderful time of year. The land was awakening from the sleep of the winter, bringing new life and light, fresh buds, shoots and colour after the darkness of the long, cold months. It was the season of renewal.

Rutherford sprinted off towards the ginger blur of a cat, but, as ever, got nowhere near it. He ambled back to Dan and jogged beside him. He had his mouth open and his tongue hung out in his smiling face. Dan patted his head and ran his hand along the dog's sleek back. He was a beautiful animal.

Another unwelcome thought intruded. What would it mean for Rutherford if there was a baby in the house? How would the dog react? Some got jealous at the competition for affection. Rutherford had never lived with anyone else. Could they trust him with a baby crawling on the floor, perhaps poking him, or pulling his tail?

Dan increased the pace of his run to try to shut out the worry. But it combined with his other concern about how he and Claire would ever find time to care for a child. Together they goaded him, attacking from opposite corners of his mind.

He tried to distract himself. Adam wanted to meet at eight tomorrow morning to talk about the case. How were they doing? They had three victims, two suspects and three of the five code words. Surely they could make some progress now?

What did "Open original memorial" mean? Could the irascible priest, or that tank of a solicitor really be the blackmailer?

An image flitted through his mind, an Alsatian bent snarling over a terrified baby. Dan blinked hard to exorcise the vision, but it hung in the air.

He forced his heavy legs to run faster still. He was panting heavily. Was he sure enough of his relationship with Claire to have a child? They weren't married, hadn't even discussed it. They'd only got as far as agreeing to move in together and they hadn't even made any real efforts to find a place yet. Was that commitment?

Dan reached the end of the lap and slowed to a jog. His heart was racing and his mind ran with it. Tiny spheres of sweat slid from his face onto his T-shirt. He stopped suddenly and stared up at the darkening sky. The bravest stars were beginning to force their way through the cowl of the night. The city was peaceful, preparing to sleep.

'What's the matter with me?' Dan whispered to Rutherford. 'Last night, this morning even, I was so happy. What's changed?'

He slipped the lead over the dog's neck and walked slowly back towards the flat. Dan didn't know where the ambush of emotion had come from, but suddenly he felt afraid of the world.

Chapter Sixteen

DAN DIDN'T HAVE MUCH time that spring Tuesday evening to compose an entry in the diary he kept of the cases he worked on with Adam. But despite all else that was going on in his life, he made sure he found just a couple of minutes, so important was it to record the headlines of what had happened.

"Caught the bloody blackmailer!" he wrote. "The case is SORTED! Great TV scoop on it too. Groves does it again. Yeah, yeah, yeah!!"

Looking back on the case of The Judgement Book, in the coming weeks and months, when he finally found the courage and strength, Dan didn't know whether to be angry or laugh at himself, so woefully naive were his words.

The day started quietly enough, with the briefing Adam had arranged in the MIR. It was eight o'clock exactly.

'I scarcely know where to begin,' the detective said, standing beside his beloved green boards. He looked at Dan. 'We've had some very interesting information come in. Your broadcast last night certainly caused a stir.'

Dan sipped at his canteen tea and flinched. It was bitingly strong, the way the police seemed to like it. Built for the beat, Adam always said.

He hadn't slept well, those goading thoughts about his future with Claire and his unborn son intruding continually into his dreams. But the two of them had managed to find five minutes together before the briefing, hidden in the far corner of Charles Cross car park, and the quick squeezing cuddle had lifted his spirits.

He'd felt his eyes ache and had to blink back the gathering tears. Where had they come from, he wondered? Even in the days when the swamp was at its most powerful, and dramatic mood swings were a familiar sufferance, he couldn't remember such mercurial emotions.

Dan focused back on Adam. The detective's face had darkened and he seemed to find what he was saying distasteful.

'Sorry, what?' Dan asked.

'I said sex.' Adam spelt out the taboo with all the distaste of an accomplished prude. 'S – E – X. Linda Cott and sex.'

Dan instinctively reached for his notebook. 'Go on. I'm listening.'

'I bet you are. So I'll remind you again. No stories without my say so, remember?'

'Yes, yes, of course. Go on.'

Adam gave him a look. 'We had an anonymous call after your story last night. It was from a woman. She said she knew why Linda had killed herself.'

'And?'

'She said it was down to sex. She claims Linda used to take part in an activity known as "dogging".'

Dan blinked hard. He liked to think of himself as a man of the world and was pretty sure he knew what dogging was, but thought he'd better check before he made a fine fool of himself.

'And dogging is?'

Claire looked away. Adam's face was reddening. He cleared his throat awkwardly. 'Sex – in public – with strangers – watched by ... other people.'

There was a pause. Dan frowned, couldn't keep the incredulity from his voice. 'Linda Cott? A senior cop? Who you all rate so highly? Doing – that stuff?'

Adam and Claire exchanged glances.

'Well – do you believe the caller?' Dan prompted. 'Is there any evidence to back up what she says?'

Adam folded his arms. 'I don't want to believe it.'

'Nor do I,' Claire interjected forcefully, shaking her head hard. 'Not one little bit.'

'But, I have to consider it might be true,' Adam continued. 'Because if it is, it certainly explains a lot. Linda's reluctance to let us see the blackmail note. Her killing herself. You can imagine the scandal if it had got out.'

Claire walked over to the window, stared out at the brightening day. Adam joined her. Down on the grey concrete steps the press pack was gathering again, photographers and reporters leaning against the railings, waiting.

The MIR had been cleaned overnight; all the bins were empty, the windows shiny, a lingering hint of polish in the air. But the pervading atmosphere Dan could sense was disbelief.

'Well – I hardly know what to say,' was all he could manage.

'Imagine how it feels for us,' Claire replied quietly.

More silence, then Dan asked, 'So – what do we do?'

Adam tapped a palm on the windowsill. 'We have to check it out. We'll send a team of detectives to look into the wonderful world of dogging. We'll see if we can find some of these ...' he struggled for the word. '... these – doggers.'

Outside, a flock of pigeons fluttered by, wheeled in unison in the blue sky, headed back for their loft. Cars crawled around the ruined church. It must have been a couple of minutes before anyone spoke.

Adam walked slowly to the boards. He couldn't keep his gaze from Linda's face, calmly staring out at him. How many eyes hid such secrets, Dan thought. And that was exactly what this case was about. Human frailty and guilty secrets.

'I'd better fill you in on what else has happened,' the detective said heavily. 'Yvonne Freedman's found a way to get her revenge on the Traditionalists, without breaking the law this time.'

He picked up a copy of the Daily Gazette from a desk. The broadsheet's front page splash was headlined, "They killed my husband". Dan scanned through the story. It was based on an interview Yvonne had given, accusing the party of gross self interest, and using people like components on a factory line.

Some of the quotes were very spicy. "Faceless party barons, interested only in the pursuit of power at any cost ... misplaced adoration for the rising stars, giving them messianic complexes ... far too selfish and dishonest to ever be trusted with real responsibility."

Yvonne had further embroidered her attack by saying that, since her husband's suicide, no one from the senior ranks of the Traditionalists had bothered to get in touch to find out how she or Alex were coping.

Dan whistled softly under his breath. It was an evisceration in print.

'A couple of developments from our background checks,' Adam continued. 'Father Maguire has suddenly become more interesting to us. He's got a criminal record, for burglary.'

'What?' asked Dan, more than a little surprised. 'Really?'

Claire opened a box file, found a couple of sheets of paper. 'It's from before he became a priest. When he was in his twenties. He had some family bereavement – his dad, I think – and went off the rails. Got involved in drugs, starting burgling homes to support his habit.'

'Blimey,' Dan said. 'Who'd have thought it? About him, and, well ...'

His words faltered. Their eyes again crept to the photograph of Linda.

'What happened to Maguire afterwards?' Dan asked quickly.

'He was spared jail,' said Claire. 'Did some community work, found God and the church. There's no further hint of wrongdoing. Quite the reverse in fact. No one's got a bad word to say about him. He's noted for being a caring and compassionate priest.'

'But,' said Adam pointedly. 'But ...'

Dan nodded. 'He's got form – as I believe you lot say.'

'Yep.'

'A possible means of getting information he could use for blackmail. From the confessional for Freedman and Linda, if not Osmond.'

'If he's been telling us the truth,' said Adam. 'If.'

'And a motive?'

'Don't know – yet.'

'So what do we do?'

'Well, his little misdemeanours were a long time ago, and he might well have left them all behind. But we keep it in mind. See what else happens, whether we need to talk to him again.'

The door opened and a couple of detectives walked in, greeted them and settled at the line of computers at the back of the MIR.

'Anything else?' Dan asked. 'It sounds like there's plenty to go at.'

Claire opened another folder. 'We've done some work on the clues we've broken so far. "Open original memorial." All we managed to come up with were plaques commemorating the Queen's Silver and Golden Jubilees – assuming the Silver is the original memorial, and the Gold the newer one, and the sailing of the Mayflower to the New World. As you know, the Mayflower steps, where the Pilgrim Fathers set off from, have been moved a couple of times, hence more than one memorial. But neither idea gave us anything.'

'There was one other thing,' Adam said. 'It came from our checks on Julia Francis.'

'Who you gleefully told she was a suspect. You didn't really mean that, did you?' Dan asked.

'Not really. But I had her checked, just in case. Her background's more interesting than I suspected. Her family are from South Africa. Her father was a prominent anti-apartheid campaigner. He was imprisoned several times, and died in jail. The family escaped to England afterwards. It seems young Julia took up the law because of what happened to her Dad. She's a prominent supporter of Freedom, the civil liberties group, and does a lot of legal work for them, all for free apparently.'

Dan wondered whether to say it, but thought he would anyway. 'Which might explain why she took exception to your interview technique.'

He readied himself for the retaliation, but was surprised when it didn't come.

'It may indeed,' Adam replied quietly. He looked almost abashed. Dan could see he was reconsidering his view of Julia Francis. It was as evident as an old-fashioned computer, a pattern of lights flashing on its frontage to indicate a program was running.

Claire got up from her desk, opened a window. A welcome breeze slipped around them, easing the room's stuffiness.

'What about the banner on the plane?' Dan asked. 'Any luck with that?'

'No,' said Claire. 'It was commissioned and made at the same time as the bill poster which exposed Freedman, paid for in cash and delivered by the company to the pilot. When I asked if it might seem odd to them, putting that drink-driving message on to a banner no one batted an eyelid. They've had much worse. They've made and flown banners about unfaithful husbands and wives, cheating business partners, you name it. Revenge is good business, apparently.'

Dan itched again at his back. He glanced down at his mobile phone. So far no call from Lizzie, but it was early. He knew she'd want another story today and he was wondering what he had to offer. Not much, given this briefing. There were some fascinating titbits, but nothing Adam would allow him to report. Not yet, anyway.

'So what do we do next?' he asked.

Adam shrugged. 'We wait. Probably for the next blackmail note, to see if that takes us anywhere.'

Dan remembered the news stands he'd passed on his way to Charles Cross. They were full of headlines about the blackmailer.

'I bet we won't wait long,' he said. 'The abuse you hurled at the Worm in the press conference, I'm sure he'll want to react. It feels to me like the person we're after is very proud of what he's doing. He's not going to take it lightly, you suggesting he's some kind of common criminal and inadequate.'

Adam yawned. 'I hope you're right,' he said. 'I feel like we're treading water, waiting for something to happen. And it's bloody frustrating.'

Dan drove back to the studios, his mind full of the briefing. There were lots of tantalising possibilities, but no hard leads. His legs ached and he could still sense a lingering fatigue. He would have welcomed a lie in bed this morning. Still, he'd seen Claire and now felt more content about their relationship. Those worries about how they'd ever look after a child remained on the outskirts of his mind, but at least they'd quietened.

He peered through the porthole window of the newsroom door before walking in. Lizzie was at her desk, working on the computer. He craned his neck to see her shoes and got a pleasant surprise. Low heels today, probably only a couple of inches.

'You got a story for us then?' she asked as he walked in. She sounded remarkably jovial. Dan noticed she was sporting a new silver bracelet. Unusual. She didn't wear much jewellery.

'Not at the moment. The detectives are investigating a series of leads and I'll hear if anything comes up.'

He didn't like lying at the best of times, and found it even more difficult with Lizzie. She had laser eyes, could see straight through him. Dan looked around for a distraction, spotted the corner of a greetings card sticking out of her bag.

'Happy birthday, by the way,' he added, trying to sound nonchalant, as though he'd planned to say it all along.

'You remembered!' Lizzie sounded genuinely touched. 'Thanks, that's kind of you. Men are usually so hopeless about things like that.'

'It's never a good move to forget your boss's birthday.' Dan began edging away, towards his desk. Time to quit while he was ahead. 'I wish you a good one.'

'Thanks,' she said again. 'A present of a story would be nice.'

'No promises today, but I'll see what I can do.'

He was surprised she let that go. It was almost worth a story in itself. She must be feeling mellow.

Dan spent a dull morning answering emails and filling in two month's worth of expenses. He'd clocked up four hundred pounds when he gave up, and was sure he was owed at least another couple of hundred more. He'd never got the hang of paperwork – far too tedious for a limited lifespan – but sometimes that could be costly.

He found himself doing a couple of internet searches for babysitters, nannies and playgroups in Plymouth. There were scores. How would they ever choose which to use? You didn't just entrust your child to anyone. A recommendation from a friend would be the best way, but it wasn't something he was going to raise with anyone just yet.

He was about to type in "animal rescue homes" too, but stopped himself. He could scarcely believe it. Was he really considering that he might have to find another home for Rutherford? Never, he would never do that. Rutherford had been a loyal friend through some difficult times and Dan resolved he would never allow himself to even consider losing him. Never.

His stomach growled. The newsroom clock said ten past twelve. He began thinking about braving the canteen for lunch when his mobile rang. Adam.

'Hello mate,' said Dan, excited. 'You got something? A breakthrough?'

'Nothing like it.' Adam sounded flat, dispirited. 'We're checking everything we can think of, doggers and all, but at the moment we're not getting anywhere.'

Dan tried to keep his eyes away from Lizzie. He could hear her voice cutting across the newsroom. She was berating a producer for his sloppy use of English. A sharpened fingernail jabbed at the air. Her charitable mood of earlier hadn't lasted. It wouldn't be long before she was hovering, hounding him for a story. "I want, I want, I want …"

'How can I help you then?' Dan asked.

'I could do with getting out of the office for a while and fancied a chat. How do you feel about lunch?'

'Great.' A prowling Lizzie meant it would be a very good time to exit the newsroom. 'See you in a while. The Ginger Judge?'

'Done.'

On the drive down to town, a car pulled out in front of him and Dan hit the horn and swore. The man waved two fingers out of an open window as he drove off, and Dan responded in kind, winding down his window and shouting too. He surprised himself. He wouldn't normally react that sharply to something so petty, prided himself on rising above the chavvish and thuggish behaviour he was convinced was becoming more common.

He was angry with himself, he thought. He felt as though he had betrayed Rutherford. It didn't need to be that way. If he and Claire were going to have this baby, they'd have to buy a house big enough for the two of them, the child and Rutherford too. They could afford it. It might not be in the area they'd most like, but it would have to do.

That word again – if. If they were going to have this baby. What did he mean, if? Yesterday, it was when, not if. Was he thinking now they might make a different decision?

Dan braked hard as he realised the lights on a pedestrian crossing had turned red. He'd hardly noticed the drive into town. A young woman crossing the road held the hands of two young children. She shot him an accusing stare.

He passed the library where the joyriders had crashed. A vision of that knife formed again in his mind, but this time the man was pointing it at Claire's bulging stomach, the tip just inches from the distended flesh. She held up her hands, begging him not to harm the unborn child, but he was smiling, enjoying his power, edging the blade forwards, almost touching her skin. Dan saw himself watching, paralysed by the sight, unable to do anything, only look.

He reached out and turned on the radio, slid the volume up loud. Music boomed from the car's speakers. He tried to concentrate on it, follow the beat. Shut the thought out, anything to force it away.

Dan parked the car on the street behind the courts, got out and bought a ticket. The parking charges had gone up again and he cursed the council as he fumbled in his pocket for change. More red anger enveloped him at having to overpay by twenty pence. It was such a con, the machines not giving change, just another way to extort money from hapless motorists.

He had to sit on a bench for a couple of minutes to calm himself before he went to meet Adam. Dan counted the branches on the chestnut tree in the graveyard behind him and watched the snowy mountains of cloud drift past.

The detective was waiting in the corner of the Ginger Judge. Sarah had given them their usual table. Dan picked up a bunch of newspapers from the rack by the bar and sat down. He handed a couple to Adam and they leafed through. The blackmailer case was prominent in the headlines, this time accompanied by pictures of the plane and its banner superimposed on photographs of Osmond standing by his car.

All the pictures were credited to Ellis Hughes. Dan could imagine the photographer doing a little dance and improvising one of those strange limericks of his. He must have made thousands of pounds.

'Never a hint to anyone whatsoever about how you found out where Osmond lived,' whispered Adam. 'If word gets out that it came from me, it would be a sacking offence.'

'Don't worry,' said Dan. 'I won't let on. You've told me worse before and I've never said a word to anyone about where it's come from.'

He reminisced about some of the other tricks they'd pulled, not noticing Adam's growing frown.

'That stuff about the serial rapist for example, that was far, far worse,' Dan went on. 'And what happened to him, and why. That would have landed us in court if it'd ever come out ...'

Adam interrupted quickly. 'OK, enough said. I've been trying to forget about that, however much he deserved it.'

He sat back and ran his hand over the spread of newspapers. 'It worked, getting the picture of Osmond in the press. He's almost forgotten his complaint against me and is going for the newspapers instead. He's talking about suing them for breach of privacy.'

'How did the High Honchos react to him being on the news?'

The flicker of a smile crossed Adam's face. 'Remarkably calmly. I got a call from the Deputy Chief asking if I'd seen your report.'

'And?'

'I said I'd caught some of it.'

'What did he think?'

'He just said, "I suppose the media do what they do."'

'Which is true.'

'Yep.'

'And sounds like Osmond's got no great support from on high.'

'Yep. He's proving an embarrassment to the force, and quite a few of the High Honchos are young and ambitious, so I don't think I need worry too much about Osmond.'

Sarah bustled up and made a fuss of them, even complimenting Adam on his tie. She was a fine hostess, the kind you rarely got now. Most pubs were so industrial. You went in, ordered a beer or some food, sat, ate and drank and left. It was production line leisure, processing people without the input of any humanity. Having someone who knew your name and wanted to have a little chat made such a difference.

'Have you seen all that?' Sarah asked, pointing to the newspapers. 'What a scandal. Everyone's talking about it. Are you still working on the case?'

'Yep,' said Adam, sipping at his beer.

'Have you got him yet?'

'Not yet,' the detective replied. 'But I will.'

'Good,' replied Sarah, crouching down next to them. Her voice fell to a whisper. 'That poor Mr Osmond. He came in here a lot you know.'

'Really?' said Adam, suddenly sounding interested. 'Was he in over Christmas at all? Can you remember?'

Sarah gave him a mock frown. 'Of course. I remember all my customers. Yes, he came in several times over Christmas, usually with that lovely wife of his. And Mr Freedman too. A very kind man he was. Always left a good tip.'

'Really?' Adam replied. 'Look, don't take this the wrong way, but you might have some information which could be important. When the lunchtime rush is over, can we have a chat? I'd be interested to know who they were with, who was sitting near them, and what they were talking about.'

'Me? Some information?' Sarah sounded surprised. 'Of course, if I can help in any way I will.'

Adam nodded. 'After lunch though,' he said meaningfully. 'I'm starving.'

Sarah took the hint and brought them a pair of menus. Dan scanned through his, then got up to look at the Specials board behind the bar. Chicken pie, some salad that he edited from his sight, scallops and roast pig.

'That's an unusual description, Sarah,' he said. 'Roast pig?'

'All local and very popular, Dan. We serve it cold with chips or salad. But I'm afraid we're out of it.'

Another little irritant for his day, thought Dan. When life wasn't running your way it really did so with style. He ordered sausage and mash instead. Adam had another mixed grill. Brain food, he explained. Dan tried not to glance at his friend's stomach. He was sure Adam was putting on weight. It was something that often happened when he was in the middle of a big case. There was little spare time for healthy eating or exercise. It was remarkable how fast it could happen when you reached a certain age.

The bar was about half full, plenty of lawyers again, but more than a few lunching ladies too. The wooden floor was strewn with a minefield of shopping bags. The sounds of a busker blasting away on a harmonica drifted from outside.

Adam began talking about something to do with a family birthday he must remember to get a card for, but Dan couldn't quite concentrate on what he was saying. Something was bothering him, nagging at his consciousness, distracting his thoughts. Claire again? More guilt about Rutherford? He didn't think it was any of that, but the inkling wouldn't go away, sat annoyingly on the edge of his mind, just out of reach.

'Err, what, sorry?' he said.

'I said, I was thinking it could be useful, talking to Sarah,' repeated Adam, tapping the table to make Dan concentrate. 'The Worm might have somehow overheard conversations his victims were having. Perhaps he even found a way to bug them.'

Dan frowned. 'A bit far fetched, isn't it? How? Slip some sort of bug into a pocket, or bag? It sounds too Hollywood for me. And how do you choose the likely victims anyway, not to mention get close enough to them to do it?'

'Ah, you're probably right. I didn't really believe it. But I do think that if we can find the link between the victims we're almost there.'

'Sure. But where is the link? That's the problem, isn't it? We don't have a link between them, or not all three of them anyway.'

Adam sighed. 'Let's leave it for now. I could do with talking about something else.'

Sarah brought their food. People had been slipping in through the door in their ones and twos and the pub was almost full. Dan was amused to see almost all the lawyers had bottles of mineral water on their tables. It was the fashion of the moment, a politically correct eschewing of alcohol. He and Adam hadn't hesitated to get themselves a couple of pints of ale. He wondered if journalists and detectives would be the last to change. He certainly hoped so. For him, political correctness was a target for attack, never aspiration.

Delicious scented steam wafted up from their plates and again Dan felt his stomach growl. He reached into the hexagonal wooden pot, fixed to the side of the table, to get a knife and fork and handed a set to Adam. His own slipped from his grip and dislodged something in the pot so it hung from the inside lip.

Dan leaned over to see what it was. The object was tiny, a black plastic oblong, the size of a pen nib. A thin black wire trailed from it down to the bottom of the pot. He carefully traced the wire, then pushed a finger down on the base. It shifted slightly under his touch. He did it again and levered up the wood. It was a false bottom. Underneath was a small, metallic box, about half the size and thickness of a cigarette packet. The wire from the plastic oblong led into one side. A dot of green light glowed from its edge.

Dan stared at it, baffled. He knew well what it was, used one almost every day. It was a radio microphone, a low powered, short range transmitter ideal for a reporter to walk around and talk, unencumbered by cables, while a receiver on the back of the camera picked up his words.

He felt his body go cold and sat back, rigid on his chair. It was a feeling that had become so delightfully familiar, since he first experienced it, back on the Edward Bray case. The sacred Epiphany moment. From blank incomprehension to beautiful understanding in an instant.

Adam looked up from his plate. 'You OK?' he managed through a mouthful of pork chop. 'Not feeling hungry? You look pale.'

'I'm fine – just fine,' stammered Dan.

His mind spun, churning up ideas. He checked through them, again and again, kept probing, kept testing. Each time the answer came back the same. It made sense, he was sure of it. He was about to look round, say something to Adam, but stopped himself. Dan knew that if his vision was correct he had to cap his excitement and act naturally.

He forced himself to pick up his knife and fork and take a mouthful of mashed potato. He was vaguely aware it was hot, but didn't taste it. His eyes seemed unable to focus on the food. He kept staring at the cutlery pot. He made himself breathe deeply and try to be calm.

Dan allowed himself a casual look around the pub. There was no sign of Sarah. She was probably in the kitchens. Had she been in the pub when he and Adam were talking about the blackmail case earlier? When they'd discussed Osmond, or the rapist investigation? He didn't think so, but he couldn't be sure.

Was that as significant as he now thought it might be?

He cut off a piece of sausage and dunked it into the gravy. He had to tame his racing excitement or he'd give himself away.

'Mmm, good sausage,' he managed.

'Great mixed grill,' agreed Adam. 'Just what I needed.'

Dan looked back at the hexagonal wooden pot. Was what he was thinking right? Surely it was ridiculous. But didn't it add up?

He took a sip of his beer and ate some more mashed potato. A drip of gravy plopped onto the wooden table, but he didn't notice. Dan made himself think, slowly and carefully.

'You sure you're OK?' asked Adam, who was now attacking a chicken breast. 'You're not eating very fast.'

'Yeah, I'm fine. Just taking it easy and enjoying it.'

Dan stared at his food as the ideas tumbled through his mind. He looked around again, more carefully this time. Still no sign of Sarah. But that didn't necessarily mean anything. She could be in the kitchens, or looking after a delivery.

He craned his neck to see the Specials board. Roasted pig. It had been some ham dish when Linda had thrown herself from the cliff. And fried local shark when Freedman had killed himself. It was disgusting, crass, ridiculous, but – but, he was convinced he was right.

Two pigs and a fried shark. A sick gloat.

How was he going to tell Adam? He had to know and now, but without blowing it. If he was right, this was the moment they could catch the blackmailer in the act.

Dan chewed on another piece of sausage and swallowed. He fumbled in his satchel and found a piece of paper and a pen, began writing.

URGENT!! Say NOTHING, this is deadly serious. I think we're being BUGGED. Just keep eating and act normally, OK?

He checked around again. Still no hint of Sarah. Dan casually slipped the piece of paper across the table to Adam and ate some more mashed potato. The detective read it and looked up, his eyes widening. He frowned, tilted his head quizzically and Dan nodded slightly.

He took another sip of his beer and wrote more words.

Get a squad of cops here. Go OUTSIDE to do it. Make some excuse about remembering something urgent.

Adam read again and stared at him. Dan quickly scribbled more words.

URGENT! Trust me!! Do it NOW!

Adam finished a chunk of lamb, stood up.

'I've just remembered there's something I need to check on,' he said. 'I'm going outside to make a quick call.'

The detective walked out of the door and disappeared around the corner of the street. Dan tried to continue eating in what he hoped was a nonchalant manner. He felt as if he was being watched and struggled to resist the temptation to keep looking around. He scanned through one of the papers he'd taken from the rack, but couldn't concentrate on any of the stories. He noticed his hands were shaking.

Around him, life continued, oblivious. Lawyers gossiped, shoppers strolled by, the bar rumbled with a dozen different conversations. In a few moments, that would all change. If he was right.

If.

Adam walked back into the bar and sat down. 'Sorted,' he

said. 'Sorry about that. Now, where were we? Oh yes, that's what I meant to ask you. Annie said would like you to pop round for dinner one evening soon.'

He wrote, *3 cops, 5 mins, what we do when they arrive?* on the paper and slid it back over to Dan.

'Sure, that sounds good,' he replied. 'Work permitting, of course.'

Dan wrote, *Run out, pull them in here, follow me, do it fast* and slipped the paper back to Adam. He saw the detective flinch and grit his teeth. His look said – this had better be good.

'OK, work permitting of course,' Adam said lightly. 'When do you think is best?'

'Next week probably. This week looks busy.'

'How about a weekend? I can usually guarantee to have at least one day off, and that also gives Annie more time to cook. You can come play football with me and Tom for a bit too. He's getting too good for just me alone.'

'Erm, yeah, a weekend would probably be best,' Dan managed. 'Shall we go for the Saturday after this one? I don't think I've got anything planned.'

'Sure. I'll check with Annie when I get home.'

They stared at each other. Both had stopped eating and looked blank. Dan couldn't think of a thing to say. He could see Adam was having the same problem. In a career full of hollow conversations, desperately pretending to be interested in dull and pompous interviewees and filling time in outside broadcasts, this was probably the worst of all the charades.

'I'm not so keen on nuts,' Dan said finally. 'If Annie's cooking, that's the only thing I don't like.'

A police car drew up outside. Adam jumped up from his chair, walked quickly to the door and beckoned the officers in.

'Where's Sarah?' Dan asked the blonde young woman behind the bar.

'Upstairs, doing the books,' she said. 'Can I get her for you?'

'No, you stay there and don't move. Urgent police business. You'll be arrested if you try to contact her. Which way upstairs?'

186

The woman gulped, pointed hesitantly to a door at the end of the bar. Dan strode towards it and pushed it gently open. A flight of wooden stairs led upwards. He leaned in, listened for any movement, but there was no sound.

'What the hell are we doing?' asked Adam. The three police officers stood behind him, looking puzzled. Diners had stopped eating and were watching them. Heads turned. Fingers began to point. The bar had gone quiet. They had to move fast.

'I think we might have found your Worm,' said Dan quietly, looking at the stairs. He watched Adam's mouth slip slowly open. 'Up there.'

'You're joking.'

'Nope. Just a guess, but a decent one. The stairs are going to be noisy, so I suggest we rush it if you want to catch her in the act. You're the cop, you'd better go first.'

Adam looked at the stairs and loosened his tie. Around them the entire bar silently stared.

'Jesus, Dan! If you're wrong, we're going to look bloody fools at the very least. In fact, it'll probably be another complaint against me. Are you serious?'

Dan tried to keep his voice calm. 'I'm totally serious. And the longer we wait, the less likely we are to get her.'

Slow seconds slid past. In the bar a mobile phone rang, but went unanswered.

Adam let out a strange low groan, then beckoned to the police officers. He bounded up the stairs, taking them two at a time. Dan followed, feeling his heart start to race with the sudden effort. The officers tailed behind him, their heavy feet thumping and clattering on the bare wood.

They rounded a corner in the stairwell. It was half lit, curls of paint peeling, and it smelt musty. Ahead, Adam stumbled and bounced off a wall. He gasped, but didn't slow.

They emerged into a corridor, a worn old carpet stretching along the floor, a couple of doors either side. Both were closed. Through an open door further ahead they could see an unmade bed and a jumbled pile of clothes.

Adam didn't hesitate. He tried the door on the left. It opened easily and he lurched in. Some cardboard boxes, brown and dusty, a jumble of beer pumps and piping, a ramshackle pile of files. An old fruit machine. A mirror, grey with cobwebs filled with their panting, sweating reflections.

Adam scanned the room, then spun around and pushed at the other door. It opened and he strode through. Dan followed, just feet behind. The room was gloomy, some old carpet rolled up in a corner, more cardboard boxes. They were full of crisps, a range of exotic flavours, all chilli and curry. Above the boxes he saw a table at the far end, right in the corner.

Sitting there, wearing a pair of headphones and bent over a notebook, was Sarah. She looked up at them. They stared at each other, just stared. The room was silent, still.

Slow seconds ticked past. Dan felt himself tense, preparing for the fight, ready for her to try to run. He quickly checked behind him. The line of cops was there, waiting. There were no other exits. There was nowhere for her to go.

She was trapped. They had her. They'd caught their blackmailer.

Still the quiet enveloped them. Still Sarah stared. Dan couldn't read her expression, wondered what she was going to do. The frozen moment stretched on.

Then, at last, she broke it, in a way they could never have expected.

Sarah's face stretched into a great, beaming smile, and she burst out laughing.

Chapter Seventeen

NEVER HAD DAN SEEN someone so delight in her crimes.

He wondered if the interview room, with all its long experience of a parade of criminals, from the most minor of shoplifters and graffiti artists, to some of the most notorious murderers the South-west had seen, could ever have known such an extraordinary series of ecstatic outpourings.

Sarah sat at the small wooden table, fixed firmly to the floor by thick metal bolts, and looked perfectly relaxed. Sometimes she leaned forwards and laced her fingers together, at others she leant back on the chair and crossed her legs. There was none of the slumped despair Dan had seen here so many times before, nor the screamed or snarled abuse of rage and fear.

The room was in the basement of Charles Cross, the only natural light a pathetic seepage from the small barred and opaque rectangular glass window, high up on the far wall. A fluorescent tube cast a sterile, flickering green-edged glow directly over the table and stretched grey shadows around it.

The floor was grainy with its brushed concrete, the walls cheaply whitewashed brick, fading and rallying in random patches of shade and light. Words echoed back and forth from the stark interior like secret whispers, passing on the details of the interrogation. The room was never anything other than cold, even on the hottest of days. It felt forsaken, the start of a journey that led inevitably to prison, usually for long years, sometimes for life.

It was a place designed for despair. But not today.

Sarah had readily confessed and seemed to be enjoying immensely the chance to explain how and why she'd carried out her plan. She'd laughed at Adam's question about whether she felt any guilt for the two people who had killed themselves because of what she'd done. It was another wild outburst of rocking, near hysterical laughter, which had left Adam nonplussed and made the detective leave the room to take a break before he went on with his questioning.

The Custody Sergeant had raised the question of whether Sarah was mentally ill. Adam sighed, added a couple of creative profanities and some of his forthright opinions about the law being more interested in the villain than victim, but reluctantly agreed to Silifant being called.

The doctor talked to Sarah for half an hour, then emerged from the cell with his verdict.

'She's perfectly fine. She's just enjoying her moment. There's a bit of release of tension at being caught, but that's perfectly natural. Common reaction.' He'd rolled his bloodshot eyes at Adam and added, 'Since this time you haven't managed to present me with your traditional options of efficiency of death or degree of pain to mark, I'll give you eight out of ten on the pointless call-out scale.'

The doctor was gone before Adam could find a rejoinder.

Dan stood by the door in the corner of the room, Adam sat at the table opposite Sarah. A recording machine, built into the wall beside him, clicked softly. Sarah yawned, making Adam look up from his notes.

'So where's this Judgement Book, Sarah?' he asked.

'I can't tell you that, Adam,' she replied calmly.

'Why not? It's all over. You might as well tell us.'

She leaned back from the table and angled her head.

'That's rather a sweeping assumption, isn't it? That it's all over.'

'Isn't it?'

'We'll have to wait and see. You never know what the Judgement Book might do next. It's filled with depravity. And that makes it very dangerous.'

'How many other people's secrets are in there, Sarah?'

'I can't tell you that either.'

'Why not?'

'Because it would spoil the fun. You've got the clues to find it. I suggest you keep trying.'

'But we've only got three, and there are supposed to be five, aren't there? And as you're here, there aren't going to be any more of your poisonous little notes. So why don't you just tell us? I can make sure the judge knows and it goes in your favour when you're sentenced.'

'Another sweeping assumption, Adam. That there aren't going to be any more notes.'

'But how can there be? Have you left something behind? Did you plan to get caught?'

'We'll have to wait and see.'

Adam sighed heavily. 'You're not making this any easier for yourself, Sarah. You're facing a long prison sentence, you know. We can make it as short as possible if you cooperate.'

'I'm relaxed about my fate, Adam. I think I've achieved something.'

'What?'

'A little justice. Probably more so than you do in your job.'

'By driving people to kill themselves?'

Now, for the first time, Sarah's voice rose. 'Osmond isn't dead, is he? Would you have uncovered his crimes? I don't think so. What happened to the others was not expected, but in a way they've purged themselves. Wouldn't you say we're better off without lying, hypocritical perverts like Freedman?'

Adam's voice hardened too. 'What about Linda Cott? She was a colleague of mine. A good woman with a fine reputation.'

'I don't think you know her very well at all, Adam, do you? Don't you believe what I put in her little note?'

'We haven't recovered your note to Linda yet. What was it you had over her?'

'I thought you said you had three of the clues, Adam?'

'She left us the answer, but not the note. What was it you taunted her with that was too horrible for her to let us see, Sarah?'

'I'll wait for you to work that one out, Adam. But I can guarantee you'll find the answer shocking.'

Silence. Adam glared at her, then sighed again and sat forwards so he was just inches from Sarah's face. Dan could see the detective's neck reddening, a sure sign he was angry and struggling to control it.

'We know how you got Osmond, Sarah. You bugged a conversation between him and his wife, while they were having a meal in the Judge.'

'Well done, Adam,' she said condescendingly. 'Very good.'

'When he drove home again, despite being well over the limit. It wasn't the first time, was it? And when his wife tried to stop him, he shouted her down, saying if he was stopped he could always make sure the cop concerned turned a blind eye. Just like the last time.'

'Very good indeed Adam. That's exactly right. So I challenge you to tell me we're not better off with Osmond being exposed for what he is. And who would have done it if I hadn't? Would you?'

Adam ignored the question. 'Is that how you got the others too? How many tables did you bug, Sarah? You couldn't do all of them, surely?'

'Two was enough Adam. The two best tables in the place. You see, that's the great thing about the pompous. They always want the best table.'

'We know how you got Osmond. What about Freedman?'

She smiled. 'It's all so painfully predictable Adam. He came in for a meal with an old friend. They had a few too many drinks and like little boys started boasting about some of the things they'd done. He spewed out the whole tale about the schoolgirl prostitute beautifully. He could hardly contain his excitement.'

'And Linda Cott? She came in to the Judge as well?'

'Yes indeed, Adam.'

'And what did she talk about that you used against her?'

'Good try, but we've discussed that. It's up to you to find out.'

'Come on, Sarah, it hardly matters now. Linda's dead and we've caught you. You might as well tell us.'

'Not yet, Adam. Let's say it's another of the riddles you have to solve.'

Adam sighed again, but kept his voice calm. 'I'll ask you this then. How many people are in your Judgement Book, Sarah?'

'You know, Adam, I've lost count. Quite a few. It seems everyone has their little secrets. Even I was surprised how fast the Book became gorged. You'll know when you find it. You might get a few surprises too. It's quite a read.'

Sarah was nodding now, the smile growing on her face. There was something wrong, Dan sensed it. She was too sure of herself, too confident.

Adam stared at her. A vein ticked angrily in his cheek. 'Like what? What surprises?'

She raised her eyebrows. 'Just think about yourself, Adam. You always wanted the best table too, didn't you? Loose talk about breaking the law to catch a rapist, giving away the address of a senior police officer to get him off your tail ... that kind of thing can cause you real trouble. I would have thought an experienced detective like yourself would have known better.'

Dan caught his breath. He waited for the reaction from Adam. He could see his friend was surprised, but was trying not to show it.

'And you too, Dan Groves,' Sarah added, looking over at him. 'You've conspired with Adam here in ways which wouldn't do your professional reputation any good, would they? I doubt you could carry on as a journalist if the public knew how close you were to the police and how they use you. Not that you seem to mind. You play along very happily. In fact ... some of the little schemes are all down to you, aren't they?'

Dan didn't know what to say. He glanced at Adam.

'That's enough of your crap, Sarah,' the detective spat, sitting back on his chair and placing his hands on his hips. 'You have nothing against us, and we are not part of this investigation. Now, back to where this bloody book is.'

Sarah shook her head, the smile never slipping. 'You know, you might just come to find you are a part of the investigation, Adam. What a lovely twist to the story it would be if both you and Dan were in the Judgement Book. You've had enough intimate conversations in the Ginger Judge to qualify yourselves eminently, haven't you?'

Adam jumped up from his chair. It screeched backwards and looked about to topple over. He shot out a fast hand, caught it, leaned forwards, into her face.

'Enough of your crap, Sarah. This is over.' His finger jabbed out at her, but she didn't flinch. 'You're caught, you're going to jail for a bloody long time, and there'll be no more of your sick little notes.'

Sarah leaned back on her chair, laced her hands behind her head. She gave him a knowing wink.

'We'll see, Adam, eh? We'll see.'

They walked upstairs to the canteen for a cup of coffee. Dan's mind wouldn't let go of what Sarah had said. He tried desperately to remember exactly what he and Adam had talked about in the Judge.

They'd mentioned the rapist case, but in enough detail for her to know what they meant? He couldn't avoid the conclusion the answer was yes. And what had they discussed during the other times they'd been in? Osmond certainly, and that was enough to end Adam's career. She was right about Dan's future too. If it all got out, his credibility would be destroyed. Lizzie would be forced to sack him.

Adam was striding hard up the stairs, taking them two at a time. 'Bloody woman,' he grunted under his breath. 'Cold, callous, scheming bloody woman.'

He sat down at the canteen table furthest from the door. Dan took the hint and got the drinks.

'There you go, two coffees,' he said, sitting beside Adam.

'Bloody woman,' the detective growled again. 'She got to me there and I should never let that happen. I hadn't thought she could have anything on me.'

'On us.'

Adam looked up from his drink. 'Yes,' he said, more gently. 'On us. Sorry.'

They sipped at their drinks. Adam began picking little semicircles from the paper rim of his cup.

'She's bluffing,' said Dan finally. He knew his voice sounded more hopeful than convincing. 'She's in here, locked up. What else can she do?'

'I'd like to think you're right,' Adam replied. 'But she's planned this bloody well so far. And she's been ahead of us all the way. It was only luck and your weird imagination that got her. I can't help but think she must have had a plan in case she was caught. Look at the clues and taunts she left for us. Fried shark and pigs! Evil bloody woman.'

Dan hesitated to ask, but knew he had to. 'Like what? What kind of plan?'

'I have no idea.' Adam stood up, straightened his jacket. 'But I'm going to find out. Let's go and talk to her again. And this time, no being sidetracked by her taunts.'

They found Sarah standing by the tiny opaque window, staring up at it.

'Saying goodbye to the world for a few years?' asked Adam, sitting back at the table. 'We can make that time as short as possible if you start cooperating with us.'

She turned and again smiled at him, but this time more wistfully.

'You know, I'm really not sure I'll miss it out there. It's a rotten place. If you'd heard all that I have over the past few months, you'd wonder if there were any decent people left. Everyone carries an invisible stain, Adam. It comes from their moment of submission to their weakness. And it lives with them in disgust, or regret, or rage. I think I've come to see it in people's faces now. Everyone's marked with it.'

'Is that how long it's been going on, Sarah? Your listening in to people's conversations? Months?'

'Yes, Adam, I can tell you that. It's been going on for months.'

'Ever since you've been running the Ginger Judge?'

'Not quite. A little while after that.'

'Why?'

Sarah looked at Adam, then back out of the window. She stretched up a hand to touch the thick, dusty glass.

'Why?' asked Adam again. 'What started it all?'

'I don't think I can tell you that yet. You'll know soon enough.'

'Is that a threat?'

'No, no. Just a fact. I'll happily tell you when the time is right.'

Adam looked over at Dan, tilted his head towards Sarah. He walked to the table and stood beside the detective.

'Is it an establishment thing, Sarah?' Dan asked. 'I remember one conversation when you talked about how difficult it was to be in business with all the regulations the government heaped on you. As far as I can see, all your victims have been establishment figures. So is that what it's all about? Hitting back?'

She turned to look at him. 'I was wondering when you were going to chip in, Dan. I know from your conversations how much Adam relies on you. While we're talking about memories, I recall one time when he told you that you were much better at the psychological bit than he was. The understanding why people do the things they do. So is it my turn to be the subject of your famous insights? You certainly do have that knack of making people talk to you. I felt it myself on a couple of occasions and had to be careful about going too far.'

Dan breathed out hard, swallowed to calm himself. 'I'm just interested, Sarah,' he said neutrally. 'It's part of my job to understand.'

'I'm flattered, Dan. But then, I suppose I'm going to be the subject of some of your reports now. Shall I consider this two interviews in one then? A criminal one from Adam and a journalist's one from you?'

Dan heard Adam snort.

'I'm just interested, Sarah,' he said again. 'It was an establishment thing, wasn't it?'

She shifted her position, leaned back against the hard, whitewashed wall.

'Yes, Dan, your wonderful insight is right. It was an establishment thing. But it was a little more than that. I could have taken what the government did to me if it wasn't for something else that happened one night.'

And now her voice was tense, strained, and Dan knew he was on the verge of discovering something important. He held her look. Her eyes were soft, misty. She was somewhere else, lost in the comfort of a favourite memory.

He let the moment run, then gently prompted, 'What was it,

196

Sarah?'

She stared at him, then down at the concrete floor. Seconds drifted by, but Dan kept quiet. The old trick, the one he'd used so many times in interviews.

The power of silence.

He stood still, waited. Finally, Sarah looked back up, said softly, 'Nice try, Dan. You almost got me … almost. But I'll leave you to think on that one. You'll find out soon enough how it all began.'

Through the glass windows of the Ginger Judge, Dan could see three white-overalled forensics officers unscrewing a table. Another pair checked the walls for wires, leads and any possible hiding places. They'd been called in as soon as Sarah was arrested. The trouble was they didn't know what they were looking for. A modern day Judgement Book could be small or large and it might not even be a book, just a memory stick, a CD, or a file on a computer's memory.

Adam stood outside and talked to the head technician, a small, reedy young man called Crispin. He seemed nervous, continually pushing his glasses up his nose. Adam explained he'd been newly promoted and this was his first time in charge of a crime scene. He would have preferred a straightforward burglary or mugging, but this was a high profile and complex case and it was making him edgy.

A small crowd of people had gathered to watch. Adam was about to have the street closed off when Dan interrupted.

'Could you wait half an hour?'

'A story?' the detective asked wearily.

'Yep. There's no way this won't get out. Give me half an hour and I can get Nigel and El here. I'll have exclusive pictures for tonight and El will get the story in the papers for tomorrow. You can put out a message that you're making progress with the case. It'll play well with the public and your High Honchos.'

Adam straightened his impeccable tie, asked coyly, 'And I suppose you'd like an interview with me too?'

'Yes please.'

'Half an hour only then.'

Dan almost smiled. He found himself wondering if Adam recorded his TV appearances, to preserve them for posterity. It wasn't beyond the detective's vanity.

He made the calls. El arrived, panting, twenty-five minutes later. He didn't even say hello, just raised his camera, loosed off some shots and then flopped heavily down on the pavement.

'Had to run all the way from the top of town,' he gasped, between breaths. 'Doing a job on a bloke who's suing the hospital after his wife died in there. She only had an in-growing toenail. Bloody car wouldn't start.'

He caught his breath and panted out a rhyme.

'It's rare to get Dirty El to run,
But he'll do it if he sniffs out some fun,
And for this blackmailer,
He won't want to fail 'er,
'coz he knows he can make some good mon–'

El waited for a few seconds, then added the missing 'ey'.

Dan pursed his lips. The paparazzo's latest masterpiece defied comment.

When Nigel had finished filming the forensics team, they interviewed Adam. He sounded positive about the arrest and search of the bar, but made it clear the case wasn't yet over. Dan again found himself wondering what Sarah could possibly do from a cell in Charles Cross. Nothing, he reassured himself. Just simply nothing. Those claims about exposing him and Adam were pure bluff, the ranting of a criminal bitter at having been caught. The case was over.

He couldn't quite convince himself. She had sounded very sure.

After that last interview with her Adam had given up, said they were getting nowhere. They'd left her in a cell, sitting on the thin, padded mattress, still wearing that whimsical smile. As the heavy steel door closed, they'd both looked back. Through the narrowing gap, Sarah had waved.

Dan checked his watch. Almost four o'clock it said, so probably about ten past. He waited outside the Judge for another hour. The forensics teams had nearly finished and he wanted the latest news to put on air. So long as he left by quarter past five he'd have at least an hour to get the story together.

He could get it edited in less, but it was always a delicate balance. The longer you left yourself, the more time there was for thought and a well-considered script. Only the reckless went for last-minute edits when they could be avoided. Besides, it wasn't good for the heart. He had to look after himself. In future, he would have responsibilities, the most important a man could know. That was if they decided to have the baby, of course.

That word again. If.

Dan's mobile rang, a welcome interruption to his thoughts. It was Lizzie and she was fizzing. He held the phone a little away from his ear as it buzzed with her voice. He didn't have a chance to get a word in until the hurricane that was his editor in full flow had abated.

'There's some kind of police raid at a pub in town. It's to do with the blackmailer case. The cops are ripping the place apart, apparently. What's the good of you being part of the inquiry if we don't get these things? The pictures sound fantastic! Really dramatic! I need them! I want them! I want to lead the show with them tonight. I want you on it at once! I want interviews. I want you live in the studio to talk about it. I want you moving! Now!'

Dan savoured the moment. Ah, the rare and sweet delight of being ahead of the game for once. He waited, waited, waited, delighted in the heady anticipation.

It was like the coming of the time to open a bottle of vintage wine, one you'd been saving for countless years.

The phone squawked again. 'Dan? Dan?! Dan?!! Are you there?'

Another beautiful pause as he wondered which weapon of choice to employ. Indignation? Hurt? Irritation? Under-statement, he thought. It would be a fine and effective counterpoint to Lizzie's tirade.

Quietly and calmly Dan said, 'I'm already here. We've got all the pictures. We've been here for a few hours, in fact. Got an interview too. All exclusive to us – naturally.'

It was interesting how edifying a silence could be. That was all he heard in return, a first for Lizzie. 'I'll be back at the studios in 15 minutes,' Dan added and hung up.

He had another quick word with Adam first. The search teams had found the two bugging systems, in the best tables in the house, just as Sarah said.

They were both radio microphones and both in the cutlery pots, linked to a receiver upstairs. There was a small digital recorder too, capable of storing hundreds of hours of conversations, but it was blank. The technicians thought it had been erased recently. Dan grimaced when Adam told him. Had it held the chat they'd had over lunch? And what others?

Adam believed the recorder was to keep a log of the conversations Sarah didn't have time to listen to when potential victims were in the bar. She probably sat down and checked them later, wrote up the most compromising parts in the Judgement Book before the recordings were erased.

A mobile phone was also found. Initial investigations indicated Sarah had been using it just before the raid in which she'd been caught. A couple of officers from the Square Eyes technical division had been assigned to find out who she'd rung and why. That was their most urgent line of inquiry, Adam said. He looked worried.

Dan well understood why. The call must have been made just after they'd been discussing how Adam had directed him to Osmond's house, and how previously they'd broken the law to catch a serial rapist. Were they such powerful snippets of information that Sarah couldn't resist passing them on? Quickly and gleefully, as excellent blackmail material. And if so, who had she passed them to? Dan tried to push Adam to talk about it, but the detective wouldn't. He seemed preoccupied, lost in his thoughts.

The teams had searched the bar and the upper floor, but there was no sign of anything that might be the Judgement Book. There was one oddity. A file of cuttings on the Iraq War and the death of a peace activist in Baghdad. Dan felt his imagination stir, but didn't have time to think about it further.

He had to get the story on air. He agreed with Adam what he could report and drove back to the studios.

He wondered whether to talk to Lizzie about turning the report into an edited package rather than him being live in the studio, but decided against it. Once set on a strategy, she wasn't easily dissuaded. It was like trying to talk a torpedo into changing course. Plus, it wouldn't do any harm to appear in person to claim obvious ownership of the exclusive.

Dan sat at the news desk, suffered the attentions of the floor manager as she clipped on a microphone, puffed some make up powder onto his face. At first, your macho instincts resisted it, but it made such a difference, stopped your skin shining distractingly in the inevitable sweat of nerves. It was especially important if your hairline was receding, as Dan had finally acknowledged – with great reluctance and annoyance – that his had begun to.

Lights flared in the metal trellis rigging of the roof and the thundering drumbeats of the title music played. Dan felt the familiar shot of adrenaline of live broadcasting, the knowledge of half a million people watching him. Craig turned to one of the cameras and introduced the story.

'We begin tonight with another exclusive on the blackmailer case,' he said. 'The police have raided a Plymouth bar and made an arrest which they describe as highly significant. Our crime correspondent Dan Groves is with us.'

Dan talked about the search of the Ginger Judge for equipment that might be used to eavesdrop on conversations and the arrest of a member of staff. Nigel's pictures ran as he commentated. Then there was a clip of Adam's interview, the detective being cautiously optimistic that this was an important breakthrough. Dan summed up with a little of the background to the case.

At the meeting after the programme, Lizzie professed herself "reasonably pleased", quite an accolade. It was one notch below the current absolute peak of her praise, an unqualified "pleased". That was reserved for exclusives of the quality of the revelation of alien life, or proof of the existence of God. She'd never understood the meaning of the word wholehearted.

In the excitement of the raid, Sarah's arrest and questioning, Dan realised he'd hardly thought about Claire or their baby. But now the image was back with him, playing football in the park with his son. It was raining, but the two of them didn't care. They were belting the ball at each other as they took it in turns to go in goal, shouting and laughing as they floundered in the morass of mud.

So, they were going to have the child again, then. What was going on in his mind that one minute they would be proud parents, the next not? They had to talk about it.

Dan fished his mobile from his pocket and called Claire. Good timing, she was almost finished at work and was about to head home. He'd tend to Rutherford and take him for a quick walk if she would pick up a Chinese take-away. As he slipped some clothes, shoes and shampoo into a bag, a sudden nervousness hit him. He didn't want to think why.

Claire unwrapped the plastic containers and spread them out over the coffee table. Dan stared at the colours of the chicken, beef and pork and realised he didn't feel at all hungry. He picked at the food and noticed she was doing the same. They weren't even drinking the glasses of red wine she'd poured, hers another conspicuously small measure. They sat side by side on her sofa and made small talk about how their days had been, the state of the investigation and Rutherford until he couldn't take it any more.

Dan put down his plate. 'This is ridiculous. We might as well just get on and talk.'

She turned to him and nodded. Her eyes were full of tears and her lips trembled. She reached out, cuddled into his neck and held him close. He felt the trembles of her sobs shiver through him.

Dan held her and stroked her hair until the crying had subsided. She sat back and looked at him, dabbed at her eyes.

'I'm sorry,' she said softly. 'I'm so sorry. I just don't know what to do. I'm not used to feeling like this.'

Dan took her hand. He weaved his fingers into hers.

'I don't know either. What can we do?'

'There are two options,' she said, after a pause. 'And I'm frightened of both.'

'Me too.'

She began crying again and he reached out and held her. Her voice was muffled by his body.

'I'm sorry, so very sorry,' she sobbed once more, the words tumbling out. 'I just don't know what to do. I hate the idea of an abortion, but I don't know if I'm ready to have a baby. I don't know where we'd live, or how we'd cope. I don't know what it might do to my career, or yours. I'm worried it might force us apart, whatever we do.'

Dan squeezed her shoulders, then sat back and took her face in his hands. He unfolded another tissue from the box. It was almost empty. There's been too much crying lately, he thought.

He dried her eyes. 'We'll work something out.' Even to him, the words sounded hollow.

She managed a weak smile and nodded. He knew she didn't believe it either. Her eyes were full of doubt.

'I know we will,' she said. 'I just feel so tired and unsure of myself. I'm all lost and helpless. Whenever I think I've made a decision, all these doubts crowd in on me and I start to change my mind again.'

'Me too. I keep thinking about having a son, then wondering how on earth we'd cope.'

'Or a daughter.'

'Or a daughter.'

'I keep imagining taking her to the hairdressers for her first proper styling. She's so bouncy and excited. She's got hair like yours.'

'I play football with him in the park. He's so full of life, always smiling.'

They cuddled back together. Outside a car raced past, hot tyres squealing in protest.

'So what are we going to do?' asked Claire finally.

Dan took a deep breath and slowly let it out. He stared at the window and the darkening sky outside. A cloud bank was gathering in the western sky, a solid line of shadow creeping across the land, its base tinted orange by the lights of the city.

'I just don't know. All I can come up with is that it's best if we have a few more days to think about it. With everything that's going on in the blackmailer investigation I'm not sure I can cope with anything else. Can we leave it a couple of days, then talk again?'

Claire cupped her hands over her stomach, gazed down and rubbed it.

'I don't want to leave it too long. I just can't. I can feel the baby growing inside me. The longer we wait, the harder it'll get.'

'Yes, of course. Just a couple of days. Let's leave it for now and try to relax. I'll see if there's a film on the TV.'

They cuddled up on the sofa and watched a documentary about Emperor penguins. Neither of them saw it. It could just as well have been a blank screen. Then they went to bed.

Dan was surprised at how well he slept. But in a dream, just before he awoke, again he saw the joyrider's knife poised above Claire's swollen stomach.

Chapter Eighteen

THE DAY BEGAN BADLY and only got worse.

'Two more blackmail notes, the two final clues to the bastards' riddle,' said Adam grimly. 'And with a little twist this time. Note I say bastards, plural. There's another worm. Sarah's got an accomplice. No wonder she was so sure of herself yesterday.'

Eight o'clock, Wednesday morning, the Major Incident Room at Charles Cross. Dan leant wearily on the window sill, Claire stood at the front beside Adam, Eleanor and Michael sat on a pair of desks. There was no banter, no chat. They'd believed, or at least dared to hope, the case was over with the arrest of Sarah. Now, this cold deflation.

Dan ran his tongue over a small but painful ulcer which had formed on the inside of his lower lip. It stung enthusiastically and he winced. Tiredness and stress, the classic causes.

'Bastards,' growled Adam again. He kept pacing up and down beside the felt boards, looking haggard. He'd shaved sloppily again with the shadow of a beard shading patches on his face.

'Everyone listening? Right! Today we work this until we've cracked it. I've had enough of these bloody riddles and being sodded about. We've got all the victims now, we've got the last two clues and we've got Sarah in custody. We've got all the info we need. So let's get to it.'

Dan took a sip of the canteen coffee. It tasted foul, worse even than usual. They always made it overly strong and he usually avoided it, but today he wondered if he might need the caffeine's help. He tried to stop working his tongue over the ulcer. The coffee had made it throb and his eyes watered. The ulcer was busy justifying one of the laws of dentistry. Small was not beautiful, but painful.

'Right,' said Adam again. 'An hour ago, at around seven o'clock, a despatch rider called at two locations in Plymouth, one a barracks, the other an office. He brought a letter to each.

The person named on the envelope was fetched, read their letter, then both immediately rang us. Forensics are looking at the letters to see what they can tell us. Copies are being made and will be with us in a few minutes. For now, I'll tell you about our new victims.'

He turned and pinned a couple of pieces of paper on separate boards. They were covered in scrawled writing, mostly capital letters.

'First, Major Anthony Robinson of the Royal Dragoons. The letter was delivered to their barracks in Stonehouse. He's a 47-year-old officer, who has been in the forces for just over 20 years, married, with two children. He's often eaten and had a few drinks in the Ginger Judge. He also served in the Iraq War. That may come to be a very important connection.'

Dan nodded to himself. The sheaf of cuttings the search teams had found at the Judge were all about Iraq. There were hundreds of them. He sensed a pattern emerging.

'The other victim is Steven Sinclair,' continued Adam. 'He's 39 years old, single, and, as you'll no doubt know, a prominent powerbroker in the Greater Wessex Strategic Assembly. He confirms the Ginger Judge is a place he regularly goes to entertain VIPs or important contacts. Ironically, he says they favoured it as it was seen as somewhere you could hold a sensitive conversation without the danger of being overheard. Both our victims deny the allegations against them, but I'm working on the basis they're true.'

Adam paused and stared around the room. He lowered his voice, and Dan leaned forwards, straining to hear.

'We have two very high profile victims. And as you'll see in a minute, the blackmailers have raised the stakes significantly. We need to get on top of this immediately. Everyone got that?'

A couple of heads nodded, but no one spoke. The door rattled with a gentle knock. 'Come in,' growled Adam impatiently.

A woman walked hesitantly in carrying an armful of sheets of paper. Adam didn't thank her and she left hurriedly. Dan began reading the first of his two sheets. The style was familiar.

Dear Major Robinson,

You are a despicable man. Like many of your kind, you pretend to be one thing in public, when the private reality is very different.

You are an accessory to murder, and quite possibly a murderer yourself. That, despite your fine talk of peacekeeping, restoring law and order in a foreign country, democracy and respect. You are utterly odious.

I know what happened in Iraq. Your troops were sick to death of the abuse they suffered. The endless taunting, the rocks and stones hurled at them, not to mention the petrol bombs, the gunfire and, of course, the booby-trapped explosives by the side of the road. Basra wasn't a comfortable posting, was it?

But your job was to keep the lads in line. However much you understood their frustrations, you had to maintain discipline. There could be no revenge and no retaliation. Even after that ambush that claimed the life of one of your young dragoons and left two more badly injured.

So, what happened, Major Robinson? Was it your idea of retribution, as well as your troops? Or did you merely think it would be cathartic, to let them vent their frustration, and so you turned a blind eye? Those two poor Iraqi lads, caught by your boys after throwing stones at them. They couldn't have been more than about fourteen or fifteen, could they?

There was no one about. A little beating wouldn't hurt. It might teach them a lesson. So you managed not to notice while your boys set about them. It was just bad luck that one of them died, wasn't it, Major Robinson?

You didn't take part yourself. But nonetheless, you are complicit. You let the lads get on with it with your tacit approval. And later, you said you understood. I can't quite decide if that makes you a killer or not. Well, we can leave that to a court martial. But we can certainly call you an accessory to murder.

So, Major, we have established you are a thoroughly despicable man. The question is, what do I intend to do about it?

You'll know by now about your predecessors in the Judgement Book, and what has become of them. The news has been full of it.

You have a chance to save yourself. I will set you a code to crack, but it is not just in your interests that you do so. The answer to your riddle, together with the other I set this morning, will lead you to the hiding place of the Judgement Book. If you do not find it by seven o'clock tomorrow evening I will release its location to the media.

For the unlucky journalists who don't get the original book, I will make sure copies are posted on the internet. I can assure you it will cause a wonderful and long-remembered scandal. I have lost count of the number of well-known people whose actions The Book describes, and the depravity of their conduct.

Here is your code. As a clue, I say this – it is very different from those which have gone before, but try a hunch, urchin. If you do, it may have the answer.

Good luck.

Dan put down the piece of paper and swallowed hard. The ulcer was throbbing. He caught Adam's look and knew exactly what his friend was thinking. Were they both in the Judgement Book? Dan took another sip of the coffee. He barely noticed it was almost cold.

He stared at the final two lines of the letter. There were no numbers, no figures, as there had been in the other two blackmail letters. So where was the damn code?

His mind flapped at it, but came up with nothing. Dan allowed himself a quiet groan, then tried to breathe deeply, find some calm. He picked up the next photocopied sheet and began to read.

Dear Mr Sinclair,
You are a despicable man. Like many of your kind,
you pretend to be one thing in public, when the
private reality is very different.
You are corrupt. That, despite your fine talk of
fairness and honesty, of building a better region,
good homes for local people, a bustling economy and
a community everyone can be proud of. You have
your hand in the till. You are utterly odious.
I know what happened with the Western Approaches
offshore wind farm. What a fine idea that is, so
important to help us meet our renewable energy
needs. Who could oppose your excellent vision? But
then, who else knows about the sizeable extension to
your own home that the company kindly built in
gratitude for being awarded the contract?
So, what happened, Mr Sinclair? What went wrong?
Did the power corrupt you? Well, you certainly
wouldn't be alone in that. I've seen so many
examples of it now.
So, Mr Sinclair, we have established you are a
thoroughly despicable man. The question is, what do
I intend to do about it?

Dan compared the end of the letter with the previous sheet. It was the same, apart from the riddle.

I predict this clue will give you the most trouble –.
See have mind good land, Plymouth.

Dan put down the sheet and looked around. All the faces were engrossed in what they were reading. Heads were shaking. There were a couple of intakes of breath at the blackmailer's words.

He rubbed at his eyes, blinked hard. He wasn't sleeping well, but that was hardly surprising given all that was going on. Dan took off his jacket; he felt oddly warm, despite the cool of the day. It was a graphite morning, the sky a dome of glowering cloud, ominous with the threat of the coming rain.

Outside, he heard a shout, then another. On the steps below some photographers were clustered around a police officer, reporters yelling questions at him. The man struggled through the pack, jogged in to the entrance. Adam swore under his breath. His mobile rang and he walked to the corner of the MIR to answer it.

His gesturing said it wasn't a pleasant conversation. The odd phrase drifted across the room. 'Yes, sir, I know the world's media are all over us. Yes, I know it's getting ridiculous. Yes, I am confident of getting a result. Yes, sir, it will be as soon as possible.'

Adam put the phone away, walked back over. His face was flushed. 'Deputy Chief Constable, keen for a breakthrough,' he explained, with impressive understatement. 'So let's see if we can give him one. OK then, what do we make of these notes?'

Claire studied her sheets. 'Clearly an accomplice, sir. Someone who shares Sarah's views on authority.'

'So we're looking for another embittered person,' said Adam.

'And smart too,' added Dan. 'Those two letters are both well written and follow exactly the same format as the other notes. We've got two clever people working closely together.'

'Any reason to suspect more than two?' Adam asked. 'We've been surprised by one accomplice – blackmailers normally work alone. Any thoughts there may be more?'

'No,' replied Eleanor. 'The more people involved, the greater the risk. That's the problem with conspiracies. This smacks of two like-minded people working together.'

'Agreed,' Adam said, sitting down on a desk. 'Eleanor, what do you make of the codes?' he added.

She studied her pieces of paper and bunched her flowing skirt. Irises today, Dan thought, although he wasn't quite sure. He'd never been great on flowers. That gave him an idea. Perhaps he should buy a bouquet for Claire. The gesture would say a lot. He couldn't remember ever having bought her flowers before.

'Well, the first one doesn't fit the pattern we've seen before, of giving us numbers. But I've got a couple of ideas. I'm guessing it's fairly simple, if my hunch is right. Which, like before, makes me suspect it might be designed to be broken easily. The second one I think will be much more difficult. It looks like it's intended to take us longer, probably because it's the vital clue in the sequence of five, the one that gives us the location of the book.'

'Which fits in with what you thought before,' Claire observed. 'The first riddle, Freedman's, was tough, to make sure he could be exposed and to start this whole thing going. The next three were easier, because they didn't matter so much. The final one is hard too, as it's the most important of all.'

'Because they want to release the Judgement Book,' Dan said. 'Despite their claims about giving us a chance. And this provides their little justification for doing so – that we couldn't solve the final riddle.'

'And taunting us all the way, and intensifying the pressure on us as much as they possibly can,' Claire concluded.

Adam let out a long breath. 'Get cracking then, Eleanor,' he said. 'We have to move fast. See if you can get anywhere with the codes.'

'I'll need a library again. I'll call you when we find anything.'

Eleanor left, Michael following carrying his laptop computer. Dan realised he hadn't heard Michael speak for several days, then remembered that wasn't uncommon. He took the old caricature of the strong and silent type to its extreme.

'Where else do we go then?' asked Adam, when they'd left.

'The despatch rider?' prompted Claire.

'Already interviewed, and no go. He's a local lad who does it on the side. He got a note through his door asking him to do the jobs, along with two hundred quid in cash. It also told him to chuck the instructions in the sea as he was helping in a test of Plymouth's security systems and it was important not to leave a trail. He did that as well. He's not the brightest.'

'Associates of Sarah's, sir?' said Claire.

'Working on that,' replied Adam. 'You can supervise it, along with the rest of the current inquiries. I'm going to talk to

Sarah again. Then we'll see Sinclair and Robinson. That won't be easy. They're both furious.'

Adam took Claire through a list of what was being checked. Dan sat on the window ledge, tried not to run his tongue over the ulcer and thought about where he'd find some flowers. A baby crawled continually around the edge of his mind, screaming for attention.

'Ready Dan?' asked Adam when he'd finished talking to Claire. 'Are you ready?' he repeated, making Dan start and mumble an apology.

'Get with it please,' the detective added tetchily. 'I need you sharp for this. Let's go see Sarah.'

Sarah was standing by the far wall of the interview room, staring up at the tiny window, just as she'd done before. She turned as they walked in.

She spoke first. 'Before you ask, Adam, no is the answer.'

'No what?'

'No, I wasn't thinking about the years in prison when I wouldn't see the outside world again. I was wondering if the plans had been carried out successfully this morning. And I see from your expressions they have.'

Dan tried to keep his face impassive, but he couldn't help being impressed. Yesterday she'd talked about his perceptiveness. But she had insight too.

Adam sat down heavily at the table. The strip light above him buzzed.

'Enough of your games,' he grunted. 'I want this sorted now.'

Sarah closed her eyes and smiled. 'It's in your gift, Adam. You've got the codes. Crack them and you find the Judgement Book.'

'We're working on them. But it'd be in your favour if you gave us a short cut and told us where it is. Then we can stop all this.'

She walked slowly over to the table and sat down opposite Adam, her face half in shadow in the dim light. 'That would spoil the fun though, wouldn't it?'

The detective's palm slapped down on the table. 'What's fun about wrecking people's lives, woman?'

'Justice,' she said simply. 'Would you have found out about Robinson's men killing that young lad? Or Sinclair's corruption?'

'If you had an allegation to make about those men, the right way to do it was come to us.'

'And be greeted by people like Osmond? What do you think he'd have done? It would have been covered up, quietly forgotten. The establishment looks after itself.'

'We're not all corrupt,' said Adam wearily. 'Most of us believe in what we do, and do it as well as we can.'

'Then it's a pity your good work is spoiled by the rest. Maybe you should join me and help to point it out.'

Adam sat back on his chair and didn't reply. Dan could see he was angry with himself for again letting her draw him into an argument. Sarah had a way of getting to him that very few managed. Perhaps, Dan thought, it was because of the detective's strong views on justice and how it should be achieved, or what had happened to Linda Cott and Will Freedman. Maybe it was simply that it was his own future under threat.

And Dan's too. He ran his tongue over the ulcer, felt it sting anew.

More calmly, Adam asked, 'Who's your accomplice, Sarah?'

'You know I can't tell you that.'

'Is it a man or a woman?'

She smiled, easy and relaxed. 'I can't tell you anything else Adam. You know now how the clock's running. You have all you need to find the Judgement Book and you've got until seven o'clock tomorrow evening. I suggest you stop wasting your time with me and get on with trying to crack the riddle. That's the only way you're going to stop this.'

Adam stared at her. He stood up quickly from his chair.

'OK, if that's the way you want it. This is your last chance to change your mind and help us, Sarah. It could see you receive a substantially shorter sentence.'

'Nice try, Adam, but I'm content with what I've done. I'll see you in court, as they say. It should be an interesting trial, with all these well-known people being a part of it.'

She looked over at Dan. 'One of the trials of the century is probably how you media people will describe it. That's assuming you've still got a job – or if you have, that you're allowed to cover it. It could be a bit tricky, couldn't it? If you were named in the Judgement Book, and it was full of scandalous details about how you and Adam worked together.'

Dan felt his tongue start working at the ulcer, but he hardly noticed the pain. He tried to keep his face set, expressionless, stared fixedly at Sarah. There had to be a way to break through her calm.

He walked over to Adam, stood by the table and put an arm on his shoulder. They were getting nowhere, succeeding only in entertaining Sarah. It was time to leave, before she drew them into another row.

She looked up at them, amused and scornful. 'You are good friends, aren't you? That's so very touching.'

Dan felt the anger bite. 'And what about your good friend, Sarah?' he shot back. 'What happened to him? Iraq wasn't it?'

Now her expression changed. There was a slight twitch in her face, only tiny, but it was there.

'A peace protester, wasn't he?' Dan went on. 'Killed in the fighting?'

She said nothing, but she was colouring, a redness creeping across her cheeks.

'A good friend, wasn't he?' continued Dan slowly. 'A very good friend?' He waited, studied her, saw the shine in her eyes.

Still he waited, then added slowly, slyly, enjoying the hurt he was sure now that his words would inflict, 'A lover perhaps?'

'He was a better fucking man than you'll ever be,' Sarah shouted, jumping to her feet.

Her chair crashed over. Adam reached out a warning arm to restrain her, but she didn't move, just stood, staring into Dan's eyes, her face screwed tight.

'He was a better fucking man than any of you bastards will

ever be,' she hissed. 'And to hear that despicable wanker Robinson talking about him as a peacenik who was just another casualty of war made me want to go and stick a fucking steak knife in his neck. But I stopped myself. I did it the right way. Everyone will know what Robinson did, and all those other bastards who're just as bad in their own shitty sordid ways.'

Sarah glared at them, then bent over, picked up the chair and sat down. She folded her arms.

'This is our last conversation,' she said with taut control. 'I'd like it formally recorded that I do not intend to say anything else. But first, I must tell you this one thing. It's been agreed and it is the final part of the game …'

'What the hell are you talking about, woman?' Adam interrupted angrily.

Sarah gave him a look of pure contempt. 'I would advise you to shut up and listen. This is very important. It was agreed at the outset you would be given this last clue. It is the final thing I will say to you.'

She paused, waited. Adam looked speechless. Dan sensed it was no time to argue, grabbed his notebook.

'If you should find all the clues that lead you to the Judgement Book, bear this in mind,' she continued. 'Our initial thoughts are often wrong, but in this case they would be dead right. Remember that. Your initial thoughts will be dead right, and will take you to your goal.'

Sarah leaned forwards, stretched, laid her arms on the table, lowered her head, closed her eyes and silently ignored every other question Adam and Dan put to her.

Chapter Nineteen

ADAM JOGGED QUICKLY, DAN right behind him. Eleanor had called them from the library. She didn't want to leave as she had more research to do and time was vital. But she'd already solved the first of the two new codes.

Dan ran his tongue over his ulcer. It was hurting more now, swollen and sore. Another thought was dominating his mind. What did Sarah mean by those bizarre words, that their initial thoughts would be dead right, and would take them to their goal? Was it a riddle within a riddle that they had to solve? The case was growing ever more extraordinary.

They jogged past a sandwich shop, a queue of people winding back through the door. A smell of frying chicken drifted on the breeze. It was getting on for lunchtime, but he didn't feel hungry. There was too much going on to think about food.

A picture of Claire slid into his mind. She was pushing a pram, then stopping, bending over to tuck some blankets around a tiny, sleeping shape. Soothing nonsense noises bubbled from her lips and the baby opened his eyes and smiled up at her. It was summer, the warming sunshine bathing them both.

A sudden cloud passed in front of the sun and a sharp wind picked up. A man came to stand beside Claire, proud and protective. It wasn't Dan. The man was younger, more handsome, with a powerful, athletic physique and not a hint of receding hair. Dan clenched his fists, forced the image away.

He glanced up at the sky, enjoying the coolness of the misty rain. The weather had finally turned. After the long spell of sunshine, a grey drizzle was drifting in from the west. It was as though a tired cloud had fallen from the sky and come to rest on the city. The cars on the streets took on a sibilant sound as they pushed their way through the enveloping dampness.

A couple of people looked on, amused at the men in their suits, jogging and panting. Adam ignored them. He was focused on the library ahead. A line of pigeons stood watching from one of its grey, decaying ledges. They were still and silent, quietened by the change in the weather. Dan felt the moisture seeping through his jacket.

Adam took the two flights of stone steps in his stride and turned into the Reference section. Eleanor sat at a desk in the middle of a row, Michael next to her. She looked up from a pile of magazines.

'What news?' panted Adam from the door.

'Shhh,' came a series of replies as heads raised from their desks in annoyance.

Eleanor got up and ushered them outside into the stone stairwell. Michael followed.

'What news?' said Adam again.

'I think I've got it,' she replied, holding up a copy of Robinson's blackmail note. 'It's simple. The reason there's no riddle is that the answer is contained in that last sentence.'

She pointed to it.

"Here is your code. As a clue, I say this – it is very different from those which have gone before, but try a hunch, urchin. If you do, it may have the answer."

Eleanor looked expectantly at Adam. When he said nothing, she prompted, 'The answer is in that paragraph. The blackmailer tells us so. That talk about try a hunch urchin, and it might include the answer.'

Again she waited for some response. When still it didn't come, with all a veteran teacher's forbearance she said, 'What's the only word hidden inside "hunch urchin"?

Dan peered at the sheet, then said, 'Church.'

'Yes,' replied Eleanor simply.

'Church?' Adam queried, with disbelief.

'Yes, church.'

'Which means, we now have "Open original memorial church." So – we're looking to open the original memorial in a church. But what church?'

No one answered. No one could. There was no answer to give.

The clock on the wall said it was just after eleven. They had less than 32 hours to the blackmailers' deadline.

'What bloody church?' barked Adam. 'There are scores of churches around Plymouth alone, hundreds if we have to go further afield. We can't go looking for an original memorial to open in all of them. We don't have anything like enough time. So what damned church?'

'We don't know,' replied Eleanor finally. 'As I suspected, that clue was made deliberately easy. They're playing with us. It's the last word, the one which gives us the location that's the vital one.'

Adam looked at her. 'And it's the one we don't have,' he said bitterly.

They walked slowly back to Charles Cross and up the stairs to the MIR. Adam didn't say a word the whole way. He'd lost the driven energy of earlier and was laboured in his movements. He didn't even look around when a police car blazed past, its siren screaming. It was his usual way to speculate on what the emergency might be, and to wish his colleagues luck.

The press pack was still clustered around the front of Charles Cross, drinking endless take-away coffees and shouting questions at any senior police officer who passed. No wonder the High Honchos were growing concerned. Dan and Adam had to use the rear entrance to slip back into the station.

He steeled himself for the lie and phoned Lizzie to say there were no new developments worthy of reporting, but ... there might be later. It sounded lame, even to him, and Dan got exactly the response he expected.

'You can come back to the studios then, and work on something else.'

'But I think there is something afoot.'

'What?'

'Not sure yet.'

'So how do you know?'

'Just a feeling.'

'Feelings don't fill programmes. Feelings don't excite viewers. Feelings don't win ratings.'

Dan tried not to sound desperate. He couldn't leave the investigation now. Adam needed him, Claire needed him. And he had to save his own career.

'Just a hint then, from the detectives here, that something's brewing,' he managed.

'Well, make it brew faster. Ferment it. I want news. I want stories. I want exclusives. I want slots in the programme filled, not vague hopes that one day they might be.'

His ulcer throbbed throughout their conversation, as if to punish him for lying. Eventually, Lizzie agreed to let him stay, on the condition he would scramble if another story broke. Dan thought about Sarah, sitting in a police cell and wondered whether she might have a point. The world did sometimes seem full of deceit.

Adam barked a series of orders to a group of six waiting detectives. They were to start checking whether any churches in the Plymouth area contained well-known memorials. Dan could see from the looks on their faces it was a morass of work for a long shot, but they moved fast, urged on by Adam. Within seconds they were all at desks and on their phones, like a line of old-fashioned switchboard operators.

A forensics report on the two new blackmail notes had arrived. Both were written by the same person, but there were no clues as to who it was. There were no traces of any fibres, DNA or hair that could be used to check if the writer was a previous offender.

'That's no bloody use,' Adam grumbled, dropping the papers back on to a desk.

Another sheet detailed the attempts to penetrate the sexual underworld, talk to doggers and investigate whether Linda might have been involved. There was little written because there was little to say. The inquiries had got nowhere.

'No use again,' Adam grunted. 'As expected. It's not exactly a scene that welcomes the law.'

He picked up another report, from the Square Eyes division about Sarah's mobile. The call made just before she was arrested was to a pay as you go mobile, which had not been used since. Such phones were a criminal's favourite. No records kept of the sale, no way of tracing who it belonged to. The report said analysis of where it had been when it received the call indicated the centre of Plymouth, but nothing more specific.

'No bloody help there either,' muttered Adam. 'They were smart. They knew that if Sarah was caught we could trace any mobiles she'd rung. They were ready for us.'

Dan caught his look. They were both thinking it. That call was about them, breaking the law to catch the serial rapist, hunting down Osmond. Sarah had been gleefully passing on the details, the faceless accomplice scrupulously writing them down, line by line in the Judgement Book.

Adam walked over to the windows and stared out. The drizzle had stopped and the sky was brightening. He said nothing, just stared and tapped on the windowsill with his wedding ring. Dan could see he was thinking and wanted to be left alone, so he took out a piece of paper and tried to work on the final clue.

"See have mind good land, Plymouth."

He started with the basics. They were looking for somewhere or something in Plymouth obviously, but what and where? How could it lead to a word, the last, most important part of the riddle? Have mind of a good land – see a good land – Dan searched his memory, but couldn't think of anywhere called or known as a good land in Plymouth.

Anyway, what did it mean, see it? Go to somewhere you could see this good land? How did that help? Would you find yourself in a place which gave you the last word of the puzzle? Some road, street or square, some landmark?

And what did those words about predicting this clue would be the most trouble mean? It must be some kind of cryptic hint about the solution, surely. But if so, how? Dan stared at the words until they lost their focus and drifted across the page. He couldn't see how they might be any help. Maybe it was just the blackmailers enjoying a gloat. He wouldn't put it past them.

He doodled a couple of notes about checking the library and on the internet for references to a good land in Plymouth, but didn't come up with anything else. He wondered whether it would be so straightforward. It seemed too literal, given the answers to the riddles they'd already solved.

'Sir? Sir!'

One of the group of detectives walked up to Adam. He flinched, as if the young man had surprised him.

'Yes, Ben?'

'No good leads on the churches I'm afraid, sir. Just about every vicar we've spoken to claims famous original memorials. To check properly, we'd have to go out and see them all.'

'No time, no time,' Adam groaned.

'One more thing, sir. The work on Sarah's background, phone calls and associations – we've got nothing to indicate anyone was particularly close to her. She doesn't seem to have any family or good friends. In short, no hint of who her accomplice could be. The only person she seemed to be close to was a man she met at university in Sussex. But he died last year in Iraq.'

Adam nodded again. 'Thanks, Ben. I know it's a long shot, but you'd better start going round the churches.'

The man didn't move, looked at him questioningly. 'Go on!' Adam snapped. 'We've got nothing else. Get moving.'

The detectives slowly filed out. There was no spirit, no sense of hope or expectation in their movements, only duty. Adam drummed on the window ledge again, a rhythmic metallic echo in the quiet of the MIR.

'What do you read into that little row you had with Sarah in the interview room?' Adam said, turning to Dan. 'That stuff about the peacenik. You seemed to think you were on to something there.'

Dan looked up from his notes on the last riddle. He hadn't made any progress beyond sketching an ink drawing of Rutherford, his tongue hanging out in his smiling face.

'Part of Robinson's blackmail conversation she overheard, I'd say. It sounds to me like he was going on about his time in Iraq. He was probably drunk and that made him indiscreet. I'd guess he was sitting with a fellow officer and they were yarning about what they'd done in their careers. Robinson talked about the beating and death of that Iraqi boy. I reckon he also mentioned the peace activist who was killed in some kind of derogatory way. Hence the peacenik bit. He must have been a friend or lover of Sarah's.'

'The man referred to in the analysis of her past? The one from Sussex University?'

'I'd guess so.'

'That was the catalyst for all this? All this blackmail and these attacks on what she sees as the "establishment"?'

Dan thought for a moment. 'Yes, I think so. It's not the whole story, but it's the start. I'd guess that enraged her. Combine it with the loss of her business and the drunken conversations I imagine she's starting to overhear in the Judge and there's your motive. It's only a small step from hearing some of the things she did to taping them, playing them back, them eating away at her, inflaming her anger and then her seeing a way to use them in some kind of grand, meaningful gesture.'

Adam loosened his tie and sighed. 'Bloody hell. And Sinclair? What do you reckon happened with him?'

'Same kind of thing as Robinson. He was in the Judge, drunk, talking to a mate or trying to impress some woman. You should pop round and see my new extension kind of thing. It's great, top of the range, huge, didn't cost me a penny either …'

They looked at each other. Outside, a pigeon landed on the ledge, glanced in at the window, bobbed its head back and forth, then turned and flew off again.

Dan broke the silence. 'Rather brings to mind the old wartime slogan that careless talk costs lives, eh? Are we going to see Sinclair and Robinson then?'

'In a minute. I need to think first.'

Dan looked back at his notes on the final part of the riddle, toyed with the words, tried to find the hidden meaning. He succeeded only in adding some vague Dartmoor background to the sketch of Rutherford. It was about time they had that walk he'd been promising.

The door opened and Claire walked in. She held one arm over her stomach as if she were protecting it. Dan suddenly felt nervous.

'Everything's drawn a blank, sir,' said Claire, talking to Adam but repeatedly glancing towards Dan. Her voice was steady but he thought her eyes were shining. He wondered whether she'd been sick, or crying again.

'No leads anywhere on who the accomplice could be,' she continued. 'Not a thing.'

'Bollocks!' exploded Adam. He strode back over to the felt boards and stared at all the pieces of paper and photographs. 'There must be something. There must be. Come on! Have we tried everything?'

'We've done all the staff and regulars in the Judge, sir. Not a hint of anything. She's never been seen with anyone in particular, no one's ever come to visit her, nothing.'

Adam ran a hand through his hair, pushing up a couple of spraying tufts. The shadow of his beard had grown darker.

'We're running out of time,' he moaned. 'We've got until tomorrow evening or the whole thing blows up in our faces. God knows who the blackmailing bastards will be implicating in their sordid scandals. We could have a dozen suicides on our hands. There's got to be something, some way we can get them.'

Adam put his hands on his hips and clenched his teeth. 'It's no good talking to Sarah again I suppose?'

Dan could see he already knew the answer. 'No chance. She's said all she wants to.'

'Yeah, but what was that crap she came out with about our initial thoughts to do with anything? She really went on about it at the end of the interview. It sounded like it was important.'

'No idea. Our initial thoughts, and being dead right … what could that mean? I can't see anything. It might be important, but it might just be a bluff. I wouldn't put it past her to try to wind us up or confuse us even more.'

Adam turned away from the boards and caught an elbow on the metal edge of a support. He yelped and rubbed at it.

'Bollocks,' he growled again. 'I'm going to get a coffee. It might help kick-start my brain. Claire, Dan, get thinking. I want ideas. Any bloody ideas. Then we're going to have our little showdowns with Robinson and Sinclair.'

The door to the MIR slammed shut behind him. Claire looked at Dan, her face crumbled and she started crying. He reached out and cuddled her.

'I'm sorry,' she sobbed. 'I thought I could handle it, but I'm all over the place. I thought I could wait to work out what we're going to do, but I don't know if I can. Every time I think about it I start to cry. I'm so frightened. I can feel the baby growing inside me.' She tenderly rubbed her stomach. 'If we're going to have it, I've got to know. If not, I can't bear it being here, alive inside me. I just can't.'

Dan squeezed her tight. He could feel the tears gathering in his own eyes, but he blinked them back.

'Claire, come on. Claire! We will work it out, I promise you. It's going to be all right.'

She pulled away, fast, sharp, a violent movement which left him standing, staring, not knowing what to do.

'"Be all right? Work it out?" Work what out? How do we work it out?'

'Claire, please I …'

'How the hell are you going to work anything out? You didn't even notice I was pregnant!'

'Claire …'

'Do you know how that felt? All those days I was waiting for you to realise. All that time, all alone. All those hints I dropped, and you never even noticed. Do you know how lonely I felt?'

'Claire …'

'You were too stupid. Too self-absorbed. Too bloody intent on yourself, your own life, your job, your damn dog, everything except me!'

And now, for once in a career and a life of talking, for Dan the words would hardly come. 'Claire, I … I'm sorry. I don't know why …'

'And every bloody day I was trying to tell you I could feel the baby inside me. Growing! Every day. And you didn't even realise. You selfish, self-absorbed, ignorant arsehole!'

Dan stood, just stood and stared. There was nothing else he could do. Claire glared back, her lips trembling, her eyes a red haze of tears. Then, she raised a fist and swung weakly at his shoulder. He caught her wrist, gripped it, and pushed her away.

'What the hell are you doing woman? I'm trying to help sort

this out! For Christ's sake, we don't even have to have this baby…'

'Is that what you want?'

The blade of her voice cut through his words. 'All I'm saying is …'

'An abortion? Is that what you want?'

'Look, I just think …'

'Is it? Well, is it?'

They glared at each other. 'I … I can't talk about this now,' Dan stuttered. 'Adam will be back in a minute. We're in the middle of a big case. I can't think. I haven't got the time. We'll talk about it later. Or at the weekend. That's it.'

'But I need to know. I have to …'

'That's it, I said. Enough!'

The clock ticked loud in the quiet of the room. Outside in the corridor, a door slammed.

Claire lowered her head, that dark bob of hair falling across her face. Slowly, she turned, sat down at a desk and started typing mechanically at a computer.

Chapter Twenty

THE MAN WITH THE machine gun eyed them warily as they waited in the car. It was understandable given the ever-present terrorist threat, although it couldn't fail but make you nervous. Dan shifted awkwardly in the driver's seat, offered a reassuring smile to the sentry. It wasn't returned. But then, in fairness, smiles and deadly weaponry seldom made easy companions.

To avoid any possible misunderstandings, he kept his hands on the steering wheel, clear and obvious in the soldier's sight.

Next to him Adam looked up. 'Bloody military,' he said. 'They're the worst to deal with. A law unto themselves. And they go out of their way to make sure you don't feel welcome.'

The Dragoons' barracks loomed above them, the façade of grey stone glowering in the day's gloom. It was pitted with roundels bearing cherubs and capped with a great portico of charging horses and chariots. Atop, the Union flag hung limp, as if waiting for a gust of air to give it life. A gold-embossed plaque brusquely informed them that they were about to enter the military's domain.

'As if we hadn't guessed,' Dan murmured to himself. 'It doesn't exactly look like a croquet club.'

The sentry marched up and down, past the car, never taking his eyes from it. Dan kept his hands firmly on the wheel.

'What are you expecting to get from this interview exactly?' he asked Adam, more to distract himself from the menacing black barrel of the gun than for an answer.

'Nothing much. Ideally a full confession, a confirmation that Sarah and her accomplice got the info from bugging him in the Judge, but most importantly some hint on who that accomplice might be.'

'And in reality?'

'I'm expecting a bucket full of bluster, an outraged denial and simulated shock that I could even have the gross temerity to put such disgraceful allegations to him.'

'What about the claim that he's responsible – partly at least

– for a young boy's death?'

'Not my department. That's one for the military.'

'But you reckon it's true?'

Adam gave him a look. 'As I said, that's their business. We've got enough on. We've got to find the Judgement Book and we're running out of time.'

As one they looked at the car's clock. Its glowing digits said half past eleven. Just over 31 hours until the Book's contents were revealed. The numbers burned into Dan's mind.

And following them came Claire. The memory of that row. Never before had she called him an arsehole, however much and however often he might have deserved it.

And the shock of the venom in her eyes.

And still they didn't know what to do about the baby.

Dan flinched as the metal gates groaned open. The sentry waved them through, and he drove carefully under the great fluted stone arches into a parade ground. A sergeant gestured to the end of a line of impeccably parked cars and they pulled up.

Adam introduced them and they were escorted along a long, white stone corridor, past lines of busts of imperious-looking men, interspersed with dark oil paintings depicting bloodied soldiers of many different periods of history holding hordes of the enemy of the time at bay. Dan was amused to see one painting showed men with rifles valiantly defending themselves against tribesmen armed only with spears.

The sergeant stopped suddenly, rapped hard on a polished wooden door. It was so bright that Dan almost had to squint. He counted off the seconds. He reckoned it'd be at least ten before there was an answer. Self-important people were always far too busy to be immediately available.

At fourteen, a clipped voice called, 'Enter.' The sergeant opened the door, ushered them inside, closed it heavily and stood to attention beside it. Dan resisted an urge to do the same.

Adam held out a hand. Major Robinson studied it as though to check it wasn't infected, then reached slowly across his desk and shook it. Dan got the same treatment. He felt the sergeant's eyes glaring into him. Adam was right. Possibly the only way to make them feel less welcome would be stringing a banner across the room reading, "YOU'RE NOT WANTED HERE CIVVIES".

Adam was about to speak when the Major interrupted. 'I understand why you're here,' he said brusquely. 'Have you ever been to war, Chief Inspector?'

'Err, no.'

Adam was clearly surprised by the question. It was an unusual one – in the normal world, anyway.

'I thought not,' the Major continued. 'It can be a dirty business. I lost three good men in Iraq. Fighting for democracy. For their country. For peace.'

Dan nearly choked, managed to turn the noise into an unconvincing cough. He wondered where, as a journalist, he should begin challenging that little speech. There was a vivid spectrum of options. But Adam had warned him before the interview that it was best if he was seen, but not heard, so he managed to keep quiet. Just.

Robinson shuffled some papers on his desk. He wasn't a tall man, but neither was he short, and he was built like a block of flats. His voice was loud and abrupt and its tone was clipped in the manner that many military officers seem to adopt. Perhaps it was a part of their training.

He looked in his late 40s, swarthy and tanned with short, sandy hair, but to Dan's disappointment Robinson wore no moustache. It would have completed the stereotype nicely.

'Major, with respect, the rights and wrongs of the Iraq war are not what we're here to talk to you about,' said Adam. 'I simply need to know if the allegations in the letter addressed to you contain any truth, and if so …'

'They do not.'

'I have to say Major, that other claims against different individuals have proved to be true.'

'These are not.'

'Major, we're not interested in investigating the nature of the allegations, merely how the blackmailers may have …'

'The allegations are false. End of discussion.'

It was a true military response to the questioning. Every probe, prod or jab was met by a barrage of heavy artillery.

Adam sighed heavily. 'Major Robinson, please …'

'As I said, end of discussion. If such allegations do merit investigation, that will be carried out by the army. As you are no doubt aware, you have no jurisdiction here. Now – before you leave – was there anything else?'

From the corner of his eye, Dan was sure the sergeant at the door was smiling.

Adam got to his feet, tried again. 'Major, I am investigating a very serious crime, and I'm asking for your help. I simply need to know …'

Robinson cut across him again, his voice now an order. 'That then ends our business.'

Adam glared at him, snapped, 'No it does not. Listen to this. For what it's worth, I think those allegations are absolutely true. But I don't care about that. You can sort it out between you – you and your army chums. All I want to know is this. When you were in the Ginger Judge, drinking and bragging about what you'd done in Iraq with your military mates, did you notice anyone hanging around you?'

'How dare you …'

'… anyone appearing to linger? Being unusually interested in you or your conversations?'

The two men were standing face to face now, competing to out-shout each other.

'How dare you –' Robinson barked.

'Did you see anything suspicious, Major?' yelled Adam. 'This is important! Did you?'

'How dare you!'

'Did you?!'

A sudden silence. The two men had shouted each other into submission. Perhaps it was a verbal version of the doctrine of Mutually Assured Destruction. Robinson's fists were clenched. Adam's neck had turned red.

When the Major finally spoke it was with a controlled calm. 'This discussion is at an end. But finally, I give you this warning, Inspector. I intend to report you to your Chief Constable for your conduct here today.'

'Go ahead,' Adam replied. 'That's the least of my worries.'

He turned for the door. Dan followed. The sergeant had stopped smiling.

Twenty minutes later they were sitting in the waiting room outside Steven Sinclair's office. It was on the twelfth floor of a city centre, 1960s tower block, one of the heights of architectural misjudgement. As such, naturally it had been endowed with listed building status, thus sparing it the merciful justice of a gang of bulldozers.

Below was a concrete plaza and series of small, oblong ponds which had been designed to add atmosphere and elegance, but which became a dumping ground for cigarette butts and other assorted litter.

To pass a couple of minutes, Dan picked up his mobile phone and sent Claire a text message. She always appreciated knowing she was in his thoughts, and after their little scene of earlier that was more important than ever. Adam glanced disapprovingly over, so Dan switched on the predictive text function to make the typing quicker. It was remarkable how its anticipation of the words could speed up the messaging ritual.

With Adam on inquiries, but thinking of you. x

He looked up at the detective. Dan wasn't sure he should ask it again given what had happened with Robinson, but thought he would anyway.

'And what do you expect to get from this interview?' he whispered.

'Roughly the same as last time, except with less military bluster.'

A secretary showed them in. The office was large, the wooden floor covered with an ornate and patterned rug, the walls panelled with austere oak. Steven Sinclair sat on one of a row of soft chairs by the large windows overlooking the city. He was six feet tall, lanky, with short dark hair and wore a navy blue suit, but no tie, the modern politician's fashion of smartness without formality. The skin on his face was taut, as if it had been stretched back from the nose, giving him a look of permanent surprise.

He'd certainly received a sizeable one that morning, Dan

reflected.

But it wasn't Sinclair who held their attention. It was the woman sitting next to him, upright, dressed in a black suit and with a large folder on her lap. Julia Francis.

The marathon they were running had just grown more arduous, as if some mischievous tormentor had kindly attached a ball and chain to their legs.

'What an unexpected pleasure,' said Adam heavily.

'Likewise,' she retorted. Neither she nor Sinclair got up from their chairs, so Dan and Adam pulled over a couple of seats from the corner of the room.

Adam hadn't even had a chance to sit down when Francis said, 'Before we begin, Chief Inspector, I give you two warnings.'

One more than last time, Dan noted. My, they were doing well today.

'First, I refer you to the objections I made when you most recently came to see me with ...' Again that disdain-laden pause, '... a journalist in tow.'

'And again I refer you to my responses,' replied Adam smoothly.

Francis nodded, her pale blue eyes even more watery in the sunlight beaming from the window. 'Further, I have advised my client to say nothing which could in any way incriminate him. That, I suspect, may mean he says nothing at all.'

Adam didn't reply, instead turned his body pointedly away from her and to Sinclair.

'The truth of any allegations contained in that blackmail note are not my concern,' he said. 'I am trying to catch the person who sent it. Thus, I must ask you –' he hesitated, seemed to be searching for a way to phrase the question, then added, 'whether you have had any conversations of a personal nature in the Ginger Judge?'

'Don't answer that,' Francis said immediately.

Sinclair glanced at her, nodded and said nothing.

Adam pursed his lips. 'I see. Then let me ask this – if you have been in the Judge lately, have you noticed anyone hanging around? Perhaps looking over at you? Getting a little too close?'

'Don't answer that.'

'Seeming like they were trying to eavesdrop?'

'Don't answer that.'

'Anyone who was talking to the landlady, Sarah? Someone who might have appeared close to her?'

'Don't answer that.'

Adam went through a series of questions, pleading the importance of the case and his need for help, much as he had with Robinson. He got the same response each time. But unlike in the barracks, he didn't get angry. Dan suspected the moment Adam saw Julia Francis he was resigned to learning nothing from the interview.

The detective leaned back heavily on his chair, shook his head, said wearily, 'Is there any point asking you anything?'

Sinclair shrugged, looked again at Francis. 'I think you've answered your own question, Chief Inspector,' she replied.

Adam got to his feet. 'Then we'll be going. I haven't got time to waste. Mr Sinclair, some of my colleagues will be contacting you regarding the allegations contained in the note. And Ms Francis, before you ask, I must warn you that yes, you are still a suspect in this case.'

It was a cheap shot thought Dan, most unlike Adam, but he couldn't blame his friend. The morning had passed and they were no closer to catching Sarah's accomplice.

The clock on the wall said the time was just after twelve. They had less than 31 hours.

To add to their frustration, when they turned out of the Civic Centre they were greeted by a traffic jam. A solid line of buses and cars tailed back from the roundabout and up the hill towards Charles Cross. The odd horn blared, but most drivers suffered the familiar irritant in resigned silence. It was the English way. As so often in a major city in modern times, it would have been quicker to walk.

Adam stared at the tailback, swore under his breath. 'Right, let's not waste time,' he said. 'Brainstorm with me. I want a list of possible suspects and ideas about how to catch our second

Worm.'

Dan pulled on the handbrake, thought for a moment. 'The most obvious possibility is the worst. That it's someone we haven't seen or even had any hint of yet.'

'Yep. But that doesn't help us. So let's work through who we have seen, and think if any of them could be involved.'

'From the start?'

'Yep.'

'As wild a possibility as you like?'

'Yes. Just start thinking.'

Dan edged the car forwards, a handful of precious yards progress. 'Yvonne Freedman.'

He glanced to his side, was taken aback that Adam didn't look surprised. 'Yep,' the detective said.

'You've considered her?'

'You know my suspicious detective's mind. What if – say – Yvonne had known about the prostitute before Freedman killed himself? What if she'd had enough of her husband? She's told us he was never there in her life, or Alex's. She might have been in the Judge, chatting to a friend, telling her about it all. Sarah could have bugged the conversation, approached her later, teamed up with her. It could even have been Sarah who told her about the prostitute.'

Dan couldn't keep the disbelief from his voice. 'You're suggesting she blackmailed her own husband? You mean to say that she guessed he might kill himself, so nicely ridding her of the man she wanted out of her life anyway?'

'Well,' Adam mused, 'she wouldn't necessarily have had to suspect he'd kill himself. She could just have calculated the scandal would have given her a good reason to divorce him and get the house and enough money for her and Alex to live on.'

Dan breathed out heavily. 'It sounds a bit far-fetched.' He tapped a finger on the steering wheel. 'But then again ...'

'Yes?'

'Well, we've tackled more bizarre crimes. I never cease to be amazed at what people will do. And in fairness, she was pretty bitter. She clearly wants some kind of revenge on what she sees as the "establishment". I suppose it could all fit.'

Adam nodded. 'You starting to be convinced?'

'Not convinced, but it's a possibility.'

Ahead, they could see flashing blue lights and a crumpled car being shunted to the side of the road. 'There's the reason for the jam,' Dan said. 'It should ease up in a minute.'

'Let's keep going for now,' Adam replied. 'Who else is on our little menu of suspects?'

They crawled forwards a couple more yards. The sun sneaked out from behind a roll of cloud, making the car feel warm. Dan rolled down a window. The sun went back in again. He sighed.

'In order of the people we've met – or in this case, haven't – Linda Cott?' he said.

'You mean, faking her death to become Sarah's accomplice?'

'Yep. Her body still hasn't been found.'

'True. But we did find her blood on the rocks below where she jumped. And as for not finding a body, that's not unusual around there. The tides are vicious.'

'She could have had a motive. We've got some evidence she was getting frustrated in her career.'

'Who doesn't? But enough to turn her into a blackmailer?'

Dan thought for a few seconds. 'Probably not.'

'And that stuff about her being involved in ...' Adam hesitated before finding the word. 'Well, dogging. That would have been incredibly powerful material to blackmail her with.'

'True.'

'And Sarah seemed very sure she had something nasty over Linda. Dogging would certainly fit the bill.'

'Yep.'

'OK then,' said Adam. 'Linda's an unlikely candidate, I agree. Let's keep going. Next?'

Dan chuckled, couldn't help himself. 'Superintendent Osmond?'

Adam rolled his eyes. 'You mean to get back at the rotten police force around him, to expose their corruption and incompetence by offering himself as a sacrifice? Being turned to become Sarah's accomplice after she taped him talking about his drink driving, and persuaded him to join her crusade to highlight all that was wrong in society?'

The two men exchanged a look. 'No,' they said together.

The traffic started to move. Dan shifted the car into first gear, allowed it to trundle towards the roundabout.

'Julia Francis?' he asked.

'I'd like to say so, but probably not.'

'She does have a chip on her shoulder about the establishment thing, though. There's her history of civil liberties work. Maybe she thinks the state is infringing too far on people's lives, just like Sarah does. And there's no hint of her being in the Judgement Book. Perhaps that's suspicious in itself. Maybe Sarah bugged her raging about how she hated the system and afterwards persuaded her to join the plot?'

Adam considered this. 'I'd like to believe it, but it's a long shot,' he said finally. 'I hate to say it, but despite all my run-ins with her I've always got the impression she's pretty straight.'

Dan indicated, turned the car towards Charles Cross. The ruined church loomed ahead.

'Almost home,' he said.

'Keep going,' Adam replied. 'This is useful.'

'OK, Sinclair or Robinson. As for motive, again to expose the rottenness of the world around them, again after being taped by Sarah talking about their own misdemeanours and her persuading them to join her great crusade. A sort of way to make up for what they'd done.'

'Possible, but a bit crime fiction. You are prone to it. That sounds like something from a book. Long shots, surely?'

'Yeah, but we don't know much about them, do we? We got nothing in those interviews.'

'We'll keep working on them, but I can't see it.'

They reached the Charles Cross roundabout. Sunlight flared through the open stone arches of the church's windows. A couple of magpies hopped across the grass. A mist of rain began drifting from the sky, conjuring a fragile rainbow over the city. The sight would usually make Dan smile, but not today. Even a brief lull of contentment felt a far distant emotion.

'Well, that's about it,' said Dan. 'I reckon ...'

'Hey!' Adam interrupted. 'I don't believe it! I nearly forgot him.'

Dan couldn't hide his puzzlement. 'Who?'

The detective pointed at the ruin standing proud in the centre of the roundabout, traffic edging around it. 'The church jogged my mind. Maguire.'

'The priest?'

'Yeah.'

'On what grounds?'

'How about – getting fed up with all the horrible things he hears in confession. Ground down by the world's endless sin. Wanting to hit back at a rotten society. He could have been in the Judge, been bugged saying something, got together with Sarah that way. And he's got form too, that previous conviction for burglary.'

'I don't know. It sounds pretty wild to me.'

'Maybe,' replied Adam. 'Until you remember the clues we've got so far.'

Dan thought for a moment, closed his eyes, groaned. 'Of course. "Open original memorial church."'

'Exactly!' Adam hissed. 'Church – what if it's his church? What if the Judgement Book's safely hidden in an original memorial in his church? Come on, quick, turn the car around. Let's go and see him.'

The little priest was on his hands and knees, polishing hard at a flagstone. He seemed intent on his work, didn't look up as they walked towards him. The church was deserted, their footsteps echoing from the stone and rainbow glass. The air was still and cooler than outside.

Still he rubbed away at the floor, the yellow cloth flicking busily back and forth. The surface was smooth, inscribed with faded letters, a name and a date, but they were faint and worn, eroded by the countless years and pairs of feet which had passed by. Dan noticed Maguire was wearing jeans under his cassock.

They stopped just feet from him, waited. Adam coughed

pointedly. 'I sense trouble,' Maguire said, without looking up.

He shifted his position, finished rubbing at a corner, then got up, dusted himself down and they shook hands. He was sweating. Dan wondered if it was from the exertion of his work, or something more.

'Police footsteps,' he explained. 'I knew it was you the moment you opened the door. You manage to walk in an ominous way. And you let the door shut a little too hard for a believer.'

Adam didn't smile. 'Why do you say you sense trouble, Father?'

'Because you haven't just popped in for a cup of bloody tea, have you, Breen?' he snapped, dabbing at his forehead with a sleeve. 'I read the papers. They're full of your blackmailer case. And they say it isn't over. I take it I'm still a suspect and that's why you're here?'

Adam knelt down, ran a finger over the stone Maguire had been polishing. Dan knew his friend well enough by now to see he was playing for time, deciding on his tactics for handling the interview. On the drive to the church, the detective had hardly spoken. He sat, staring out of the windscreen, silently thinking.

'What are you going to say to him?' Dan asked finally, as they rumbled down the hill towards the church.

'A little test, I think,' was the cryptic reply.

Dan bent too, studied the writing. He could just make it out. The light seemed to slide from the polished stone, only briefly held in the shallow grooves of the words. They were in loving memory of a Thomas Hubball, a notable parish priest from some time in the 1600s, although the exact date was too worn to discern.

Adam tapped a finger on the stone. 'A memorial,' he said slowly.

Maguire folded his arms. 'I certainly can't fault your ability as a detective.'

'Do you have many in the church?'

Dan studied the priest's face. He was peering at Adam, but there was no hint of a reaction to the question. His silver hair shone in the mellow church light, making it appear as if he was wearing a halo.

'The church dates from the thirteenth century, Breen,' he said. 'So yes, we've clocked up one or two over the years.'

'Are there any which are particularly famous? Or important?'

Maguire raised his eyes to the fluted columns of the church's roof. 'Holy Father preserve me. They're all important, man. That's why they were created. To mark the passing of our better fellows into the arms of the Lord.'

He crossed himself with the same sense of theatre he'd shown when they had first met.

Adam took a deep breath. 'Then let me rephrase that. Are any of your memorials particularly famous?'

The question received due consideration before the reluctant reply, 'No, not really. We're in Plymouth, not Westminster Abbey.'

Outside, two sets of feet crunched on gravel. Adam nodded to himself. The preamble was over. Dan sensed the sting of the interview coming.

'Then have any been duplicated?'

'Duplicated?' The priest's voice was sharp with scorn. 'What the hell are you talking about now, man? This isn't a bloody factory. We don't knock off copies of our memorials to stack the shelves of our local Ecumenical Discount Store.'

Dan gritted his teeth to stop himself from grinning. A suspect he may be, and as such the rules dictated he had to be treated with dispassionate neutrality, but despite that, Dan couldn't help rather liking Father Maguire.

Adam frowned, but answered patiently, 'I'm sorry, perhaps I'm not making myself clear. Have any new memorials been created to anyone already remembered here? Perhaps by their family? Or for some occasion like the anniversary of their death?'

Again no sign of a reaction from Maguire. If he knew what Adam was hinting at, he was hiding it well. He didn't look in the least guilty or worried, just mildly puzzled and more obviously irritated. 'Not that I know of. Not that's happened in my time here, anyway. Why do you ask?'

'Just – a possible line of inquiry.'

The priest regarded Adam with suspicion. 'I've heard that one before,' he barked. 'On the TV it's normally a prelude to someone being arrested. What are you up to, Breen?'

'Nothing, Father, nothing. Just thinking out loud.'

'Got me down as your number one suspect, have you?'

'No, Father …'

His voice rose. 'Blackmailer Maguire? The priestly extortionist? The latest in a long line of Catholic Crooks? If it's not the choir boys they're after, it's cash.'

Adam held up his hands calmingly. 'Father, please. I'm only following a possible lead, that's all. We'll leave you in peace now.'

The tone of the detective's voice had changed, become softer. Dan had seen it before. The interview was over. Maguire didn't know the contents of the blackmail notes. He thought they demanded cash. Unless he was the finest of actors, the priest wasn't Sarah's accomplice.

The church's bell rang one, a jarring loudness in the quiet. The morning's precious time had been wasted. There were now just 30 hours until the contents of the Judgement Book were revealed and they were no closer to finding it. Dan was growing ever more sure that he and Adam were both in there.

There was an invisible clock, counting down the time to the end of their careers. It followed wherever they went. And its ticking was growing ever louder.

Chapter Twenty-one

IT WAS TWO O'CLOCK and the sun that had spent the morning battling to free itself from the shroud of cloying clouds had finally won through. The hurrying umbrellas disappeared from the city and shirt sleeves and cropped tops took their place, making their way to their destinations with easy leisure. From the window of the MIR, high above Plymouth, Dan wondered at how a change in the weather could transform spirits in an instant.

On the window sill was his piece of paper with the final, most important riddle. He'd written the words in as many different combinations as he could think of, looked for anagrams, acrostics and patterns of any kind, wondered whether there could be hidden numbers or place names contained there, and come up with precisely nothing. He still had no idea what the solution could be.

"See have mind good land, Plymouth."

No matter how many times Dan looked at it, in how many different ways, he couldn't see any hidden meaning.

Lizzie had rung again, demanding a story. It was a quiet news day and they were desperate for anything he could provide. Dan had just about managed to fob her off with more vague talk of something being likely to happen and him needing to be with the police to make sure they got the exclusive. But being fobbed off had never become his editor. She was growing increasingly agitated.

He found himself strangely tempted to tell her the truth, about the two new notes, the deadline for solving the riddle and tomorrow's promised release of the Book, complete with its section on a certain Dan Groves. He wondered why. Perhaps it was the classic spin doctor's art of preparing the ground for bad news, or simply to make an early appeal not to be sacked?

He'd ended the conversation by telling her something seemed to be happening and that he had to go and see what it was. He'd call her back later with some kind of story, he said.

But he had no idea what.

All he knew was that he had to be here. With Adam to do his best to break the code, find the Book and save them both, and with Claire, to support her as they decided what to do about their baby. Dan raised a hand, wiped his forehead. It felt strangely hot, as if there was too much going on in his mind. There were just 29 hours to their deadline.

Eleanor and Michael sat at two desks next to each other, studious like children in a class. She had a small pile of books, he had his laptop. But both had also come up with no ideas about what the final code might mean. Dan worked with them on his thought about seeing a good land. They'd checked reference books, thick works on Plymouth's history and the countless computer memories gathered on the internet, but they'd got nowhere.

At the front of the room, Adam either paced back and forth in front of the felt boards or sat heavily on the edge of a desk, his head bowed. He was a study in thought. Each time a telephone rang, he jumped for it. Each time there were no new leads to report.

Claire worked at the phones, coordinating the inquiries they had left to cover. The team checking the churches had come up with no famous original memorial and not even a hint of a lead. A couple of technicians from the Square Eyes division had been working on the internet to see if they could trace any web site which might be used to post the Judgement Book. They'd found nothing. The list of possible suspects Dan and Adam had discussed earlier in the car had yielded no progress.

They all knew it, but none would say. No one dared.

The investigation had stalled.

Claire and Dan exchanged occasional glances. She looked pale, and her eyes were still red. One hand rested automatically over her stomach.

They'd had a brief chat earlier, agreed to leave the row behind. Such emotions were inevitable; her hormones were racing, he had never been in this position before, they were amidst the tension of a major investigation.

Dan was almost convinced that all was more or less OK.

Almost.

More or less.

It was hardly the most romantic of moments, huddled in a narrow gap between two police vans in the yard behind Charles Cross. Dan very much wanted a hug. But all he got was tears.

'I can't go on like this,' Claire sobbed. 'I just can't. We've got to get it sorted. It's eating away at me, every hour, every minute, every second. I can't think about anything else. What are we going to do?'

And he'd had no reassuring words to give her, no magical solutions, nothing but more uncertainty. 'I don't know. I just don't. I keep thinking of what having a baby would mean. I don't know how we'd cope. Your job, my job, Rutherford, where to live. Any of it.'

She buried her head into his neck, didn't reply, just whimpered. Dan held her close, but she didn't squeeze him back and he couldn't still her sobbing.

'We'll work it out,' he tried to soothe. 'We will. I promise. We'll work something out.'

'But what? What?!'

And that was the fatal question, the one without an answer. Dan hugged her tighter, tried to think. And then, with vindictive timing, a policeman had jogged up to one of the vans, muttered some excuse about a call out, and driven it off.

Dan tried to stop her, but Claire walked quickly away, her face buried in a handkerchief. All she could say was, 'We have to get it sorted. I just can't go on like this any more.'

And the words hadn't stopped resonating in his head.

He gulped hard, was about to get them all another round of teas and coffees when his mobile warbled. Lizzie again, and this time she was fizzing.

'Need you on a story. Urgent!'

'What?' He tried not to panic, instead find another excuse. 'But I'm at Charles Cross, waiting for developments on the blackmailer case. It's a cracking story. We don't want to lose sight of it, and I reckon...'

She cut in. 'Do you have any developments?'

Dan stared over at Claire. She was looking at him too, and

242

he could see her face was ready to crack. It felt like the weight of emotion it held back was growing too powerful to resist. He couldn't leave her now, not to go chasing some stupid story. He had to be here with her. She needed him, her eyes were full of it.

The icy voice on the phone again. 'I said, do you have any developments that will make us a report for tonight?'

If only he could tell her about the two new notes, the final riddle. It was a fantastic story. But Adam wouldn't let a word get out. They had to concentrate on the investigation, couldn't afford the distraction of the media frenzy it would create. The pack of reporters and photographers was still hanging around the front of the police station.

'I'll take that as a no then,' came the merciless voice once more. 'Get moving. Now! North Devon Zoo. They've had a break in and lost loads of their rare animals. Great TV story. It's our lead for tonight. Nigel will meet you there. I'm sending the outside broadcast truck too. I want a report and a live.'

'But Lizzie, I …'

'Enough! I know how much you love playing detectives, but this is breaking news. I shouldn't have to point out it's your job. Get going. Now!'

Dan could feel Claire's eyes fixed on him. Her lips were trembling.

'But Lizzie, I don't want to lose sight of this case. It's one of the biggest stories we've ever had. I think …'

She interrupted again, and her voice was acid calm. 'It's very simple. Go do the story and do it well or start looking for another job.'

She hung up. He stared at the mobile, felt a sudden screaming desire to fling open a window, hurl it out, enjoy the sight of it shattering on the street below. But he knew he had no choice. Dan briefly closed his eyes, took a breath and stepped down from the window ledge, the noise echoing around the silent room.

'Got to go,' he said to Adam, but couldn't help himself looking at Claire. 'There's a story I have to do in north Devon.'

Adam shrugged. He looked tired and defeated, his shoulders

slumped. 'Go ahead,' he said wearily. 'You're hardly missing anything.'

Dan walked to the door, paused, looked back at Claire. Her head was bowed over her desk, her hair falling across her face in that way he always found irresistible. She didn't look up.

The drive to north Devon took two hours. It was one of the worst in the region, full of frustrating twisted and sinewy roads with only the rare release of some dual carriageway. And when you were in a rush you could always guarantee at least a couple of tractors and caravans to get stuck behind. It was one of the hazards of the South-west, tourists and farmers, both working to a pace of life at least fifty per cent slower than the rest of the world.

Dan couldn't concentrate on the story he was going to cover. All he could think about was Claire. He kept seeing her with that other man, hand in hand, pushing a pram.

The newsroom rang to update him on what happened. A gang of raiders had burst in, tied up the staff and filled a van with animals. They knew exactly which ones they wanted. Two breeding pairs of Galah Cockatoos had been taken, a colony of dozens of Geffroy's marmosets, nine black-eared marmosets, a pair of Rainbow Macaws and two yellow-winged Amazon parrots. The animals were worth tens of thousand of pounds and probably destined to be sold to collectors.

Dirty El also called. He too was on the way to the zoo. All the national papers wanted pictures. Not even the usual tormented entertainment of his burbled and painful limerick cheered Dan.

'El, he always loved the zoo,
The creepies and the crawlies too,
But now they're out,
Up goes the shout,
Get us pics, pursue, wahoo!'

Loud was already there when Dan arrived, Nigel standing beside him. They'd been in the newsroom when the tip-off came through and Lizzie had scrambled them first. Dan checked the cameraman's watch. Almost five o'clock. They had an hour and a half until they were on air.

Such deadlines, and so merciless, Dan thought miserably. Tonight's programme, and the countdown to the release of the Judgement Book.

'I've got you a few pictures already,' Nigel said. 'So that takes the pressure off us a bit. I've done lots of general shots of the zoo, plus plenty of the animals that are left. You can talk about "cockatoos and marmosets similar to this" being stolen. The boss is bringing me some old photos of the actual animals. I'll film those in a minute.'

Dan thanked him and excused himself to go to the loo. It was a priority after that long, frustrating drive. His mouth was dry too, and his ulcer was stinging hard. To save time he called Claire while he was in the toilets. He had more bad news and he wanted her to know now.

'I'm so sorry,' he began. 'I really am. But I couldn't get out of it. It's a big story for us.'

'It's OK, I understand.' She sounded flat, distant, almost indifferent.

'Claire, I'm sorry, really. It's the worst time for something like this to break. I want to be with you, not here, believe me.'

'It's OK,' she repeated. 'I'll see you later. I'll wait up.'

Shit. Just – simply – shit. How the hell was he going to tell her? He couldn't put it off, he didn't have a choice.

'Claire, I hate to say this, but I'm not going to be back tonight. They want me to stay up here to do a follow-up story for tomorrow.'

The mobile line hummed and clicked. Dan thought he heard a gulp, but couldn't be sure.

'Claire? Claire!' he urged. 'I'm sorry, I really am.'

'It's OK,' she said again finally, and her words sounded hollow, empty of feeling. 'I'll be fine.' Her voice caught and she struggled to finish. 'I'll see you tomorrow. Got to go.'

'Claire! Claire, please,' Dan shouted, but she'd hung up.

He twice tried to ring back, but got her answer machine. Dan glared at his mobile, then put it back into his pocket. He'd have to call her again later. He loosed off a machine-gun string of expletives, making an old man walking into the toilets stare and shake his head. It was an effort not to lash out at him, vent the seething venom.

Dan walked with Nigel to see the layout of the zoo for the outside broadcast and did a quick interview with one of the keepers. Other journalists and photographers were arriving, El amongst them. He had his biggest lens on the front of his camera and stroked it lovingly as he clicked off his snaps, the trademark sleazy grin shining on his face.

Dan sat in the outside broadcast truck to edit the report. Loud was wearing a shirt adorned with strutting Rainbow Macaws and kept giggling, pointing at them, then the monitor screens. Dan scarcely noticed. He had to force himself to think about the story he was writing, be professional. He wondered if this would be the last report he produced. The theft of some animals from a zoo wasn't exactly the blaze of glory he'd always had in mind for the end of his career.

It was half past five. They'd need 15 minutes to prepare for the live broadcast. They only had 40 to cut the report.

Time to shift. Stop worrying about craft and polish, just cut and burn. News was the art of the possible.

He started the story with pictures of the cockatoos and macaws, their spectrum of plumage lighting the monitors, and talked about them being worth thousands of pounds and probably stolen to order. Their breeding programme had also been destroyed, almost twenty years of work gone in the few minutes of the raid.

Then came a clip of interview with the keeper. He could have been an actor, played the part perfectly, broke down and cried, right on cue. Dan felt tears forming in his own eyes as his mind ran once again to Claire. He imagined her sitting alone in a dark cubicle in the toilets at Charles Cross, trying to stifle her sobs.

Loud laid down some pictures of the marmosets, while Dan talked about how vulnerable they were to shock, how they could easily have died already because of the stress of the raid. Their tiny, human-like faces looked pitiful to match his words. He finished the report with some general pictures of the zoo, writing about how and when the gang had struck and the photos

Nigel had filmed of the actual animals, asking the viewers to keep an eye out for them in newspaper adverts and pet shop windows. Loud spun the edit controls and they watched it back.

'Not a bad report,' the engineer grunted begrudgingly, his forest of a beard twitching. 'Almost worth coming all the way here for.'

It was a quarter past six. Time to plan the live broadcast.

'I've got it all rigged up,' said Nigel. 'We're going to use the radio link camera. That way you can do a little walk through the zoo wherever you want without any problems with cables.'

Dan hopped down from the truck and thought fast. 'I reckon we start with me by the empty cages and I go on about how they should be full of birds,' he said. 'Then they can bring in my report. During that time, we relocate to another cage with some birds or animals behind for a live interview with the owner.'

Dan tried another call to Claire. He got her answer machine again and swore to himself. She was deliberately avoiding him, she must be. Two swelling emotions collided in his mind, anger and guilt. He felt like running to his car, jumping in and gunning the engine back to Plymouth.

He called Adam. Still no progress on the investigation. That last, vital clue to the riddle was the key the detective thought, but Eleanor and Michael had had no luck in solving it. They'd worked through all the reference books on Plymouth, all the web sites they could find and even spoken to local historians. Michael had put it through every computer program he had, but hadn't found any hint of an anagram or hidden meaning in the words.

The sentence taunted Dan. "See have mind good land, Plymouth."

Something in Plymouth or about the city, it had to be. But what? He knew he had no idea. And if Eleanor and Michael, with all their knowledge and experience couldn't solve it, what chance did he have? Twenty-four hours, that was all they now had to crack the code or the Judgement Book would be released and with it the end of his career and Adam's too.

And if he was honest, "end" was a masterpiece of modesty.

It would be a crash, a spectacular, a fireball of flame. There would be shock and scandal. Dan would be pursued by the press pack, become notorious, his name always branded with the story of the Judgement Book.

He must get back to Plymouth first thing tomorrow morning. He'd have to find a way. Perhaps convincing Adam to put out a story on the new blackmail victims would be the best idea. That would give him a reason to return. Dan needed to be with the investigation, and Claire too. But what story could they release that might help them solve the code?

He could think about it later. He had to concentrate on the outside broadcast. But he knew that whatever happened he was going back to Plymouth tomorrow. If Lizzie really wanted to sack him, so what? He was going to be out of a job the moment the Book was released anyway. He might as well get back home, be there to try to find the thing and save his relationship too.

'Studio to Dan, do you hear us?' came Emma's voice in his earpiece. He bit his ulcer and gasped at the stab of pain, but at least it forced him to concentrate. 'Two minutes to on air, Dan. Standby.'

'You OK?' asked Nigel. 'You're looking a bit out of it.'

'I'm OK.'

His friend's look said the attempted reassurance was hopelessly unconvincing. Dan could feel his mind again drifting to Claire. He tried to concentrate, focus on his words.

'A shattering blow for one of the region's best known zoos tonight,' came Craig's voice. 'Raiders have stolen scores of rare and highly valuable parrots and monkeys from North Devon Zoo. Our Crime Correspondent Dan Groves is there live for us.'

'Cue Dan,' Emma prompted.

'Yes, Craig, these cages,' he said, gesturing behind and beginning to walk past them, 'should have been full of life here this evening, birds stretching their colourful wings, chattering to each other, feeding and settling down for the night. Instead, they're poignantly empty, as are many others in the zoo, the animals stolen in what looks like a well planned raid.'

They cut to his report. Two short minutes to reposition

themselves for the interview. Dan and Nigel marched over to the zoo's owner. He was standing in front of a cage of lazing cheetahs.

'One minute to you, Dan, come on, hurry it up,' came Emma's harassed voice.

Nigel manoeuvred the two of them around to get the animals in the background of the shot.

Emma again, 'Thirty seconds, come on, come on!'

Nigel spun the focus and exposure rings on the camera and finally gave a thumbs-up. Dan gazed at his reflection in the lens. Was it his imagination, or did he look forlorn, lonely and lost?

A shout in his ear. 'Cue Dan. Cue, man!'

He was spurred instinctively into action. 'With me now is Oscar Kennedy, the zoo's owner. The viewers will understand the financial loss. But for you, it's more than that, isn't it? It's the loss of years of work.'

The man stared, and Dan wondered if he was going to dry up. But he began talking, softly and hesitantly, and all the more powerfully for it.

'For the last twenty years I've been building up a breeding programme here. Day in, day out, I've tended these animals. There've been so many long days' work I've lost count. Sometimes it seemed it was never going to work. Then, a couple of years ago, we had our first successes and I was elated. All the work was worth it. Now, with a few people's criminal selfishness I've had those twenty years taken away from me.'

Dan couldn't think of anything else to ask, so he played it simple and safe. He thanked the man and handed back to the studio, telling the viewers if they had any information that could help the police they should call Crimestoppers. It wasn't perfect, probably wasn't even a good outside broadcast, but it was adequate, and for now that was all he could aspire to.

Nigel and Loud had been detailed to stay the night too, so they drove to the nearest village and booked three rooms at the local Inn, the Milkmaid's Daughter. Normally, a night away on expenses was a pleasant perk, but Dan could scarcely find the enthusiasm to try to enjoy himself.

The pub had fine beer and they ate venison pie, the deer from Exmoor. Dan even discovered that when the pressure of work eased, Loud could shed his sulkiness and become mildly entertaining. He never suspected the engineer had a passion for ballroom dancing. After a couple more pints, he talked movingly about meeting his wife at a dance and even to this day, almost thirty years on, enjoying waltzing her across a polished wooden floor.

The tenderness in Loud's voice again made Dan think of Claire and he excused himself, went outside and tried to call her. She still wasn't answering. He left it a few minutes and walked up the hill to stare at the Exmoor countryside. It always struck him just how vast the sky was here. Living in Plymouth, densely packed with buildings and polluted with the hazy smog of the leaking light you never got to enjoy the simple pleasure of the full wondrous canopy of the heavens.

The night was clear and a luminous half moon shone in the east. Only the boldest stars could compete, studding the sky as occasional pinprick diamonds. Dark rolls of hills slid towards the sea in the north. The night lay silent, punctured only by the odd bleat of a lonely sheep.

That was another thing he missed, the tranquillity of living away from the eternal, grumbling traffic. You only realised how ubiquitous and ugly it was in its absence.

He turned to the south, towards Plymouth and thought about Claire. What was she doing? Raging at him? Sobbing on her sofa? Watching a film, trying to forget? Just sitting there, her arm across her stomach, her mind blank?

He tried to call again, but once more got her answer machine. He left a message asking her to ring and hung up. Dan tried to keep the upset and anger from his voice, but wasn't sure he'd succeeded. After a few seconds staring blankly at the phone he surprised himself by letting out a loud groan. It went on and on, turning into a wail.

Just like a mad dog howling at the sky.

He checked his watch, noticed his vision was blurred with the beginnings of tears. The Rolex said just after nine, so probably a quarter past. Less than 22 hours before the contents of the Book were revealed.

Dan wondered how Adam was feeling. Sitting at home with Annie and Tom, trying to be a contented family man with all this on his mind. He must be suffering just as badly, maybe worse. Dan took another couple of deep breaths of the still and silent air and walked back into the pub.

He had another pint to be sociable and then went to bed. It was early, only just after ten, but he didn't feel like sitting and chatting. He wanted to do some work on the last part of the riddle and see if he could come up with a plan which would get him back to Plymouth.

The bed was old and creaked every time he moved, but it was comfortable too. The down pillows folded themselves around his head and neck. The landlord had kindly left a miniature bottle of sherry on a cabinet, so Dan lay back, sipped at it and thought about the riddle and Claire. He glanced at his mobile.

No calls, no messages. He closed his eyes.

And again came the memory of that row. How she had called him a selfish arsehole.

And the nagging fear that she was so very right.

He pushed his thoughts back to the puzzle to distract himself. "See have mind good land, Plymouth." Dan tried to spin the words in his head, read them backwards, forwards and in a series of random orders. Nothing came to him about what they could possibly mean.

Tomorrow, he would go back to Plymouth and drive all around the city, to see if he could find any hint of this good land he had to see or have in mind. It didn't matter what Lizzie said, he was going back. Why not? He only had tomorrow to save his career and relationship.

There was nothing left to lose.

Chapter Twenty-two

DAN WOKE EARLY, NUDGED from his dreams by the new sun seeping through the faded curtains. He hadn't slept well, but he felt OK. Neither refreshed nor tired, he thought, just about all right. He wondered how long that would last. It had been a punishing few days.

He ran his tongue over the inside of his mouth. The ulcer seemed to have eased its assault, or perhaps it was just taking longer to wake. He looked over at his phone, but there was no call or message from Claire. He hissed to himself. The clock on the wall said it was a quarter past six. Outside, a cockerel crowed, welcoming the day.

He knew what he was going to do. He would get up and drive back to Plymouth. There was no choice. He had to be there to help in the search for the Judgement Book and to see Claire. There were only 12 hours left to solve the riddle and save himself and Adam. He didn't want to think how long he had to save his relationship.

Dan yawned and stretched in the duvet's comforting cocoon. Should he try to call her again? No, it was early and she would ring when she was ready. If she was ready – if she even wanted to.

If …

He gritted his teeth. She would ring. She would. But he wanted Claire to know he was thinking about her when she woke. He could send her a text message.

He picked up the phone, plumped up his feather pillow and lay back. So – what to say? It was never easy to get it right with a text. Without the grins and winks and verbal inflexions that were the basis of so much communication, they were all too easily misunderstood. Dan didn't want to risk that here. He had a sense the stakes might be too high.

Best to keep it simple, but straightforward, he thought. Something like, "Am on way back to Plym, need to be with you. Call me when you can."

He typed in "am" and the predictive text program came up with "an", so he hit the button to change it. Dan kept typing. "Am coming home" he wanted to say, but the phone interpreted "home" as "good". He went to press the key to change the word, but then stopped.

He was never sure why. The only explanation could be that he felt the indefinable something. The hint which whispers from a dark corner of the mind. The sense of a moment of realisation. Incomprehension to understanding. The wondrous step from darkness to light. He could feel its tingling presence, close, flitting through his brain, but not quite ready to deliver its thrill, not yet.

Dan steadied himself, forced his mind to calm. Take it easy, stage by stage. What had triggered the shock of excitement?

He'd seen that word "good" an awful lot in the last day or so. It was from the final clue in the riddle. He'd thought about it so many times.

"See have mind good land, Plymouth."

But what did that have to do with anything? He still had no idea where or what the good land could be. And this hardly helped. The cold deflation spread fast. He felt his excitement wane.

Shit.

Dan was about to start typing the rest of the message when again he stopped himself. The itch was still nagging. He'd never understood it, but he'd also learned never to ignore it. It was telling him he'd stumbled on to something important.

He tried to clear his mind and let the thought settle. He imagined Rutherford, probably asleep on his side, soon to be woken and walked by the ever-obliging downstairs neighbour. He was looking forward to seeing his dog again, he had been neglecting him too much of late. When he got back home they'd go for a long Dartmoor walk as a treat. It would be official bonding time, good for them both.

The flitting thought insisted on more attention. Like a wailing baby in his mind it prised his thoughts back from Rutherford. What else was in that clue? The blackmailer had written something about predicting it would be the most difficult to solve. Could that be a hint?

Dan couldn't help but doubt himself.

So, the predictive text function on his phone made the word home into good. So what? It meant nothing, was just how the program worked. He stared at the phone, but the idea continued to form, gained momentum, tumbling fast through his mind.

Hope rekindled. First just a flicker, then a flare, spreading defiance. Give it a try – have some faith – believe. What is there to lose?

Dan clenched a fist. So then, the other words in the clue. What would the predictive text make of them?

It couldn't be that easy, surely? But it was often said the simplest way was the smartest. It worked in his profession. The oft-repeated mantra, the acronym drilled into cub broadcast journalists. Kiss, keep it short and simple. It had saved him yesterday in that broadcast at the zoo. Perhaps it could do so again now.

Dan noticed his hands were shaking. He knew he thought he was on to something, but he couldn't allow himself to believe. Not yet. It was too far to fall if he was wrong. He ran his tongue over the ulcer and began typing the words of the final clue into the phone, checking what the predictive text made of them.

See gave him the options red or ref. Have offered gave, hate or gate. Mind came up with mine or nine. Good gave a range of choices, hoof, hood, gone or home. Land was lane, Jane or lame.

He felt his belief falter. It looked random, hopeless, nonsensical. But he didn't dare give up. Not now. Not yet.

Dan reached over, grabbed a piece of paper and pen and wrote down all the possible words in columns, trying to sense a pattern.

see	have	mind	good	land
red	gave	mine	hoof	lane
ref	hate	nine	hood	jane
	gate		gone	lame
			home	

His hands were shaking more now and he felt breathless. He was convinced there was a message in there. But there were too many combinations and possibilities to be sure he'd found the answer. What could help him?

Dan stared at the words. Plymouth, that had to be the clue. "See have mind good land Plymouth," was the original riddle. He was looking for a sentence that made sense in the context of Plymouth. It had to refer to somewhere or something in the city.

The first word must be red. Ref made no sense. So if the first was red, the second had to be gate. Nothing else fitted.

Red gate … it was making sense, he was sure of it. They were looking for a red gate, somewhere in Plymouth. Was that the hiding place of the Judgement Book? Maybe the four other riddles were just diversions, part of the blackmailers' game. Was this the only clue that really mattered?

The third word had to be nine. It must be, nothing else worked. So the fourth should be a street, road, or place. It had to be Hood or Home Lane. He wasn't sure if there was either in Plymouth, but as Plymouth Argyle's ground was Home Park, that must be it. Home Lane.

Dan sat back on his pillows and gazed at the piece of paper. He circled the words, then wrote them out again to be certain.

Red gate, nine Home Lane, Plymouth.

That was where they had to go. His heart was thumping so loud it was like a bass drum beating in his ears. He was sure it was the answer, sure.

His imagination flew. In the next couple of hours he'd be back in Plymouth. They'd find the Judgement Book, save his and Adam's career and the lives of the countless other unknown victims. He'd give Lizzie the exclusive of her life by revealing the Book's hiding place and he'd be back with Claire too.

All would be well. A true Hollywood ending.

Dan gulped a drink of water from the glass on the bedside table, tried to steady himself. It was almost seven o'clock.

There were just 12 hours to go to the blackmailers' deadline.

Dan didn't notice the drive back to Plymouth. His head was full of the red gate at nine, Home Lane. He wondered if it even existed. And if so, what they would they find there.

He imagined the end of a tree-lined road and an arched, wooden gate, tall and imposing, himself checking over it, then, by the hinges finding a secret compartment which sprung open when he pressed the right place on the wood. For the first time in what felt like days he managed a weak smile. It sounded like something from the children's books he used to read so many years ago.

He'd had a quick wash, dressed and hurriedly left the inn. Dan called Adam on the way and was unsurprised to find the detective already in Charles Cross.

'Can't speak for long, I'm driving. Any news?'

'Not a bloody thing. And no leads either.' Adam's voice sounded husky with tiredness and frustration. 'I'm sitting here trying to work on the case and I've got sod all to work on. We've only got hours before the Judgement Book's released to the media. And you know what happens then.'

Dan didn't want to think about it. A vision of the headlines floated in front of his eyes.

"THE POLICE'S REPORTER", would be one of the more polite banners. Others would be harsher; "COPS' TV STOOGE," or "INSPECTOR HACK". They would be accompanied by a photo of Dan, talking to a TV camera, the picture doctored to show him wearing a smart police uniform. He noticed the car's speed creeping up.

'I think I might have something,' Dan said.

'What?'

'Can you check if there's a Home Lane in Plymouth?'

'A what?'

'A Home Lane.'

A disbelieving pause, then an angry torrent. 'For God's sake, Dan! What the hell are your talking about? A huge scandal's about to erupt, we're going to lose our jobs and you're ...'

'Shut up, Adam! I know all that. Damn, I bloody know it! I haven't thought about anything else. I think I might be on to something. Just do it, will you?'

'If you're wasting my time for some ...'

'Just do it!'

Dan heard Adam loose off a couple of profanities, but he could also hear the detective's footsteps walking across the MIR. There was a city map on the wall. Dan accelerated the car around a milk lorry and tried to enjoy the beauty of the rising sun stretching across the emerald fields. A herd of black and white cows plodded towards an open gate, a man walking behind them, shepherding them along. Such an anachronism would usually make him grin, but not today. Dan tried to count the animals to distract himself from the tortuous wait.

It didn't work. Not in the least.

Finally the footsteps returned and the phone crackled. 'Yes, there is,' came Adam's voice, calmer now. 'It's down in Eggbuckland, near the Deer Park Forest. Why?'

Dan tried to keep his voice level and convincing, explained about the predictive texting. There was another silence on the line. He could feel Adam weighing it up.

'Sounds a bit wild to me,' he said finally.

'It did to me too. But I still reckon it's right.'

Adam sighed. 'What else have we got? OK, we'll give it a try. Why the hell not? I'll get going …'

'No! Not without me. I've got to be there.'

'We don't have time.'

'Adam, I've got to be there! It's both our futures riding on this.'

'How long?'

'I'll be at Charles Cross in an hour and a half.'

The detective swore again. 'No longer then. This case is like bloody torture.'

Dan made one more call, to the duty journalist in the newsroom and told him he was on his way back to Plymouth. Highly significant developments were breaking in the blackmail case he said, and he had to be there. He didn't expect to produce a report for the lunchtime news, but certainly for Wessex Tonight. The producer promised to pass the message on to Lizzie when she got in.

He thought about Claire, imagined her just waking up, going through her breakfast ritual. Was she thinking about him? Had her mood passed? Dan realised he didn't have much history to judge for how long she could remain angry. They'd only had a couple of rows in the time they'd been together, and they'd been very minor, dissipated within an hour or two.

He wondered whether he should try to ring her again. It was a quarter past seven. Too early. She would call him when she was ready. Or he hoped she would. He hoped.

The Peugeot reached the M5 and Dan relaxed a little. Fast roads all the way back now, no more of the Devon countryside's charming but frustrating green lanes. He thought about the gamble he was taking. He had to be right about the last clue, he had to convince Adam he could report a story on it and it had to be good enough that Lizzie would accept he was right to leave Exmoor.

Dan swallowed hard. It was a hell of a lot to hope for. He turned on the radio and found some music to dampen the fire of his thoughts. He had a sense this drive back to Charles Cross was the classical calm before the oncoming storm.

Adam was waiting in the police station car park, pacing back and forth and looking over every time the gates drew back. His tie hung well down his neck. He'd called Dan three times on the drive to check his progress. The detective climbed straight into the car as he pulled up.

'Let's go,' he said. 'Home Lane. Quick. I've just about convinced myself your guess is worth a try. We've got nothing else.'

Dan noticed a patrol car swing out from the underground garages and follow them.

'In case we need them,' Adam said. 'Couple of uniforms. Big lads. You never know. I wouldn't rule out a trap.'

Dan drove north, past the shining glass of the University, along Mutley Plain and up to Eggbuckland. The outbound traffic was light, most of the roads filled with people commuting into the city. The sun still hung in the sky, rising quickly now, the day warming fast.

Dan found himself wishing he had rung Claire. He'd been hoping for five minutes with her in the police station. An exchange of smiles in a hidden corner, a quick cuddle of reassurance and the world would have been habitable again. He wondered what she was working on. He'd half expected her to come to Home Lane.

'Where's Claire?' he asked Adam, trying to make his voice as easy as possible.

'I've given her the morning off. She said she needed some time to sort out a couple of things. She has been working a lot of hours lately.'

Dan felt his body stiffen. He pictured Claire collecting his stuff from her flat, taking it round to his place and removing her possessions. Saying goodbye to Rutherford, then posting her key back through the letterbox.

In a few sharp seconds of fret he'd managed to convince himself he would get home later to find his toothbrush, shampoo, bed T-shirt, spare socks, pants, work trousers, shirt and tie and even tins of emergency beer from her cupboard, all dumped in the hallway. He wondered if there'd be a sorrowful note.

"Dear Dan, I couldn't bring myself to say this to you in person, but …"

He gripped the steering wheel and ran his tongue over the ulcer. It felt like a small pit on the inside of his lip, starting to throb again.

He tried to calm himself. She'd probably just gone to the doctor. She'd said she was going to. After all, they needed to know how long she'd been pregnant. She just wanted to talk it through with a professional. That was all.

Dan couldn't help feeling annoyed. He'd wanted to go with her, to hear the news as she did, be there to hold and support her.

'Right turn here,' said Adam, pointing. Dan swung the wheel and the patrol car followed, almost on their bumper.

A mildewed white sign said Home Lane. Dan slowed the car to look for number nine.

The lane wasn't so different from the way he'd imagined. The houses were large and modern, a mix of detached and semis, all set back from the road. A line of young chestnut trees ran down the gentle hill towards the Deer Park, a misnomer if

259

ever there was one. It was just a patch of woodland in a housing estate which had stolen the name to disguise itself with rural appeal.

The area was far too urban for such wildlife. Any deer that found itself here would quickly have put up a "For Sale" sign and started looking at properties elsewhere.

'That was fifty-five,' yelped Adam, pointing to his left. 'Keep going, we're almost there.'

They counted down the houses. They were too far back for Dan to see ahead to the colour of the gates, but he found his hands shaking again as they neared number nine. They'd know if he could be right the moment they saw its gate.

'Nineteen, seventeen, fifteen, thirteen, eleven,' reeled off Adam, his head locked to the left. Dan stared straight on, couldn't look.

Adam began opening the door even before the car had stopped. 'Nine – number nine, there it is.'

Dan steadied himself, got out of the car, counted silently to five and then allowed himself to look. It was a detached house, shining white, a grey slate roof and a couple of cars parked outside on the tarmac drive. The double gates were both open. They were bright red. Dan closed his eyes, then opened them again, just to be sure. The gates were still red. He leaned back against the Peugeot in relief.

'Well that's half the battle,' called Adam over his shoulder as he strode towards the house. 'Now the important bit.'

The patrol car pulled up behind them. The two officers didn't get out, but rolled down the windows and watched curiously. Adam was moving fast, almost at the gates.

The door of the house opened and a middle-aged woman stepped out. She was wearing a blue dressing gown and picked up two bottles of milk from the doorstep.

Adam bent over and began examining the left hand gate. It was wooden and arched, reaching up to head height, just as Dan had imagined. But the wood was cheap and thin, and there was no place to hide a book, nowhere at all.

Dan stopped walking and stared back and forth between the two gates.

What if there was no Judgement Book here? No book, no story, no way to solve the riddle. Then what would they be left with? The words echoed in his mind.

No future.

His tongue found the ulcer again and he winced with pain.

No future.

Adam had shifted around to the back of the gate and was checking the supporting struts. His hands ran over them, his face just inches from the wood. Dan could see from the rapid way he was moving he hadn't found anything. The woman took a couple of hesitant steps towards him.

'Hello?' she said nervously. 'Can I help you? What's the police car doing at the end of our drive? Is there something wrong?'

Adam stood up from the gate and showed her his warrant card.

'Nothing wrong at all, madam,' he said with his usual extreme politeness. 'We've had a tip off there may be some information hidden in your gate which is important to an inquiry.'

Her face wrinkled with bafflement. Dan could see she'd put on some blue eye shadow, but hadn't yet got to the rest of her make-up. Preparations for work interrupted by the need for a morning coffee, probably. He understood well. It could be irresistible, deferring the demands of the day.

'Have you found anything?' she asked.

'Not a thing,' replied Adam bitterly. 'Have you noticed anyone tampering with your gate lately? Anyone hanging around it, acting suspiciously?'

She shook her head, making the damp ends of her hair flap. 'No, and I'm sure we would have. We've got motion sensors, which light up the drive if anyone comes close to the house.'

Dan let out a low moan.

She hesitated, seemed to think for a moment. 'You could ask the Charleses I suppose, but they haven't said anything about anyone acting strangely.'

The word was like a shock. Charles.

Dan felt the sudden energy of fresh hope propel him

forwards. He walked quickly and joined Adam. The detective was still glaring at the gate as though it had offended him.

'I'm sorry, did you say there was a Charles family living here?' Dan asked.

'Yes,' she replied, turning to him. 'The house is split into two. The Charleses live in the other half, around the side. We get on fine. The only problem we've ever had was the post, but we've sorted that.'

'How? How?!'

She looked at him, even more puzzled now. 'We just put a little post box on the pillar by the side of the gate.' She pointed. 'So their post goes in one side and ours goes into the box on the other.'

'Where?' asked Dan, then again, 'Where?'

She shook her head at the stranger's interest in such mundane, domestic matters, checked a look at Adam. He nodded, so she walked to the far corner of the right hand gate and pointed. There was a small wooden box fixed to the edge by the pillar.

'It works fine,' the woman went on. 'The only problem is when we have a relief postman. They get confused. So we wrote the Charleses' name by the box.'

She pointed again and they followed the gesture. To Dan, it felt like slow motion, his shifting gaze taking in every foot of the ground until it found its target.

There, on the gate, by the box, in neat, handwritten white paint was the simple word "Charles".

They stared at it. Just stood and stared.

'Can I help you any more?' the woman asked. 'Only I've got to get ready for work, and it's going to be a busy day.'

Adam flinched. 'No, no thanks. We may have to pop around for a chat later, but don't worry. It'd only be brief.'

She walked back into the house, still casting the odd quizzical glance over her shoulder. Adam crouched down by the box and slowly touched the word. His fingers traced the small, white letters, almost reverentially.

'Charles,' he whispered.

Dan knelt down and joined him. He looked up at the clear

blue sky and nodded as if to say thanks. Hope had returned.

'Charles,' Dan repeated. He couldn't suppress the excitement in his voice. 'Which I think gives us, "Open original memorial Church Charles." We've cracked it. We've cracked it!'

They stood up, and without thinking Dan reached out and hugged Adam. The detective didn't resist, patted a hand on Dan's back. Only a loud cough from one of the officers in the patrol car prompted them to disengage.

'Charles Church,' said Adam. 'Charles bloody Church. The Judgement Book's in the memorial in Charles Church. It's their final taunt. It's just yards from the police station. They've been taking the piss out of us in a spectacular way. The damned thing's been under our bloody noses the whole time.'

Dan drove fast, back to Charles Cross, Adam urging him on. They were close now, the detective kept repeating, he was sure of it. The case could be wrapped up by tonight, the Judgement Book found, the second blackmailer safely in custody, their venom neutralised. To Dan, his friend sounded obsessed, almost demented.

But he understood exactly why. Of all the cases they'd worked on together this felt the most personal, the first one he had a real stake in. With the rest it was justice they were fighting for; a concept, an ideal, something desirable but often debatable too, and always on behalf of others. This time it was themselves, their lives and their futures.

Adam had shaved even more sloppily today, his stubble casting patches of pronounced shadow around his neck and chin. His face was taut and lined with fatigue, his tie was low on his neck and he made no attempt to tighten it. There was a slight staleness in the air around him, as if he'd washed only carelessly. In the mirror, Dan saw the patrol car following them.

When they got back to the police station, Adam sent the two constables to get a toolbox. He went to find a forensics officer and returned with Arthur in tow. He was again prattling about how he should never have been forced to retire. The technician kept interlacing his fingers and looked excited. He repeatedly told Adam he wasn't a field man, but he was honoured at the assignment and would do his best, as ever.

Dan's mobile warbled. It was five to nine. He knew who was on the phone. He'd been expecting the call and for once was surprised to find he didn't particularly care.

Lizzie would have come in to work ten minutes ago, been briefed on what was going on by the morning producer and Dan would be top of her list of matters requiring immediate attention. He paced over to the corner of the car park, faced into the brick wall, steeled himself for battle and answered.

A raging Lizzie never bothered with introductions. She expected her staff to know who it was and why she was calling, and invariably they did.

'What the hell do you think you're doing?'

'My job.'

'Your job's what I say it is.'

'My job's to be right on top of the big crime news. It doesn't come any bigger than the blackmailer. A huge story's breaking and I need to be here to cover it for us before anyone else gets it.'

A pause on the line. Dan wondered if Lizzie had been taken aback by his reaction. You fought her fire at your peril. Usually, by far the best policy was to accept the assault and hope it would quickly pass. He could feel her torn between an innate desire to maul him and her curiosity about the story. They were both powerful instincts. He waited, let himself cool a little. He thought he knew which would win.

Finally, more calmly, she asked, 'What's the story?'

'I think the cops are going to find the Judgement Book,' he replied, hoping desperately that was exactly what they'd do.

She almost shrieked. 'What? Find it?'

'Yep.'

'And we can have this all to ourselves?'

'Yep.'

'And we can get pictures of the book?'

Dan hesitated. He hadn't talked to Adam about any of this. They weren't even sure they were going to find the Book.

He heard himself say, 'I think so.'

'You'd better make sure so. If this story comes off, and if we have pictures of the book, I might just forget about you disobeying my express instructions. I want the exclusive, I want the Book, I want the cops talking about it, I want a good, long, award-winning report and I want it all by tonight. You got that?'

He agreed and hung up, then stuck two fingers up at the phone. But Dan was amazed he'd escaped so lightly. Now it was just a matter of selling the idea to Adam. The detective was pacing back and forth in front of a patrol car, kicking out at the occasional imaginary stone.

Now wasn't the time to raise it. Later, he could do it later. When they found the Judgement Book. When, Dan thought, when. Please let it be when. It had to be when. He couldn't allow himself to consider the alternative of if.

He tried to distract himself, think about something pleasant, enjoyable, fun, something to look forward to when this ordeal was finally over. Nothing came to calm his racing mind.

Dan tried a quick call to Claire, but her mobile was turned off. He looked at his phone in surprise, checked it was working. She must be having a lie in bed, he thought. She rarely turned off her phone. Maybe she needed to catch up on some sleep, didn't want to be disturbed. Or did she need time to think about the future of their relationship?

Whether they had a future.

He looked over towards the Hoe and Claire's flat. It was only half a mile away. The momentum of his fear was growing fast. He must see her soon, and he would. But first they had to find the Judgement Book.

The two policemen emerged from the station's back door carrying a large silver toolbox between them. They were already sweating. Adam barked an order to follow him and they walked quickly out of the car park. Dan broke into a jog, caught up with Adam and marched alongside him.

They walked down the hill towards the ruined church, standing serene in the spring sunshine, unaware of the burden of hopes weighing upon its ruined shell.

Chapter Twenty-three

THE CHURCH ROSE LIKE a mirage, growing out of the haze of heat and traffic fumes from the surrounding intersection of roads. A spectrum of colour buzzed around it, the cars, vans, trucks and bikes of the people following their daily routines. Dan wondered how many ever really saw the church and thought about what it meant, the hate, prejudice and insanity that overcame Europe, the destruction it left behind and the countless lives it stole.

The sun was high in the morning sky now, generous in spreading its warmth across the city. Dan felt a sticky sweat seeping over his body. He took off his jacket and carried it on his shoulder. Adam did the same. Behind them, the two police officers stopped for a quick break, fanning themselves with their caps. They lowered the toolbox onto a wall, then picked it up again when Adam looked back at them. Arthur followed, chattering away to the policemen. Motorists began to stare at their strange convoy, heading down the hill.

They reached the edge of the roundabout. The traffic was relentless and there was no way over, apart from crossing the road. Adam shouted to one of the policemen who gave him a look, then stepped confidently out with his hand raised. The procession of cars reluctantly slowed and they crossed.

It felt surreal, a small haven of green in the midst of the concrete bustle of a modern city. The grass surrounding the church was carefully trimmed and speckled with the white dots of daisies and yellow stars of dandelions. A couple of patches and lines of cream and butter daffodils ran along the banks towards the old walls. A semi-spiral of stone steps led down to the main tower, at the western end of the ruin. Adam jogged down and they followed.

A black iron gate hung open at the arched entrance to the tower, its once sharp spikes blunted by years of rust. Dan looked up, to where the peal of bells would have hung. There was only a square of distant sky. He imagined the lost spire, reaching into the night, the German bombers droning above it.

A pigeon fluttered, the beating echo of its flapping wings surprisingly loud in the hollowness of the tower. The flagstones at their feet were covered in dusty guano. In one corner were a couple of empty cans of lager and a crumpled pair of lacy black knickers. Dan couldn't suppress a smile. He saw a Saturday night and a drunken young couple with nowhere to go. Very Plymouth, he thought. Scrambled sex in a ruined church, surrounded by speeding cars. It wasn't the pinnacle of romance.

'Here, over here.' Adam had walked into the main part of the church, what would have been the chancel. He shouted to the two policemen.

Grey-green ivy climbed the pitted walls, spreading skywards as if trying to escape the ruin. The empty, fluted arches of the windows stared sightless, gouged out by the screaming shrapnel of the murderous past. Dan's feet slid on the smoothness of the flagstones, worn away by generations of worshippers, and, after the Blitz, the pummelling of the relentless rain. Some bore faint inscriptions, too tired now by the years to be legible. Stray patches of grass edged across them, as though trying to pull the stones back into their earthly home.

Adam stood, hands on hips, staring at a circular black plaque on the wall. It looked fresh, new, incongruous with its aged surroundings. Dan joined him and together they read the words.

It marked the fiftieth anniversary of the Blitz of Plymouth and was dedicated to the honour of the 1200 citizens of the city killed as a result of the air raids.

'That can't be it,' Adam said doubtfully. 'It's too modern. The answer to the riddle was "Open original memorial". Is there another one?'

It was Arthur who answered. 'Yes, Mr Breen,' he said hesitantly. 'It's over in the other corner.'

He explained that local history was a passion, something he'd begun to take an interest in following his retirement. The new plaque had been forged to demonstrate the past should and would never be forgotten, a fitting way to mark such a significant anniversary of the Blitz. But there was an older plaque too, dating from just after the war. It must be that to

267

which the riddle referred.

Arthur shuffled off towards the opposite corner. There, at head height on the stone wall was another dark plaque, this time oval in shape.

"Charles Church. Built 1641. Consecrated 1665. Completed 1708. Named in honour of King Charles I. Ruined by enemy action, 21 March 1941. Partially restored 1952, by the city in cooperation with the Ministry of Works. The idea of restoration having been sponsored by the Old Plymouth Society, as a memorial to those citizens of Plymouth who were killed in air raids on the city in the 1939 – 1945 War."

'That's it,' said Adam, his voice strangely quiet. 'That's it.'

Dan shifted forwards to stare at the plaque. It was fixed to the stone by two thick metal screws. He could see from the shining wear marks across their heads that they'd recently been removed.

The policemen creaked the toolbox open, found a large, cross-headed screwdriver and positioned it over the plaque. One tried twisting it, but the screw wouldn't give. The other man had a go. Still no movement.

'Come on, come on,' muttered Adam impatiently. He wiped some sweat from his forehead. Dan chewed on his ulcer but didn't notice its stinging pain. All he could concentrate on was the plaque.

One policeman found a rag in the bottom of the toolbox, wrapped it around the screwdriver's handle and tried again. His face creased with the effort. The other joined in, forcing his weight around the tool. This time the screw grated and gave, just a little. Panting, they tried again. Now it started to unwind, slowly at first, then smoothly. After a few seconds the screw dropped onto a flagstone. Arthur bent down and picked it up.

The policemen went to take a brief rest, but Adam chided them on. The detective couldn't keep still, his black shoes continually shifting on the smooth stone.

The second screw gave easily. One policeman held the plaque as the other kept working the screwdriver, turning it rhythmically. The shiny metal protruded further and further as it eased out. The thread was almost free. The policeman stopped working, the two officers glanced at each other, then over to Adam.

He held the look, breathed out hard, nodded. Finally he said simply, 'Do it.'

They lifted the plaque from the wall.

Something fell from behind it, a blur of motion, streaking down the stone, thudding softly into the ground. Their eyes followed as it bounced and settled.

It was a black book, plain and the size of a pocket diary. It had fallen so some of the pages fanned open. Dan strained his eyes, but couldn't see any writing. The tension in his chest was such that he was struggling to breathe. He noticed he was trembling.

He started eagerly forward, but Adam reached out a warning arm. 'Arthur,' he prompted hoarsely.

The technician had snapped on some plastic gloves. He knelt slowly down by the diary and picked it up, then slid it into a large, clear plastic bag and sealed the end.

'You can have a look now, Mr Breen,' he said, holding it out.

Adam took the bag and through it turned some of the pages of the book. Dan took a couple of fast steps forward, stood over his shoulder, chewing hard at his ulcer. The two policemen sat down on the toolbox and watched. One shook his head, as if wondering at all this fuss about a small black book.

Adam kept turning the pages. The first few were blank, then the next, then the next. He got to half way and still no writing. He turned some more pages. They remained blank.

The book was almost finished and still nothing written there. Not a word. Not a thing.

Dan felt himself start to sweat harder. Where were the tales of sex and lust, lies and deceit? Where was his entry? Where was Adam's? Where was the report he needed for the programme tonight?

Adam got to the final page and now, at last, there were words, scribbled in blue ink, but clear and familiar. It was the same handwriting as the final two blackmail notes. Adam held the pages open, Dan's face close by his shoulder, reading too.

"Good try," it said. "But the Judgement Book lives on. Remember your initial thoughts if you want to find it. They would be DEAD right. This is your final chance."

Adam stared at the open pages, then threw the book down onto the flagstones.

Dan squinted in the sunshine. The lines of red dots of the digital clock above the post office said it was just after ten. Chimes started to ring out from St Andrew's Church. He had to force his mind to remember where there was a florist in the city centre. He'd never had to find one before. He was struggling to concentrate on anything, but some small logic in his brain told him that if he was going to lose his job he should at least try to save his relationship.

He found a florist by the banks, a small place, but full of the rich scents and colours of fresh flowers. It was doing a healthy trade. Men who neglected their partners, prompted by the sight of flowers as they withdrew money from the cashpoints, he wondered? It was a clever location for a shop that often traded on guilt.

Dan had no idea what to buy, but went for the safety of half a dozen red roses. The old lady who ran the shop seemed to find his confusion amusing and recommended he should buy flowers for his girlfriend more often.

If I still have her I will, he thought.

He walked south, out of the city centre and towards the Hoe. The sun had climbed higher in the sky now, and the day was growing hotter. People sat at tables outside cafés and laughed together. The sunshine was infectious.

Adam had stalked back to Charles Cross. Dan asked him what he planned to do next and was surprised by the answer. Adam rarely swore, and when he did it was usually at the mild end of the range. This explosion of profanities would have made a navvy nod with respect. The upshot was he was going to go back through all the case material they had and try to think of what he could do next.

He wasn't hopeful. There were only nine hours before the Judgement Book was released to the media. They had very limited time and no leads.

Dan had asked for half an hour in town to sort out a couple of important matters. He'd been prepared to plead urgent personal reasons, but Adam had just said 'whatever'. He looked defeated, his shoulders hunched and his tie hanging low on his neck. Dan watched as his friend took out his wallet and stared at a picture of Annie and Tom. He'd never seen the detective look so forlorn.

Dan tried to come up with some grand vision to solve the case as he walked to Claire's flat, but his brain was utterly lifeless. What chance did he have if Adam couldn't think of anything? They needed to find the Judgement Book, it was as simple as that, and they had no idea where it was. He thought of Sarah, sitting in her cell, laughing at them, then ducked as a seagull wheeled over his head. It had become an instinctive reaction. Twice in the last year he'd been hit by their stinking, flying droppings, once right in the face.

The anger of the memory stirred his brain. There must be another way to help themselves. Lateral thinking, he'd always prided himself on it. When he'd bought his flat, there were three other people who wanted it and they'd all had to submit blind bids. It looked to Dan like a game he could easily lose, and he'd never cared for such lotteries. After remarkably little agonising, he bribed the estate agent to tell him what the other bids were and won the flat by a convenient five hundred pounds.

It had become a motto. If you can't win by the rules, there's only one thing to do. Change them.

He wondered if there was any way to change the rules here. Well, if they couldn't find the Judgement Book, how about the other blackmailer? That would be just as good. It would stop them releasing the book and give the police a chance to find it. A tiny hope sparkled in Dan's mind. Not a bad idea, not bad at all. But how the hell would they find the blackmailer?

He felt the brief glow of optimism fade. He knew he had no idea.

Claire lived on the first floor of a converted Victorian house, dating from the 1850s. It was the way the Hoe had evolved, just

271

like in countless other cities, from the showy family homes of the affluent Victorians to the flats of the young and modern middle classes.

The area was popular, close to the city centre and the sea, but suffered with the clutter of cars all competing for scarce parking spaces in its narrow lanes. It was a haven for seagulls too, who never seemed to rest. After his first couple of sleepless nights staying over and raging at their screeching cries, Dan had bought himself a pair of earplugs. Claire, who could sleep through anything, had never stopped ribbing him for it. The memory made him smile, until he remembered why he was here.

He fumbled for his key, let himself in to the exterior door and slowly climbed the carpeted, wooden stairs. They creaked with the rhythm of his steps. Outside the door to her flat, he paused. He felt nervous, jittery, just as he had when he came to pick her up for their first date. It was a sign of just how far he feared their relationship had deteriorated that he didn't put his key in the door and walk straight in.

Dan bent over and rested his ear against the door. Inside it was silent. He knew she wasn't there, but he knocked anyway. There was no answer, so he opened the door.

The flat was tidy, apart from a couple of mugs and plates on the side of the sink. A chat with a friend over a cup of tea, most likely. Another thought surfaced in his mind and he tried to force it away, but it wouldn't go, kept nipping at him. Another man …

No, it couldn't be. Claire wasn't like that. But the fear wouldn't quieten. It kept whispering snidely – how many other men had been sure their partners weren't like that?

He shouldn't snoop, he knew it, however strong the temptation, but he had a quick look around to see if there was anything that might indicate where Claire had gone. Nothing.

Dan put down the roses on the coffee table and debated whether to leave a note. No, there was no need. She'd know they came from him. The flowers said more than words.

He'd been trying to keep his eyes away from it, but he couldn't help looking at the photo of them together on

Dartmoor, Rutherford sitting between them. It was her favourite, taken at Christmas, patches of snow on the wiry moorgrass and distant hilltops. Claire liked the way their hair was being blown back by the mischievous Dartmoor wind, how glowing and happy they looked. Her strange little family, she'd called it.

Dan stopped himself before he could wonder whether they would still be together for a photo next Christmas, or the one after, and whether there might be an addition to the family in that picture.

He remembered the day well. It was one of those rare photographs that felt genuine, captured their happiness, no need for forced smiles. It'd been taken by a passing rambler he'd waylaid. For once they hadn't even had to struggle to get Rutherford to sit still.

They'd gone for a walk out from Princetown, around King's Tor, then back to the Spray of Feathers Inn for a pint and a pie. Rutherford had got himself stuck in a gully and they'd had to pull him out. Claire fell backwards as the dog escaped, Dan had burst into helpless laughter and she'd tripped him, pulled him down with her and they'd rolled together in the snow.

And now her voice was in the room, screaming and vicious, bouncing from every wall. The two words from that row, in the MIR.

"Selfish arsehole!"

Dan felt a sudden urge to pick up the photo and throw it against the door, enjoy the cascading shards of shattering glass crashing around him.

Where the fuck was Claire? Why was she ignoring him? Avoiding him? Tormenting him? How could she do this?

He felt like running around her flat, kicking out at the TV, the stereo, the bookshelves and the CDs, picking up the plates and glasses and bowls in the kitchen and smashing them onto the floor.

Dan stared at the photo. He took a couple of deep breaths, turned away, closed the flat's door with an exaggerated calm and walked slowly down the stairs, one leaden foot automatically following another. It was over, his career, his relationship. He might as well start facing it.

Unless …

He could never explain where the idea came from, how the defiance fired so quickly through his mind. Perhaps it was the instinct of survival, the human willingness to believe. All he knew was that it was there, a firework in the night. It was a chance where before there was only hopelessness, a possibility where previously there was none.

Dan stopped, reached out a hand, gripped the banister.

The idea was growing.

The only thing they had was that they'd solved the riddle. It might not have led them to the Judgement Book, but that was all part of the blackmailers' plan to humiliate them. To get another one over on the establishment. To lead them to a false book and laugh at them. To enjoy their defeat and despair.

So would the second blackmailer be able to resist if they were offered the chance to witness such a humiliation in person?

The thought gathered impetus. Dan started jogging down the stairs.

One last chance, he thought. Maybe we've got one last chance to save ourselves. But we'll have to move fast.

He didn't notice he'd already stopped thinking about Claire.

Chapter Twenty-four

THE MIR SMELT OF defeat. It was hot, despite the open windows and the air tinged with the sour staleness of dry sweat. Dan was reminded of a night spent covering the last General Election, the local Traditionalist Party headquarters, a group of dedicated and driven people who had stayed up all night in hope to await a result which had rendered all their months of work worthless.

Now it was apparent in the MIR. The movements of the people slow and laboured, lacking urgency or energy. There was nothing left to try for. And it was captured in each expression. No belief, no spark, no hope.

Adam stood, head bowed over a pile of files and a spread of papers. The bin beside him was full of empty coffee cups and screwed up balls of paper. He didn't look over when Dan walked in. There were a couple of other detectives on the phones, but their voices were hushed. One kept glancing over at Adam, as though worried for his superior's sanity.

Dan tried to force some enthusiasm into his voice. 'How are you getting on?'

'We're not,' said Adam curtly, shaking his head. 'We're stuffed. We've got no leads and almost no time left.' He looked up at the clock on the wall. It was exactly midday. 'Seven hours and no leads. We're stuffed.'

Dan knew he couldn't talk in front of the others. He had to get Adam somewhere private, and fast. He didn't have much time. The lunchtime news was on air at half past one. If he missed that, his plan was finished before it had begun.

'Can I have a word?' he asked the detective.

'Go ahead. I haven't got anything else on at the mo,' Adam replied sarcastically. 'Just trying to catch a blackmailer, save a few more people from suicide and myself from humiliation and the sack.'

The anger that made him want to smash up Claire's flat singed Dan again.

'It would be better – if I could have a quick word – in private,' he said in a strained voice.

'I'm not leaving the MIR until there's no hope left.'

One more try, thought Dan. Hold your temper. One more.

'It'll only take a minute,' he said determinedly. 'Please.'

'Here or nothing,' replied Adam dismissively, looking back at the papers on his desk.

'Adam, for fuck's sake!' shouted Dan. The two detectives stopped talking into their phones. The room fell silent. Adam looked up, his eyes narrowing. Dan couldn't tell if he was surprised or angry. He wasn't sure he cared.

'I've got a fucking idea that might just help us and I want to talk to you about it in fucking private! Is that clear enough for your thick cop head?'

Adam glared at him, stood up and strode out of the MIR. Dan followed, checking the door was shut behind. The detective stopped sharply in the corridor outside.

'Who the hell do you think you are?' he snarled. 'Never talk to me like that, or you're out of here and we don't speak again. Got that?'

Dan saw his finger jab out at his friend's chest. 'Then never put me down like that again – who the hell do you think you are?'

'I'm a senior detective with a vital investigation to run …'

'And you've asked me here to help! And I'm as much in the shit as you are! And I've got an idea, and we haven't exactly got anything else, have we?'

Adam's mouth opened as he tried to snap back, but Dan didn't give him a chance. 'I'm only in this because of you! It's not just your bloody life that's on the line here. It's mine too. So do us both a favour. Lift your head from the pit of your selfish misery and listen to me, will you?'

The two men glared at each other, their faces set just a few inches apart. Neither blinked. A ridiculous thought grew in Dan's mind. Were they going to fight, here, in the police station? Then Adam closed his eyes for a second and nodded.

'OK,' he said quietly. 'I apologise. I shouldn't have done that.'

Dan felt the rage cool. 'I'm sorry too. I shouldn't have lost my temper.'

Adam put out a hand and Dan hesitated, then shook it. 'Let's forget it,' they both said at the same time.

'OK, what've you got?' asked Adam.

'It's got to be quick if it's going to work. You ready for this?'

'Go on.'

'We need to find the Judgement Book, but we don't know where it is. But wouldn't finding the other blackmailer be just as good? It would stop them revealing the Book and give us a chance to find it.'

'True. But there's just the one tiny problem. We've got no idea who or where he or she is.'

'Right. So we have to make him come to us.'

Adam couldn't keep the incredulity from his voice. 'And how do you plan to work that little miracle?'

'Our blackmailers want to humiliate us. So let's give them the chance to do it, and to a huge audience. I don't think they'd be able to resist.'

'Meaning?'

'Meaning we've cracked the riddle and we know it's a fake. But they don't know we've cracked it. So let's use that.'

'How?'

Dan thought fast. 'Here's how it runs. I go live on our lunchtime news to say you believe you've worked out where the Judgement Book's hidden and you'll be going to recover it later this afternoon. I guarantee the other blackmailer is watching. They know how close you and I are. They're bound to want to see what I'm up to and how you're getting on with the case.'

Adam sounded more interested now. 'OK. But how does putting all that out help us?'

'The blackmailer knows we're going to find a fake book. They'll know we'll look stupid. They'll know that once I've put it out on the TV that all the television cameras, the snappers, the whole of the press will be there to witness it. They'll know lots of ordinary people will also turn out if it's somewhere as public as Charles Church. I reckon they'll think they can blend in with the crowd and so come to witness our humiliation in person. I tell you, they'll find it irresistible. There's your trap.'

Adam nodded slowly. He reached for his tie and pulled it up to his collar and straightened it. Dan almost smiled, almost. He'd didn't think he'd ever been so glad to see his friend's little idiosyncrasy.

'So we put lots of plain clothes cops in amongst the crowd,' the detective said. 'And tell them to keep an eye out for anything suspicious.'

'Yep,' said Dan.

Adam breathed out heavily. 'It's still a long shot.'

'Yep,' repeated Dan. 'It is. But the simple point is this. What else have we got?'

The detective nodded. 'I think that's the winning argument. Come on, let's do it.'

Dan drove straight back to the studios, slewing the car around the back streets and rat runs, avoiding the inevitable tailbacks of the city's main roads. He knew he was going too fast, but he hardly noticed.

It was half past twelve. The lunchtime bulletin was on air in an hour. He parked badly, across two spaces, and ran up the stairs, his head full of how he needed to play his idea. He had to get it just right. Lizzie was standing in the corner of the newsroom, talking to the sports team. Talking at might have been a better description. Her animation said it wasn't an amicable conversation.

'Got a story for you,' he panted to Lisa, the lunchtime news producer.

'I'm OK for lunch thanks,' she replied, looking up. 'I've got enough stuff.'

Dan gritted his teeth in irritation. Producers who were only interested in filling their slot were a treasured hate. Never mind the quality of what was being offered, they were happy just to have any stories to take up their allotted time. They were computerised hacks, working automatically to a template without the input of thought, and there were far too many of them.

Plus, if his plan was going to work, he had to make it on air. There wasn't much time to argue the case. He usually hated melodrama and fuss, but on this occasion it might not be a bad strategy.

'For Christ's sake!' Dan shouted, as angrily as he could. He noticed only a few people had turned to look, so he slammed his satchel on the floor and flung his arms up into the air for added affect. 'Give me strength!' he bawled.

That was better, more heads were turning now. The newsroom was quietening, but most importantly Lizzie hadn't noticed. More histrionics were required.

'I've come running back in here to offer you a corking exclusive and all you do is tell me you've got enough stuff!' Dan ranted, his voice even louder. Out of the corner of his eye, he saw Lizzie's head snap over.

'It's a great story, a really top exclusive,' he yelled. Lizzie was moving now, walking fast towards the producer's desk. 'You'd be mad not to run it, absolutely barmy.'

Lisa gaped at him, raised her hands placatingly.

'OK, what's all this about?' Lizzie cut in. She was standing beside Dan, and tall today he thought. Bad news, that meant big heels. He had to get his spin in first.

'I've just come running back with a great story about the blackmail case and our alleged lunchtime producer here tells me she doesn't want it.'

Lizzie glared at him. Dan could hear a stiletto grinding into the carpet.

'What is it?' she snapped. 'It had better be damn good after all this fuss and leaving Exmoor without my say so.'

'It is damn good. I told you it would be.'

'So then?'

Dan bent down and fumbled in his satchel for his notebook. He knew exactly what he was going to say, but he wanted Lizzie to think he was quoting it, word for word, from a secret source.

'The police have worked out where the Judgement Book is. They've solved a series of riddles which have led them to it.

279

They're going to recover it this afternoon. It's the end of one of the biggest and most bizarre cases in the region's history.'

The whole newsroom had gone quiet. Everyone was watching.

'On air,' she barked. 'Lead story. Go on then, get writing. What are you waiting for?'

'You,' she added, turning to Lisa. 'Get a better nose for news or get looking for another job.'

Dan walked over to his desk, logged in to the computer and began working on his script. He kept his head down to avoid having to look at Lisa's tears. He put a note in his diary to take her for coffee tomorrow, explain and apologise – if he still worked here tomorrow.

'Some breaking news this lunchtime on the blackmailer case,' began Craig. 'We have an exclusive report for you on extraordinary developments. Our crime correspondent Dan Groves is with us.'

A camera spun and focused on him. Dan put on his most sonorous broadcast voice and intoned, 'Craig, I can tell you this. The police think they have discovered the secret location where the Judgement Book is hidden. I'll say that again, because of the importance of the story. The police believe they have discovered the location of the Book that's been used to blackmail several prominent local people, led to the suicide of two, and is said to contain the scandalous secrets of many more.'

Craig nodded, and put on his serious face. Every time he did it, when introducing stories of death and disaster, Dan couldn't help thinking back to Christmas, the newsroom party and the presenter's drunken karaoke of Jake the Peg, complete with bizarre dance. If only the viewers knew what really went on, he thought. And that applies just as much to the way I work and the things I do, probably more so in fact. Much more.

Which is why I'm about to say what I am.

'Dan, what more can you tell us?' Craig asked.

'The police want to keep the Book's location a secret, so they don't have large crowds of people and the media to deal with when they recover it. But I can tell you this. They believe the Judgement Book is hidden right in the centre of Plymouth, at a well-known landmark, probably one of the city's most famous. In fact, Charles Church …'

Dan stopped, only for a second, just enough to make the mistake clear, to let it linger. He tried to force his eyes to widen as though shocked with himself and put a false fluster into his voice.

'I'm sorry,' he continued. 'What I meant to say was the police believe the Judgement Book is hidden in a well-known Plymouth landmark and they intend to recover it sometime around four o'clock this afternoon.'

Dan had to sit for ten minutes in the studios' relaxation room after the broadcast. The base of his back was damp with sweat and his heart was racing. The trap was laid. The only question now was whether it would work.

He closed his eyes and lay back on the reclining chair. The room was quiet, still, soft with its thick cream carpet and matching curtains, but the peace just amplified the barrage of his thoughts. His mind oscillated like a frantic pendulum, from thinking it was a great plan which couldn't possibly fail, to ridiculing himself about how stupid it was.

The only conclusion he came to was that they'd see soon enough.

Adam called after the lunchtime news. He'd watched the bulletin from Charles Cross and praised Dan's act. He found it convincing he said, and he wasn't alone. They'd had scores of calls from journalists asking if the police really were going to recover the Judgement Book from Charles Church at four o'clock this afternoon. The official line was "We do not comment on irresponsible press reports", but the implication was clear.

The media would be there.

Many other people had rung the station as well, to ask if they could watch. They were told the police couldn't stop them from gathering at a public place. It was their right.

Adam had made his plan. He, and a small team of police and forensics officers, would walk into the church and down to the

281

plaque where they would go through a charade of trying to unscrew it. They would take their time, making it look as though detailed forensics work was slowing their progress. Plain-clothed police officers and detectives would fill the crowd, searching for anyone who might be the blackmailer.

Dan wondered how they could do that. The blackmailer wasn't exactly going to advertise his presence. But Adam was confident his officers would spot someone behaving suspiciously or nervously. It was a large part of a cop's job, he said. It became second nature.

Onlookers would be kept behind a cordon thrown around the walls of the church. The edge of the roundabout made a natural boundary which limited the number of people who could watch. That was their hunting ground.

Dan thought about getting a sandwich from the canteen, but he didn't feel hungry. He couldn't stop wondering whether the blackmailer would come, and what the next few hours would bring. He ran his tongue over the ulcer. It was smaller now he thought, and wasn't hurting. Or it could just be that he was too distracted to notice the pain.

To try to occupy his fretting mind, Dan logged into the internet to look up a new Dartmoor walk to take Rutherford on at the weekend. They hadn't been up to the north moor for ages. Perhaps somewhere around Taw Marsh. The river valley was a wonderful natural amphitheatre, bursting with colour and life in the springtime. They could even go to see the Ted Hughes memorial if they felt like a longer hike. He'd hardly been since he discovered it five years ago, the great granite rock etched with a dedication to the extraordinary poet.

Dan was proud of the find. It had taken several years of work and many miles of walking, but finally he'd tracked it down, to a barrow of grass, in a secluded valley, high on the lonely moor by the trickling source of the River Taw. Walks to the memorial were now included in all the local guidebooks, a few even crediting him with finding it.

A thought grew in his mind that it would be a better day for being with Claire, but he blocked it. He had to concentrate on work, not her, had to keep his mind on the trap they were setting for the blackmailer. Anyway, it was hard to face, but he might soon have to begin thinking about life without her. What other explanation was there for her silence?

Dan stared hard at the computer screen and the map of the area around Belstone. There was a good pub in the village, he remembered it from previous walks. Maybe he could book in for the night. He and Rutherford could walk to the memorial, then come back, have some dinner and a few beers and crash out.

His mobile bleeped with a text message. Claire's name flashed on the display. Dan sat up straight, instantly nervous.

Even after all these hours, waiting and wanting to hear from her, he wasn't sure he was ready to know what she had to say.

Whether he could face it.

His hand was shaking.

He hesitated, then pressed the read button.

"Feeling ill so staying home. Know you're busy, but any chance you can pop round? Really need to see you."

Dan tried to call her. The phone rang, but her answer machine kicked in. He tried again with the same result. The anger roared back.

What the hell was she doing, ignoring him? What the fuck was she up to? How dare she?

She was pregnant with his son. What a despicable way to behave, to just disappear, not want to talk to him, then to think she could click her fingers and summon him with a text message.

He wanted to rage at her, tell her to forget it, get lost, leave him alone, not be so selfish, so vindictive, so vicious, so foul. Instead he placed the phone down on the floor, lay back in the chair, closed his eyes, tried to force himself to be calm. Whatever happened between them she was pregnant with his child, and that at least they had to discuss.

It was quarter past two. Less than five hours left until the Judgement Book was released. Just under two until they made their attempt to trap the second blackmailer.

For now, all he could do was wait. Dan had an hour before he and Nigel went down to Charles Church to film the police

283

opening the plaque. His mind was full of Claire.

He had time to get to her flat.

Dan stared at Claire's door. He checked his hair in the reflection of the blue gloss. He looked OK he thought, reasonably calm, but his chest felt rigid with a steel tension and his forehead hot as the racing blood pumped its seething resentment through him.

He felt like wrenching the key in the lock, letting himself in, slamming the door, then storming around, flailing his arms, shouting at her, screaming, venting his anger, raging until he could enjoy the satisfaction of her tears. He thought of their son, playing football, their daughter, having her hair cut and tried to calm himself. He reached out an unsteady hand, curled it into a fist and knocked.

Inside, he heard uncertain footsteps. They paused. He counted off the seconds. He'd begun to wonder if she would answer, what to do next, when Claire slowly opened the door and stood looking at him. Her eyes were ringed with angry red circles. She held one hand over her stomach and she was visibly shaking. Her lips trembled, her cheeks too. She looked ashen, almost colourless.

Claire reached out her arms and Dan hesitated, fighting the anger. Her lips mouthed the word, 'Please', but her voice couldn't find the strength to project it.

Still he stood, staring. The seconds passed. Again her lips formed the words. 'Please. Please ...'

His resentment broke and he stepped forwards and hugged her. She collapsed into him, sobbed against his shoulder, uncontrolled, wracking gasps of breath and tears. His eyes found the photo of the two of them together, Rutherford between them and he stared at it, not daring to allow himself to speak. Slowly her breathing grew more regular and the sobs subsided to whimpering.

Dan took her hand and sat her down on the sofa. Shame and anger crashed together in his mind, like two mighty armies in an ancient battle. He wanted to tell her what she'd put him through, but also to reach out, to comfort her.

The red roses lay untouched on the coffee table, some of the tips of their graceful petals beginning to droop and fade. He stretched over, picked them up and put the bouquet in her arms. She stammered a low, 'Thanks.' She was still trembling and started crying again, the tears speeding their silver trails down her face.

Dan put a hand on Claire's and tried to calm her. She closed her eyes and lay back on the sofa, that protective arm never leaving her stomach. He waited, but she just lay there, still whimpering, the occasional tear dripping softly onto the armrest.

'Claire,' he whispered gently. 'Claire – what is it? What's the matter?'

She said nothing, just lay there, her eyes closed, the lids occasionally fluttering.

'Claire,' Dan said again. 'It's just your hormones. That's all. It's bound to happen when you're pregnant. Your hormones are all over the place. That's what's making you feel so strange. It's perfectly natural.'

She opened her eyes and reached out for him again. Dan took her and cuddled her, squeezing the shuddering body into him. She was trying to talk, mumbled gasps of words, so he leaned back and looked into her eyes, did his best to summon a reassuring smile.

'Claire, it's OK. I'm here. I'll look after you. Don't worry. We'll sort it all out. We'll work it out together.'

She looked at him, her lips trembling hard. She went to mouth some words, then stopped, tried again, faltered.

'Claire, what is it? What's the matter? I'm here now. Everything's going to be all right.'

She bowed her head, stared down at the sofa. A tear hit the fabric, spreading into a tiny dark circle. Dan watched it grow.

Sunlight flared in the room, then faded.

The silence edged on.

And then came the words. He would never forget them.

'I've had an abortion,' Claire said quietly.

Dan felt himself go numb. His eyes, hands, mouth, nothing would move. Even his brain was frozen. He wanted to ask questions, leap to his feet, wave his arms, shout, scream, but nothing came. All he could do was sit, rigid, staring at her.

Claire looked up at him, her eyes glazed. She began crying again, the strangled words struggling through her sobs.

'I'm sorry,' she gasped. 'I'm sorry. I didn't know what else to do. I'm so sorry.'

Dan began to shake. It started in his chest, then spread fast, out across his body, infecting every artery, vein, organ, muscle and limb. He couldn't tell if he was breathing or not.

He saw the joyrider's knife plunging into Claire's swollen stomach. He saw his son, playing football in the park, screaming with triumph at scoring a goal past his father, his daughter's proud excitement as she stepped from the salon after her first hair styling. He saw Claire, alone, in a hospital bed, crying, a faceless surgeon stalking towards her, holding something metallic, silver.

He shut his eyes to try to escape the thoughts, but they danced around his mind, circling him, taunting him.

Claire reached out her arms. Her mouth opened, but no sound emerged. Dan started to back away. He kept moving, sliding inch by inch until he was up against the arm of the sofa, as far from her as he could get. He was still shaking, couldn't speak, just stared.

Outside he heard the thump of a football against a wall and the joyful shout of a young boy.

Dan forced his rigid legs to stand. A sickness swirled in his stomach and his eyes wouldn't focus. It felt as though the body he inhabited was no longer his. He had to concentrate to force it to move.

His slow eyes found the blue gloss of the door and he fixed his gaze upon it until it was all he could see, a shining oblong at the end of a blurred tunnel. He picked up the roses and walked out.

Chapter Twenty-five

HIS MOBILE RANG A dozen times before he noticed it. Dan swirled the last of the hypnotic liquid in the bottom of his glass, finished it, smiled contentedly and answered. It was Nigel.

'Hey, old friend, how you doing? Good to hear from you. I'm just …'

'Where the hell are you?' Nigel cut in. 'We're due down at the church in a few minutes. Lizzie's going nuts.'

Dan forced his eyes to focus on the empty glasses in front of him. Three pints and two whiskies. A vague thought drifted through his mind that it wasn't a bad tally for only an hour's drinking.

'What's the time?' he managed, trying not to slur.

'Almost half past three!'

Dan wondered why his friend sounded so agitated. He loosely recalled he had been due to cover some story, but surely it wasn't going to get in the way of this lovely beer. Something to do with some case he'd been working on, wasn't that it? It was supposed to be important too. Some corruption thing – some murder? No, that was it, blackmail. Suicide. The Judgement Book. And that was the punch line. He remembered now.

He featured in it.

Dan laughed out loud, making a couple of the men propping up the bar look over. One raised a glass to him and Dan grinned and waved back.

'Where the hell are you?' came the irritating voice on the phone again.

'In the pub mate. In town. In the beautiful pub. It's warm and cosy and safe and …'

'Well get out of there and get to the church. And sober up.'

The word "sober" drifted through Dan's mind. He imagined a battery of anti-aircraft guns blazing away at it, trying to shoot down the dangerous foe. He gazed at a line of horse brasses on the bar's wall. We had some of those in the pub where I grew up. Pure 1970s' tat he thought, and giggled. But I used to get extra pocket money for cleaning them, so I shouldn't knock them. The ones here could do with a polish. I might get a cloth and give them a rub when I get up for my next pint, just for old times' sake.

The nagging voice was back in his ear. 'Dan! We've got a job to do. Come on man!'

These driven people were such a pain. Damned zealots, continually running around chasing some pointless cause. Always making a fuss. Selfishly trying to distract others from the simple business of enjoying life.

What was the point of anything? He had no partner, no child and soon no job. He was about to become famous – maybe infamous – celebrated in that Judgement Book thing. He'd be all over the newspapers.

Dan giggled again. It would be quite a show. Maybe he could bum a free beer or two by telling the story.

There were always upsides, if you looked hard enough. It was important to maintain a positive attitude.

He should be safely sacked by then. That was good too. Staying here would be far more pleasant than the tedious, mundane routines he'd endured for so long. No need to fight and fight. There was only one certainty in life. You always lose in the end. Better sooner than later. Get it done with.

That was settled then. Good. It had been surprisingly easy. Dan smiled happily. It was time to slip away into blissful oblivion.

A memory of a time he'd once interviewed a recovering alcoholic slipped into his lazy mind. The man had talked about "the slide". Now Dan knew what he meant. And here he was, sitting at the top of it. What a fine place to be. It was warm and comfortable and the view was getting better by the pint. Time to ease himself gently down.

'Dan, get moving for God's sake,' came the carping voice again. 'I'll see you at the church in five minutes. You'd better be there.'

Dan looked down at the bunch of roses on the chair beside him. He ran a finger over a red petal. He had an important question to answer and could do without petty distractions. What beer to have next? That was the wonderful thing about ales. There were so many to choose from. And a whisky too, maybe? Or perhaps not this time. The taste was good, the warming shock of its bite, but he didn't want to incapacitate himself too soon. He had many more lovely hours of drinking ahead if he paced himself.

He checked his wallet. Damn, he was out of cash. How very inconvenient. Dan looked over at the bar. Tarnished horse brasses, a faded and threadbare burgundy carpet and sticky wooden table tops. It wasn't the kind of place to take a card. How annoying.

He'd have to get some more money before he could have his next drink. Well, it was a pleasant day outside and a walk to another pub wouldn't be a bad thing. The beer tasted better with a change of scene. The exercise would burn off a little alcohol and help pace his session too. Dan was about to get up when another man walked in, being pulled by an energetic Alsatian.

The dog looked just like Rutherford. A little smaller perhaps, but remarkably similar. He even had that tongue-hanging-out smiling face. Their mothers and fathers must teach them it as soon as they're born, along with other useful expressions like the forlorn, "I never get fed or loved" look, so very handy for begging titbits.

A feeling broke through the haze.

His dog. He hadn't spent any quality time with his beloved dog for far too long. What about that weekend walk on Dartmoor he'd planned? He'd been neglecting Rutherford because of Claire. And where had that got him?

Claire.

Claire.

Fuck Claire.

She could do whatever she liked, but he wouldn't let his faithful dog down. And he wasn't letting that bastard blackmailer get the better of him either. He was the one who'd come up with the plan to trap the second Worm. He was going to see it through.

He got up from the chair. His legs wobbled a little, but they were mostly OK. It was only a five-minute walk to Charles Church and he could do with some water to sober him up on the way. But he had no money left.

Dan smiled at the woman behind the bar and traded the roses for a small plastic bottle of mineral water.

It could have been the loving reassurance of the beer, it might have been the angry defiance burning in him, but Dan was sure that in the next couple of hours they were going to catch the other Worm. As he walked fast to the church, he wondered who it would be.

The suspects he'd discussed with Adam formed a procession in his mind. Yvonne Freedman, Linda Cott, Leon Osmond, Father Maguire, Julia Francis, Major Anthony Robinson, Steven Sinclair. Dan found he couldn't settle on one as his favourite, the most likely accomplice. Somehow, for some reason he didn't understand, he just knew that whoever it was would soon be caught.

He paused for a second as he rounded the corner of Exeter Street and saw Charles Church. Today, for once, it wasn't lonely. The green of the roundabout was covered with people, hundreds of them, a multicolour ring of expectant humanity, waiting in the spring sunshine. Most were standing, a few sitting, pointing, some under shades, others sipping from bottles and cans. It was like a crowd waiting for a concert.

The plan was working.

Nigel gave him a friendly scolding, but offered the opportunity for a chat if Dan needed it. He thought he would, but not today. Perhaps over the weekend, or when his feelings had settled down a little. He could still taste the emotions spinning inside him, but he could hold them at bay with the pursuit of the blackmailer. For now ...

They would assault him again when the time came. And he knew he was frightened of what they would do to him.

Dan tried to focus on the story, the case, to help block out the echoing thoughts of Claire. They needed a high shot to get a sense of the mass of people surrounding the church. He led Nigel over to the police station and they climbed the steps up to its entrance.

'Perfect,' Nigel said. He positioned his tripod and swept the camera back and forth in a couple of pans while Dan counted the numbers. He estimated at least three hundred people had gathered. He wondered how many were detectives.

The ruin itself had been cordoned off, the blue police tape fluttering around it. Uniformed officers patrolled up and down the walls, to make sure no one tried to get inside. Dan noticed another couple of TV crews in the crowd and a line of photographers, Dirty El amongst them. Even from this distance Dan could see he was grinning.

Nigel unhooked the camera and they walked down to the roundabout. A policeman was stopping traffic to let people cross the road to the church. It was like a circus. Roll up, roll up, come see the show. Watch the true-life drama unfold, and all for free.

It was just before four, almost time for Adam to make his appearance. Nigel hauled the camera onto his shoulder and filmed some shots of the police cordon and close-ups of the expectant faces of the people around them. Dan's gaze drifted over the crowd. How did you spot a blackmailer in this lot? Everyone looked absolutely ordinary. Couples, families, older people, children. The person they wanted was obviously clever and wouldn't just give himself or herself away.

He started to doubt whether they would even come at all. Why not just avoid the risk and watch it on the TV later? Claire forced her way back into his mind too, joining forces with his other fears. Dan screwed up his eyes, tried to blink them away.

The sun was high in the sky and the day was hot. Most of the people wore sunglasses and hats. That was going to make spotting the blackmailer even more difficult. A few groups of families and friends had sat down on the grass and a couple even munched away at sandwiches. Dan felt a tug of hunger. He was surprised how quickly he'd sobered up. His mind felt clear and sharp, ready for what the next few hours might bring.

Nigel finished his close-ups and they pushed their way back through the throng, up the bank, to the edge of the grass. It was higher here, giving them a clear view of the church and the crowd around it. They could see into the ruin through some of the open arches of the windows. Perfect. They would be able to film anything that happened anywhere on the green. The other TV crews came to join them, as did several of the photographers. The pack mentality always tended to bring them together. Journalists were paranoid creatures.

In just a few minutes the crowd had grown noticeably, as ever some people leaving it to the last minute to get to the show. A young couple, hand in hand, ran across the road, zig-zagging through the traffic, hurried on by the blaring of car horns. There must be at least five hundred people surrounding the church now, few gaps in the tightness of the packed mass.

'Alert!' yelped Nigel, and Dan sprung to his side to avoid the wheeling camera. The rest of the line of lenses spun too, following Nigel's lead. Adam was crossing the road to the roundabout, behind him a couple of uniformed officers and two white-overalled forensic technicians. Arthur was one, but Dan didn't recognise the other. In the distance, clear above the rumble of traffic, the bells of St Andrew's Church struck the hour. It was exactly four o'clock.

The procession pushed their way slowly through the crowd, every curious face turning to watch them. Many held up cameras and mobile phones, taking photographs and videos. A policeman lifted the tape and they marched into the interior of the church. They stared at the plaque for a few minutes and there was some discussion and pointing. Dan knew it was all an act, but it looked convincing. Around him, everyone was intent on the performance.

A series of plastic sheets were laid down beneath the plaque, the group stood back and there was more pointing and conversation. The two technicians walked forwards, began making a play of examining it, fingers probing the smooth metal edges, faces pressed to the stone wall. Dan heard the whirr of the camera's motor beside his ear as Nigel zoomed in his shot.

Dan counted the minutes, wondering at how slowly they passed. For every one that ticked by he imagined himself and Adam being eased ever closer to the end of their careers. At seven o'clock the Book would be released. They had less than three hours. Claire too stalked the fringes of his mind, one hand protecting her swollen stomach but her head held high, never looking at him.

Around him some people sat down on the grass, stretched out, settled to watch the scene inside the church. Dan tried sitting too, then quickly stood up again. Relaxing was not an option. He shifted a foot back and forth, tapped at the odd daisy, scratched tetchily at an itch on his back. The time passed slowly with the drag of expectancy.

For half an hour, the technicians dusted away at the plaque and picked around its sides. Arthur got down on his hands and knees and crawled around on the flagstones beneath it, his hands scouring the smooth surface. Adam stood back, arms folded, watching. Occasionally he would look round and scan the crowd.

Dan noticed a series of men and women walking slowly amongst the onlookers, stopping occasionally as if to gaze at the church. CID he thought, they must be. There'd be others, standing back from the crowd and probably some overlooking the area from the police station too. From where he stood with Nigel they could see all around the church. There was no hint of anything suspicious.

A rumble of conversation buzzed through the crowd. People were turning to their neighbours, exchanging excited whispers, some pointing. The technicians had begun unscrewing the plaque, slowly, painstakingly. It was a little looser on the wall now and they held it, checked the gap behind, probing it with tiny brushes. Dan had a sense of the people around him craning their necks to get a better look. Most had gone quiet. They could feel the moment was coming.

If only they knew.

Dan looked over at Dirty El. The photographer had his camera trained unerringly on the technicians. He stood perfectly still. That would be the shot that told the story, the golden picture, the one that sold. The moment the technicians removed the plaque and held up the Judgement Book. El wouldn't risk missing it, not even by daring to wipe his sweating face.

'I wish they'd get on with it,' whispered Nigel. 'I take it we want to get this on tonight?'

'Yep,' was all Dan could reply. His throat was dry and he felt too tense to manage anything else.

It was just past five. They were on air at half past six. Time was growing tight. He knew Adam would eke out the operation for as long as he could, until he thought there was no chance left for an arrest. But how much longer could that possibly be? Some of the crowd had already grown bored and begun drifting away.

Still the detectives slowly swept through the mass. A young man whom Dan thought he recognised had just edged past the press pack, subtly checking them over. He was making his way along the edge of the roundabout, sipping at a can of drink, smiling at a couple of families gathered there.

Less than two hours until the Book was released. And so far, no hint of anything suspicious. His great plan was starting to feel very hollow.

Dan wondered what he would do tomorrow, the first day of unemployment he'd ever known in his life.

'You'd better give Lizzie a call,' Nigel said. 'She was keeping the Outside Broadcast truck on standby in case we needed it.'

Dan picked up his phone. He was about to ring the newsroom when a distraction nudged at him. Someone was talking to El and the photographer was trying to reach into his back pocket, while keeping his lens trained on the plaque. He handed a small rectangle of white paper to the person, who walked away and sat back down on the grass verge.

It was a woman: Dan could see a tail of bunched dark hair under the back of her baseball cap. She wore black shades, but Dan thought there was something familiar about her. Someone he'd interviewed, or vaguely knew? He tried, but couldn't bring the memory home.

The technicians were still checking the edges of the plaque. They couldn't stall for much longer. Any minute now they would have to remove it from the wall. The charade was nearing its end. The crowd would disperse, there would be no

Judgement Book, no hope left of catching the blackmailer. It would all be over. The final gamble lost.

An instinct tingled, but Dan had no idea what it could mean. He looked over at El. He couldn't be sure it wasn't just petty curiosity. Few women spoke to the paparazzo.

Dan put his phone back into his pocket and walked down the grassy slope to see his friend. He picked his path through the crowd and kept his eyes away from the woman. He wasn't sure why, he just felt he should. The feeling wasn't letting go.

He offered the photographer his bottle of water. El put out a hand, took it, sipped gratefully, then handed it back, never letting his lens waver from the technicians.

Dan leaned over so he could whisper into El's ear. 'What did that woman want?'

'To buy a snap,' El replied quietly. 'She wanted one of my pictures of the cops unscrewing the plaque. Big one, full colour, said she needed much better quality than you'll get in the papers. I gave her my card and told her to call me tomorrow.'

It was an effort not to turn and stare at her. Dan thanked El, made a vague arrangement to go out for a few beers at the weekend and walked as nonchalantly as he could back up to Nigel.

Now the instinct was shouting.

'I'm going to ring the newsroom,' Dan said, walking further up the slope, away from the crowd, right to the edge of the roundabout.

He struggled to find the number in the phone's memory, so badly was he trembling. He called Adam and kept his eyes fixed on the church as the detective picked his phone from his pocket.

'I think I've got her,' Dan said breathlessly. He didn't have time to wonder about what he'd said, it just came out.

'What?' snapped Adam. 'Her? What are you on about? The other Worm you mean?'

'Yes. I think it's a woman and I think I've got her.'

Adam turned and looked over at the crowd surrounding the church.

'Where are you?'

'See the line of TV cameras, at the top of the bank?'

'Yep.'

'Up from them, and towards the police station.'

Adam's eyes travelled up the slope.

'Got you. Why do you think it's her?'

Dan explained about the photo. His voice was thin and wavering.

'Blimey, it's scarcely conclusive,' the detective said finally.

'Have we got anything else?'

'No.'

'Any hint of anyone who might be the other blackmailer?'

'No.'

'How much longer can you eke this out for?'

'Not long.'

There was a pause. 'Then I reckon it's our best shot,' said Dan finally.

'OK,' replied Adam. 'We haven't got anything left to lose. If I humiliate myself by arresting an innocent spectator in front of the world's media, it'll hardly matter when the Judgement Book's released. Where is she?'

'Down the slope and to my right, next to the fat bloke in the Union Jack T-shirt, but don't look.'

Adam snorted. 'Thanks, mate. I had thought of that. OK, go stand somewhere behind her, but not too close. In a couple of minutes I'll make as though I'm taking another call. I'll walk out of the church and back towards the police station. When I get near, you move in on her from the back so I know I've got the right one and I'll arrest her.'

Dan felt his heart begin racing. A memory of their pursuit of the joyrider hit him. He swallowed hard, could say only, 'OK'.

He slid back over to Nigel, whispered to be ready to film some activity on the grass in front of him. The cameraman raised an eyebrow, but didn't say anything. Dan watched and waited, his eyes set on the church, counting off the seconds. They crawled by, one limping after another.

Eventually Adam put his mobile to his ear, then turned and walked out from the church's gate and climbed the stone steps.

Dan slipped slowly over to behind the woman and edged

towards her. She was sitting, her arms folded around her legs on the grass, watching the technicians intently.

He couldn't help himself wondering what the hell he was doing. Could she really be the blackmailer? The evidence he had consisted solely of her wanting a photo of what was going on. She might be a relative of one of the technicians, a freelance journalist, a local historian. She could have a thousand reasons for wanting a picture. And they were about to arrest her in front of a crowd of hundreds of people. If they were lucky, she'd only make a formal complaint. Worse, she could sue for defamation and wrongful arrest.

But there was no way back. It was all they had, one thin, vague chance based on guesses, hopes and a hunch, nothing more. The longer he thought about it, the more ludicrous it sounded.

Adam was near to the woman, still looking ahead as he walked, pretending to talk into the phone. There was no hint he was interested in her. He moved on, was even closer now.

Her head snapped towards him. She appeared to flinch, stiffen, glanced quickly to her sides, started to scramble to her feet.

Dan felt a sudden flare of excitement, a hot rush of wonderful hope. He could see she was alarmed, looking for a way out. And she could easily get away and escape into the crowd. They might yet lose her, still fail when they could be so very close to success.

He had to stop her.

There was a family in front of him, a couple of young men, one older, a woman holding the hand of a small girl. They stood tightly together, formed a barrier in his path. He didn't have time for politeness, had to move. He aimed for the young men, shouldered them out of the way, ignored the angry cries, rushed forwards.

She was just ahead now. But he was still too far away, the gap too great to reach out and grab her. And she was moving, turning, getting ready to run into the crowd. He had to do something.

Dan lunged forwards, gathered his breath and bellowed, 'Oi,

blackmailer!'

She spun, startled. The hesitation was just enough. Adam sprang, reached out, clutched at her, scrabbled a firm grip on her arm. The woman struggled and tried to pull away but he held her tight. She went to hit out at him, but Adam ducked the swipe, pivoted and pinned her arms together.

She swung a leg and he pushed her away. She fell back onto the grass, gasping, winded, panting desperately, her chest heaving. Her sunglasses slid slowly from her face and dropped. The woman glared at Adam, breathing heavily, her eyes wide with shock and venom.

'Jesus,' Dan heard Adam gasp. 'I don't believe it.'

The woman lying on the grass, staring up at them was Inspector Linda Cott.

Chapter Twenty-six

DAN GOT BACK TO the studios at five to six and ran panting into the newsroom. He felt dizzy with the exertion and disbelief that the plan had worked. He hardly dared to hope he and Adam were safe from professional ruin and media ridicule. That at last it was the end of the blackmailers' game, and that they would finally now find the Judgement Book.

Claire was with him too, invisible but everywhere he looked. She prowled around the edge of his consciousness, always just out of sight, a dark, stalking figure.

Lizzie's eyes were on the newsroom door. She sprung up as soon as she saw him and barked, 'Where the hell have you been? We've been trying to call you. What's going on?'

Dan fished his mobile from his pocket. He'd forgotten he switched it to silent just before they closed in on the blackmailer. Seven missed calls. No wonder she looked thunderous. Lizzie's hands were fixed on her hips. She wore a scarlet shirt, making her arms form two perfect warning triangles and her lips were even thinner than usual.

'Really sorry, it's been so busy I didn't have a chance to talk,' he gasped. 'Got some great stuff for you though.'

Her expression eased, just a little and a hand lifted to point a sharpened nail between his eyes. 'You've got pictures of the Judgement Book?'

'No,' he managed, trying to catch his breath.

A stiletto ground into the carpet.

'What then?' she asked ominously.

'I've got pictures of the arrest of the other blackmailer. There were two, and the cops have now got them both. It shouldn't be long before they get the book too.'

The stiletto stopped grinding.

'Lead story, you live in the studio, pictures of what happened for you to talk about,' she snapped. 'Go on then, get to it, what are you waiting for?'

Dan sat with Jenny and they cut a sequence of shots. A little build up to add drama first, he thought. That was an important part of the story, the anticipation of the crowd, no one knowing how the afternoon would unfold. Adam and the technicians inside the church, a couple of images of the police officers watchfully on guard. Then pick up the pace, the plaque being unscrewed, people looking on keenly and then to the arrest. Dan jotted down a few notes of what he'd say and checked them against the pictures. He had to complement them, explain what the viewers were seeing.

6.20, just under ten minutes to on air. He'd better get down to the studio and prepare. It always took a few minutes to settle, and for the engineers to check the camera and lighting positions. He couldn't afford to get this story wrong.

The dizziness was still swirling in his head and his mouth felt dry. Dan gulped down a glass of water and nearly choked. A camera swung onto him and lights flared and died in the metal lattice of rigging above his head.

6.27 now.

'What questions do you want?' asked Craig calmly.

'What happened today is the first one, and what does it mean for the investigation is the second.'

Dan scribbled a couple more notes, changed a few words and switched the order of a sentence, then read it through again. The rough script seemed to make sense. The opening music of Wessex Tonight boomed out across the studio and Craig drew himself up in his chair.

'First tonight, more extraordinary developments in the blackmailer case,' he intoned. 'An arrest in front of hundreds of people, as the police searched an area in the centre of Plymouth where they believe the Judgement Book had been hidden. Our Crime Correspondent Dan Groves is with us. Dan, you were there, tell us what happened.'

Dan took a final look at his notes. 'Craig, as you said, I witnessed the whole thing and it was a quite extraordinary afternoon. The police had received information leading them to believe the Judgement Book was hidden behind a plaque in the ruin of Charles Church.'

He looked down at the monitor screens. Emma had taken her

cue and run the pictures of the church, the people watching and the technicians.

'Forensics officers began checking this plaque, and as you can see, as it's such a prominent area hundreds of people came to watch. Well, for an hour or so, the police didn't make much progress. They just worked slowly at the plaque, unscrewing it from the wall. They were probably taking it gently so as not to destroy any possible forensic evidence. Then came the remarkable twist, and here we can bring you exclusive pictures of it.'

Dan paused for a couple of seconds to let the pictures breathe and the drama of his words settle on the viewers. Only amateurs babbled on when the images were so striking they required no words of embroidery.

'The man in charge of the investigation, Detective Chief Inspector Adam Breen, walked out of the church and into the crowd. All appeared absolutely normal when, suddenly, he grabbed a woman who'd been watching and arrested her. I can now reveal the woman is suspected by the police of being the second blackmailer. Detectives think two people working together produced the Judgement Book.'

Craig nodded gravely, asked. 'So, what's the significance of this arrest for the investigation?'

'It could be highly significant. First, it should mean there'll be no more blackmail demands on prominent people in the area, which will come as an enormous relief to many. Secondly, it should help the police find this Judgement Book in which all the secrets are said to be recorded. In effect, the arrest could signal the end of the case.'

At the after-programme meeting, Lizzie professed herself "contented" with the story to such an extent that she would buy everyone one drink in the studios' bar. She emphasised the "one". The taste of those earlier beers was still with him and Dan would have loved a drink, several in fact, but he'd promised Adam he would return to Charles Cross as soon as Wessex Tonight finished. The detective wanted to start questioning Linda Cott.

Lizzie didn't offer to buy drinks very often and he didn't

want to miss out, so Dan picked up a tin of ale on her account and slipped it into his bag for later. His mind wandered to Claire. It brought an ache to the back of his eyes, so again he blocked the thought. It wouldn't be long before he had to face it, but not yet. Instead he looked for a distraction. He thought of Cott and wondered what turned her into a blackmailer. He imagined a Dartmoor walk with Rutherford and a few beers with El at the weekend and tried not to think that was exactly how he used to fill his time before he'd met Claire.

The interview room looked as unwelcoming as always, except the flickering fluorescent tube had finally been replaced. It had much the same cheering effect as someone adding a coat of paint to a crypt. A steady green glow now tinted the chairs and table and the two people sitting there. Dan stood in his customary position by the door.

'Why, Linda?' Adam asked quietly. 'It's as simple as that. Why?'

Cott sat up on her chair, her arms folded on the table in front of her. She stared straight ahead and Dan couldn't read her expression. She wasn't quite there, as if she was taking solace in a mental refuge. She answered Adam's questions impatiently, as if they were annoying distractions that had to be dealt with in the hope they would soon go away.

'I'm not saying anything. If you want to charge me, go ahead. But Sarah will already have told you we don't intend to answer any questions.'

'You don't know what Sarah has told us.'

'Don't bother trying that one. I'm a cop too, remember. Or I was. I know about playing people off against each other. I have a statement for you, but that's it.'

Adam rubbed his neck and stared at her. She looked back, quite still and unblinking.

'Give us your statement then, Linda,' said Adam wearily. 'And we'll take it from there.'

Dan half expected her to take out a piece of paper, but she began talking as if it were a verse she'd been taught as a child, something so familiar it flowed without thought.

'When I began my career as a police officer, I really believed in it. I wanted to make a difference. But as the years went by, I started to realise I was lonely in that aspiration. Many of my fellow officers just wanted to do as little as possible, serve their time, then pick up a fat pension. Others were actively corrupt and abused their positions. My efforts to bring this to the attention of my senior officers were ignored or rebuffed, so I sought another way to let people know what was going on. Those are my reasons behind the creation of the Judgement Book.

'No one suffered our attentions who did not deserve them. Our methods may seem extreme, but we were forced to adopt them. They were the only way to win attention in an uncaring world. All we have sought to do is for the public good. We are different. We try to be better. We are fair. To emphasise that, as you know we have agreed we will give you one final chance to find the Judgement Book. As we have said, to do so you must follow your initial thoughts. They would be dead right. That is all I have to say.'

Adam nodded and slowly scribbled a note on a piece of paper in front of him.

'How do you know Sarah?'

'No comment.'

'Why the faked suicide?'

'No comment.'

'How well do you know Superintendent Leon Osmond?'

This time Dan thought he saw a hint of reaction, a quick blink of her eyes, but the reply was the same.

'No comment.'

Adam sighed heavily. 'Is there any point in asking you anything else, Linda? I don't have to tell you that all this is over and you might as well cooperate.'

'No comment.'

'Where's the Judgement Book, Linda?'

'No comment.'

Adam shook his head sadly, got up from his chair and walked slowly out of the door. They climbed the echoing stairs to the canteen. Dan steeled himself and ordered two coffees.

The acrid, wafting smell from the polystyrene cups warned him it was as strong as ever.

They sat at a table in the far corner. To the west the sun was dipping towards the horizon, a flaming orb in a dying blue sky. Claire picked at his mind again, memories of their early days together and evening walks on the Devon coastline.

How far gone were those days now.

'It's pointless,' said Adam. 'She was a cop. She knows all the tricks I can use. We're not going to get a thing out of her.'

'At least they can't reveal the book to the media now,' replied Dan. 'Come on, we have made some progress. We've got them both.' He looked over his shoulder, checking to make sure no one could overhear. 'We're safe, as is anyone else who might have been … compromised.'

'For now, maybe' Adam replied, loosening his tie and sliding it down his neck. 'I don't know about you, but I still feel it's like a death sentence hanging over me. It could be carried out at any time. We've got to find the Judgement Book before someone else does. The case isn't closed and we're not safe without it.'

'You really think so?'

'How do we know they don't have another accomplice out there who can release the Book? How do we know Linda hasn't sent a letter to some newspaper or journalists saying where to find it? They might have set up a computer program to tell a load of hacks. There are hundreds of ways to release it.'

Dan grimaced. 'But surely …'

'Surely what? They're smart and embittered. And they've planned this damned well. I wouldn't put anything past them.'

Adam leaned forwards, lowered his voice to a whisper. 'Let's take the best case. Even if they haven't arranged to release the Book now, what about when they get out of prison? Off they go, pick it up and then tell the world what's in it. Or someone could find it first. Until we've got that Book, I won't relax. Every day I'll expect the phone to go and it'll be some journalist asking if I've got any comment on the allegations in it. I don't know about you, but I can't live like that.'

There was a silence. Dan sipped at his coffee and recoiled.

'Yeah,' he said finally. 'You're right. So what do we do?'

'No bloody idea. I have had a guts full of this case. It's haunting me. And it looks like it's going to go on doing so. For weeks, months and bloody years until the Book's finally released and we're ridiculed, humiliated and finished. Just as we've been expecting for so long.'

Another thought of Claire flitted through his mind, and Dan rested his head in his hands, tried to think. But his brain felt slow, lethargic, as if punch-drunk from the relentless pounding of the last few days.

'Look,' he managed, 'They've obviously agreed in advance what they'll both say if they're caught. The only clue they've given us is that stuff about our initial thoughts, and them being dead right. Just like it was written in that note when we found the false book. How they put "DEAD" in capitals to emphasise it. What does that mean?'

Adam shrugged. 'No idea. It might be nothing, just another taunt. And to tell you the truth I'm sick of their bloody games.'

'Sure, but it's got to be worth thinking about. It must be something to do with initials. But initials of what? Is there any point going back over the blackmail notes to see if they contain anything?'

'Maybe.' Adam sounded anything except hopeful. 'But Eleanor and Michael have been through them though, and if there was anything there they'd have found it.'

Dan pushed the coffee aside. It was making his ulcer sting.

'There is just the one possibility,' he said. 'Linda flinched when you mentioned Osmond, and the only time we got anything out of Sarah was when she got angry. We could try winding Linda up.'

'It's worth a try,' nodded Adam. 'But let's not mess around. When we talk to her again I'll go straight for the jugular. If we don't get anything I'm going to call it a day. I'm tired out.'

Dan felt a sudden fear of the coming night and spending it alone. It was when the thoughts and memories would come. The dark and vulnerable moments. He got up from his chair and wearily followed Adam back down the stairs.

Linda looked up when they walked in to the interview room.

She glanced pointedly at her watch.

'Are you ready to talk now?' Adam asked abruptly.

'No comment.'

'Then do you mind if I ask you a couple of questions? There are some things I'd like to know.'

'No comment.'

He let the silence run, then said quietly, 'Why did you betray us, Linda?'

'Don't give me that,' she shot back. 'You betray yourselves.'

'How?'

'No comment.'

'Osmond?'

She glared at Adam. Dan sensed she was balanced between a desire to talk, to justify herself, and another to stay quiet.

'Osmond?' prompted Adam again. 'Did you know?'

'Yeah, I knew,' she said finally. 'Some of the younger cops confided in me. I raised it with my bosses. And guess what? It was hushed up and swept under the bloody carpet. They all look after each other, that lot. That's what we were exposing. Now, no comment.'

'Why the faked suicide?' asked Adam.

'No comment.'

'I'm guessing it's because you thought Sarah might get caught, and you had to be free to carry on the game? Being dead is a good way to be beyond suspicion. You took a little of your own blood and left it on the rock, to look like you'd hit your head when you jumped, didn't you? To help convince us you were dead. That was a nice touch, Linda.'

'You might think that, but no comment.'

'But why do it anyway? Why not stay inside the force, quietly, to keep an eye on our attempts to solve the case? Wouldn't that have been more useful to you?'

A snort.

'What does that mean, Linda? Apart from contempt?'

'No comment. Except – Osmond.'

The detective nodded slowly. 'I see. If the allegations about him had been made on their own, they might have been ignored.

306

He could have hushed it up, bluffed it out – again. But after your "suicide", because of what we thought the blackmailer knew about you, we'd have to take another attack on a cop much more seriously, wouldn't we?'

'No comment.'

'You used your reputation, didn't you? Because you were popular and respected, you knew your "death" would galvanise us, your fellow cops, to try to find the blackmailer. You knew it'd mean the claims against Osmond would be thoroughly investigated, and he'd be exposed. And likewise with the others in the book. There'd be no chance of them using their influence and power to cover it all up. That was the reason for your "suicide".'

'How very clever you are. But no comment.'

'And Sarah didn't really have anything on you, did she? You weren't sent any blackmail note. We thought it was so awful you'd destroyed it, but there wasn't one. You were just in it together. You left that suicide note so we would believe there was a riddle set for you, you'd solved it and you wanted to help us by leaving it behind.'

'Still no comment.'

'And that stuff about the 'dogging'. That was rubbish. It was Sarah who made the call to us, wasn't it? To make sure we weren't on your track. To give us a good reason to explain why you might kill yourself, so we wouldn't suspect you'd faked your death.'

'No comment.'

'Just like it was Sarah who rang in to report your "suicide" in Cornwall?'

'No comment.'

'And that bomb hoax in Plymouth city centre. I'm guessing Sarah planted the rucksack. It could hardly have been you. Someone might have recognised you. It was part of your little game, wasn't it? To give us notice of what was coming. And to have another little laugh at us.'

'No comment.'

'Where's the Judgement Book, Linda?'

'No comment.'

'Am I in it? Is Dan?'

'You'll find out one day. And maybe sooner than you think. But for now no comment.'

'What do you mean, sooner than you think?'

'No comment.'

Dan could hear the words echoing from the bare bricks. "Sooner than you think."

Adam was right. They would never be safe until they found the Book.

The detective sat back on his chair. 'There are just a couple of things that still puzzle me, Linda. I can see your motive now, and I can see how you did it. But why throw away your house and life in England? If you'd got away with it, you could never stay here.'

'No comment.'

'I know you didn't have any family, and not even many friends. Were you lonely?'

'No comment.'

'Was this all a cry for attention?'

Linda rolled her eyes. 'Is this going to go on much longer?'

'Until I get some answers.'

'Then try this. No comment.'

'I'm guessing you were so disillusioned with life here that you were going to go abroad. Start again. And maybe send us some letter, or video, as another taunt.'

'How very wonderfully perceptive you are. But no comment.'

'What brought you and Sarah together in the first place?'

'No comment.'

'You know how police officers get treated in prison, don't you, Linda? You know what will happen to you?'

'No comment.'

'Even in a women's prison dreadful things happen to police officers.'

'No comment.'

Adam stared at her. She looked back, expressionless.

'You were a colleague, Linda,' Adam said, and Dan thought he sounded genuinely saddened. 'A highly regarded colleague.

We're not all corrupt and idle you know. Some of us work hard, believe in what we do and try to do it well. Perhaps you should recognise that and give us a chance to find your Judgement Book?'

'You have your chance. Remember your initial thoughts. They'd be dead right. Now, no comment.'

Adam stood up. 'OK, that's enough. We're getting nowhere. We'll get you to the cells and leave you to think about your future.'

She shrugged. Dan stared at her, thought fast. Again that emphasis on the word dead. He was sure it was significant. But how? And how to get to her?

'Linda,' he said and she looked over, her face full of contempt. He could see exactly what she thought of him and it settled his mind. 'Was it the old story? Were you and Sarah lovers?'

Her face creased into a slow snarl. 'No we bloody weren't. Only a disgusting bloke like you would think that. You foul hacks love your sleaze, don't you? You're as bad as all those others we exposed. Your fantasy is it, two women together?'

'All men though, weren't they?'

'What?'

'They were all men you exposed. No women.'

'So?'

'So – why might that have been?'

She glared at him, slowly shook her head. 'Maybe it was because it was all men who were the corrupt ones. I'm so sorry to disappoint your sordid little fantasy, but it's this simple. Sarah and me were just two people who shared a purpose. If you really want to know, Sarah approached me after I'd had a meal at the Judge. I'd been moaning to a friend about corruption in the force and she wanted to know if I would like to help her to do something about it. I did and I'm proud of it. That's all there is to it.'

Dan nodded. It was time to try his last question, but even now he knew it was hopeless. She was angry with him, even genuinely disgusted, but she was in full control.

'And where's the Judgement Book?'

Linda smiled coldly, looked back and forth from Dan to Adam. 'You'd love to know, wouldn't you? So you could sleep safely at last. But I'm afraid that's to be denied you, unless you can prove yourselves worthy by solving the clues. And it's written all over your faces that you can't. So, no comment – or rather, no further comment except this ...'

She paused, that emotionless smile still on her face. Dan leaned forward, wondering what she would say, couldn't help himself. He sensed Adam was doing the same.

And when at last the words came there were only three, but they were vicious and penetrating, summed up exactly what they would both go through, today, tomorrow and for countless days to come, until the guillotine blade that hung above them finally fell.

'Enjoy your torment.'

Chapter Twenty-seven

THE FINAL BRIEF HOPE was extinguished as soon as they walked back into the MIR. Eleanor and Michael looked up from the laptop and pile of books they were working on. Each slowly shook their head. No one spoke. No words were necessary.

Adam sat on the edge of a desk, studying the floor. Dan pulled out a chair, slumped into it, stretched out his legs. They felt painfully heavy. He was aware of the dull pounding of a headache gathering momentum in a corner of his mind.

At least they'd resolved one question, something which had been bothering him from the start. The blackmail notes and their intentions. From the first one, there was a sense of a dual purpose, almost a confusion, about the crime. It was as if the Worm, as they thought of the blackmailer then, wanted to taunt her victims, but also give them a chance to solve the clues and save themselves.

Dan wondered if he should have seen it before. There was not one blackmailer, but two, and both with slightly different agendas. And as in the rest of life, be it the infamous working party, focus group or sub-committee so beloved of the bureaucrats, they'd reached a compromise over exactly what it was they were trying to achieve.

Both wanted to make their statement, and that they certainly had. But Sarah was the one more filled with anger, keener to taunt, while Linda, as had been her reputation in the police, was fairer, and felt the need to give the victims a chance, albeit so very slight.

It was effectively a composite crime, the first time he'd faced one. Dan told himself he would write it down in his diary later, to remind him in case he came up against anything like it again.

But then struck the ruthless impact of reality. He would never be working on another case. Soon he would be sacked, as would Adam too.

His head thudded anew, and Dan heard himself let out a low

groan.

The atmosphere in the room was stale and rank, the air thick and heavy. Dan looked across at the windows, the reddening sun settling on the western horizon, but couldn't find the strength to get up and let in some air. His eyes found the picture of Linda Cott on the felt boards, her expression impassive, as though she was monitoring them with scientific detachment, mere ants she had provoked to run around hopelessly as part of a grand experiment. He expected to feel anger or hate, but nothing came. There was only numbness.

Michael's laptop let out an electronic warble. Adam's head snapped up. 'Got something?'

The young man hesitated, then replied softly, 'No. It's just telling me it's finished its program. It hasn't found a thing.'

'Nothing at all?'

There was a silence, then Eleanor stood, smoothing her flowing skirt. 'I'm afraid not. We haven't found even a hint about what the answer to their last riddle could be.'

'And you've tried everything?'

Adam's voice was hoarse with tiredness. Eleanor took a couple of steps towards him, laid a gentle hand on his shoulder. 'Yes. Everything we've got. Everything we can think of. We've looked through all the blackmail letters for any kind of hints or patterns, anything to do with initials or death. We haven't managed to find a thing.'

Dan screwed his eyes shut, tried to focus. He picked through the memories of each note, the death of Freedman, the bill poster, the plane's banner exposing Osmond, the letters to Robinson and Sinclair, the interviews with Sarah and Linda, but no thoughts, no ideas, not even any possibilities came to him. He felt as though he just wanted to sleep, to slip away and find some brief refuge from this never-ending ... the word formed fast, despite his attempts to resist it.

The word Cott had used, and from which he knew he could not escape. The word which would keep returning to him.

Torment.

Every day knowing the Book was hidden somewhere, full of your destructive secrets. Every day expecting it to be found and its festering contents revealed. Every day expecting it to end your career in a blaze of scandal. And always knowing that one day, be it sooner or later, it would surely happen.

Torment.

Adam's low voice interrupted Dan's thoughts. 'Then we're done, aren't we?'

Eleanor managed a sympathetic smile, but it was brief. 'I don't think there's anything more we can do. I wouldn't be surprised if there is no final riddle, just a last way to taunt us.'

'Well it's bloody working!' Adam snapped.

Eleanor looked surprised, and the detective apologised. 'I'm sorry. It's just – this case, I think it's got to me. It's felt as if they've been ahead of us in everything. And even when we do seem to get a break, to be getting somewhere, they're ready for us. It's felt so hopeless. And so bloody personal.'

'I understand,' said Eleanor gently. 'But for what it's worth, I think you did everything you could.'

Adam didn't reply, just went back to studying the floor. Eleanor packed up her pile of books, then said, 'If it's all right with you, we'd better be going. There's another case where it looks like we're needed.'

Adam nodded, got up, shook Michael's hand and gave Eleanor a hug. Dan did likewise. He wondered if Adam was thinking the same as him. Whether they'd ever work together, perhaps even see each other, again.

The door clicked shut.

Dan wondered what to do, whether to try to talk to his friend, but sensed he wanted to be left alone. He walked over to the window, stared out at the sunset. The day's death throes were lighting the land a bloody red, the fading sun slipping fast below the horizon. Thoughts of Claire again started to form, the sunset walks they'd enjoyed together, and Dan instinctively blocked them. He tried to think instead of the blackmailers' final riddle. They had to find a way to solve it.

Nothing came. The numbness persisted. He bowed his head and let out a low groan.

The door swung open, crashing into the wall. Dan spun round, startled. Osmond hobbled into the MIR. He was glowing

313

with sweat and panting.

'Have you found it, Breen?'

Adam looked up wearily. 'Found what?'

'Don't play your bloody games with me, man! The Book! I saw it on the news.' He nodded towards Dan. 'That you'd caught the bastards. But where's the Book? Where's the damned Book?'

'Aren't you supposed to be suspended – Superintendent?'

'Don't give me that crap, man! Where's the bloody Book?'

Adam stood up quickly, his voice suddenly angry. 'We don't know. We don't have it. We haven't found it. OK? Your sordid little secrets are still out there somewhere. Now get out of here before I have you thrown out.'

Osmond reached out an arm, went to push at Adam's chest, but the detective grabbed his fleshy wrist. He squeezed it hard until the hand whitened under the pressure, then pushed it away.

'Go home,' Adam growled. 'Before I let myself tell you what I really think of you.'

Osmond glared at him, then turned for the door. He paused and shot back, 'You're a loser, Breen. A no-hoper. You know shit about policing. They've been running rings around you. You're pathetic.'

The door slammed shut behind him. Adam stared at it for a moment, then walked over to the window and uttered a word Dan had never heard him use before.

'Wanker.'

They watched the setting sun in silence. Dan glanced at his friend. His eyes were red and looked swollen. In the years they'd known each other, through all the traumatic cases they'd worked on, for the first time he sensed Adam was close to tears. Dan felt a sudden need to help, to lift his spirits, to do anything to stop that. It was as if the last barrier to despair was breaking. If the detective cried Dan knew it would take him too, and he wondered where it could possibly stop.

'Superintendent Wanker, surely?' he managed.

Adam snorted, said only, 'Yeah.'

The last lines of sun disappeared, the sky now darkening fast, ready to welcome the coming night. An occasional star began a faint shine.

'So?' Dan asked.

'So what? There is no so. There's nothing. We've got no leads, no hope of finding the Book. It just sits wherever it is, hidden, until …'

Adam didn't need to finish the sentence.

'But – there must be something. Surely – something …'

'What? How? Have you got any ideas?'

Dan breathed out heavily. 'No. But we can't just give up. We can't go on every day knowing the Book's out there, waiting to be revealed.'

'Can't we? What choice have we got?'

Dan couldn't find any words to answer.

'Then –' said Adam, turning from the window and heading for the door. 'Then, I think we'd better start getting used to it.'

Back in his flat, Dan lay on his great blue sofa watching a flock of clouds chase each other across the glass expanse of his bay window. Their undersides were lit with streaks of silver from the reflected glow of the city. He counted them as they sped past, urged on by the breeze that had bustled in with the evening.

He told himself when he got to a hundred, he'd decide how to reply to the text message from Claire. His phone lay on the coffee table, neatly placed in the corner, and occasionally he would reach out and touch it lightly. Dan kept counting the clouds. A century came and went, then another, and still he didn't move. He was hardly aware of the time passing. Only Rutherford's insistent wet nose on his drooping hand made him stir. He got up automatically, let the dog out into the flat's garden and forced himself to look again at the phone. He heard Claire's voice as he read the words.

"I'm sorry, so very sorry. I'm in such a state I don't know what I'm doing. I'm scared to call you, but please can we talk?"

Dan felt assailed by emotions. He didn't know whether to call her, go to her and hold her or scream at her to fuck off and never contact him again, never ring him, never come near him. He longed to erase her from his memory, his history, forget her name, that she had even once existed in his life. He imagined painting over the last two years in his mind until there was no sign, no hint of what had once been. He wished he could be like a computer, hit just a couple of buttons and the contents of its brain were gone for ever, clean and ready to start anew.

Then Dan would imagine himself running to her, holding her, stroking her hair and drying her tears. He'd protect her and heal her, ease her fears and hurt, soothe it all away with his whispered words and tenderness. They'd go back to her flat, he'd cook some food, fuss over her, not allow her to move from the sofa as he made up for his crassness and stupidity. He'd be alongside her wherever she went, to protect her from the past and to guide her, and himself, to a better future.

Rage and pity battered him. One moment he could raise his fists to attack Claire, the next open his arms to hug her. Rutherford trotted back in through the half-open door and he reached down and stroked the dog's head, then walked into the kitchen, poured himself a large whisky and paced leadenly back into the living room.

Dan lay on the sofa and closed his eyes. Now a new image came. A huge book, all in black, the size of an ancient monolith. It loomed above his frightened figure and the pages slowly turned. His name was there, in capitals at the top of each. Below were lines and lines of text. He picked out the occasional word. "Rapist, murder, connived, blackmail, conned, cheated, deceived, lied."

Dan groaned and turned his head into the fabric of the sofa, but the image refused to die. Now Linda Cott appeared by the book, dressed as a Master of Ceremonies, smiling broadly. Hundreds of people surrounded her in rows of theatre seats. She was introducing the pages, gleefully telling the crowd what scandal each contained.

He couldn't shut out what Cott had said. That he and Adam would find out what was written about them, and maybe sooner than they thought. His panicked mind imagined the possibilities. Someone discovering the Book and selling it to a newspaper. Sarah or Linda found not guilty at their trial, or sentenced to just a few months or years in prison, the Book patiently waiting for its moment when they were freed. An unknown accomplice releasing it …

The Judgement Book's toxic contents could be unleashed at any time. If he and Adam didn't find it, it would be like a ticking clock within them both, counting down the minutes until detonation.

Dan sat up again, reached out and cuddled Rutherford. The dog nuzzled into him, letting out a low whine. He felt his eyes start to sting.

The glowing clock on the stereo system said it was almost eleven. Dan turned on the television and tried to watch a film, but hardly registered it. He closed his eyes again, but the visions crowded straight back into his mind. He sat up and stared out of the window. The cleansing breeze had cleared the night and a glowing half moon hung in the darkness of the sky. He was frightened to go to bed, to lie and think and dream.

'Fancy a walk?' he asked the dog. 'I could do with trying to clear my head.'

They crossed the road to Hartley Park. Dan wandered slowly around the tarmac path while Rutherford bolted back and forth across the grass, skidding to a halt, then turning and sprinting off again. Dan watched but couldn't find his usual smile for the dog's antics. He sat down on a wooden bench by the swings of the children's play area and rested his head in his hands.

A cultured voice cut through the peace of the night, startling him. 'I say, are you all right, young man?'

It was a middle-aged woman wearing a rainbow-coloured shawl, Wellington boots, a Fedora hat and walking a fat black Labrador. The fabled English eccentric was alive and well and had apparently moved to Plymouth.

'Yes, sorry, fine,' he said, trying to sound reassuring. 'I was just thinking, that's all. I've got a lot on my mind.'

'Good,' she said jovially. 'I was a little concerned.'

'No, I'm fine. It's been a long week, that's all. Thanks for the young man compliment too, I don't get called that very often.'

She smiled indulgently and turned to go. 'Just one thing,' said Dan. 'I don't have my watch on. Could you tell me the time please?'

'Of course.' She lifted a sleeve to reveal a classical, square-faced watch and angled it to catch the light of the streetlamps. Dan noticed the numerals were Roman. 'Half past eleven,' she said and walked briskly off.

Dan watched her go, the Labrador waddling after her. Half past eleven. Or VI past XI, as her watch would have it.

Rutherford wandered back and sat down, facing towards the flat.

'I get the hint, old chap,' said Dan. 'We'll go home in a minute. But first answer me this. Why is my mind full of Roman numerals?'

The dog looked up at him, yawned, lay down on the tarmac. Dan didn't move. What did Roman numerals have to do with anything? It had to be the blackmailers' riddles. They were full of numbers. He tried to think methodically. What numbers had he seen recently that were important?

There was that house number, the Charles family and their red gate. It was number nine. He searched his mind but couldn't come up with anything that helped. Dan wondered what he was trying to do. The only riddle they had left was Sarah and Linda's talk about their initial thoughts being dead right. How could that fit with Roman numerals?

Dan breathed deeply at the night air, tried to use its freshness to instil new energy into his tired mind. Once again he worked through the case.

1200 drifted into his brain. Where had he seen 1200? That was it, the number of people killed in the Blitz of Plymouth. It was inscribed on the new plaque at Charles Church, on the wall opposite the original, the one they'd opened. The number of people dead.

That word again – dead.

Dan stared up at the white moon, not seeing it, just thinking. What was it the blackmailers said about their initial thoughts? That they'd be dead right, would lead them to the Judgement Book. But the initials of what?

What about the five parts of the riddle they'd originally been set? They had the answer now. It didn't help, it led to a fake

318

Book, but they had it. Perhaps it could be important after all. Were they looking for a riddle within a riddle? It sounded far-fetched, absurd even, like something from a spy film, but he wouldn't put anything past Sarah and Linda.

Open original memorial Church Charles.

That was the answer to the five clues. The words twisted and bounced in Dan's brain. He forced the letters to dance, imagined patterns and anagrams, but couldn't see anything significant.

Initial thoughts ... why did the blackmailers make such a point of talking about their initial thoughts? That they were dead right. It was their last taunt, their final victory. To them it must be the most important part of the game.

Open original memorial Church Charles.

The initials.

OOMCC.

Dan felt a seeping excitement start to fill his body. It began slowly, just an imperceptible awakening, then quickly gathered momentum and seemed to fill him with new life. He felt instantly fresh, his mind clear.

The sacred power of the epiphany moment.

OOMCC.

Roman numerals.

But – a vague memory from long-gone schooldays. The Romans didn't have zeroes.

So call it MCC.

Or 1200.

Twelve hundred. The number of people killed in the Blitz of Plymouth. The number of dead. The number inscribed on the new plaque in the ruin of Charles Church. Not the old one, the original memorial where they'd thought the clues led and where they'd found the false book, but the new plaque.

And how very like their two Worms. To hide the Book not where they thought it was, but just a few yards away.

Dan swore loudly, jumped up from the bench, jogged back to his flat and called Adam.

They met in the car park at Charles Cross. Adam was carrying a bulky holdall. He explained it contained some of the kit from the toolbox. It was a good job his friend was a Detective Chief Inspector, Dan thought, or they risked being arrested for going equipped for burglary.

'I'm sorry if I woke you,' he said. 'But I couldn't wait.'

'You didn't wake me,' Adam replied. 'I was sitting up thinking.'

Dan nodded. He knew that was exactly what Adam would have been doing, just as he himself had. He scarcely dared to hope that tonight they would find the Judgement Book and save them both that familiar torment in the weeks and months to come. It was something you could ease from your mind temporarily, for a few hours, even, after a while, maybe for a day or two. But you could never forget it.

'Annie knows something's wrong,' Adam went on. 'I reckon even Tom does. I haven't exactly been myself of late. I've not told them yet. I just said to Annie I've been called out on a job tonight. But if we don't find the Book, I will have to tell her everything. How it's all going to hang over me – how I could be exposed and sacked at any time. The scandal, the outcry, the photographers at the door. The bloody lot. I know she'll stand by me, but ...'

Adam shook his head and his voice tailed off. Dan patted his shoulder. He wanted to reassure his friend, tell him that this time he was sure they were going to find the Book, but the words wouldn't come. With all they'd been through over the past few days, Dan wondered if he was losing the precious power of hope.

The metal gate to the car park ground open, the noise surprisingly loud in the quietness of the night. They walked down the hill to the church. The bag Adam carried clunked as they strode.

Across the city, a chorus of church bells struck midnight. The moon was high in the clear sky, surrounded now by a halo of haze. A few drunken revellers staggered along the pavements, and music thudded from the open doors and windows of the late bars. A police car streaked past, its blue light strobing over the pale stone of the ruined church.

Adam turned away. This wasn't a time to be recognised by his colleagues. They crossed the road to the roundabout and walked down the steps into the church's open innards.

A young couple were grinding together in the hollow bell tower.

'Church patrol,' barked Adam, holding out his warrant card. 'On your way and this time you won't be arrested.'

Even given all they were going through, Dan had to stifle a laugh. It was truly an impressive feat, the detective managing to make the ridiculous words sound so pompous. The couple trotted away up the steps, hand in hand. They looked no more than about fifteen years old.

Dan and Adam stood and stared at the plaque. It was an oval, head high, and held on to the stonework by four screws. Adam took a step closer and scrutinised them.

'They've certainly been moved lately,' he said. 'There's no rust on the heads. They're shiny.' He tapped the plaque. It sounded hollow. 'Plenty of room there to slip something in behind too. Come on, I've had enough messing about. Let's just do it.'

He handed Dan a screwdriver, took one himself and they began work. The screws came out easily. They removed the left and right ones first, then the bottom. Within a couple of minutes the plaque was being held on to the wall only by the top screw. Adam slowly undid it while Dan supported the plaque. The screw fell out and rolled over the flagstones.

The two men looked at each other.

'You ready?' asked Adam.

Dan felt himself begin to tremble. His eyes were aching.

'Yep,' he said, as confidently as he could.

Still though, they waited. It was as if they each feared being the one to make the discovery, that there was nothing behind the plaque, or worse, another fake book. Hopes raised and again shredded.

There had been so much of that lately.

Adam let out a low hiss, gave Dan a quick glance. He hesitated, then nodded and they lifted the plaque away from the wall.

An object fell and hit the flagstones. They followed its path, watching it settle. It was wrapped in a thin white plastic shopping bag, but it was obviously a book, pocket diary-sized. Dan knelt down and touched it. He was surprised by his own reverence.

It was as though they'd finally found the sacred relic at the end of a long and arduous quest. He'd expected something bigger, more powerful, more deadly. In the countless times he'd imagined it, it had towered over him with its dominance. But it was mundane, utterly ordinary.

Adam knelt too, picked up the bag and carefully slid out the diary. It was bound in cheap black leather, just a plain cover, so very innocuous. It couldn't have cost more than a few pounds over the counter of any average store. Dan gulped hard.

Surely not another of the blackmailers' tricks. He wasn't sure he could take another one.

Claire rushed back into his mind, tearful, on her knees, begging for his help. He blinked her away, concentrated on the small black diary. One corner was slightly frayed, as if it had seen far more use than the year's work it was designed for. Dan wondered how many times it had been opened. By Sarah, or Linda, or both of them, sitting together, side by side, glorying in the fetid words and the justification of their grand purpose.

Adam held the book in both hands. 'Are you ready then? Do you want to open it, or shall I?'

'You open it,' said Dan, his voice croaking. 'You're the detective. Besides, I don't know if I can.'

Adam's fingers found the corners of the diary. Outside the ruined church there was a screech of laughter followed by angry shouting. Dan could only make out the word "kebab". A howl of pain echoed through the night. A vague image came to him of people fighting over a take-away. He'd seen it happen often enough before.

Adam opened the book and the two of them stared at the first page. There, on the top line, in capitals, were the words WILL FREEDMAN MP. Below, in neat handwriting were the details of the night he'd spent with a young prostitute in a hotel in Blackpool.

Adam's hand was shaking, the damning words blurring a little with the motion.

'This is it,' the detective said simply. 'We've found it. The Judgement Book.'

Dan didn't know what to say. He expected to feel exhilaration, delight, joy, happiness, even simple relief. But nothing came. There was just emptiness.

'Let's have a look at what else is in here, shall we?' Adam asked. Dan only nodded. He seemed to have lost his voice.

Adam leafed through the pages. They saw the names they expected, Leon Osmond, Steven Sinclair, Major Anthony Robinson, the details of the crimes they'd read about in the blackmail notes the men had received. There were other names there too, some very familiar.

Dan saw one that surprised him. Christopher Parkinson, the pub baron. That pleasurable night conning him out of thousands of pounds for charity seemed a very long time ago now. Dan reached out, stopped Adam turning the pages and went to read, but the detective closed the book firmly.

'Enough,' he said. 'We've done quite enough trespassing into the laments of people's souls these last few days. We've all got our guilty secrets and secret is how they should stay. There's only one thing that really matters to us now.'

He opened the diary at the last page. It was blank.

'If we're in here, we should be towards the back,' Adam continued. 'You want to have a look?'

Dan knew they didn't have a choice, but he still couldn't find anything to say. A cold and familiar fear filled him. Claire sprung back into his mind again, the loss of his unborn son, the words the book could contain and the effect they would have on his life. The last few days felt unreal.

How his world had changed in such a short time. How fragile was the hold on human happiness.

'We've got to look,' Adam said grimly. He started leafing through the back pages. Dan watched intently. The pages were blank, two, three of them, then ten.

Dan felt his whole body shaking as Adam slowly turned the sheets of paper. Still they were blank. Then he came to a page with a heading, neatly written in blue ink.

ADAM BREEN / DAN GROVES

Dan closed his eyes. He imagined himself standing on a scaffold, the gallows waiting. It was a sunshine day and hundreds of people ringed the wooden structure, all clapping, smiling, laughing. Lizzie was reading aloud from the Book, the crowd quietened by her words. The waiting hangman took off the enveloping hood. It was Claire and her face was impassive.

He opened his eyes and stared at the page. There were just three blocks of writing. A pigeon fluttered past, but he hardly noticed. He had to read the words. They blurred in his sight, but Dan forced his vision to focus.

"Adam Breen gave strictly confidential information to Dan Groves about a police investigation into a rapist. Groves deceitfully and illegally secured a DNA sample from the main suspect under the pretence of interviewing him about police harassment. This sample was used to help convict the man. But that wasn't enough for Breen. He also leaked information that the man was a child molester, to ensure he suffered a dreadful time in prison. The man was eventually killed in jail by other inmates – probably as a result of Breen and Groves' actions.

"Further – Breen appears to have told Groves the address of Leon Osmond, as retaliation for the Superintendent's complaint about the investigation into him. This allowed newspaper and TV pictures of Osmond to appear, in connection with his corruption in evading a drink driving charge – a story already documented in these pages.

"Breen and Groves are clearly very close, far more so than is healthy and certainly more than their professions should allow. They have worked on a number of cases together. Further investigation into exactly what happened in those should prove most interesting."

Dan stood up. He hadn't realised his knees were aching. He watched a car screech around the roundabout, music pumping from inside its blackened windows.

'They've got us,' he said finally.

Adam nodded heavily. 'Yes. It's not everything by any means, but it's plenty enough to finish us. And if anyone looked up the rest of the cases we've worked on together, it wouldn't take long to realise some of the other things we've done.'

Another long pause, then Dan said. 'So what do we do? I take it the contents of the Book have to become known? You can't just take Sarah and Linda to court on the basis of the blackmail notes they sent to the victims they actually chose?'

'The contents would certainly get out. The Book would be the most important exhibit in their trial. Then it becomes a public document, nicely on the record in black and white for anyone who wants to see. It'd make all the papers, radio and TV, the works. They'd doubtless report what it said about each person named. It'd be a huge scandal.'

Dan walked over to the wall and leaned back against it. A leaden weight of tiredness had crept over him. He lowered himself and sat cross-legged on a flagstone. Adam followed and sat beside him. He dropped the Judgement Book in front of them.

'So what do we do?' asked Dan, gazing at the diary. 'There's important evidence in there. Can we just rip out the page that contains the stuff on us?'

Adam shook his head sadly. 'No. The book's got our fingerprints all over it and our DNA too now. I should have been more careful, but I suppose I didn't really believe we'd find it. And when we did, I just wanted to see what was in it. If a page disappeared, and the book was in my custody, it's pretty obvious where the finger would point. Sarah and Linda would make sure it was raised in court, what that page contained.'

They sat in silence and stared at the diary. Just a book, cheap leather and paper, small and innocuous, but full of so many secrets and with a hold over so many lives.

Dan poked at it with his foot. 'Do you need the Book to convict them?'

'No. We've got more than enough evidence. I'm sure they'll take it all to trial so they can trumpet their so-called mission and get their final blaze of publicity, but we've got plenty to convict them. That's not in doubt.'

Dan drummed a couple of fingers on the flagstones.

'Well, you and I are the only ones who know the Judgement

Book's been found ...' he began, and let his voice falter.

Adam bowed his head between his knees. Dan stared up at the moon. He wondered who would look after Rutherford if he were sent to prison. He couldn't bear to see his friend incarcerated in the concrete and wire cages of an animal home. He'd be given away to some stranger, forget all about Dan. If only Claire was still around, she would have taken the dog in and waited for Dan to walk free again. He screwed his eyes shut to escape the thoughts.

Adam finally lifted his head. When he spoke, his voice was quiet and so subdued that Dan had to strain to hear.

'You know, we have connived together in ways which have been both illegal and immoral. Sarah and Linda are quite right about that. But I'm convinced that everything we've done has ultimately been in the interests of justice. Whatever happens, I'm content I've always acted for the best.'

Dan kept quiet, his mind running back over all they'd been through together. He wanted to believe Adam was right, but he knew it was something he'd argue about with himself in the times to come. He tried not to wonder if that would be in a prison cell, or the dark corner of some dingy bar.

Adam got to his feet. 'I'm going to screw this plaque back on to the wall,' he said. 'And I suggest you go home. It's been a hell of a few days. But on your way back, be a good citizen and pick up some of this horrible litter that's spoiling one of Plymouth's most important memorials, will you? And make sure you dispose of it well.'

There was an odd silence. Both men held a look.

Dan reached out a hand to his friend and Adam pulled him up. The detective took the plaque and started screwing it back on to the wall. He didn't look round as Dan slowly climbed the stone steps, crossed the road, walked over to the police station, got into his car and carefully drove home. The dashboard clock said it was half past one. He yawned and ran his tongue over the ulcer. It had stopped stinging.

He let himself into the flat and was greeted by a panting, yelping Rutherford. Dan knelt down, gave the dog a cuddle and felt a sudden, sweeping urge to burst into tears. He hid his face in the soft fur so Rutherford wouldn't see the salty trails leaking from the corners of his eyes.

He got up, poured a glass of whisky, found a box of matches in the kitchen, crumpled up some newspaper in the grate of his fire and set it alight. He added a few other bits of waste paper and rubbish that he found around the living room. Orange flames rose and danced, flickering their reflections through the room. It was remarkable how fast it all burned, became only a small pile of black and grey ash.

Dan let Rutherford out into the garden and stared up at the moon as he waited for the dog to return. He walked back inside, cleared the ash from the grate, brushed his teeth automatically, got into bed and drew up the courage to close his eyes. Before he did he reached out for his mobile and looked again at the text message from Claire.

He read it, then read it once more, stared at it, debated with himself, and finally decided he would ring her in the morning.

Dan lay back on the bed, switched off the light, but knew he wouldn't sleep. He let a series of slow minutes slip by, took the phone, found Claire's number and called it.

Each ring felt like a step towards a crossroads of his life.

Epilogue

THE COUNSELLOR SAID TO write it all down, everything I feel, as honestly as possible, and she'll talk it through when we meet next week. I'm not sure about this at all, but, here goes.

Deep breath –

He's still there, in my life, but I can only see him in the distance. He's like a castle on the horizon. The keep is tall, the walls are made of thick stone and heavily defended. And around those walls are more walls, more rugged stone, all topped with barbed wire and ringed with a wide moat.

He's that far away, and he protects himself so well. But just occasionally I can reach him. And sometimes he reaches out to me.

We haven't spoken. Not since that night, five months ago, when we said too much. But there is the odd text message. I know it doesn't sound much, but, for him, it is. And so it is for me too.

What's important is that there's still a link, a connection. It's fragile, but it's there.

I think I've come to realise the castle isn't just keeping me out. It's imprisoning him too.

I'd like to help him escape it. But I think only he can do that. So I wait. It's all I can do.

Even now, these months on, I still find myself looking down at my stomach and running a hand over it. I can't go back there, to that dreadful day, and it'll be a very long time until we can talk about it, if, perhaps, ever. I'm still not really sure why it happened. But I hope he doesn't think he's the only one who was so very wounded.

And even more filled with regret.

I keep going, day by day. I try to focus on my job. Some days are better than others. The most recent have been a welcome distraction.

The trial of Sarah and Linda finished last week. Both were jailed for twelve years. When the judge passed sentence, Sarah just laughed at him. But Linda looked stunned. I wonder if I could see some remorse in her face for all that she did.

There was an extraordinary moment when, giving evidence, Sarah told the court where the Judgement Book was hidden. All the reporters stampeded out and ran down to Charles Church, all except Dan. He just sat there, on the press bench, with his head bowed.

We heard later that the journalists didn't find the Book. It must have been yet another of the blackmailers' games. That's one of the most enduring mysteries of this case. What became of the Judgement Book? Perhaps some day we'll get to know. But I'm not really sure I care.

Mr Breen is still the Detective Chief Inspector here, and has been given a commendation for his work on the inquiry. Those complaints against him, by Osmond and Robinson were found to be baseless, and quite rightly so. He was doing his job on a very difficult case, and doing it well.

The death of that Iraqi boy was investigated by the military. I'm not the only one who wonders just how thorough and committed an inquiry it was. They concluded there was insufficient evidence for anyone to be charged. Well, surprise, surprise. When I heard that, I did wonder whether Sarah and Linda had a point in what they were trying to say about the "establishment".

Sinclair was investigated by some colleagues in the financial crime unit, and was jailed for five years. He's in Dartmoor Prison now, and doing his best to make amends, working in the education service and teaching other inmates how to read and write.

As for Osmond, I don't quite know what to say. He never returned to work, instead he took early retirement. The gossip is that the High Honchos did a deal to save a scandal, and to protect the poor cop who caught him drink-driving. It was an awful situation for him to be put in.

For what it's worth, I'd like to have seen Osmond publicly disgraced, but I think the way it was handled was about as good as it could have been.

So, work is going fine. The flat's fine. My friends are fine.

Everything's fine.

The only problem is him. And what happened between us, and why, and whether it can ever be worked out.

I have to believe there's hope. There's always hope. While there's belief, there's hope. And believe me, there is belief.

So, that's it. That's how I feel, as honestly as possible.

And that was where I was going to end this, all ready for my first counselling session, whatever good it may do.

But now comes the twist, the little sting in the tale.

I've just had a phone call. An urgent one.

For the first time in five months, I'm going to see him again. We're being thrown together on the biggest inquiry either of us has ever worked on, a terrorist atrocity in a sacred place.

We'll be investigating a dreadful case. We'll have to see each other. At last, we'll have to talk.

And I'm wondering just what the next few days will bring.

About the author…

Simon Hall

Simon Hall is the BBC's Crime Correspondent in the
south-west of England. He also regularly broadcasts on
BBC Radio Devon and BBC Radio Cornwall.

Simon has also been nominated for the Crime Writers'
Association *Dagger In The Library* Award.

For more information please visit Simon Hall's website

www.thetvdetective.com

Also by Simon Hall

The Death Pictures

A dying artist is murdered before the answer to a riddle hidden in his series of ten paintings can be revealed, while a serial rapist is taunting the police.
The TV reporter covering these stories, Dan Groves, is drawn into the investigation, breaking the law to help the police, as he tries to solve the riddle and find the murderer.

ISBN 9781906125981
Price £ 6.99

Evil Valley

A psychopath is out to teach the world a shocking lesson and the clock is ticking. Can the police crack his cruel riddles and stop him from committing the ultimate crime?
Chief Inspector Adam Breen and crime-fighting TV reporter Dan Groves are reunited in the hunt for a masked man who boasts of plans to commit a crime so evil it will shock the nation.

ISBN 9781906373436
Price £ 7.99